A TIME THAT LEAPS INTO LIFE . . .
A MAN YOU WILL NEVER FORGET . . .

MAX

"An absolute page-turner. . . . Mr. Fast has worked [a] kind of narrative magic. . . . In Max Britsky and in Sally Levine, the woman he marries, we have two characters who are disarmingly real. . . . They are authentic in every respect, and we can no more give up on the story of their private lives than we could close our ears at the family table to the latest gossip about Uncle Max and Aunt Sally."
—*The New York Times Book Review*

"Howard Fast has done it again. . . . Max is the epitome of the major creators of motion pictures. . . . MAX [is] a vivid picture of the times and the men and women who made them and made possible the giant entertainment medium that flourishes even mightier today." —*San Diego Union*

"A memorable character in a classic tale of America, land of opportunity." —*Publishers Weekly*

"A great fast-paced hit . . . pure entertainment."
—*The Cincinnati Enquirer*

D0010988

BOOKS BY HOWARD FAST

MAX

THE LEGACY

THE ESTABLISHMENT

THE MAGIC DOOR

SECOND GENERATION

THE IMMIGRANTS

THE ART OF ZEN MEDITATION

TIME AND THE RIDDLE

A TOUCH OF INFINITY

THE HESSIAN

THE CROSSING

THE GENERAL ZAPPED AN ANGEL

THE JEWS: STORY OF A PEOPLE

THE HUNTER AND THE TRAP

TORQUEMADA

THE HILL

AGRIPPA'S DAUGHTER

POWER

THE EDGE OF TOMORROW

APRIL MORNING

THE GOLDEN RIVER

THE WINSTON AFFAIR

MOSES, PRINCE OF EGYPT

THE LAST SUPPER

SILAS TIMBERMAN

THE PASSION OF SACCO AND VANZETTI

SPARTACUS

THE PROUD AND THE FREE

DEPARTURE

MY GLORIOUS BROTHERS

CLARKTON

THE AMERICAN

FREEDOM ROAD

CITIZEN TOM PAINE

THE UNVANQUISHED

THE LAST FRONTIER

CONCEIVED IN LIBERTY

PLACE IN THE CITY

THE CHILDREN

STRANGE YESTERDAY

TWO VALLEYS

MAX

A NOVEL BY

Howard Fast

A DELL BOOK

Published by
Dell Publishing Co., Inc.
1 Dag Hammarskjold Plaza
New York, New York 10017

Rachel and Avrum
Blessings

Dell® TM 681510, Dell Publishing Co., Inc.

ISBN: 0-440-16106-1

Reprinted by arrangement with Houghton Mifflin Company
Printed in the United States of America
First Dell printing—September 1983

[ONE]

NOVEMBER
1891
—
Max at the
Age of Twelve

AS WITH MOST of those who enter this world, Max Britsky did so violently and unwillingly, and once life had been smacked into his small red behind, he screamed out his anger and resentment with a voice and strength that surprised Dr. Segal, who held him upside down by his two small feet.

"I'll be damned," Dr. Segal said under his breath. "Scrawny little beggar, but full of life. Can't be an ounce over six pounds, but by golly, he's alive."

The birth had taken place in Abraham Britsky's apartment on Henry Street, on the Lower East Side of New York City, on the fifteenth day of November in 1879. It was before the time when most children would be born in hospitals, and the mother, Max's mother, Sarah Britsky, lay in her bed, staring at the fuzzy vision of a small, froglike bit of pink and red flesh dangling from Dr. Segal's hand by its heels, her first son. Sarah Britsky was not yet twenty-three. When not exhausted, colorless, sweating, splattered with blood, and still trembling in the aftermath of having given birth, she was a reasonably attractive young woman, with regular features and a good head of thick brown hair. Her husband, Abe, was five years older, much more frightened than she. When he was at work — which, barring today, was six days a week — he was a cutter in a garment factory, a sweatshop which paid him seven dollars a week for a twelve-hour day.

Max was his first child, but Abe Britsky was a virile man, and after Max had blundered into existence, brothers and sisters appeared almost by cosmic schedule. Freida was born in 1880; twelve months later, a stillbirth died unnamed. Reuben appeared in 1883, and somewhat less than three years after, in 1886, Sheila saw the light of day. Esther was born in 1888, and fourteen months later, in 1889, Benjamin Britsky joined the burgeoning population of the United States.

While the country had territory in abundance, the tiny cold-water flat on Henry Street was not expandable. It had two closet-sized bedrooms, a small living room, a small dining room, and a small kitchen. Since the rooms were lined up, one behind the other, with no taste of the outside except a narrow, dark airshaft, it was called a railroad flat, even as it was called a cold-water flat because the landlord supplied no hot water. For a year after the birth of his sixth child, Abe Britsky vowed that he would ask for a raise, demand a raise, plead for a raise; but alas, all of his virility seemed to repose in his gonads, and each time he approached his boss, his courage failed him. Taking the one alternative that appeared reasonable to him and within his powers, he found a Sunday job as deckhand and general cleaning man on the Pennsylvania Railroad ferry to New Jersey; but working seven days a week proved too much for his already exhausted constitution, and at the age of forty, he dropped dead at work, a victim of a massive coronary thrombosis.

Max was approaching his twelfth year when his father died, leaving Sarah Britsky with six small children, a railroad flat on Henry Street, and twelve dollars and twenty cents in the brown jug in the kitchen, which acted as the Britsky bank. Since the Britsky store of savings had passed the fifty-dollar mark only once since Max's birth and was frequently as low as two dollars, a net worth of twelve dollars was not unusual. Both Abe and Sarah Britsky were immigrants, he from Lithuania, she from Poland, both of them launched across the sea and into the New World through the collective energies of families that had remained behind. Through the years, there had been a lingering hope that other members of their families would eventually join them, but since this did not come about, the hope finally faded. When Abe died, the Synagogue Beth Sholom raised the money for a simple funeral, then Sarah went home with her children and pondered whether she should kill herself. There was, in that time, no relief, no social welfare, no aid to the poor except for private charities, and what private charities touched the Lower East Side of New York City were outside Sarah's world. So, still a bit short of his twelfth year, Max Britsky became the head of a household of seven, their pillar of life and hope.

Max accepted his role. While his mother wept and shrieked her grief, terrifying her five younger children, Max acted. He was in the sixth grade at the public school on East Broadway, and he silently, subjectively, terminated his schooling. He conveyed his decision to his mother tersely, thus: "It'll be all right."

"You're telling me!" Sarah cried. "I'm dying and you're telling me it'll be all right!"

She said this in Yiddish, her English still poor and not to be attempted under such great emotional stress, and then she slapped Max. That was to be expected. If her love for a man, now departed, who had kept her pregnant for most of the past thirteen years was somewhat less than heartfelt, the enormity of the tragedy she now faced could not be exaggerated, and the effrontery of this skinny twelve-year-old turned grief into anger. In his own way, Max understood this and accepted the blow without resentment.

Years afterward, Max's life would become the subject of a great deal of social and artistic inquiry, but none of it took into account the factors that made him — the factors that made the child, who became the father of the man. The man, in later years, was often accused of dishonesty, but he was not dishonest and neither was he a thief. The child was once a thief, if one excludes pilfering, but a real thief only on a single occasion. The pilfering consisted of following the milk wagon, in the small hours of the morning, in the wealthy neighborhoods around Gramercy Park, in the north, since milk deliveries hardly abounded in the environs of Henry Street, and the two or three quarts of milk that followed such excursions were looked upon bitterly by Sarah but accepted silently. Max's single venture into actual larceny was greeted with more vocal anger.

It happened the day after his father's funeral, the day he told his mother that things would be all right, the day he faced the necessity of immediate cash. There was some food in the apartment, brought there by people from the synagogue who had a vague tribal affiliation but were otherwise strangers, for Abe Britsky had possessed neither a social nor a religious life worth mentioning. There was bread and cheese and a bag of potatoes and a salami, but with the normal hunger of the Britsky family, it was not much more than a day's ration. And there was no cash. Max Britsky was a realist, and while at his age he did not have too many courses of action open to him, he was able to face those that represented a part of his reality. He did his thinking on the front stoop of the tenement that housed his family, a small, skinny boy, with a long, narrow head, a sharp nose, a wide full-lipped mouth and pale blue eyes. His light brown hair covered his ears in a shaggy mop. His shoes were worn to holes at the toes and at the soles. His stockings were loose and torn, his short knickers worn through at the knees, and a dirty, worn shirt and a ragged sweater completed his costume.

It was late September, so he did not yet have to confront winter weather, an uneasy future since his last year's coat had already been made over for his sister Freida. But one thing at a time and one day at a time. Today he required cash for survival, and having considered the alternatives, Max moved into action.

It is about a mile and a half from the tenements of Henry Street to the shadowed canyons of the financial district, which lie to the south. Max might have paraphrased a later thief, who explained that he robbed banks because that's where the money was, and in this single instance of overt crime, Max moved into the financial district for much the same reason, his quarry a stout man with a protruding belly. While such might be found in the vicinity of Henry Street, ghetto bellies did not support watches and heavy gold watch chains. At the corner of Pine and Nassau, Max found an appropriate belly, enclosed by a white damask vest and crossed by a heavy gold watch chain of indisputable quality. The owner of this gold chain was engaged in deep conversation with another gentleman, and neither of them noticed the skinny kid who moved up to them, grabbed the gold chain with all his ten fingers, then yanked. The vest snapped open, buttons flying, the buttonhole which held the chain tore through, and the heavy pocket watch at the end of the chain bounced out of the stout man's vest pocket. Before either of the men could gather their wits and begin to shout, "Stop thief!" Max was off into the press of people.

The street was his element, street nourished, street wise, and when the cry of "Stop thief!" finally did come, he was a block away, cutting into an alley. A man running attracts a crowd; a boy running attracts no one, and Max ran all the way to Moe Splenski's hock shop on Rivington Street. He had been there before with brass fittings, doorknobs, hinges, and brackets dug out of the dump on South Street, but never with anything worth more than ten cents. The watch and chain Max pushed through the wire grille to Splenski were worth a good deal more than ten cents. Splenski examined it closely, snapped open the watch cover, moved the hands, and then offered Max two dollars.

"Go fuck yourself," Max said. "My father died yesterday. My mother's got six kids. I want twenty bucks." It embraced the entire situation, and Splenski, studying the boy's cold blue eyes, stroked his beard and nodded.

"Ten dollars," Splenski said. The watch and chain were worth at least a hundred.

"Gimme it," Max said, reaching.

Splenski pushed the watch and chain out of reach. "Your father died yesterday?"

"That's right."

"Twelve dollars."

"Like I said, go fuck yourself."

"Suppose I call the cops?"

"Call them. Tell them I want to hock my father's watch. Then tell them where the other merchandise comes from."

"You're a snotty kid."

"Yeah. Give it to me in one-dollar bills, all of it in one-dollar bills. And I know how to count."

As of this day and this moment, school was in the past; Max was now in the business of survival, and being in that business, he recognized the fact that job opportunities were few and far between for a twelve-year-old, nor would any of them pay what would be needed to support a family of seven people, six of them children blessed with healthy appetites. Max had to be an independent operator, and as such he required capital. The result was that when he returned to the Britsky flat, he placed only eighteen dollars on the table in front of his grieving mother, retaining two dollars for himself.

"What's this?" Sarah demanded.

"That son of a bitch Himmelman, he been here yet?" Himmelman was their landlord.

"Don't use dirty language!" Sarah exclaimed.

"He been here? That's all I'm asking."

"Yes."

"So what did he say?" Max asked her.

"So what did he say — so what did he say!" she cried angrily, forgetting that she was talking to a twelve-year-old boy and talking to him as she might have talked to her husband, in a fierce, almost threatening whine. "What should he say, that prince of evil? To-morrow the rent is due. Pay the rent or get out. He smells death like a dog smells filth. They say he lives uptown with the fancy rich Jews, but he was down here knocking on my door before poor Abe was cold in his grave. He'll turn us out on the street!" she cried, her voice rising.

Little Benny Britsky, one year and a half in age, lay in the crib that had come down from birth to birth. The four remaining Britsky children stood in the kitchen, partaking of the awful drama that had taken them up into itself, watching, listening, trying to comprehend the message of doomsday.

Max pointed to the money. "Eighteen dollars," he said. "You got nine dollars to pay the rent and you got nine dollars for food. So nobody ain't going to kick us out into the street."

"Where did you get this?" she asked, handling the money.

"What's the difference? I got it."

"You little bum, you stole it!" And she slapped him, but there was no force in the slap.

"We won't starve," Max said, "and nobody throws us out into the street."

There have been worse declarations of intent.

• • •

It was a conceit of Max to declare in later years that he had been weaned on show business and that it was in his blood. The small operation he embarked on, along with other independent enterprises, had only a tenuous connection with show business, but like others of his enterprises, it partook of imagination. Max thought of things that escaped others. But in his case, imagination was narrowed and directed with the intensity of a laser beam. If Max had been put to introspection and forced to declare why he should have accepted the responsibility for the survival of the seven lives that constituted the Britsky family, he would have been unable to come up with an answer. But the question was not put to him, not by another and not by himself.

Show business, on the other hand, thrived in New York City in the year of 1891. There were, aside from the English-speaking theatre, four Yiddish companies, two German companies, an Italian company, and a Czech company. The czar's expulsion of the Yiddish theatre from his realm a few years before had led to a veritable explosion of Yiddish drama on the Lower East Side. In the English language, over forty theatres thrived on a succession of bad plays, interspersed now and then by the work of Shaw, Ibsen, Barrie, and Shakespeare as well as Strindberg, Hardy, and other accomplished Europeans. The age of the native American theatre was still in the future, but the love of and obsession with theatre was very much a part of the time. New Yorkers adored the theatre. Everyone who could put the price of a ticket together went to the theatre at one time or another — except for European-born shopkeepers, whose long hours and difficulties with the language made them indifferent to the English-speaking theatre.

Of this, Max was well aware, and to this end he had preserved his capital of two dollars. Each morning after his father's death, Max left the house at half-past six, his eight-year-old brother Ruby tagging along with him. They were the two Britsky children old enough to say Kaddish, the Jewish prayer for the dead, which the son repeats each morning and each evening for a year after his father's death. Max made Ruby his surrogate, dropping him at the door to the synagogue with the observation that nobody yet ate a prayer.

They ate bagels, however, the hard, indigestible ring-shaped pieces of bread that had been brought to America in the eighteen-seventies by the Eastern European Jewish immigrants; and since it was still too early in the morning for Max to embark on what would be remembered as his entrance into show business, he went instead to Kurtz's bagel factory on Broome Street. He had been there once before on a Sunday morning with Shutzie Levine, seventeen and tolerating Max as an assistant whom he paid off with ten cents for the morning's work. The East Side sweatshops worked twelve hours a day, six days a week, giving the Jewish workers only one day off, Saturday, and since Shutzie was still in high school, Sunday was the only day he could ply the trade, namely, the sale of hot bagels to the workers.

Max, whose schooling was in the past, entered the business on a weekday. He moved into the bakery almost unnoticed, savoring the smells hungrily, watching the bakers mold the bagels in one swift yet intricate motion, dropping them then into the pots of boiling water, from whence they were fished out and thrust into the oven to be baked to a golden brown.

Finally, someone noticed him and asked him what he wanted.

"One hundred bagels," Max said, flattening a dollar bill on the counter.

"Why ain't you in school?"

The whole world of adulthood was nosy, officious, and suspicious. Storekeepers were walking into the place and walking out with huge bags of bagels. No one questioned them. Their money was sufficient.

"School don't open until nine o'clock."

At Stylish Shirtwaists, Inc., on East Broadway, it was the same thing. A fat janitor, sitting at the door of the old loft building, demanded to know why Max wasn't in school.

Unspoken, Max thought, Up yours, you old shithead. Aloud, he poured out the tale of his dead father and the many mouths to feed.

"Costs you twenty cents to go in there." The janitor was unaffected by sentiment and beyond compassion. He lived in a world of lies and liars, and Max would have been surprised if he had accepted the story as the truth.

"Ten cents," Max countered.

They settled for fifteen cents after Max informed him that it could be a daily source of income. Upstairs, between the clattering rows of sewing machines, Max sold his bagels, still hot, charging two cents for each and making a hundred percent profit. When the floor boss would have thrown him out, the women at the machines took pity on him and defended his right to sell his merchandise. He elicited pity and sympathy. He could assume an air of wistfulness that made his face quite lovely; he was small and skinny. When he explained his case to the women workers, their hearts went out to him. In that one building, from Stylish Shirtwaists to Sylvan Frocks to Ben's Blouses, he sold his hundred bagels, and with his capital increased almost fifty percent to three dollars, less the fifteen cents he had to pay the janitor, he went on to his beginning in show business.

* * *

In those days, when a theatrical piece opened in New York City, they placed showcards in the windows of hundreds of retail stores. The showcards were usually eighteen by twenty-four inches, and they announced the name of the show and the lead players and included a puff about the contents. In return for the use of his window as a display place, the merchant was given two tickets to the performance. Most of the merchants on the Lower East Side were indifferent to the English-language plays, performed in another world that existed uptown, and as often as not they gave away the tickets or sold them for a few cents. Once, in a grocery store on an errand for his mother, Max saw a woman pay fifty cents for a pair of tickets that the storekeeper would just as soon have given away. But since the woman was a prostitute, the storekeeper exacted payment as a sop to his moral indignation. Max, who had never seen a theatrical performance and who had no desire to see one, could not understand what a woman in his neighborhood, where money was spent on food and clothes and not much else, was doing when she put out good money for theatre tickets. Reasoning simply and directly, he decided that whores were addicted to the theatre. While this was very poor deductive reasoning, it was a lucky guess, for among the hundreds of prostitutes who plied their trade on Allen Street and Orchard Street and Ludlow Street, the uptown theatre was very much in vogue. It was their lifeline to a little class, a veneer of culture and a glimpse of life outside the ghetto.

Thus, balancing one need against another, Max made his approach directly and specifically. He went into Sal Marietta's shoe repair place and said, "How about the tickets for them showcards in your window? I'll buy them."

Sal had neither the time nor the inclination for the English-speaking theatre. "I hear your poor mama pass away."

"My papa."

"Worse, terrible." In Italian, he observed that this place stank, that life was an oversized outhouse, and that the poor ate shit. Max nodded in agreement, his wide blue eyes moist and vulnerable. "I give you this," Sal said, offering Max a dollar. "Helps, maybe."

"I don't want money," Max said. "Thanks, Sal, but that ain't what I want. I want the tickets for the showcards."

"What for? Your mama's dead, you go see shows?"

"My papa. I buy the tickets. Two bits a pair."

He left Sal's with two pairs of tickets, one for a performance of *Devil May Care*, starring Lucy Demar, and the other for a rerun of *The Mikado*, by Gilbert and Sullivan, which had a triumphant opening in New York some six years before.

He explained to Sal what he intended to do with the tickets, feeling that Sal would not screw him. Even then, Max was a fair judge of human nature. Sal promised to save the tickets for him in the future. In some way, Max understood the barrier between these hard-working storekeepers and the uptown world of the theatre, of glowing gaslights, of fine restaurants, of men in dinner clothes and ladies in their evening gowns. The nearest theatre center was on Fourteenth Street, which was either a mile away or a continent away, depending upon who you were, and the newer theatre centers in the Twenties and in the Forties were even more unapproachable. It would never have occurred to Sal Marietta to go to the theatre, even as it would never have occurred to Max.

• • •

Max's mother, Sarah, had been born in 1856, transported at the age of sixteen to the Lower East Side of New York City. Years later, Max would remember and try to comprehend what life had been for Sarah. She was only thirty-five years old when her husband died, but already worn and defeated, the juice of life squeezed out of her, the fragile bit of youthful beauty she had once possessed gone forever. She was boxed into a room with no exit; she was beyond planning or hoping or dreaming, and the thought that this strange, alien, skinny boy could provide for her and her family was untenable. The ability to love had also been squeezed out of her, replaced by fear and rage and frustration. Left to her own devices, she might well have waited for death or extinction. A woman in her situation in another ethnic group might well have killed herself and her children; Sarah might have allowed life to perform the execution at a slower rate.

But Max brought in money, and they survived. It was an affront to the normal monstrousness of life, and instead of being grateful, Sarah snapped and whimpered and raged at her son. Strangely enough, Max understood this.

But his understanding and acceptance of his mother lay buried deep in his unconscious, almost animal-like; as a despised dog clings to loyalty, Max clung to Sarah. He never asked himself whether he loved this shrike of a woman because in some strange way he was wise enough to understand her. He was guilty of denying her the horrible extinction that would revenge her on life and circumstance. He gave her a preposterous gift — continuing existence — and incredibly, yet naturally, this was something she could not forgive him. He denied her the small, terrible logic of her impending fate and doom. Explicitly, neither of them actually comprehended this; but in the process of living, it became central to their relationship to each other. With his brothers and sisters, it was another matter.

Max never separated himself from the six human beings who depended upon him. Their survival was his survival; their fate would be his fate. It was a fact, not of compassion or duty, but of reality, because he was unaware of any other reality; and as he accepted this, he also accepted his mother's anger and irritation. He tried to protect her. He wrote notes for his sister Freida, thirteen months younger than he, to bring to school, and he lied to his mother about his truancy. When it caught up with him after a visit from the truant officer, he accepted his mother's slaps and her tongue-lashing.

"You're a bum," she told him. "You're a little bum." But her rage was weakening; she was emerging from the miasma of despair. Days and weeks had gone by since her husband's death, and still they survived and there was food on the table.

"I do what I got to do," Max told her. "I'm not a bum, Mama."

"Twelve years old with whores!"

"I don't do nothing with whores, Mama. I sell them tickets."

"Mr. Greenbaum says you pimp for them."

"He's a liar! I'm not a pimp." He hated the word. He had understood the finances of pimping and prostitution since he was eight years old. It was all part of the streets, and even if he had been less than clear about the emotions and desires that went with the oldest profession, all of it existed within walking distance of his home, where pimps and prostitutes abounded. Once he had guided a customer to Suzie Brinkerhoff, but only once, and Suzie had given him a dollar. Suzie was a large, voluptuous woman in her mid-thirties, with peroxide-dyed blond hair. She was sentimental. She knew the story of Sarah Britsky and her six children, and she adored Max. She was so sentimental that her eyes brimmed with tears every time Max approached her with tickets, for in her eyes Max was not a scrawny little boy but the image of the thoughtful and selfless lover she had never known as well as the wonderful child she had never given birth to. She was indifferent to his ragged clothes and his gutter speech; she clothed him in her own fantasies. And she always bought whatever tickets he offered, cheerfully paying two dollars for a pair. When other prostitutes made obscene remarks to Max, Suzie told them to keep their lousy mouths shut, and she said to Max, "Stay away from them lousy whores, because they stink with social disease." Then she proceeded to deliver an explicit lecture on the nature of syphilis and gonorrhea, leaving nothing out and describing the prognosis of both diseases with fervor and color.

In a way, she adopted Max. "He is my mascot," she told the other whores, and the market for his showcard tickets broadened. At the same time, he added to his bagel business. Most of the loft factories were barred to him, but he did manage to find two more places to add to his clientele, Garden Dresses and Birdie Blouses. In each instance he had to bribe the janitor, yet within months after his father's death, Max was selling a thousand bagels a week, which yielded him, expenses deducted, a net profit of about eight dollars. The first week after his father's death, leaving aside the income from the stolen watch, he presented his mother with nine dollars. The second week, it had increased to twelve dollars, and the third week, he brought home fourteen dollars and sixty cents, more than his father had ever earned — and with this, retaining his capital for the bagel business. Not every week was so profitable, yet from week to week, the six Britsky children and Sarah, their mother, managed to eat and pay their rent.

Sarah relented. The incomprehensible miracle of a skinny, wiry twelve-year-old boy keeping them from death and starvation had to impress her. She shouted at Max less frequently, and her slaps and anger were directed toward the other children. And once, with tears in her eyes, she managed to say to Max, "Thank you, thank you."

Yet Max had seen her, on many occasions, showing the love and tenderness that one would expect from a mother, but directing it toward his brothers and sisters. There was no way in the world that Max could comprehend what was taking place, nor could he conceivably ask her why she was kind to the others and so dismally unkind to him, nor could he speculate that having replaced her husband as a provider, he was not only denying her own role of motherhood and caring but abandoning his own position as one of her children. None of these thoughts or conclusions were possible for the skinny little boy, and therefore, when his mother made her feeble gesture of gratitude, Max failed to respond.

His lack of any response, either pleasure or annoyance, did not indicate a lack of human equipment. Only saints continue to love where no love is returned, and Max was hardly a saint. What he felt for his mother and his brothers and sisters was a sort of tribal bondage, a clannish binding, not love, not even emotion, but a glue of circumstances that he never tried to evade. That his mother managed to swallow her bitterness and resentment long enough to thank him meant nothing; his only satisfaction came from her reduction as a nuisance. When he thought about her, it was only to express a desire for her to leave him alone, not to get off his back — they were all of them on his back forever — but to leave him alone.

The kids Max knew — a bit older, a bit younger — all of them worked, some more, some less. There was no happy, easy childhood of carefree play on the Lower East Side. The kids sold papers, delivered packages, collected tinfoil and sold it, found bits and pieces of work at the East River fishing docks, opened the doors of hansom cabs downtown for penny tips, collected junk for the junk dealers, all of this after school hours, these and a hundred other odds and ends of work; and if there was a dollar a week to be made, it was good pay. And other kids stole things, and there was not much more than a dollar a week in that either. They existed in a teeming, squalling, turbulent, overcrowded world of rotten jerry-built tenements and garbage-strewn, pushcart-lined streets through which an endless procession of horses dragged carts, wagons, trucks, hansoms, fire engines, black Marias, vans, even an occasional carriage, lost or detoured, and all of the horses pissing until the gutters ran with an endless yellow flow, defecating the food of thousands of sparrows and pigeons who made this enormous eddy of humankind their natural habitat.

It was not for Max. He spent each day until he was ready to drop from fatigue, but he sold his labor to no one. In his pragmatic philosophy, there were two approaches. You sold your strength for a dollar a week, or you sold other things and used your brains. But when you used your brains, you provoked other people to thought, and that could hurt. If this kid was willing to pay twenty-five cents for showcard tickets, he would also pay thirty-five cents and fifty cents. There was no endless flow of honey out of this particular hive, and not until a year later would Max begin to organize other kids as bagel distributors and add hot coffee to his menu. In the time between, he wandered farther and farther afield in his search for showcards.

That way, he came to Rowdy Smith's penny arcade, on Second Avenue just south of Fourteenth Street. In New York, a few blocks made a neighborhood, and ten blocks could be a universe apart; and while on one or two occasions, Max had wandered as far north as Fourteenth Street, it was well out of his usual world. He had a vague image in his mind of Rowdy Smith's place, but only that, and now to his delight he discovered a dozen showcards lined up in the wide windows of the penny arcade. None of the many and varied delights in the penny arcade attracted Max, not the cheap gambling wheels, the carny games, the miniature bowling, or the kinetoscopes. Yet they were there and they registered, and as Max put it long, long afterward, "I went in there and I changed the world. Don't make any mistake about that, because that's where it began, back there in Rowdy Smith's penny arcade." But that was long after, when the penny arcade had disappeared and Rowdy Smith had been taken to his ancestors.

But in 1891, Rowdy Smith was very much alive, a big, white-haired Irishman of sixty or so, his face as red as fire from enough whiskey to float a battleship, his paunch enormous from enough beer to float a fleet. He stood in his cage at the entrance to the arcade, collecting a two-cent fee from those who were persuaded to enter and share its many delights and occasionally thundering through a megaphone in a voice that could be heard blocks away. His wife, almost as large as he, paraded back and forth through the place with an apron full of pennies. Smith's own pale blue eyes met Max's, whose chin barely cleared the counter of the cage, and something in the waif's orbs of innocence made Smith smile with pleasure.

"What can I do for you, boyo?" he asked. "Either you got two cents to come in or you got to watch from outside."

"All them showcards in your window," Max said. "What do you do with the tickets?"

"And what's that to you?"

"I'll buy them. I'll give you two bits a ticket."

"And then sell them for twice that?"

"Nah. I make a nickel or a dime on each. But I find the customers."

"It's an old game. Get on line, sonny." He waved Max away. "Stand aside. Paying customers behind you." Two customers paid their fee and entered, then Max was back at the cage.

"Still here," Smith said. "How old are you, boyo?"

"Twelve."

"It's two o'clock. Why ain't you in school?"

Max studied Smith thoughtfully, then he told him the truth. Smith laughed and shook his head. "That's a lot of horseshit, sonny. You know that. You telling me you support your mother and five other kids? How long now?"

"Since September."

Smith's wife came over to the cage. Business was slow during the day. He told her Max's story.

"Poor lad," she said.

"If he's telling the truth."

"What's he after, money?"

"He wants to buy the showcard tickets."

"Oh?" She turned to Max. "And what for, if you're that miserable?"

"I sell them."

"And how much would you pay?"

"A quarter each."

"Sell him the damn tickets!" she snapped at her husband. "You give them to any bum who asks you."

"Yeah, and don't I save them for your sister's husband?"

"He's the worst bum of all. Sell them to the lad."

After that, Max returned to Rowdy Smith's place each week. Smith and his wife took a liking to the boy, which was somewhat strange, since Max was not the most likable of children — indeed, if the word "child" could be applied to him at all. In the years that followed, the concept of childhood remained cloudy in Max's perception, a land he had never truly entered or departed from and from his point of view a fostered illusion. Smith had a mixed-breed street dog that he kept in his cage with him, and if he made an image of Max in his mind, it was as a sort of human counterpart of the dog — tough, shrewd, street wise, and capable of viciousness if pushed too far. He watched in silent and objective interest once, when Max was cornered just outside the penny arcade by two Irish kids, both of them older and larger than Max. Max did not merely fight back; cornered and provoked by their anti-Semitic slurs, he went at them like a wild animal, driving an elbow into the groin of one boy and leaping onto the other, arms around his neck, teeth biting through an ear. There was a kind of mad yet calculated frenzy in the way Max fought, not the way a kid fights, but drawing blood and exacting pain. The two boys pulled loose and ran, and shaking with his effort, Max came into the arcade and faced Smith's inquiring look.

"No fucken mick's going to call me a Jew bastard," Max said.

"You're absolutely right," Smith agreed.

It was about two months after Max had first come to the arcade when Smith said to him, "You're too damn serious for a kid, Max. Why don't you try some of the pleasures here? It's a place for fun."

"I ain't got money to spend on fun," Max said.

"Go on, go on, you're a kid."

"Yeah."

"Go on, try the kinetoscope. It's a wondrous thing."

"Yeah."

"It's only a penny."

"Yeah."

"Here's a penny," Smith said, pushing the coin toward him. "Go on, try it."

Rowdy Smith had received his kinetoscope machines only a few months before he encountered Max, and already the business was such that he had ordered a sign reading KINETOSCOPE PARLOR to be put in place over his penny arcade entrance. Actually, the machines he rented were not the famed kinetoscope of Thomas A. Edison, but one of a half a dozen imitators that had come on the market. Some four years earlier, Edison had set himself the task of creating a machine that would enable people to look at photographs that moved. In his workshop, a contrivance was put together, but he came up against the need for a proper carrier to feed in pictorial images. Concurrently, George Eastman, working in Rochester on a means of improving his Kodak camera, found a new material to put on the roll, a material that Edison was able to restructure for his kinetoscope. It was a boxlike structure, twelve by twelve by forty inches. There were eyeholes, and when one put one's eyes to the holes and cranked the handles, an image inside the box took on the illusion of motion. Once Edison had created the little machine, he lost interest in it; later, when a promoter, Tom Lombard by name, talked him into allowing the manufacture of ten of the peep shows for the Columbian Exposition in Chicago, Edison first agreed and then regretted his involvement in what he felt was a cheap carnival gimmick. However, without infringing on his patent, imitations of the peep-show machine began to appear. The simplest type was the machine in Rowdy Smith's penny arcade. When the handle was cranked, a series of photographs on cards were flipped in rapid succession, giving a jerky illusion of what, in most cases, was the process of a woman undressing to get into her bath, or being undressed by a lover, or some variation of the same. Always, the process stopped short of full disclosure, and since the whole thing lasted only ten seconds, actual prurience was for the most part avoided. Nevertheless, for the price of a penny, the novelty of motion combined with a suggestion of pornography was very enthralling, especially to the younger set.

In Max's case, there was no sexual innocence to be titillated. For months now, he had been in effect a theatre ticket agent for prostitutes, and he had encountered them in all stages of dress and undress. The female anatomy held no erotic secrets for him to explore as a voyeur, and when he cranked the handle of the kinetoscope, his attitude was more critical than appreciative. When Smith asked him how he liked it, he shrugged.

"They don't really move," Max said.

"What do you want for a cent, the folly boojare?"

"Not some stupid machine that's kidding you into believing you see pictures that move."

"You're a tough little son of a bitch, Max, ain't you?"

"Maybe. But I don't piss my money away."

"That's a fact. I'll tell you something, sonny. They tell me Thomas Edison's working on the real thing, that he's got a peep show you look into and they really move. So when we get some of those machines in here, I'll blow you to another show."

"Sure," Max said. "Sure, why not?"

[TWO]

1897

Max at the Age of Eighteen

IN 1897, on a fine afternoon in March, Max and Suzie Brinkerhoff were having dinner together in the Empire Dairy Restaurant on Second Avenue. Although they served an excellent table d'hôte dinner for thirty cents, economy was not what drew Max there. It was the potato soup. As he explained to Suzie, "I am not a gourmet, believe me — hey, I pronounced that right, didn't I?"

"You got me. What does it mean?"

"Having class when it comes to food. I mean, my mother is a lousy cook, the world's worst, so I developed a taste for good food. Does that make sense?"

"I suppose so."

"And the potato soup here — Well, I don't know, maybe if you set it up at Delmonico's they'd hold their noses, but by my judgment, it's the tops, absolutely the tops."

Suzie shook her head and smiled affectionately. "You're a funny kid, Maxie. Sometimes you make me feel that you got a lot of class, not just about food but about other things, too. Three or four of the girls, we was talking about it, and they all agreed that if you'd get a place, we'd all rather work for you than for anybody else. It wouldn't have to be any kind of great, fancy place, just a place —"

Max shook his head. "No, forget it."

"Why?"

"Because I'm not a pimp. I hate pimps. I never knew a pimp, I didn't want to kick his face in."

"That's only because pimps are rotten people."

"So? And you want me to be a pimp?"

"You're different."

"No, no, not in a hundred years, Suzie. Forget it." He rose, took out his wallet, and dropped a dollar on the table. He enjoyed that; he liked being a large tipper. Waiters remembered him, and he liked that, too. They scrambled to serve him when he came in.

"Where you rushing to?" Suzie asked him. "I thought we had a date."

"We got a date, but it's showtime. You want I should pass you in? You sit through the show, and then afterward, me and you and Bert, we'll go out for coffee and cake."

"I seen the show, and your friend Bert I can live without."

"We got a new routine for tonight, two new jokes."

"You know, Maxie, you set up with me and two or three of the girls, you can make yourself maybe three, four hundred a week. That ain't hay. That is big, big money."

"I told you no!"

"O.K., O.K., don't get sore. Thanks for the dinner." She turned on her heel and started away.

"Hey, where are you going?"

"I'm a working girl, Maxie. I don't improve my income sitting in that flea-bitten Bijou and watching you tell dumb jokes."

• • •

The Bijou, which was located on West Broadway between Prince Street and Spring Street, was a music hall, which meant that it was the workingman's theatre and that it catered more to the English-speaking population than to the immigrants. It had been built in 1823, and its footlights had once been candlelights. Now they were gaslights. The style and manner of the Bijou's entertainment — and, incidentally, the entertainment of most of the other music halls in New York City — had been lifted originally from the British music halls and then adapted to fit the local taste. The evening of entertainment consisted of a mixture of what would someday be called vaudeville and what would be known as burlesque, except that the acts were never overtly lewd or obscene. The meat and potatoes of music hall comedy was a kind of vulgar *double-entendre,* which the less prurient-minded could pretend not to understand, and the songs were mostly ballads, some brought over from London and reworked, since there was no international copyright protection at that time. The Bijou had five hundred and forty seats, and it played two shows every evening, double matinees on Monday and Wednesday, and two matinees and three evening shows on Saturday. For the comedy routine which he did with his partner, Bert Bellamy, Max and Bert were paid forty-four dollars a week, twenty-two dollars each. It was good pay. There were music halls that paid a lot less for their acts.

Max had met Bert Bellamy at Rowdy Smith's penny arcade four years before. Bellamy was fifteen at the time, a year older than Max, tall, freckled, with a small snub nose and gray eyes. He worked at the arcade evenings between eight and ten, which were the heaviest hours of business, and he had been taken on by Smith after worsening arthritis had diminished the amount of hours Mrs. Smith could put in. Bellamy was given an apron with huge pockets filled with pennies, and each night he wandered through the place making change and looking for cheaters.

He and Max became friends. Indeed, he was the only friend Max made in all the years of his clawing his way out of childhood into the beginning of maturity. Max was fascinated with Bert Bellamy. He came from a background as poor as Max's; as with Max, childhood with its supposed carefree joys had slipped by him unnoticed, and like Max he was a survivor who survived through his wits and street-wise cunning. But unlike Max or any other kid within Max's limited world, Bert Bellamy was a white Protestant American — Presbyterian — and the product of over ten generations of American-born white Protestants. Every other kid Max had ever known or fought with was either Jewish or Catholic and always the child of an immigrant. Bellamy was something else and from elsewhere, another place, planet, and culture — or so Max saw him and understood him. Actually, Bert Bellamy was the son of an alcoholic father and a mother he could not remember. The mother had disappeared when Bellamy was two years old. The father, a carpenter, drank himself to death when Bellamy was sixteen, after which Bert gave up the basement residence that could hardly be called an apartment and spent his nights in a tiny storeroom behind the penny arcade.

But because he had been on his own, more or less, ever since he could remember, the death of his father made little difference. He and Max had a great deal in common: they were both products of the streets; they were both tough and tough-minded, survivors, and cunning in the paths and ways of survival; and they both had the gift of mimicry. They were both skinny, wiry, long-limbed, and they were well coordinated. They could pick up any dance step in minutes. When Max was sixteen, Bert talked him into working out an act and began to drag him around to the music halls. They never paid to go in. They would tell the stage door keeper that they had a date with the manager to show him a gig, and even when they were thrown out, they usually had enough time in the wings to watch the acts. They got their first tryout after practicing for almost a year, and by now they were reasonably successful as a song, dance, and joke team.

Bert was made up and waiting for him when Max came in this evening, and petulant over the fact that it was only eight minutes to curtain.

"Take it easy," Max said soothingly. "I took Suzie out to dinner."

"You still hanging around with that big floozie? Come on, come on, change." Bert was already dressed in the oversized checked trousers, the loose celluloid collar, pink waistcoat, and black tailcoat that made up his costume. Max climbed into green pants and purple jacket.

"She's my friend."

"Do you get it from her? What do you get, Max? I offer you some of the nicest ass in little old New York, and you turn your nose up at it."

"I don't sleep with her, and what you consider nice ass, I don't."

"Right. You listen to a different drum."

"What?"

"Nothing, nothing. I read it in a book or something. I wanted to go through that new routine, and now we ain't got time. We're on."

Applying makeup quickly, Max said, "Go on, go on, we'll wing it."

"You sure?"

"I'm sure." He gave Bert a friendly shove. "Go on, go on. I'm not playing high and mighty, old buddy, I just got a nightmare thing about getting a dose."

"Never been there myself," Bert said. "Just lucky." He did a soft-shoe out of the tiny room to face the manager, who whispered hoarsely, "Where the hell have you been?"

"Way down upon the Suwannee River," Bert sang.

"Funny, funny."

Bert was onstage. A ripple of applause from behind the gaslights; no one expected very much from a two-man song and dance team. They were just part of the scene.

Bert bowed. "Bellamy and —" He looked around him, nonplussed. "Bellamy and —" He began again. Still he was alone on the stage. The repeated double-take drew some laughter from the audience. "Well, here I am," Bert said, spreading his arms in despair, "the only one-man two-man song and dance team in New York."

It was a new opening. Bert could see Joe Guttman, the manager, standing in the wing, chewing on an unlit cigar. He was drawing it out too much, and in another moment it would go flat. Where the hell was Max? Why did he always allow himself to be talked into things by that smartass little Yid? Then Max appeared, shuffling out onto the stage, the very picture of dejection and rejection. Bert was not acting when he snapped at him, "Where the hell have you been?"

"A man wants to be loved for himself —"

"Can that! Here I am on the stage of the Bijou Music Hall, trying to introduce a song and dance team, of which I am a part, and I say, 'Introducing Bellamy and —' and what?" Past Max, Bert saw the scowl on Guttman's face. He was taking it straight, with no idea that they were doing a new opening. The man was a fucken cretin, but they should have anticipated that and warned him, and now he could just drop the curtain on both of them. "And nothing," Bert said desperately.

"So I was late. You know what happened to me?"

"How do I know? I'm here at the Bijou."

"Well, I'll tell you what happened to me. Just calm down. I'll tell you what happened to me. Two blocks away, right on the corner of West Broadway and Canal Street, I'm stopped by a beautiful girl."

"Beautiful girl. What was her name?"

"How the hell do I know her name? We wasn't introduced. I wasn't taking her home. I was stopped by her."

"You were stopped by her. Canal and Broadway. Go on." Bert breathed a sigh of relief. The rhythm of their patter had gotten through to Guttman even as he was moving to drop the curtain. He paused and turned to listen.

"I said, 'Lady, I don't do that kind of thing.' "

"That's a lie. What did she say?"

"She says, try it. Otherwise, you'll never know what you're missing. So I tell her I'd like to, but I'm on my way to work."

Bert licked his lips. "So she says, 'What a coincidence! We can work together.' "

"How do you know that was what she said?" Max demanded.

"Was that what she said?"

"I said that was what she said. Then she says, 'Let's work together.' "

"And you're not even beautiful."

"That's what I told her. She said it don't matter."

"Did you tell her you don't know up from down, boys from girls?"

"I told her. She said it don't matter."

"Well, what happened, what happened?"

"I told her I didn't have no money."

"You told her that? What did she say then?"

"She said, 'Get out of here, you lousy little bum, or I'll call a cop.' "

There was a long moment of silence, and then the audience applauded. It was strong applause. The new opening worked.

• • •

Whenever Max saw a school, either a public school or a high school he experienced a sense of loss, a sadness without definition, a dejection that placed him on the defensive. Like a reunion with an old lost love who loved no more, it provided no space for understanding or accommodation, and his love-hate of school was too complex for him to unravel. He could have been given to introspection; he had enough imagination and instinct; but introspection was too threatening. It interfered with a simple, workable credo: he did whatever he had to do.

Today he had to go to school because there was a note from Ruby's teacher asking Mrs. Britsky to come to see her and discuss certain difficulties she was having with Reuben Britsky. Reuben was now fourteen years old, in the eighth grade of public school. Describing his brother succinctly, Max read the letter and said, "He's a little bum. He always has been."

"What use to say that?" Sarah asked him, speaking in Yiddish. "When you're home he's at school, and when he's here you're working."

"So it's my fault?"

"I didn't say that. Only, no one disciplines him. He's too big, and he don't listen to me."

"He'll listen to you. I'll break his goddamn neck. You can be sure he'll listen to you.",

"I can't go to school."

"Why not?"

"Max, what do you want from me?" she asked him. "I can barely speak English. You want me to go to a school and speak to a teacher? How can I? If your saintly dead father —"

"All right, I'll go!" He could not bear hearing his father described as saintly. "I'll go!" He stamped out of the kitchen in anger. It was the same kitchen, the same roach-infested tenement flat, the same stinking smell of urine in the hallway outside the apartment door, the same filthy, noisy street outside — all the same, all stinking to high heaven of misery and poverty. Nothing changed, not even the public school, the same school he had attended through the sixth grade.

A block from the school, across the street but with the school in full view, Max paused and studied it, realizing that for years he had detoured around it, refused to face it. Now he faced it, a four-story red brick building, standing there in Clinton Street as it had for the past half-century. Max could visualize the place precisely without setting foot in it. The building had been turned into a hospital for Civil War soldiers soon after its completion, and the kids still called it sickbay, a nickname that had stuck through the years. The schoolrooms on the second floor of the building all had sliding walls, and when assembly took place, all the schoolroom walls were rolled back, turning the entire second floor into an assembly hall. The walls were on rollers, each section eight feet wide and ten feet high, and four kids were assigned to roll each section. During his last term in school, Max had won an assignment to a section. With some disdain, he recalled his pride at the achievement. Big deal, he said to himself. The privilege of pushing a wall. Then he crossed the street and entered the school.

The office was on the main floor, and on a bench outside the door to the office, three kids sat, staring sullenly at the floor. It was a time when the free public school was a sort of holy place, the teacher's word accepted as law, the whole system and structure sacrosanct in the eyes of the immigrant children and their parents. There were few breaches of discipline, and when they occurred, the school itself was turned into a jail of sorts, with the offending child kept sitting in his classroom for hours after closing time, writing the nature of his offense over and over. Yet this was not the source of order and obedience in the schools; rather, it was the fact that the immigrants themselves, the Irish and the Jews and the Italians who composed the bulk of the parents, regarded the free school as a shrine, an incredible and unbelievable gift to their children. Whatever they themselves suffered and endured, the filth, the poverty, the cold and hunger, there was the school as a promise for their children. And within this system, the offender was sent to the office, as these three kids had been, sitting on the bench outside and awaiting their turn and fate.

Max paused to glance at them. At least today Ruby wasn't among them. Inside the office, a matronly woman looked at him inquiringly.

"I have a letter from Miss Sally Levine to come here," Max explained.

"You're too young to be a parent," she said suspiciously.

"Yeah," Max agreed. "That's right. It's about my brother Ruby. He's in Miss Levine's class. My mother got a letter, she should come. Well, my mother can't come."

"Why?"

"She's sick," Max said, choosing the shortest explanation.

"I'm sorry. Yes, I suppose you ought to talk to Miss Levine.

You'll find her in Room Three twenty-two. That's up two flights, and when you come out of the staircase, you turn right.''

Max nodded and left, pausing outside to grin at the three sinners. "Mind your manners, little bastards," he said softly. On his way up to Room 322, he silently vented his anger against Ruby. "Little son of a bitch, making me come to this stupid place!" Yet he too was in the grip of the place, directed and constrained by the mythology that permeated the old building. He opened the door of Room 322 gently and tentatively.

The door was at the back of the room, so only the teacher and one student saw him enter. Max was surprised at the youthfulness of Miss Levine. His last appearance in school had been at age eleven, and at that time Miss Levine's twenty-two years — as he learned later — would have appeared quite mature; at age eighteen, he might have described her as a kid. She had good features, brown eyes, a small, delicate mouth, and a great mop of rich brown hair that she wore in a large bun at the back of her neck, a severity that was *de rigueur* in her profession. The same severity accounted for her high-buttoned white blouse with long sleeves and a long gray skirt, yet in spite of the severe and colorless costume, Max had the impression of a slender yet well-rounded body.

Miss Levine stood at the front of the room at one side. Between her and Max, at the back of the room, there were six rows of desks six in a row, with an aisle down the center separating three from three. Each desk was a single unit, bolted to the floor. The student at either end of the group of three could slide out; the student in the center was trapped until one of the others gave way. Even as a kid, Max had considered it to be a silly system. The whole front wall of the room was covered with a blackboard, upon which was neatly chalked: "The sonnet is a poem of fourteen lines. The rhythm of the words it contains is called iambic pentameter. It must have a rhyme scheme, which can vary but which must conform to certain historical restrictions.''

Max had never heard of a sonnet, and he had no notion of what iambic pentameter meant. He felt a sudden rush of fury against his goddamn little son of a bitch kid brother who had all this handed to him and showed his appreciation by lousing it up, and at the same time, thinking this, he listened to the fourteen-year-old girl, wide-eyed and open-faced, standing in front of the class opposite Miss Levine, declaiming:

> Milton! thou shouldst be living at this hour:
> England hath need of thee: she is a fen
> Of stagnant waters: altar, sword and pen,
> Fireside, the heroic wealth —

The girl noticed Max at the back of the room, hesitated, stopped; and now the other students followed her eyes, turned in their seats to look at Max. He tried to put it together — the writing on the blackboard, the poem the girl was reciting, which made no sense to him, the fact that Ruby was not present, for by now all the faces had turned to him, and Miss Levine striding toward him.

"Who are you and why are you interrupting my class?" She was certainly not the timid type, at least on her own ground.

"I'm Max Britsky. You wrote a letter about Ruby, my brother."

She was speaking while he was speaking: "Ruth, please go on. 'The heroic wealth of hall and bower.' Continue with that line."

Ruth recited:

> — the heroic wealth of hall and bower
> Have forfeited their ancient English dower —

Against her voice, Miss Levine said sharply, "If you will please wait outside, Mr. Britsky, I will join you in a few minutes." She opened the door for him and practically propelled him into the hall, and there he stood, angry, frustrated, deflated with the awareness of his own ignorance in terms of an eighth-grade class, telling himself, That bitch — that hard-assed stuck-up little bitch! Where the hell does she come off pushing me around like I'm dirt in front of a broom? I ought to go in there and tell her the right time right in front of her class.

But he didn't do that. He remained at the door, waiting, and when Miss Levine finally appeared, Max mumbled, "Sorry — I didn't mean to bust in there like that. In the office, they said I should come up here."

"Yes, of course, and that meant march in and disrupt my class."

"I didn't mean to disrupt your class," Max told her, his anger returning. "Damnit, what was I supposed to do? They tell me, go up to Room Three twenty-two, and now you're ready to take my head off!"

She looked at him thoughtfully, then she nodded. "Yes, I've been rude, haven't I? I don't know whether you can understand, but this poetry session is the most meaningful thing in my teaching. To have that child, who comes from a background where no English is spoken . . . Well, to have her stand up in front of the class and recite from memory Wordsworth's ode to Milton, well, it's just something incredible, and that's why I was so short with you, Mr. Britsky. Please accept my apology."

Listening to her, Max was thinking that she was very attractive and very different from anyone he had ever spoken to. Her words were different, her manner of speaking was different, and there was no frame of reference to lock it into. He tried to recall his teachers at age eleven, but where a woman was observed as a woman, there was no subjective connection between age eleven and age eighteen. Miss Levine's name indicated that she was Jewish. Max had never heard of anyone with the name of Levine who wasn't Jewish, but neither had he ever met a Jewish girl who was not the product of the Lower East Side ghetto; and if this had produced Miss Levine, why did she look and talk the way she did? And how did she happen to be a teacher? In the six years of his life between entering public school and leaving it, Max had never encountered a Jewish teacher.

Max stared at her without replying, and Miss Levine went on to point out to him that she could leave her class only for a limited time. "I asked for Reuben's mother," she added.

"Well," he said uncertainly, "my mother —" He was suddenly acutely conscious of the fact that he pronounced it *mudder*, and he tried to correct himself as he went on. "My mother's from the old country. She don't speak much English, and she'd be afraid to come here to a place like this."

It wasn't at all what he had intended to say. He had anticipated no need for an explanation. He would simply say that his mother was sick and now he couldn't quite comprehend why he had said what he had said, but Miss Levine simply nodded and said that she understood.

"Most immigrant women live in a state of fear. It's a wretched thing, but it's so." Max listened and nodded, not entirely sure that he knew what she meant. "Still, you're his brother, and you have taken a day off work, so I can see that his education means something to your family."

"Well, no, not exactly. I didn't have to take a day off work. I'm an entertainer." He was bogged down, enmeshed in his attempt to manufacture an explanation. "I mean, that don't mean I'm not interested in his education. But today I got no matinee."

"Oh?"

What did the "Oh" express? Contempt? Disdain? "What's wrong with Ruby?" he snapped.

"Yes. You see he's not here. Is he ill?"

"Hooky. That —" He bit off the words.

"It's not simply truancy, although that averages at least a day a week. He forges notes from his mother, well written but transparent. You see, it's not that he's stupid. He's very clever, but he's boisterous, unruly, and very disruptive. I almost breathe a sigh of relief when he is truant."

"I wish I had known this," Max said grimly, so grimly that Miss Levine smiled at the stern, stiff-necked young man who faced her. "No more hooky, you can be sure of that, and no more fooling around. He's going to toe the line."

"It will certainly help the class deportment, Mr. Britsky."

"Yeah, I'll take care of it."

"Thank you. I must go back to the class now."

• • •

It wasn't until late afternoon that Max returned to the apartment on Henry Street. It was almost five o'clock, and as he entered the kitchen, Ruby was on his way out and Sarah was shouting at him, "Now, five o'clock, and you're going out, and it's practically time for supper."

"I don't want no supper, Mama."

"What is this, you don't want no supper?"

They were all there in the kitchen, spectators at the scene between Ruby and his mother, Freida fifteen already, blooming, tight in her clothes like a ripe plum in its skin; the two other girls, Esther and Sheila, nine and eleven respectively, Esther with unexpected red hair, Sheila skinny and long-legged, built as Max was; and the baby, Benny, almost eight years old — all of them alive and healthy because Max had kept them alive and healthy, all of them integrated as parts in the high-pitched drama that their lives had become, packed as they were into the tiny apartment. They lived in clawing contact with each other, and they screamed and fought and bitched because they were without space or privacy and because they lacked any blueprint to define their lives; yet at the same time they were keenly aware and intrigued by the electric and dramatic quality of their disputes.

"So you're going out," Max said to Ruby.

"Yeah."

"Going out for dinner?"

"Yeah. Maybe."

"Tell him!" Sarah cried. "Tell him he can eat dinner at home!"

Max ignored her. "You going maybe to Delmonico's?"

"What's Delmonico's? No. I'll pick up a hot dog on the corner."

"With what for scratch?"

"I got thirty cents. Big deal."

"You are goddamn right!" Max exploded. "You are goddamn right, you miserable little shithead! It's a big deal. You got thirty cents, you put it down there on the table and Mama buys food. You stole it, you little bastard."

"Max, I didn't —"

"Shut up! Put it on the table, or I'll give you a mouthful of teeth for dinner!"

"Max, please," Sarah begged him, but facing his brother's rage, Ruby emptied his pocket and threw a quarter and five pennies on the table.

"Now get to hell inside and do your homework," Max said.

"I ain't got homework."

"You're damn right. And you know why — because you played hooky today. And how many other times? Now you listen to me. You miss another day of school or make another *wisenheimer* crack to your teacher, and I will personally beat the living crap out of you. Now get to hell in there and do your homework, and if you ain't got any, invent it!"

• • •

For the following three days, Max thought of little else than Miss Levine. He held fantasy conversations with her in which he mysteriously emerged as a student at either Harvard or Yale, both of them places about which he knew only the names and certain fuzzy connotations. Or he became a tycoon, a builder of railroads and factories, wealthy beyond measure, driving her through the city in a marvelous open two-horse carriage. Max and his partner, Bert Bellamy, had once tried bridling, as it was called, at Delmonico's restaurant at Fifth Avenue and Twenty-sixth Street. The bridler was a kid who grabbed the bridle when the carriages lined up outside of Delmonico's waiting to discharge their dinner guests, his pretense being that he kept the horse from rearing, and sometimes there was a half-dollar tip. But the competition was fierce and the doormen were brutal. When they caught a kid, they beat him unmercifully, and after Bert had been trapped and beaten, he and Max gave it up. But Max remembered the carriages, the men in their evening clothes, the women bejeweled in pearls and diamonds and overdressed in their expensive and incredibly ornate gowns of silk and moiré and taffeta and lace. To Max, they were neither overdressed nor vulgar, only enviable, and he saw himself and Miss Levine descending from one of those carriages. Yet his fantasies foundered upon the fact that he did not know her first name.

What had he done with her letter? Her name had been written there, yet he had read it in such a flush of irritation that he had not even noticed her first name. He searched everywhere in the apartment for the letter, to the tune of, "Max, what are you looking for?" from the others in the family. But the letter was gone. He even contemplated asking Ruby what Miss Levine's first name was, but thrust the notion aside. When he told Bert about his dilemma, Bert said impatiently, "Schmuck, go ask her."

Max paused in the act of smearing his face with pancake makeup and said, "What? Are you nuts?"

"Not me, buddy. You're the guy who's gone loony over this skirt."

"Hey — don't call her that!"

"Jesus, Joseph, and Mary, forgive me!"

"I can't ask her."

"Why not? Ain't she a skirt? O.K., I apologize. She's a dame, ain't she?"

"Yeah."

"So?"

"She's older than I am."

"Maxie baby, ease up. I never fucked a lady wasn't older than me. Otherwise, what have you got? Jailbait."

"She ain't that kind of a girl."

"Oh."

"Look, I don't want to talk about it. Forget it."

• • •

The first time Max went to the school after his visit on behalf of Ruby, at exactly ten minutes after three P.M., and hid himself inside the hallway of a tenement across the street, he proposed to himself that he did so to make certain that Ruby was attending classes. But if so, why at ten minutes after three, when most of the students had already left the school? Why not at ten minutes before three? The hell with it, he said to himself. I'm here, ain't I? So I'm late.

It wasn't until ten minutes to four that Miss Levine emerged, flanked on either side by a lady teacher, and so flanked proceeded down the street and out of sight. Safely concealed in the darkness of the tenement hallway, Max could watch her through the glass pane in the door that led to the street. The following day, Max admitted to himself that he went there to watch her come out of the school, but that day and the next two days, Miss Levine was securely protected by the two lady teachers who walked on either side of her. Not until the fifth day of watching did Miss Levine emerge from the school alone and unescorted.

It was not until she was halfway down the school block that Max screwed up his courage sufficiently to follow, taking long steps, half running, and then blurting out, "Hello, Miss Levine!"

But his voice came forth a quavering squeak, and Miss Levine paused to turn and regard him with astonishment. He stood foolishly, smiling.

"Mr. Britsky."

He nodded.

"Were you coming to the school? It's much too late, you know. It's after hours."

"No . . . well, yes. I mean, how is the kid acting?"

"The kid?"

"My brother Ruby."

"Oh. Yes. Yes, I think he's trying." She looked at him strangely "Yes, he's trying. It's nice to have met you." And then she started to walk off.

Walking alongside of her, Max said, "Is it all right if I walk along with you?"

Again she paused, looking at him thoughtfully.

"I guess it looks to you like I'm acting crazy," Max said.

This time Miss Levine was at a loss for words.

"Yeah, I know, because I guess I am acting crazy, because couldn't think of any other way to get to meet you."

"But you have met me, Mr. Britsky, and if you wanted to see me again, all you had to do was to send a note into the class."

"That ain't what I mean. I mean that isn't what I mean, no exactly." He noticed the shadow of a smile when he replaced "ain't" with "isn't," and somehow it reassured him. "I mean meet you — just meet you — not because some kid I'm connected with act like a little bum. Do I make any sense?"

"Yes, I think I understand."

"So can I buy you a cup of coffee? Can we sit down somewhere and talk?"

"No, I don't think so."

"Why not?"

"For one thing, I'm on my way home, where I have things to do."

"Are you married?" he demanded.

"That's really none of your business, is it, Mr. Britsky?"

"Yes, it is."

"Well, I would dispute that," she said. "But if you must know I am not married." She stared at him again, her dark brown eye searching his face. "Do you always do that, stop people on the street and ask personal questions?"

"You know I don't. You're making fun of me, aren't you?"

"No, but you invite it, you're so nervous and frightened."

"Me?" Max demanded indignantly. "Me frightened?"

"I live on Tenth Street in Greenwich Village," Miss Levine said "It's a long walk, but when the weather is good I do like to walk home."

"Can I walk with you?"

"Yes, if you wish. If you have the time."

They began to walk. For Max, it was a new experience, this sensation of deep satisfaction and great accomplishment flowing out of the simple act of walking alongside a young woman. Yet he realized that a moment or two before, she had been on the point of dismissing him out of hand. He couldn't help asking her what made her change her mind.

"I told you. You were so frightened."

"That's crazy," Max said. "I'm not frightened. I'm — I don't know how to even talk to someone like you."

"You are talking to me, Mr. Britsky."

"Yeah, sure. You're not from here, are you?"

"From here?"

"Here — the East Side?"

"No, I was born in Brooklyn. That's not so far away, but too far for a daily journey, and since I've been teaching, I do live here."

"Yeah, sure. I guess to you I look like some kind of hoodlum."

"No. Well, I am curious about you. You said you were an entertainer. But you're very young —"

"Eighteen. That's not young."

"But you can't be out of high school more than a few months."

He was silent for a while, then he told her that he had left school at the age of twelve.

"Why?"

"To work."

"I know children work, but you could have gone to school."

"My father died," Max said flatly. "He left my mother and six kids. We had no relatives, nobody, nobody who'd lift a finger or care whether we lived or died. Someone had to take care of them."

"A woman and six children?"

"Yes."

Miss Levine paused, slowed her walk, and then stopped to stare at Max as if she were seeing him for the first time. "And you did that — at the age of twelve?"

"I'm not lying," Max said defensively. "Nobody else did it, and they're still alive, right?"

"I didn't mean to suggest that you were lying. It's just so incredible, so incredible."

• • •

That night Bert said to Max, "You mean after that you just walked home with her and walked away? Maxie, baby, you got brains — you know where you got brains, in your pants."

"All right. This is not tail. This is not a piece of ass."

"They're all tail, they're all a piece of ass. You introduce me to that twist, and I guarantee you that in twenty-four hours I'll have my hand in her bloomers."

"And I'd kill you, you bastard!"

"Ah, the boy's serious. You're in love, buster."

But Max's relationship to love, romantic or otherwise, was cloudy. He was knit to his family, but he had no love for them, and since leaving school he had not read a book, whereby his notions of romantic attachment were unembellished by literature. He read the newspapers only in a desultory fashion since he was uninterested in politics, racing sheets more frequently, *Cockfight Specials,* which dealt with dogfights as well as cockfights, throwaways on pink paper, and now and then, *Dirty Dillies,* which was a crude pornographic magazine; but reading played a very minor role in his life, and notions of love as projected in the music halls were hardly inspiring. Still and all, something moved him and compelled him as he had never been moved before, and once again he approached Miss Levine as she was leaving the school.

If Max's world was a very narrow one, he nevertheless knew it and explored it, and he accepted enlargement with a totally open mind. Max knew how the floozies dressed, he knew how girls from his own background dressed, and he even knew how uptown ladies dressed; and if Miss Levine dressed somewhat differently from any of those groups, Max could balance the lot and accept her costume and learn something from it. Her ankle-length gray worsted skirt was well cut and appeared to hang and flow gracefully with her movements. She wore a dark blue spring coat and under it a white blouse, the jabot of which was just visible, and she carried both a briefcase and a purse. This time Max ignored the fact that she walked with another teacher. He fell into step alongside of her and said, "Please, let me carry your briefcase." And then he took it from her before she could properly protest.

She was taken aback and somewhat flustered as she introduced the other teacher: "Miss MacClintock, this is Mr. Britsky."

Max lifted his hat, nodded, and said, "Ma'am. How do you do?"

He had never before in his life greeted anyone in precisely that manner, and he thought he brought it off rather well.

At the next corner, Miss MacClintock left them to continue across town while they turned uptown; and Miss Levine said, with some asperity, "Really, Mr. Britsky, this can't go on. I will not be accosted by you whenever I leave the school."

"I only done — did it once before. This is only the second time. That's not whenever you leave the school."

"Twice is enough. What on earth do you want?"

"I guess I just want to know you, to be your friend."

"What!" Her surprise and indignation hit Max like a severe slap in the face. Apparently she realized that she had struck home, because when Max stopped dead in his tracks, she walked only a few steps before she turned around and went back to him.

"I'm sorry," she said.

"For what? For nothing. You got this East Side hoodlum annoying you and you tell him to buzz off. That's all right. It's a free country."

"That's not what I meant."

"Sure it is. Don't you think I know what I am? I'm Britsky, which is nothing to write home about. I got no education and I got no class, and with a puss like mine, I don't have any looks either."

"You're a very nice-looking young man, Mr. Britsky, and you're just making too much of this. I am four years older than you, and I would think you'd be better suited to a young lady of your own age."

"I know. I get the message."

Now Miss Levine smiled slightly and said, "You know, I was going to walk away a moment ago and leave you with my briefcase, and I guess that does indicate that I trust you. It's very kind of you to carry it. Would you like to walk home with me?"

"Yes."

"All the way up to Tenth Street? It's a good-sized walk."

"You don't mind?"

"I asked you because I'd like you to."

"Right."

They walked on for another block in silence, then she said to him, "What is your first name, Mr. Britsky? You do have a first name?"

"You like to kid me, don't you? Sure I got a first name. Max."

"Max?"

"That's right. And your name's ———?"

"Sally."

"So if you called me Max and I called you Sally, the world wouldn't come to an end, would it?"

"I suppose not."

"So?"

"So what?"

"So would you call me Max and let me call you Sally?"

They had now reached Houston Street, and they turned west toward Broadway. Once again, Miss Levine paused and faced him. "To what end, Mr. Britsky?" she asked him.

"Damnit!" he blurted out. "I want us to be friends! I want to go around with you the way a guy does with a girl. I want to see you again without standing outside that lousy school like some total dumbbell. I want to take you out to dinner."

"That's quite impossible," Miss Levine said primly.

"Why?"

"I don't think we ought to go into that. You're a very young man. I am much older than you, and I think we would have very little if anything in common."

"Yeah, if you count the years, you're four years older, but if you count what it takes to grow up in this rotten city, I'm ten years older than you, and maybe you figure I'm just a hoodlum, so there's nothing we got in common, because I left school and I don't speak the way you do, but —" He was grinning at her now.

"But what?"

"But I'll grow on you, I bet. Look, let me take you out to dinner tonight and I'll bet you twenty bucks you'll like me enough to do it again."

"Oh? All right. Not tonight. Tomorrow night."

"What? Hey, is that straight goods?"

"Yes, I said you could take me to dinner tomorrow night. But I want you to understand that I do this with some trepidation. We have never been formally introduced."

Max was not certain what trepidation meant, nor was he quite clear about the social meaning of a formal introduction. He was certain that she had agreed to a date on the following night. "O.K.!

Great! Right now I'm introducing myself." He bowed, removing his hat. "My name is Max Britsky. Right now I am nobody but I intend to become somebody. You can't go wrong with me, believe me. Max Britsky introduces himself!"

His enthusiasm was such that Miss Levine broke into laughter.

"Sally?" he said.

"Yes?"

"You see — Sally. I am calling you Sally. Try Max."

"What?"

"Try calling me Max. Just try it."

"Max."

"See, it don't hurt."

"It *doesn't* —" She swallowed it.

"Go on," Max said.

"No, I'm being dreadful. I'm correcting your speech."

"Do it. I got to learn."

When they reached Washington Square, they were much more at ease with each other, and Sally pointed to the houses on the north side of the park. "When you become that great wealthy millionaire Max Britsky, you can buy me one of those houses."

"Oh?" Glancing at her sharply.

"Just as a gift. We'll still be casual acquaintances, but just the way Diamond Jim throws his jewels around." She had changed, thrown off the austere mantle of the teacher.

"Which house?"

"That one will do," she said lightly, pointing to a lovely red brick mansion.

"I'll remember that."

.   .   .

Frustrated, fuming in the tiny bedroom that he shared with Ruby, both of them sleeping together in an ancient three-quarter bed, his two suits hanging from a hook on the wall, his linen stuffed into the drawers of a battered chest, Max tried to construct a bow-tie knot and failed. He rooted in the drawer and came up with a wrinkled four-in-hand. It needed ironing, but Sarah was otherwise engaged. Max listened to his mother scream at his sister Freida. Cramped and crowded into the little cold-water flat, cheek by jowl with an endless and undefeatable army of roaches and bedbugs as well as each other, they lived with tension. They screamed and raged at each other, and now, hearing his mother, Max contemplated bringing Miss Sally Levine into this madhouse. "Come right in, Miss Levine, this is my mother and my sisters and my brothers." Sarah had just finished denouncing her daughter Freida, fifteen and a half years old, as a tramp and a bum.

Freida defended herself in the only way she knew, by attempting to outscream her mother. "What am I?" she demanded. "Am I some kind of freak? We're not in Europe! I'm not a prisoner of yours, you should decide who I see and who I marry!"

"God forbid!" Sarah interjected.

"A boy looks at me, right away I'm a tramp. That's all you ever got to say to me, I'm a tramp. Beautiful words!"

"You act like a tramp, you dress like a tramp, you're a tramp!" Sarah stated. "You hang out with bums at a candy store! Who else does it but a tramp? Tell me. Just tell me."

"All right! From now on I go to cotillions. At the Waldorf, naturally. You will please arrange my debut! Or should I sit here with you every night and bite my nails?"

Unable to endure it any longer, Max stamped into the kitchen and shouted, "Will you two stop that! Every time I come in here, you're screaming at each other."

"You two! You two!" Sarah exploded. "Suddenly, I'm not your mother! I'm something called you two! I'm nothing! I'm dirt!" She grabbed a dishtowel and tried to wipe off the bit of rouge that Freida had applied. Freida fought back. Max pulled the two of them apart.

"You're demented, both of you. Crazy."

Sarah began to weep. "I'm crazy," she sobbed. "I got a son, he's a bum who runs around with whores and actors, and I got a daughter, she's a tramp, but I should be happy. So I'm not happy, I'm crazy."

Max put his arms around her. "Mama, I don't mean you're crazy. It's just you're making me crazy." He waved Freida away, and she slipped out. "No, I don't mean that, only you shouldn't upset yourself over nothing."

"Nothing, what's nothing? What's the clean shirt for?" she demanded.

"I'm going out."

"Every night you go out —"

"Mama, I work at the music hall. You know that."

"Five o'clock? And you need a clean shirt to work at the music hall? My food ain't good enough? You got to eat the poison from the Chinks and the Italians?"

"It's not poison, Mama."

Suddenly Sarah discovered that Freida was gone. "Where is she?"

"So she went out, Mama. She'll be back in an hour," thinking to himself, Poor kid. It's a lunatic asylum.

Freida, on the other hand, renewed herself each time she escaped from the flat on Henry Street. Whatever romantic fantasies she cherished, the only reality she knew was the street outside and its population. The candy store was on the corner of Pike Street, and it was run by Mr. Rabinowitz. The times were innocent of dope, and if one wanted to ease out of the torments of the world, one could buy Lydia Pinkham's Vegetable Compound quite legally, laced though it was with opium, not to mention a dozen other products dispensed from drugstore shelves and equally modified with opium. But the kids, born of the new immigrants who had pushed across the Atlantic to populate New York City's East Side, were not given to dope or whiskey. In their eager adolescence, they stepped into the twentieth century with nothing more deadly than sweets, leaving aside their gang wars and petty thievery. Mr. Rabinowitz had a counter stocked with over one hundred varieties of penny candy, nothing more than a penny, and for a nickel you could eat yourself sick with licorice, candy sticks, mints, creams, buttons, gumdrops, hard candy, soft candy, twists, streamers, jawbreakers, gunshots, sponges, hard toffee, soft toffee, and dozens of other varieties whose names are lost in the mists of time. In the warm months of summer, Mr. Rabinowitz would always have an enormous cake of ice in his store, and for two cents, he would scrape a large lump of crushed ice onto a paper plate and then flavor it with one or two of a shelf of colorful flavors, shaking the flavoring out of the same type of bottle barbers used to dispense hair tonic. The rest of Mr. Rabinowitz's shop was taken up with newspapers, magazines, cigars, and the pads, pencils, and crayons school kids required. Mr. Rabinowitz and his wife, small, gray-haired, gray-faced people, accepted their store's role as a hangout for the kids. There was no other. It was the norm. If the store became too crowded with kids horsing around, pushing, shouting, stealing, Mrs. Rabinowitz would take a broom to them and chase them out onto the sidewalk.

But it was mere formality. They were on the sidewalk now when Freida joined them, Rocky, Joe, Shutzie, Stumphead, Izzy. Lizzie was there. She was always there and appeared to have no other home. She was called Lizzie-snatch, and she was easy, even to the point of inviting gangshags, which meant having intercourse with all the boys, one after the other. Miriam, like Freida, fought the boys off, or pretended to or attempted to, and there were two or three other girls, Josie and Becky and Clara; but aside from Lizzie, it was mostly necking and horsing around, and when they got bored horsing around in and out of the candy store, they drifted over to South Street and the river and the docks and the fishing boats, but always in a group. They were Jewish kids, and when they moved they had to be wary of Irish territory and Italian territory and in particular of the cops, who would beat up on them just for the sake of beating up on them.

This was Freida's escape, her land of romance, her relief from the closeness and stink of the flat on Henry Street, her reward, as she felt it, for enduring life. By her lights, there was no other escape. Yet there were moments, when they all went over to the East River and sneaked out to the end of a wharf and sat there and saw the stars in the sky and the shimmering reflected city lights on the water and the riverboats passing by, when Freida tasted a moment of another reality. But it never lasted.

· · ·

Long after this, recalling her first date with Max Britsky, Sally told an interviewer, "It was the manner of the man. He had a grand manner, if you can think of an eighteen-year-old kid whose world was confined to the ghetto of the Lower East Side as having a grand manner. Not manners. I don't mean manners — he had no manners; he was crude — I mean the manner, the bearing. Max never felt inferior. Perhaps that was his secret. Where did we go? Who can remember! I think it was an Italian restaurant . . ."

It was Mama Maria's restaurant, over on Elizabeth Street, which was on the edge of the newly burgeoning Italian ghetto. Dinner was thirty cents, table d'hôte, and included antipasto, pasta, a main dish of veal or chicken, dessert, and coffee. The bottle of red wine which Max grandly ordered was twenty-five cents.

The price was of no consequence; it was the gesture and manner that counted. This was a new and different and intriguing Max Britsky, and in the light of the candle that stood in the center of the checked red and white tablecloth, he was quite handsome, his lean face with its pointed chin and hawklike nose and bright blue eyes reminding Sally of illustrations she had seen of buccaneers and Spanish conquistadors. That image combined with his intensity and confidence gave her a feeling of excitement she had never experienced with any other man. It was exciting and frightening all at once. The small, skinny, and very young man had turned into a person of power and persuasion, and she, on the other hand, responded to this as a very different Miss Levine.

She had abandoned the white blouse and the drab skirt of the schoolteacher and now she wore a pretty blue dress of crêpe de Chine, and while no makeup was noticeable on her face, Max suspected that there was a flush of rouge across her cheeks. She thought the little Italian restaurant was "delightful" and the food "quite delicious." "But I don't have so many dates with young men, Mr. Britsky," she added, her open honesty very charming, "that I would dare pose as a connoisseur. Perhaps someday, when you have achieved your Mount Olympus, you'll let me see some of those places like Delmonico's and the Albemarle and the Brunswick."

Max was sensitive enough to realize that she was doing her best to impress him. Though he was uncertain of the precise meaning of connoisseur and totally blank concerning her reference to Mount Olympus, he nevertheless felt that he was sitting opposite a very innocent and unsophisticated young woman. It gave him the courage to insist that she call him Max.

"No more of this Mr. Britsky," he reminded her. "You're Sally and I'm Max. And don't think this is a line I pull with every girl, because the truth is you're the first girl I ever had this kind of a date with."

She stared at her plate for a long moment, and then asked him what he meant by this kind of a date.

"Well . . ." His voice trailed off. He decided that you didn't tell

Sally Levine what you meant by this kind of a date. He switched the conversation to the subject of his job, and he discovered that Sally had never been to a music hall.

"Why?"

"You know why," she said. "Of course you do. Young ladies don't go to such places."

Max didn't contest this statement by mentioning the number of girls he saw in the theatre each night. Much of his interest in Sally Levine derived from his concept of her as a person from another world, and if in her world young women did not go to music halls, Max was delighted to accept that. Still and all, he worked in a music hall.

"Just once," he said. "I mean, you might just want to come out of curiosity. I don't think there's anything there that would offend you."

"Perhaps some other time."

"But I got you a ticket for tonight. It's the best seat in the house."

"Oh, no. I couldn't."

"Why not?"

"Alone? Max, how could I go in there alone?"

"You won't be alone. I mean, I'm not sitting next to you, I'm up on the stage, but nobody's going to bother you. Maybe you think a music hall is some kind of a sinful, terrible place. It ain't. Families go there."

She shook her head.

"Please. Look, we go on, me and Bert, fifteen or twenty minutes after the show starts. There's just a long dog act and then we're on. So all you'd have to spend there is maybe forty-five minutes, and then I change and pick you up, and you said yourself how did I learn to do what I do, when I had no experience or training."

"Well . . ." She was wavering. "You would take me in? I wouldn't have to go in alone?"

"Absolutely. And then I come around and you leave with me. I got you an aisle seat in the fourth row, so there's no problem. And then I got two and a half hours before the next show, so we can have a cup of coffee, and if you want to I'll bring my partner, Bert, along, and then I take you home."

She was torn between curiosity and the conventions. Ever since she had left her secure, peaceful home, the little frame house in

Flatbush where she had been born and had grown to maturity, convention had been her shield and protector. Her father and mother had come to America from Vienna a few years after the Civil War. They were Jewish, but, as they saw themselves, a very different breed from these Eastern European Jews who were pouring into America by the thousands and had become a seething mass of slum-ghetto humanity in New York City's Lower East Side. Sally had gone into this ghetto full of trepidation; this was the jungle, but it was also a wonderland and a place where all things were possible; and while the Lower East Side was only miles from Flatbush geographically, culturally it was a world away. In Brooklyn, there was no Washington Square, no Madison Square, the two incredible and marvelous centers of wealth, culture, and excitement that had turned New York into a rival of London.

Convention-bound and insecure Sally might be, but she was no frightened mouse, and when they arrived at the Bijou Theatre, Sally felt a delicious flutter of excitement. There had been boys who came calling to the house in Flatbush, but they were stodgy, stolid creatures, destined for law or medicine or Wall Street in the best German-Jewish tradition. There had been no one like Max, no one with that air of wildness and daring, and since she had been living and teaching in New York, she had had no dates until Max appeared. Though New York City teemed with men, Sally had no idea how to meet them, and most of the other teachers at the school were women. Thus it was very exciting to be here at night, in all the lights and bustle of West Broadway, with painted women — whom she labeled as streetwalkers — and flashily dressed men all about her, and the pushcarts and the hawkers and the three-card-monte operators and the peanut vendors. It was all wonderful and exciting and alive, and to Sally, who had been reading Émile Zola, it appeared to be very much the streets of Paris transplanted to the New World. And there she was, walking into a music hall with one of the performers, with Max's strong hand around her arm.

• • •

Bert was already in his cop costume and making up his face when Max entered the dressing room and said to him, "What the fuck are you up to?"

"I think I'm coloring my puss. What do you think?"

"The cop suit."

"We're doing the tramp and cop. There's a character outside from the Alderman Circuit. If he likes our act, he can give us twelve weeks outside this shithole, Philadelphia, Boston, Chicago — Kansas City. You know what we get for three nights in Kansas City? Three hundred dollars for the act. Guttman says fine, we can take the twelve weeks if this guy from Alderman likes us and come back here to work when it's over. Maybe we don't come back here. Guttman figures it gives the Bijou class to have an act in Chicago or somewhere, but who knows? Maybe we move up to Madison Square."

"Oh, Jesus!"

"What's eating you?" Bert demanded. "It's a good routine. You know that."

"I got Sally out in the audience."

"Sally?"

"You know. The teacher."

"So what? Educate her."

"She's not a tramp. She's a lady."

"I don't believe you. I just don't. Man, you are deluded."

"We can do something else."

"No! Now look, Maxie, this is our break. Don't piss all over it. Guttman told this guy from the Alderman Circuit that we're going to do our three cop and tramp routines. He knows what they're about, and he's waiting."

"Oh, shit, shit, shit," Max moaned.

• • •

The man next to Sally Levine kept glancing at her. She decided to ignore him. His knee then moved slowly, almost imperceptibly, toward her until it touched the crêpe de Chine. She jerked her own knees away, grateful that the aisle was on her left. Her whole body tightened as she watched the trained dogs perform, and when the curtain finally went up on Bellamy and Britsky, she had passed out of her receptive mood and was staring critically and tight-lipped at the stage.

The backdrop was a scene in a park, old and faded with cracks in the paint and some stitched repair work. In front of the backdrop, a park bench, and on the bench a tramp and a blowzy middle-aged woman. They were seated about a foot apart, and between them, on the bench, the woman's handbag reposed. Sally was hard put at first to recognize Max as the tramp. He had put on a bulbous, clownish red nose, and his face was shadowed with a week's growth of whiskers. He wore baggy patched pants and an ancient patched jacket, and after the curtain rose, the two of them, the tramp and the woman, sat motionless and silent. This in itself brought a nervous response from the audience, a ripple of applause.

Then the woman picked up her bag, opened it, and near-sightedly peered into it. Then she screamed — a succession of howling, hair-raising screams. The tramp did nothing — no response, no motion. For reasons Sally did not comprehend, the audience burst into laughter, laughter which increased as a policeman came onstage. So this was Bert Bellamy, about whom she had heard so much! He carried an overlarge nightstick, which he pointed at the blowzy woman, telling her, "All right, lady, you can stop screaming now."

She stopped screaming and pointed wordlessly at the nightstick.

"It's me nightstick," Bert said. "Have ye never seen a nightstick before?"

"Not that large."

"You're damn right." He spoke in a heavy Irish brogue, and by now the audience was convulsed with laughter. "Now what the divil were you screeching about?"

"He stole my money," she said, pointing to Max

"Me? Me? Me?" Max cried indignantly.

Bert poked him with the nightstick. "Give it back, ye dirty scut, or I'll turn yer head into a trap drum."

"I never took nothing. She's crazy."

"And what's that bulge in yer pocket?"

"Bulge?" Max stood up, staring, puzzled, at the bulge in his pocket.

"My money!" the woman cried, and thrust her hand into Max's pocket. Then she collapsed in a faint.

"What have ye done to her, ye dirty swine?" Bert shouted.

"Me? Nothing."

"What's in your pocket?"

"Pocket? Who's got pockets?" turning out the ragged fringe that was left of each pocket.

The curtain dropped to a roar of applause and laughter, and Sally rose and left the theatre. On the street outside, she hailed a hansom cab, hoping that she had enough money in her purse for the fare. She did, and when she reached Tenth Street and walked up the stoop of the brownstone in which she rented a furnished room, she sighed with relief and said, "And that's the end of Mr. Britsky."

But, of course, it was not. An hour and a half later, Max knocked at her door.

"What do you want?" she demanded angrily. She had changed into a long quilted robe, and her rich brown hair, combed out, reached almost to her waist.

From below, her landlady's voice called out, "Is everything all right, Miss Levine?"

"Yes, Mrs. Schwartz."

"It's eleven o'clock. That's too late for callers. I trust I rented your room to an honest and moral person."

"It's my brother, Mrs. Schwartz," and then she whispered to Max, "Please get out of here before you ruin my reputation entirely."

"I would have come before, but I had to do the second show."

"Please go."

"I want to talk to you," Max pleaded. "I must talk to you."

"No. We have nothing to say to each other."

"Let me come inside for five minutes. That's all I ask, five minutes." She appeared to hesitate, and he pressed the point. "Only five minutes. Since you've decided never to see me again, five minutes can't be so terrible."

"Very well, five minutes."

She opened the door and then closed it behind him. The room was small but not unpleasant; and to Max it was full of color and invention and unlike any room he had ever stepped into. On the walls were three oversized posters by Parrish and Mucha. The Mucha was of Sarah Bernhardt, while in the gardens on the Parrish posters, people of the art nouveau frolicked improbably in flowing gowns. Yet the posters were bright and charming, as was the pink and yellow bedspread and the rag rug on the floor. Max guessed that these and other pleasant touches did not come with the furnished room but spelled out the taste of Miss Levine, and he entered the room tentatively, more abashed than ever before in her presence.

"I know I struck out," he said. "I messed things up, and I guess the one thing in the world I wanted was to make a good impression with you, and don't think I don't know how dirty that *shtick* was, but I swear to God I never intended to play the cop and tramp *shtick* tonight, but there was a guy in from the Alderman Circuit, which is eleven theatres around the country, and Bert and Guttman, who runs the Bijou, promised him we'd do it and there just wasn't no way out of it, and all right, if you think I'm a cheap bum, there's nothing else I can say — what are you laughing at?"

"That is —" She choked again with laughter. "That is absolutely the longest run-on sentence I ever heard and possibly the least intelligible."

He stood facing her, silent, his lips clenched.

"And I've hurt you. Oh, Max, how stupid of me. I'm so sorry."

"Why don't you just tell me I'm not good enough for you? Why don't you tell me I'm a bum and throw me out? You know what my mother says about German Jews? She says they look at us like we're animals, like we're not even human."

"Max, Max, we're not German Jews, we're Austrian."

"Same thing."

"Poor Max, I've hurt you so deeply." She went over to him, placed her hands on his cheeks, and kissed him lightly on his lips. "Do you forgive me?"

"Jesus! Wow! You really kissed me."

"Yes."

"I'm not going to wash my face. Not for weeks."

She pursed her lips. "Ugh."

"You kissed me — yes?"

"Yes." She turned him around and pushed him toward the door. "Now go home. I'll see you Monday if you wish."

"I wish, I wish, but we're booked right out. We got twelve weeks — Buffalo, Chicago, Kansas City, New Orleans, and Philadelphia. But I'll be back. You bet your sweet patooties I'll be back."

[THREE]

1898

—

Max at the Age of Nineteen

MAX HAD NEVER HIT his sister Freida before. He slapped Ruby around when he needed it, and when Ruby cried out in protest against his brother beating up on him, Max countered, "And if I don't teach you the right time, who in hell is going to?" There was some mutual ground and comprehension there, as there was when he had to slap some sense into Benny, age nine. But Freida wailed, "Stop it! Stop it! You got no right to hit me!" He had laid a stinging slap on each cheek, her face not her ass, and she whimpered, "You're not my father. You got no right."

"Right? You tell me my rights? You — you little tramp!"

"I'm not a tramp. It happened. It just happened."

"What in hell do you mean, it just happened?"

"I didn't know how to stop. I couldn't stop."

"You couldn't stop," Max whispered hoarsely. "You dumb little bitch! You haven't got the sense of a sow! Almost eighteen years old, and you get yourself knocked up, and then you tell me that you couldn't help it."

She threw herself on the bed, sobbing, and Max loomed over her, drove his finger at her, and shouted, if a hoarse whisper can be a shout, "You know what you're going to do? I'll tell you what you're going to do. You're going to marry him."

Her sobbing ceased. She sat up. "What?"

"You are going to marry him."

"Are you crazy?"

"Me? Me? Oh, no, baby, crazy is in front of me."

"He's a dumb kid."

"Oh? And you?"

"I'll die first. I'll kill myself. I swear —" Her mood changed; the brief defiance turned into supplication. "Maxie, Maxie, please help me, please."

"Help you? What's to help you? You want a dowry? You want me to rob a bank so you and that horse's ass who knocked you up can start life together?"

"I'll kill myself."

"Bullshit."

"Please, please help me."

Now Max looked at her, and possibly it was the first time in his life that he had really looked at her and actually seen her: the reddened tear-swollen eyes, the pink cheeks, the cupid bow of a mouth, and the large, firm breasts bulging her blouse. She was a woman and lush and desirable, and something out of this discovery reached him and touched him.

"Don't tell Mama," Freida sobbed.

"All right."

"You'll help me, Max?"

"Maybe. I'll see. But if this ever happens again —"

"Never, never, never!"

"Yeah, sure." He spun around suddenly, grabbed the door to the hall, and jerked it open. Ruby almost fell into the room, and Max, grabbing him by his shirt collar and twisting savagely, hissed, "You little bastard!"

"I didn't hear nothing, Max," Ruby pleaded. He was fourteen, heavily built, almost as tall as Max.

"One word about this," Max whispered, "I'll make you wish you were never born. You hear me, you little bastard?"

"I hear you, I hear you. Max, you're choking me."

"I ought to. One word."

"I swear to God —"

"Fuck off and keep your mouth shut!"

He slammed the door again and turned back to Freida, who was staring at him now with the first glimmer of hope in her eyes.

"Where are you?" Max asked grimly. "What month?"

"I think — the third."

"You don't know, you dumb little bitch?"

She began to weep again, and Max told her, "Stop that. All we need is Mama should come in here and find you crying."

"You'll do something, Max?"

"I'll do something."

"You'll help me?"

"I told you I'd help you."

He was late already. He looked at his watch. It was a fine, Swiss pocket watch, closed face with the bas-relief of a stag upon its surface, which snapped open at the touch of a hidden spring, the case of fourteen karat gold. He had bought it for twelve dollars from a fence called Louis Harelip, who operated out of a cellar on Pearl Street and who swore it was European merchandise; in other words, stolen in Europe and resold here. True or not, Max was proud of the watch. The hands now informed him that it was 5:45 P.M.

"Take it easy," Max said.

He had to pass through the kitchen to leave, and there his mother sat, weeping at the kitchen table. Sitting at the table with her, totally subdued by Sarah's weapon of tears, bent over their notebooks and doing their homework, were Benny, eight, Esther, ten, and Sheila, twelve. They had no defense against their mother's tears, and Sarah knew quite well that tears were her weapon of the last and increasingly first resort.

"Mama, what are you crying about?" Max demanded, losing his determination to stride silently by her and out of the apartment.

"I should laugh?" Sarah moaned.

"I'm not telling you to laugh, but what in hell is there to cry about?"

"Don't swear at me with your fine American language. You fight with your sister and hit her, and I shouldn't cry? What did I raise, animals?"

Without answering, almost yet not entirely immune to his mother's manipulative sobbing and whimpering, Max started for the door.

"Where are you going?"

"Out."

"Out. Out. I cook for you and you go out, to eat in some filthy restaurant."

He fled, slamming the door of the apartment behind him, taking the stairs down the darkened tenement stairwell two and three at a time, hurtling out of a prison into the freedom of the street. He rarely questioned his bondage, which society called responsibility and which was rooted in dim and distant tribal and religious persuasions and taboos. His partner, Bert Bellamy, who was white and Protestant and fairly free of such mysterious burdens, had once said to him, "I'll be damned if I know why you put up with that squealing, whining mob. You're not their father. If I was you, Maxie boy, I'd cut out and say screw the lot of them. Serve them right. Teach them a lesson." But that was Bert, to whom the thousand threads of bondage were invisible; yet at a moment like this, he could almost entertain the notion.

His face still bore traces of home when Sally Levine opened the door of her furnished room for him, and she asked him what had happened.

"Nothing happened."

"Oh? You just decided to be miserable tonight?"

"O.K. So that's what I decided."

She bent over the chair he had dropped into and kissed him on his forehead. "All right, Maxie," she said. "If we go on this way, we'll have a fight, which we don't want, do we? So we'll just start all over from the beginning and forget that I ever asked you what was wrong."

He couldn't stay angry when she was around, and he grinned and asked her whether he should get up and come into the room again.

"If you wish."

"Jesus," he sighed, "I'm not twenty years old and I got five kids and a mother who never gets off my back, and sometimes I get to feeling that I'm ready for the nuthouse."

"Why don't you think about what a good, noble thing you're doing?"

"Noble?"

"I think so. No, I don't want to go on talking about that. I made some lamb stew, to show you that I really can cook, and you don't have to buy me dinner every time we spend an evening together, and it's not very fancy. All I have is this one little burner. But I do think it's good, and then we don't have to rush. The Chautauqua is at Cooper Union, just a few blocks away."

"The what?"

"The Chautauqua? Well, it's just a fancy name for an assembly or a lecture, and you remember that I told you about it. All the teachers from our school will be there —"

"Oh, no! No, sir. You want me to meet all your fancy, educated friends and make a horse's ass out of myself —"

"Oh, Max, come on. I told you about this long ago, and you were really interested. And you don't have to meet anyone if you don't want to, and it's not just a lecture, it's a demonstration."

"Of what?"

"Do you remember, you once told me how excited you got when you were a kid and you looked into a kinetoscope?"

"Yes, at Rowdy Smith's place. I wonder if the old guy's alive or dead."

"Well, tonight at Cooper Union, the New York Educational Alliance is showing something very new and exciting. It's like a kinetoscope, but it's an improvement on it, and people are talking about it. It's called a moving picture."

"A what?"

"A moving picture, just as I said." While she spoke, Sally placed two small tables in front of chairs. A straw mat on each, a bowl of lamb stew and a glass of wine. "It's a very simple meal, but in one room — Do you like soft rolls?"

Max had long ago decided that whatever Sally did was right. The one room she lived in was his other world. If he had the expression, he would have said that she had taste; his own world was tasteless. He didn't think about it in precisely those terms, yet that was his view of her.

"This is good," Max said, tasting. "What about this moving picture?"

"It's something that was invented by a man named Thomas Alva Edison, the same man who invented the electric light bulb."

"Come on, you got to think I'm an idiot. I know who Edison is."

"Well, I don't think you're an idiot. I think you're so bright it frightens me sometimes, and you know that. But I'm a teacher, and I can't shake the habit of explaining everything."

"What's a moving picture?"

"The pictures in the kinetoscope moved, didn't they?"

"So that's it. I seen it. Big deal."

"Will you stop being the tough, know-it-all street kid for a moment and let me explain."

"Yeah, explain," he allowed, waving an arm.

"All right. I'll try not to be didactic if you'll stop being a smart East Side Jew."

He didn't know what didactic meant, and he put her down with the observation that an East Side Jew kid was just what he was, take it or leave it.

"Oh, Max," she said, "why does this happen? You're so sensitive, and you always think people are being superior. Well, I don't feel superior, not a bit, and all I wanted was for you to enjoy tonight because it's just the kind of thing that interests you. It's new. You've seen the magic lanterns we use in school. Well, this is something like a magic lantern, as it was told to me, except that the picture moves. It really moves, and not in a kinetoscope but on an enormous screen."

"I'll believe that when I see it," Max said.

* * *

He sulked on his way to Cooper Union, and he muttered about her friends and a word like "didactic," and how did she think he felt when she spoke to him and used words no one ever heard of before?

"Didactic, Max."

"Didactic."

"All it means is to teach. People who can't stop teaching attitudes, even in ordinary conversation, are said to be didactic."

"Then why didn't you say 'teaching'?"

"Because it's not exactly the same thing. That's the beauty of words, the delicate shades of meaning. Don't be impatient, Max. You pick up everything so quickly, like a chameleon —"

"There you go again."

They were at Cooper Union now, fortunately for Sally, who was regretting her comparison of Max to a lizard that changed color at the drop of a hat, and she busied herself with introductions. Max smiled and nodded and said little; and as he met the teachers who were Sally's colleagues, his respect for her grew. He couldn't place any other among them as being Jewish; they were for the most part the ladies he remembered from his own schooldays, tight-lipped, tightly corseted white Protestant ladies, many of them spinsters. He felt that the ease with which Sally greeted them and moved among them was absolutely wonderful. It was a strange, different world he was entering here, and he noted every aspect of it with care and curiosity.

He followed Sally and her colleagues into a large room on the main floor. Evidently, its normal use was as an artist's studio, for there were easels against one wall and racks packed with canvases. For tonight, six rows of folding chairs had been set up, a dozen chairs in each row. A large sheet of white cloth, about eight by eight, had been nailed to one wall of the room, facing the chairs, and at the back of the room, two men were working on a curious machine, which reminded Max of an oversized camera with three large wheels and a crank. A tangle of wires led to a converter and from the converter to an electric light socket.

Max, fascinated, paused to stare at the projector until Sally whispered that soon there'd be no seats left, and pulled him away to a seat in the very last row.

"You can examine it later," she told him. "That's Mr. Benton," nodding at a stout, baldish man who had taken his place at the front of the room and who stood there now, polishing his pince-nez and waiting for the murmur of voices to cease. "He's our science teacher for the eighth grade. Most science teachers are men. I suppose they feel that a woman couldn't possibly master any science."

As if he had heard Sally's words, Mr. Benton nodded, smiled slightly and finished polishing his pince-nez, placing them not on his nose but in a small case he took out of a breast pocket. Then he rubbed both his hands together, gazing upon the audience with beneficence, pleased that he had prior knowledge of the world they were about to enter. "Good evening and welcome," he said.

There was a slight ripple of polite applause, and Mr. Benton went on. "I'm Mr. Benton, and I teach science at Public School Nine. Those of you from our school know me and my sometimes unorthodox methods. To those of you who do not know me, I must say that I try to incorporate the latest developments in the field of science into my teaching. However, I am not sure that my regular students are ready for this development, unless of course it can be directed toward the goal of a new area in education. This is indeed the thought of Mr. Enoch Rector, who was kind enough to arrange this evening for us and who will welcome your response and suggestions —"

"How long is he going on?" Max asked impatiently. Faces turned toward him disapprovingly. Sally squeezed his arm, whispering, "Just be patient."

Mr. Benton was asking his audience to be broad-minded, to see the implications of the method beyond the content. "We could wish for other content," he said, "but alas, this is the only motion picture — well, perhaps not the only one, but one of two or three in the country. 'Motion picture' is possibly a term you have never heard before. It is a new term, or, I should say, one of two new terms, 'moving picture' and 'motion picture,' of which I prefer the latter, and it is used to define the difference between what we shall see tonight and what you may have seen in the kinetoscopes of the penny arcades — if indeed you frequent such places. Ah, the difference! Tonight, you will see a magic lantern that moves. And I will not try to explain or dilute the magic in any way. Let the magic take over of its own accord." He paused to allow his words to quiver under their own weight.

"He's a real big talker," Max whispered. "He's going to talk the whole evening away."

Benton spread his arms, and Max twisted around to see the men at the projector in the back of the room. They stood there, shaking their heads and looking bored.

"However," Benton said, "I cannot apologize sufficiently to the ladies present for the subject of tonight's exhibition. The moving pictures you are about to see were taken at the prizefight between James Corbett and Bob Fitzsimmons in Carson City in Nevada —"

He paused for the ripple of excitement, shock, and expectant disapproval to work its way through the audience. There were whispers everywhere now, among them Sally whispering to Max, "I just can't believe it — a prizefight! I don't think I would have come if I had known."

Max sat back, relaxed, an evil grin spreading over his face as here and there in the audience ladies stood up to leave. Mostly, they were elderly and exceedingly prim, and perhaps a dozen of them pushed past those who remained seated, their mouths set in tight-lipped disgust, their faces conveying their opinion of those who remained.

Benton pleaded in vain. "Ladies, ladies," he begged them, "you are not at a prizefight, which I regard as un-Christian and degrading. You are at Cooper Union, one of the great educational institutions of this city, and privileged — privileged — to witness this scientific discovery, this incredible invention, of Mr. Thomas Alva Edison, as firm a Christian as any of you."

It was no use. Benton gave up and allowed the indignant ladies to leave without further pleading. Most of his audience remained, and, rather deflated, he explained that altogether, eleven thousand feet of film had been taken. "But to see it all would keep us here for hours, and I doubt that even you whose devotion to science keeps you here would want to witness the whole of anything as bloody and brutal as this prizefight. We will show two reels, sixteen hundred feet of film, and that will take about twenty minutes, after which I propose to lead a discussion. Now I am going to turn off the lights, since we must have darkness for the projector to work properly."

Benton then switched off the lights, after which there were a few moments of darkness and a good deal of nervous tittering and whispering — all of which turned into astonished silence as the screen lit up with the figures of two men in a prize ring, two men bruised and bloodstained and battering away at each other with sullen, tired ferocity. What amazed Max was the absolute validity of it. Nothing was faked here, nothing was contrived. He was literally watching the famous Fitzsimmons-Corbett fight where Bob Fitzsimmons, the New Zealand blacksmith, the lumbering "Limey Bull," as they called him, knocked out America's lithe and lovely "Gentleman Jim," who was all things most unlikely in a prizefighter. He knocked him out not with a clean, upright American blow to the jaw but with a typical British sneak blow to the solar plexus, which left poor handsome, decent Gentleman Jim paralyzed and unable to lift a hand in his defense. Max had bet money on the fight, lost money, argued the fight a hundred times, with never more than the vaguest notion of where Carson City, Nevada, was located, and now here, miracle of miracles, were the two heavyweights, battering each other right before his eyes. The marvelous, incredible, and unbelievable impossibility of it took hold of Max as nothing else ever had, and he sat staring at the screen in a kind of trancelike intensity.

He was impervious to the cries of protest that began to be heard from the assembled teachers. Afterward he would say to Sally, "Those dumb bitches! They watch a miracle and they want it to stop."

In all truth, they did want it to stop. It mattered not one whit to them that they were watching a process that few human beings had ever witnessed before and even less that they were granted the opportunity of watching perhaps the most skillful boxer that had ever set foot in a prize ring. None of that weighed against their horror of this cruel sport of prizefighting, brought over from England and still illegal in most places in the United States. "Oh, enough! Enough!" began to be heard, and other voices saying, "It's too horrible" and "How can they? How can they?"

Benton should have known. Even in those places like Hoboken and West New York, where illegal prizefights could be staged, no one had ever dreamed of inviting a woman to view one. A tall, lean lady with a commanding voice reminded Benton of that, rising and telling him in no uncertain terms: "This has gone far enough, Mr. Benton."

"But, madam," Benton argued, "we are watching a process, not a prizefight."

"We are watching a prizefight, Mr. Benton, and if this is what your great scientific advance is to be used for, I for one deplore it!"

They were pushing through the aisles to leave, and Benton, bowing to pressure, flicked on the lights. The men at the projector halted its operation, and the teachers began to leave. They had to push past Max, who sat rigid and unmoving, oblivious to Sally's whispered suggestion that he rise and let others past.

"Max —"

He stood up now, staring around the room, where clusters of people were still engaged in heated discussion and where Mr. Benton was hotly defending himself. Without a word to Sally, Max walked to the back of the room, where the two projectionists were rewinding the film. He stood watching them, and since he was one of the few males in the room, one of the projectionists said to him, "What the hell is this, some kind of temperance outfit?"

"Teachers."

"Oh. Yeah, that figures."

Max moved up to the projector. "Can I look at that?"

"Be my guest."

The other projectionist said to Max, "Come on, buster. We got to pack it up and get out of here."

Sally stood to one side, watching Max as he circled the projector, for all the world like a predatory animal circling its prey. Suddenly he turned to the projectionists and demanded, "How does it work? What makes it work? How do you get that moving picture up there on the wall?"

"Look, buster, it works. You pay your money and you take your choice. We're electricians. We ain't teachers."

"We got to pack up and get out of here," the other one said.

Max reached into his pocket, came out with his money, and counted off five singles. "Five bucks," he said angrily. "That ought to pay for ten minutes of your time. I'm not asking you to bust your asses. All I'm asking is to show me how that damn thing works."

"Take it easy, sonny."

"And don't call me sonny!"

The room was empty now except for Mr. Benton, two young lady schoolteachers who were evidently standing firm with Mr. Benton's interest in science, and Sally and Max and the projectionists. Benton and the two teachers moved over to join Sally and watch, and the other projectionist took the five dollars and said, "I didn't know we had any high rollers tonight. O.K., my boy, you paid your money and you get your wish. This here thing is called a moving picture projector, and it was put together by Mr. Edison's company out in Jersey. Now you want five bucks' worth of how it works, just listen carefully. Inside here is a lens. It is what we call an objective lens. Now you look at these pictures on the celluloid and you'd think they was negatives — I mean if you know anything about photography. Not so. They are positives. Now take a gander at this wheel, and you can see how these sprockets fit into the holes in the celluloid. The wheel with the sprockets is driven by this crank. Now watch. I turn the crank, and this shutter flips back and forth. Without the shutter, you'd just get a blur, but the shutter separates each picture, gives it a separate identity, as we say, and allows it to impinge on the eye of the beholder. Now maybe you been in one of them honky-tonks where they have kinetoscopes with the fancy ladies taking off their clothes. Ever been there?"

Max nodded.

"O.K. Now you can make a cheap kinetoscope, instead of the fancy one that Edison makes, by just taking a series of action pictures, putting them together with a little trigger that flips them over one at a time. You shine a light on it, and the picture seems to move. Well, this is not so different. When these pictures of the Fitzsimmons-Corbett fight were taken, they were taken with a new kind of camera. Instead of having a photosensitive plate or piece of film inside of it which is exposed when you click the shutter, this camera employs the same kind of device we got here on this projector, film wound around a reel. The shutter clicks at a set relationship to the passing film, and so you get a continuing series of pictures, and the faster the shutter clicks, the more pictures you get — of course, in relation to how fast the crank is turned."

"It ain't as easy as it sounds," the other projectionist put in. "Say we want to run this projector for a whole hour. Well, no, that's too long. I guess the realistic time limit is about twenty minutes, and then it tends to heat up, because the whole problem of putting enough light inside the projector to project the picture clearly is very difficult to solve. It ain't that Mr. Edison can't come up with a bright enough bulb. He can do that easy enough, but how do you vent the heat? This little fan here helps, but the projector still gets hot as hell."

"Not to mention," the first one said, "that you got to keep turning this crank, and you got to turn it in synchronization with the guy who took the picture, and you just hope that he stuck to the rhythm given to him, except that it's impossible to get it perfect, and that's why the pictures are so jerky." He pointed to the small holes that lined the film. "These give us trouble too, because we still don't have a way to punch them absolutely even, but we're working on that."

"You work for Mr. Edison, then?" Max asked him.

"That's right."

"Does he make the film?"

"No, but he handles it. It's made to his specifications, but the film's no good without the camera. You got to have a special camera, and I guess there ain't but half a dozen anywhere. Well, how about it, sonny? You got five bucks' worth?"

"Was it worth five dollars?" Sally asked him when they got outside.

"You bet your life."

"But why? I do think it's extraordinary, but the sight of two men beating each other to death — I could live without that."

"No, that's nothing. I don't give a damn about the fight. It's the camera and the projector. Can't you see, it's the beginning of something that never existed before."

"It's just a trick, Max. We've always had the magic lantern. This is a magic lantern that moves, that's all."

"Yeah, that's all it is."

"Where are you?" she asked him as he turned east down the street. "You're going the wrong way."

"Oh?"

"Max, what's come over you?"

"I don't know —"

· · ·

"You got to be crazy," Bert said to Max. "You got a brain in your head, you'll leave it alone."

"It's my sister."

"So it's your sister. So it's the queen of England. It's the nature of a broad to get knocked up. Where's it get you to beat him up?"

"He learns. It's the only way."

"There are times," Bert said, "when you show a nasty streak."

"That's the way I feel."

"You could make him marry her."

"I need that. I got her on my back, I don't need two of them. Anyway, she says she'd kill herself first."

His name was Joe Greenthal. Max got his name out of her by the simple process of threatening to turn his back on her if she tried to protect the boy or cover up for him, and then he went down to the corner outside the candy store on Pike Street and he asked around for a boy called Joe Greenthal. Compassion was not something Max had a large store of, but he almost felt sorry for this kid called Joe Greenthal, who was pudgy and had a round face and soft brown cow-eyes, and he might have walked away from it had he not spelled out his position to Bert. In all truth, what he had spelled out was only what he could articulate: the complex of pride, of family honor, of his own male macho, of his feelings about the stupidity and witlessness of the rest of his family with only himself to put some stamp of worth and importance upon them — these things he could not put into words.

Nevertheless, they drove him to acts hardly basic to him. He had a deep inner disgust of violence that was almost genetic and certainly tribal and cultural, but he told the boy, Joe Greenthal, that he had to talk to him, alone, concerning Freida, walking him away from the candy store toward the river.

The boy was frightened. "Geez," he whimpered, "I didn't know it was going to happen. I didn't mean anything bad. I like Freida."

"That's why you knocked her up? Because you like her?"

"I didn't know it was going to happen, I swear I didn't."

"So what do you think? The stork does it, right? So I'm going to teach you different. I'm going to teach you there ain't no stork, just snotty little shits like you." And with that, Max drove a fist into his belly. When the boy doubled over, Max brought up his knee and laid him flat on his back. He lay on the pavement, doubled up, whimpering with pain, and Max shouted at him, "Stay away from her, you little son of a bitch, or I'll come back and break both your arms."

The next day Freida said to him, "You're a crazy lunatic. You knocked out two teeth from Joey. I hate you. I'll always hate you."

"So you hate me. He has to learn. He learns. You learn."

But Max hated himself, which was also a new sensation. He kept thinking of the boy's soft cow-eyes. A few days later, placatingly, he said to Freida, "I didn't want to hurt him. I had to learn him."

"Oh, big shot!" Freida exclaimed. "You're so goddamned great. You think because you're keeping company with that fancy teacher, you're too good for all of us, but you can't even talk right. I had to learn him. You don't learn people, you teach them. You're so smart. Why don't you tell your teacher friend how you beat up a kid because he liked me."

Max was impressed. He had never thought of Freida as someone with enough guts to talk back to him.

Freida's anger turned into self-pity, and she began to weep. "Oh, Max," she wailed, "what will I do? What's going to happen to me? All I can think of is that I have to kill myself."

"Don't kill yourself," Max said.

"What do you mean, don't kill myself? What else?"

"I'll take care of it."

"What do you mean, you'll take care of it? You think you can do anything, you think you can twist the whole world around your finger, you're so goddamn smart and sure of yourself!"

"I said I'll take care of it."

That night, sitting before his dressing room mirror, staring at his lean, hawklike face, Max felt a wave of disgust that included the rouge and cream he was smearing on his face, the ridiculous baggy checked pants he wore, the routine waiting for him and for Bert when the curtain rose, the whole way of a living that brought life and sustenance to the six members of his family. Sally, trying to smooth his rough edges, read poetry to him on occasion, hoping it might interest him. There was a long poem about an "ancient mariner" and a line that went: "Instead of a cross, an albatross about his neck was hung." They were all of them his albatross.

"Do you know what a ransom is?" he asked Bert, who was using a lipstick to double the size of his mouth.

"Kidnap money, you mean?"

"You got it. I need a million dollars' ransom."

"Who'd they kidnap — Vanderbilt?"

"Me, and I'm sick of it. I'm sick of this shit. I'm sick of everyone's *peckle* on my back."

"What's a *peckle?*"

"Yiddish for burden."

"Your sister really got to you, didn't she?"

"Eh, she's nothing. Dumb, stupid kid. I found someone to take care of her, but it's got to cost me fifty bucks."

"How do you find someone like that?"

"Suzie. You got to hand it to those floozies — when you're being squeezed, they come up with something. They always do. But fifty bucks down the drain, that hurts."

"Are you so broke?"

"I'm not broke."

"Then what are you crying about money for? A lousy fifty bucks is not the end of the world. If you need money —"

"Yeah, I need money, but not to square Freida. I can take care of that. It's peanuts. Right now, I need money like a kid needs his mother's milk, and I ain't got it. I got maybe two hundred bucks put away, and how the hell I managed to squirrel away two yards with six yelping, shrieking hungry mouths, I don't know. All right, I did it, and it wasn't enough anyway, so what the hell!"

"Enough for what?"

Max turned to Bert, staring at him as if he was seeing him for the first time. "You're not even married. What do you do with your dough?"

"I live it up."

"Ah, bullshit. You're no looser with a buck than I am. How much you got soaked away, Bert?"

"Why?"

"I got an idea. I been living with it for weeks, eating on it and letting it eat out my guts. It's an idea that maybe it works, we can end up millionaires." He thrust a finger at Bert. "Throw in with me, huh? This lousy, stupid life is getting us nowhere. It stinks. It's degrading."

"What's degrading?"

"This shit we go out there and do every night, shoving a broomstick up our pants to get a laugh, cheap *double-entendres* and dirty jokes, pratfalls — fuck the whole stupid routine! I need a thousand bucks. We'll forget we ever saw a music hall."

"Max, you need fifty bucks for your sister, you got it. But don't come to me with any get-rich-quick baloney. I'm a street kid, like you. You don't like what we do — shit, it's better than a goddamn sweatshop or being a stock clerk. So I'm happy."

"You're happy?"

"You are damn right."

"So be happy," Max said sourly. "But let me talk frankly, and just remember what I say. I say you got shit in your blood — friendly, because we're old buddies — but I still say you got shit in your blood. Now remember, you won't work with me in something like this, then you know what?"

"What?" Bert asked amiably.

"You'll be working for me."

"As long as the pay is good," Bert said.

• • •

He had gone to Suzie, Suzie the floozie, as the kids called her. He had always gone to Suzie when he was troubled. At the age of fifteen, he had been introduced by Suzie into the world of sex. She loved Max — as much as she could love any man and perhaps because he was more a little boy than a man — and she told him, "You stay away from the whores or I'll break your neck, because if you get a dose, you are washed up and your whole life is washed up, because there ain't no cure, and anyone who says there's a cure is sweet-talking you. Every snatch in this town is dirty, and don't you ever think any different." She provided a prophylactic and instructed him: "This is the only thing that'll keep you clean. Any other way, you got a dose, and then it's yours until they put you away in the booby hatch."

"But you're clean, aren't you?" Max argued.

"Like shit I am. I could have been, but I'm no damn good and I pissed away my life. The Brinkerhoffs are just as good as the Kuhns and the Lehmans and the Strausses or any of the classy uptown Jews, and I could have been in silks and velvets all my life and eating in Delmonico's and having a carriage ride me up and down Fifth Avenue, but I had to piss it all away and become a floozie, but I'm not going to dose a nice kid like you. I'll just give you a little loving for your sake and because I like you."

She was telling the truth. Max had heard the story from other girls many times, that Suzie was the daughter of one of those half-mythical German Jews who had come to America two or three generations before the flood of Eastern European Jewish peasants, who had garnered wealth and influence, who ran great banking houses and industries and who lived in brownstone and granite mansions on Fifth Avenue and on Madison Avenue. What had happened to turn Suzie into a ghetto whore he didn't know, nor did he ever have the courage to ask her; and now Max was no longer a kid of fifteen, and Suzie was a fat, aging whore in her mid-forties who clucked with sympathy.

"I should have broken her ass," Max said.

"Why, you stupid jerk?" Suzie demanded, suddenly enraged. "Because you're a man with a stinking little pecker that don't know a damn thing except to fuck? Suppose you were a girl. Did you ever ask her how she felt, what she needed, what her life is in that hole on Henry Street?" She shook her head helplessly. "Ah, what do you know! What do any of you know! I never met a man who was more than an oversized stiff *putz* attached to a whimpering, whining baby. All right, I'll help you. I'll tell Mrs. Kaner that you're coming to see her."

"Who's Mrs. Kaner?"

"She used to be a midwife in the old country, and now she takes care of kids who got your sister's disease, but it will cost you."

"How much?"

"Fifty."

It hurt. He told Freida how it hurt. "You know what," he said to his sister, "all my life I broke my ass to feed this lousy family and maybe put a few bucks aside. It took a year to put away fifty bucks."

"I'm sorry," she whined. "I'm sorry and I'm so scared. What are they going to do to me, Max? Are they going to cut me open?"

"Stop it! There's no they, just this Mrs. Kaner. She was a midwife. She knows what she's doing. So stop crying. You only got yourself to blame."

"I think Mama knows," Freida wailed.

"Mama doesn't know. For Christ's sake, will you stop that!"

The tenement in which Mrs. Kaner functioned was on Orchard Street, and to reach it, Max and Freida made their way through a tangle of pushcarts, screeching kids, carthorses urged on by demented, cursing teamsters, garbage, shoppers, dogs, cats — and eyes that turned to them as they went into the tenement. Evidently, Mrs. Kaner's profession was public knowledge, and Max led a trembling Freida through a hallway that stank of urine even more than their own domicile on Henry Street to a ground-floor rear apartment. The door opened a crack to Max's knock, and a heavily accented voice asked who it was.

"Max Britsky. Suzie Brinkerhoff sent me."

The door opened a few inches wider, and two suspicious blue eyes peered out of a wrinkled face. "That's your sister?"

"Yes."

"Suzie told you how much — fifty dollars?"

"Yes."

"You got it?"

Max nodded, and Mrs. Kaner opened the door, ushered them in, and closed it behind them. The kitchen, always the first room in a cold-water tenement, was fairly clean.

"First you pay me," Mrs. Kaner said firmly.

Max took out his billfold and counted out ten five-dollar bills. Mrs. Kaner counted them again, folded them, pulled up her skirt to reveal a skinny leg in a black stocking, and put the money under the top of the stocking, held firm by a surprising pink garter. Then she patted Freida's shoulder.

"Stop crying, darling," she said to Freida, pronouncing it *dollink*, a word she favored, "will be all right, darling, maybe five hundred times I done this, and nobody ever died from it."

This last was certainly a lie, and Freida very nearly died. She developed an infection, and for three weeks lay in bed with a high temperature, sweating, burning, in the hot airlessness of the apartment on Henry Street. Max blamed himself. "Only get better, Freida," he told her, "I'll make this up to you, I swear I will."

"It's all right, Maxie," she whispered. "You didn't mean for this to happen. You helped me. What I said was true: I'd rather die than marry that little dope."

But she didn't die, and for years after, she recalled the event with a curious mixture of bitterness, anger, and gratitude. For Max, on the other hand, it added another piece to the lifelong puzzle that was his mother, Sarah Britsky. For while he accepted as his normal due that Sarah blamed him for what had happened to Freida — not that she ever knew exactly what had happened — he was amazed by the care and sympathy Sarah lavished on Freida during the course of the illness.

Max could never decide whether Sarah guessed what had happened to Freida. If she had suspicions, she never voiced them, and through the three weeks that Freida lay in bed, her mother nursed her gently and patiently. For all of their poverty, the Britsky children were a healthy lot, and aside from the common childhood diseases of the time, chicken pox and measles and mumps, they had been spared serious illness. Freida's bout with death was the first that had appeared in their household, and Sarah met it without hysteria. She sat for hours beside Freida's bed, washed her arms and legs with cold water to cool her in the heat of the miserable little room, kept cold compresses on her brow, cooked broth to feed her, and generally displayed a degree of caring and tenderness that Max had never witnessed before. And while she tempered this by increasing the intensity of her bitterness toward Max, she nevertheless gave Max the impression of his mother as another kind of person. Which added to his confusion, but not to his understanding.

[FOUR]

1899
—
Max at the
Age of Twenty

THERE IS A SCHOOL of thinking which holds that individuals influence history and the course of what we call civilization and another school which denies this and hews to a theory of implacable forces. But Mr. Isaac Schimmelmeyer was less than an implacable force, possibly less than an individual of any consequence except as a pious Jew and a member of the human race, for his ideas were few, his imagination limited; yet he played a curious and not insignificant role in creating that unique process which came to be called the culture of the twentieth century. But his act of creative input was shrouded. He had given no thought whatsoever to the fact that at the age of sixty, he stood at the threshold of the twentieth century. He knew nothing of a peace conference being held at The Hague, held so that this new century might be a passage without war; he knew nothing of the Filipino resistance fighters who had taken up arms against the American invader in that year of 1899; he knew nothing of the fierce resistance of the Boers in South Africa, tearing to shreds the British troops sent against them; and he knew nothing of the Anti-Imperialist League founded in this very city and backed by representatives from every political party, that this nation might soil its hands no more.

What Mr. Schimmelmeyer did know and what he felt almost to

the point of paralysis was the death of his wife, Sadie. She had been the force, the brains, the power, behind his business enterprise, which was a fairly large retail store on West Broadway just south of Broome Street. Mr. Schimmelmeyer's business was findings. A large sign across the front of the store read: SCHIMMELMEYER FINDINGS. Perhaps nothing on earth in the way of retail stock is as complicated as the stock of a findings store, which sells at least a thousand items, among them ribbons, buttons in a hundred sizes, stiffening, lining, belting, lace, thread, needles, snaps, hooks, eyes, interfacing, pattern cloth, pattern paper, tapes, scissors, bindings, pins, bobbins, marking chalk, and on and on and on. In an era when most women made their own clothes and most of their children's clothes, the findings store was the key to successful sewing, but it was before the age of the computer, and it took a special mind to operate a findings store. Mrs. Schimmelmeyer had had such a mind; her husband did not; whereupon after her death, bogged down and hopelessly entangled in the complexity of findings, Mr. Schimmelmeyer decided to sell his store and go to live with his daughter in Philadelphia, thereby contributing to the unique fabric of the twentieth century. He put up a sign which proclaimed: GOING OUT OF BUSINESS SALE. And in smaller letters: *Entire Stock at Half Price.*

Since Max passed by Mr. Schimmelmeyer's store every day, sometimes two or three times a day, he could hardly remain unaware of the sign. At first it did not connect, because what Mr. Schimmelmeyer had was a store and not a theatre, but then another piece of causation fell into place. This was the Congregation Beth Sholom, where Max had gone half a dozen times after his father's death to say a prayer for his father's soul — not out of any conviction of the efficacy of prayer, but in response to his mother's pleading. The Congregation Beth Sholom was a *shul,* the Yiddish word for the combination of synagogue and school that Orthodox Jews had used as a community center from time immemorial. When the great flood of Eastern European Jews came to America toward the end of the nineteenth century, their first need — as great as their need for food and shelter — was for houses of prayer and teaching. Vaguely, they knew that the rich uptown Jews, the German Jews who had come to America half a century before, had built great houses of worship which they called temples; but for the Orthodox Jew, the temple was an abomination and the Reform Judaism of these uptown Jews was almost as alien to the Orthodox as Christianity.

In any case, they were a community of paupers with no money to build anything, whereupon they put their small funds together and rented stores here and there all through the East Side. Each store was given a proper holy name, furnished with homemade benches and a pulpit, and turned into a quickly contrived house of worship — all done in ignorance of the fact that the Quakers and the Congregationalists had done more or less the same two centuries before. It was the memory of this functional alteration of space which combined with Mr. Schimmelmeyer's sign and propelled Max into the action which determined the course of his life.

Ever since he had witnessed the film of the Fitzsimmons-Corbett prizefight, Max had been under its spell, utterly enthralled by the fact that pictures of people in motion could be projected onto a screen. To him, it was one of the most exciting moments imaginable, and his fancy had spun endless variations of what might be projected.

"Don't you see?" he pressed Sally. "There's never been anything like this."

"Max, the kinetoscope's been around for years."

"This isn't a kinetoscope."

"Max," she said patiently, "no one wanted to stay there and watch that dreadful fight. Half the audience walked out."

"Because they were teachers and because it was a prizefight. But the idea — don't that excite you?"

"*Doesn't* it, Max," she said, correcting him. "Not very much, no."

Still, he refused to allow himself to be swayed by Sally. If he could be so enthralled and excited, so could other people, and if people paid money to watch the cheap and mindless routine he and Bert did each night at the Bijou, then they would more eagerly pay for motion pictures. That was the notion that excited Max and which he brooded over for months. He made inquiries about cameras and projectors, and he discovered that it would be difficult but not impossible to get the Edison equipment, possibly somewhat less difficult to buy French equipment. There was also a man called Dickson, who had worked for Edison and who had now patented his own projector. One Sunday, Max made a trip across the Hudson

River on the Erie Ferry. It was the first time he had ever taken the ferry across the river to New Jersey, since his trip to play the West was north from Grand Central Station, and the trip on the boat plowing across the vast river thrilled him. He would have to take Sally on a ferry trip, but this resolve slipped from his mind once he reached West Orange in New Jersey and saw the place where Edison made his moving pictures. It was a workman there who mentioned Louis Lumière, who had developed cameras and projectors independently in France, and grasping at the name, hardly able to pronounce it, Max went to the import-export houses down on Pearl Street to learn how one bought something from France or, indeed, how one communicated with people or companies in France. He had little knowledge of anything and no background for anything, and strangely enough, none of the people he spoke to had any notion that a motion picture might be something that people would pay money to watch.

In New Jersey, Max looked at some of the Edison motion pictures. Their length varied from three to six minutes. One was of a girl dancing. Another showed two puppies playing. Another showed two acrobats and two jugglers. It cost him ten dollars to get into the studio and get the men there to run film for him, and after the prizefight film, this stuff was disappointing indeed. The same workman who had mentioned Lumière, Sam Snyder by name, a round-faced young man of twenty-seven years, allowed Max to buy him a beer in a saloon in West Orange and informed Max that the process had been around for three years. Did Max know where Koster and Bial's Music Hall was?

"Maybe I didn't know where West Orange is," Max said, "but I sure as hell know every music hall in New York. That's way uptown on Thirty-fourth Street. Me and my partner, Bert, we played five nights there. We work mostly at the Bijou."

"Hey, you're a music hall guy?" Snyder asked excitedly.

"Yeah."

"Well, I was going to mention that Mr. Edison put on a motion picture exhibition there three years ago, which was supposed to be the first exhibition of moving pictures, except that two guys in Germany, Skladanowsky by name, put something on the year before. They're supposed to be pretty good, but Mr. Edison's show was a washout. How come you're so interested in this stuff?"

"I think that if you opened a theatre to show just moving pictures, people would pay to watch it. I think there's a lot of money in it."

"I heard that before," Snyder admitted, "but nobody thinks it could work."

"Suppose I could pull it off," Max said. "Would you come to work for me?"

Snyder grinned. "Sure, if you pay me enough. But I think you got a lot of opium in your pipe and a lot of pipe dreams."

"Mostly it's the theatre," Max said. "Do you know what it costs to rent a theatre? I think if I had a theatre, I might work out the rest of it. Except," Max added, "the kind of people I'm thinking about, they never get to a theatre. They can't afford it, and even if they could, most of them wouldn't know what's going on."

"Which leaves you where?"

"Up shit creek, I suppose," Max muttered.

A week later, walking down West Broadway, he saw Mr. Schimmelmeyer's going-out-of-business sign and remembered his visits to Beth Sholom to pray for his father's soul.

He was adjusting these two possibilities in his mind — a findings store going out of business and a synagogue in a storefront on Hester Street — when Joe Guttman, his boss and the manager of the Bijou Theatre, asked his opinion on the question of motion pictures. "I hear from Bert you are a little crazy on this subject, maybe a *mayvin*? Yes?"

"I'm interested," Max said carefully.

"Oh? Me, too."

"You mean you might turn the Bijou into a moving picture place?" Max asked eagerly.

"I should be so crazy. No, never! But in the Keith places and on the Procter Circuit, they put in projectors to show three-minute films between the acts."

"I know," Max said with disgust. "They're schmucks! They don't know what a moving picture is!"

"So they're schmucks and you know, I see."

"You think when you sell a ticket for thirty-five cents and fill a music hall, that's the end of the world? Like hell it is! I'll tell you something, Mr. Guttman, there are millions of people never set foot in a music hall because they never had thirty-five cents to spend on a ticket, and maybe because they're afraid to go into a music hall, especially with kids."

"Ah-hah! Tell me, Mr. Mayvin, how much should I charge?"

"A nickel — and three cents for the kids."

"A nickel. Go have your head examined, Max. Go do your *shtick* and leave high finance alone."

That night, Max did his *shtick*, and when he left the music hall, he walked over to Mr. Schimmelmeyer's findings store on West Broadway and stood in front of it for at least half an hour, brooding, counting, calculating.

The following morning, Max was up at seven instead of sleeping until eight-thirty or nine o'clock. When he joined the family at the breakfast table in the kitchen, Sarah said, "Ah-hah, look who's here, our actor, he does us the honor." In all truth, it was the first time in weeks; but on the other hand, his mother's remark was in character. He could not remember a kind word from her. He lived with the feeling that she blamed him for his father's death and, unreasonable as it was, blamed rather than felt grateful to him for their survival.

The four youngest Britskys — Benny, now nine, Esther, now eleven, Sheila, thirteen, and Ruby, sixteen — finished eating and scrapping and went off to school. Freida, recovered and healthy, but hardly her old cheerful self, and now with a job in a shirtwaist factory on Houston Street, got ready to leave while Sarah removed the dishes from the table. Max said to her, "Mama, let the dishes stay for a moment. I want to talk to you."

"Sure. Let them stay. They wash themselves."

"A few minutes."

She faced him, a cup and a saucer in her hands, staring at him without pleasure. "Go on." At the door, Freida paused to listen, her curiosity piqued.

"Mama, all these years I been giving you money . . . You put away a few dollars, didn't you?"

"Did I?"

"I'm asking you, Mama."

"So if I did? Who's going to take care of me?"

"I take care of you, Mama. I take care of the whole family. I always did. But right now I need money, and if you could give me a few hundred dollars —"

"I should be so crazy?"

"Just for a few months and then I pay it back."

"And you go away and we starve."

"Mama, why should I go away?"

"You're no different from the bums you're with, the actors and the whores —"

"Max," Freida said, "I got sixty dollars saved. You can have it."

"You got sixty dollars!" Sarah yelled.

"Forget it," Max said.

"Everyone's got secrets," Sarah wailed. "I slave for you, and that's how I get paid, with secret money I never see."

"I'm sorry, Mama. Forget it," Max said and left the apartment.

"You can have the money, Mama," Freida said. "You were so good to me. I was saving to buy you something."

· · ·

Mr. Schimmelmeyer told Max of his despair. "It ain't the location," he explained. "You stand on West Broadway, and the whole world walks past, but look at the size of this place. Findings. A thousand items, maybe five thousand — who could count them. My wife, may she rest in peace, she knew everything and where everything was and what the price was. Where do you find someone like her? Me, I'm going crazy. There are ten more days to the month, and I don't pay another month's rent. Either I sell out by then or my whole stock goes to that *goniff* Meyers, over on Orchard Street. Five hundred dollars, he says to me, take it or leave it. I got five thousand dollars' worth of goods here if I got a nickel's worth, but what should I do, kill myself?"

"Absolutely not," Max said. "And I'm sorry to hear all this, Mr. Schimmelmeyer, I certainly am. Tell me, who owns the store?"

"Adolf Schmidt, and he ain't Jewish but he thinks Jews are rich. I tell you something, he's rich. You know what they call a building like this, a storefront with one story over it? They call it a taxpayer. Schmidt bought it for peanuts from an old Yankee, name of Culbertson. Some taxpayer. His taxes are three hundred dollars a year. From me, he collects a hundred dollars a month, twelve hundred dollars a year. Upstairs, he has three apartments. Two flats he rents, twenty dollars a month for each, and the other one he lives in. So he has a hundred and forty dollars a month without lifting a finger.

My wife, she should rest in peace, and myself, we work our finger to the bone and we have a profit of maybe sixty, seventy dollars a month. So just don't let him tell you he's poor and Jews are rich."

Which was exactly what Adolf Schmidt said to Max. "You Jews," he said, "you're all rich. I'm a poor man, struggling. The rent is eighteen hundred a year." Schmidt was having his lunch in the kitchen of his apartment over the store. He was a very fat man and his wife was a very fat woman, and as a gesture of either good will or good business, he invited Max to join him and help himself from a platter of white sausage and red kraut. Max refused the food and accepted a bottle of beer.

"I know," Schmidt said. "Sausage, it ain't kosher."

"Neither is the price," Max said. "Schimmelmeyer pays a hundred dollars a month."

"So you talked to Schimmelmeyer. I tell you something about Schimmelmeyer. He has an old lease from that stupid Yankee, Culbertson. The store is worth twice what he pays."

"I could buy his lease," Max said, venturing a shot in the dark.

"So you get three months more the lease has to run, and then we ain't friends. We are enemies. Now I like us to be friends."

"Sixteen hundred a year," Max said.

"Seventeen hundred."

"Sixteen hundred and I sign a lease for five years."

"Seven years."

"Six years."

"Seven years."

"Seven years," Max agreed. "You're a hard man, Mr. Schmidt."

"You deal with Jews, you got to be a hard man or you're out of business. You pay me a month's rent, you can open up first of next month. Hilda," he said to his wife, "give me my receipt book."

Max counted out one hundred and thirty-four dollars, which left him with a total available capital of sixty-one dollars. Schmidt counted the money, wrote out the receipt, and signed it. As Max was folding it into his wallet, Schmidt said to him, "I hope Schimmelmeyer didn't bleed you for his stock. He pleads he don't know nothing, but he's a cunning old man, believe me."

"I'm not buying his stock," Max replied.

"You're putting in a whole new stock? What's wrong with Schimmelmeyer's stock? You can buy it cheap."

"I'm not in the findings business."

"Oh? Didn't you say —"

"No."

"So what kind of business you're putting in the store?"

Max was sorely tempted to tell Schmidt that he intended to turn the store into a synagogue, but he resisted the temptation and said shortly, "A moving picture theatre."

"A what?"

"A moving picture theatre."

"What's a moving picture theatre?"

"A place where you show moving pictures."

"I never heard of such a thing."

"Neither did anybody else. We're the first, Mr. Schmidt."

"You're crazy. A store ain't a theatre."

"This one will be."

"Take your money. I don't want any business with you."

"You took my money and gave me a receipt," Max said with a confidence he did not wholly feel. "It's as good as a lease, and you try to back out and you'll have a damn big lawsuit on your hands."

"So you trick me," Schmidt said. "I should know better than to do business with a Jew."

"You should," Max agreed. "You certainly should."

· · ·

"Yankee" was the word used throughout the Lower East Side as a sort of negative designation. When dealing with a person who was obviously not Jewish or Polish or Hungarian or German or Russian or Rumanian, or any of the various other ethnic groups who inhabited the area, one dealt with a Yankee. Mr. Hodgkins was a Yankee. He sat behind his desk at the Rivington National Bank and regarded Max dubiously as he informed him, "A bank, Mr. Britsky, does lend money. In that surmise, you are absolutely right. However, it appears to me that your experience with banks is somewhat limited. We lend money for reasonable enterprises, but we require collateral."

Max took a deep breath, cursed his own ignorance, said to himself, Fuck you, mister, so you think I'm a schmuck, and then asked, "What is collateral?"

Unable to control a curl of amusement at the corner of his mouth,

Mr. Hodgkins explained that collateral was a thing, a bond, a piece of property worth at least thirty percent more than the amount lent by the bank, which was taken over by the bank as security for the repayment of the loan.

"In other words," Max said, "you operate the same as a hock shop."

"A what?"

"A pawn shop, Mr. Hodgkins. I come here with an idea that's maybe unique, and you tell me to bring you this collateral of yours. Mr. Hodgkins, if I had something worth a thousand bucks, I'd hock it and not come brownnosing around a horse's ass like you."

"I went to three more banks," he told Sally that evening. "The same thing." They were in Sally's room. "Let's get out of here," he said to her. "I feel choked. I feel the whole goddamn world is choking me."

"Where, Max? Where do you want to go?"

"Out of here! One goddamn little furnished room!"

"I don't complain. It's my home."

"What's a home? I spend my life in that shitbasket on Henry Street! Seven of us in that lousy, roach-infested flat, pissing on each other —"

"Max," she cried, "I won't have you talk like that! I won't have such language here, and if this room isn't good enough for you, you can just get out of here and go back to your hooligans!"

The unexpected ouburst of anger and independence on Sally's part amazed Max. For a long moment he stared at her, then he exclaimed, "You're right! I ain't in your class, Miss Levine! Where does the *gossen jung* come off, consorting with a high-class schoolteacher?" And with that, he stormed out of her room, slamming the door behind him, and leaving Sally bewildered and frightened. She had forced the issue, and now he was gone. She had never been able to accept the fact that she wanted Max; now she felt an awful shudder of fear. He was gone, and perhaps he would never return.

In the downstairs hall of the boarding house where Sally lived, there was one of the marvelous new instruments called telephones. Mrs. Schwartz, the landlady, had it installed the year before after fighting the demands and persuasions of her guests for months. An hour and a half after Max had fled from her room, Mrs. Schwartz knocked at the door, complained about having to run up and down stairs for that rotten telephone, and told Sally that there was a call for her. Sally ran down the stairs, but it was not Max. It was Bert, calling from the Bijou, and he wanted to know where the devil Max was.

"I don't know," Sally said, half hysterical.

"Are you crying?"

"No. Yes, I guess so."

"Did you and he have a fight?"

"I guess so."

"That was a stupid thing to do!" Bert yelled. "Max ain't just Max! He's part of an act, and what the hell do I do now, go on by myself?"

"I didn't do it on purpose."

"Where is he?"

"I don't know."

Sally flung herself on her bed and gave in to uninhibited weeping. Each Friday night, Sally had dinner with her mother and father in Brooklyn. She was an only child, and her mother and father, Lillian and Arthur Levine, emigrants from Vienna and proprietors of a grocery store, made her the adored center of their universe. A few months after she began to see Max on a steady basis, she told her parents about him. They in turn withheld judgment until Sally was ready to present him to them; however, they could not refrain from suggesting that a penniless vaudeville entertainer who had left school at the age of twelve was hardly a fit match for a young woman from a good and substantial family — they owned their own home in Flatbush — with a normal school education and a firm job in the New York City public school system. Their comments were very mild, no more than a pointing to the obvious, but enough to affect Sally, who made a vow to herself that she would end her relationship with Max. But she did not end it, and in all truth, she had no other suitors, and the few male acquaintances of her family who had suggested dates paled into such insignificance against the drive and energy and excitement of Max that Sally had no difficulty making a choice.

She continued to see Max, and now, faced with the thought that it was finally over, and that she herself had driven home the wedge that finished it, she was utterly devastated. Now she recalled the positive qualities of Max, his brightness and alertness, his unshakable confidence, his sense of authority — putting aside his ignorance, his vulgarity, and of course his place of origin, the hideous apartment on Henry Street which she had never seen. Once again, he assumed a romantic image, fed and shaped out of Sally's reading, and finally, in the exhaustion of her tears, she fell asleep — to be awakened by someone knocking at the door. It was Max, and it was almost midnight.

"That bitch downstairs wouldn't let me in at first. I had to threaten to break down the door."

Sally threw her arms around him.

"That don't mean I'm not mad anymore," Max said.

"Bert called."

"Yeah. I missed the show. I missed both shows — first time it ever happened." He dropped into a chair. "I didn't care. I ain't got you — fuck the whole thing."

"Max!" He had never used that word in front of her before.

"I'm sorry, I'm sorry. It just slipped out. It's bad enough I can't talk straight English, I got to swear in front of you."

"It's all right."

"What am I doing up there on that stage like a monkey, telling stupid dirty jokes and acting like a clown? Do you think I want to spend the rest of my life that way? I want something. I can't spend the rest of my life in that lousy bedbug-infested hole on Henry Street. I never told you, but once with Ruby and me — we both sleep in the same bed, even now — and that time, about six, seven years ago, the sheets were covered with blood from the damn bedbugs driving us crazy, so we got some kerosene and poured it over the bedsprings and lit it. God Almighty, a wonder we didn't burn the house down, and maybe we should have, with my mother screaming at us — Oh, hell, what's the use?"

"How can you say that, what's the use?" Sally demanded, alive once again now that Max had returned.

"How? How? I'll tell you how. Finally, I see a way out. I got an idea that's going to turn the world over. You know what the idea is? Now listen to me, Sally! You going to listen to me?"

"Of course I'm listening. I'm so glad you're back. But it's so late."

"I don't care how late it is, because if I don't talk to somebody about this, I'll go out of my mind. You remember when we went to

Cooper Union to see the pictures of the Fitzsimmons-Corbett fight. Your teacher friends were shocked out of their petticoats, but I got so excited I almost peed in my pants. There I go again. I'm sorry. I won't do it again. But I been thinking about that ever since, and you take all them thousands and thousands of people live here on the East Side, and other places too, and they don't go to the music halls, because most of them don't think it's really decent, and anyway they can't afford it, and they can't afford the theatre either, and most of them don't understand English so good, so even if they went to the theatre it wouldn't make much sense, even if they could afford it, which they can't. But here's pictures. Pictures. And I could open a place and just charge a nickel for grownups and three cents for kids, and I could make out — No, I'd make a fortune." His bright blue eyes were sparkling, his lean body vibrant with excitement.

"Oh, Max, how could you? I don't want to throw cold water on your schemes, but you dream —"

"No! No, I don't! Now listen! In the whole world, I had a hundred and ninety-five dollars and sixty cents. That's what I had in my savings account at the Bowery Bank. I drew out a hundred and fifty dollars. Over on West Broadway, there's a findings store run by a guy, his name is Schimmelmeyer. He's going out of business. So I went to his landlord, who is a Kraut named Schmidt, and I make a deal to rent Schimmelmeyer's store, with a lease for seven years. That's how sure I am. Seven years, and I give Schmidt a hundred and thirty-four dollars for the first month's rent, and so he can't slide out of the deal — that's how sure I am of what I'm doing. And what am I doing? Now listen. I put two hundred folding chairs into Schimmelmeyer's store. Plenty of room. I made a deal with a guy, name of Sam Snyder, works for Edison out in New Jersey. Edison pays him peanuts. I agreed to pay him fifty dollars a week, twenty dollars more than he gets from Edison, also five percent of my profits. He don't think I'm crazy. He's a projectionist. He knows where we can get a projector, where we can pay it out for ten dollars a week, and also he has lined up six different pieces of film, moving pictures — one is of monkeys, very cute, and another is of this guy who tries to jump off a barn and fly with a set of crazy wings, and another shows a magician with tricks — that's the longest one, six minutes. But altogether, we got twenty minutes of moving pictures. Now you mean to tell me anywhere there's a grownup won't pay a nickel to see it, and suppose you got five kids. You pay fifteen cents and a nickel for yourself. And it's nice and clean. The rabbis and the priests won't scream it's filthy and stay away. You know how much I'll take in — just in that one store on West Broadway? Ask me. Ask me."

"All right, Max. I'll ask you."

"I'm not guessing. I swear to God, I'm not guessing. I worked it out carefully, every detail, estimating how many will see the show twice, and if I open twelve o'clock noon and close eleven o'clock nighttime, I got to take in two hundred dollars a day weekdays and maybe four hundred a day Saturday and Sunday, and that's not crazy but real. So why don't I do it? Because they've thrown me out of every bank south of Fourteenth Street. One thousand dollars. You want to borrow money, Maxie, my boy, give us collateral. You know what collateral is?"

Sally nodded.

"It ain't enough they want nine percent interest like the bloodsuckers they are, but collateral. Would I come to you if I had collateral? That's what I ask them. Ah, what's the use?" He shook his head hopelessly.

"You're giving up?"

"What can I do, Sally? I tried. I want to marry you."

"You never asked me. How do you know I'd marry you?"

"Well, wouldn't you? Wouldn't you? You're the only girl I ever wanted to marry."

"Max, Max, you're twenty years old."

He leaped to his feet, waving his arms. "The hell with that! So I'm twenty years old! You want me to sit down in a closet and wait until I'm fifty? I was never a kid. I was twenty years old when I was twelve years old." Suddenly he dropped his arms to his sides and stood staring at her hopelessly, for all the world like a small boy about to burst into tears.

"Max," she said gently.

"Yeah?"

"Max, I have been saving money since I started to work. I have almost fourteen hundred dollars, which includes a gift of three hundred dollars from my Aunt Lucy, but it's mine for whatever I want, and if you need a thousand dollars and you believe so strongly in this moving picture thing, then I can lend it to you."

"What?" Max asked stupidly.

"Didn't you hear me? I can lend you a thousand dollars."

"You never told me you had all that money," he said indignantly.

"You never asked me."

"You think I'm going to take your money? You think I'm a pimp?"

"Max, Max, what's come over you? I don't think you're a pimp. I would never, never in a hundred years think anything so terrible about you. When you walked out of here before, I was so unhappy I could have died."

"You mean you missed me?"

"Of course I missed you. I guess you've become a part of my life."

"You mean you love me?"

"I think so. I guess so. Yes."

He went to her and took her in his arms. It was the first time he had ever embraced her in this manner, folding her into his arms and body, kissing her fully, not the little pecks they had exchanged before, but a deep, lush kiss, their mouths open, their breath interchanged; and once caught in the clutch of that kind of passion, he couldn't stop. Max was not tall, but he was wiry and strong, and he picked her up in his arms, carried her to the bed, and then he was stretched beside her, pawing at her clothes, touching her breasts for the first time, managing to get her blouse open while she begged him, "No, Max, we have to wait. We have to. We can't do it. It would spoil everything."

He realized that, and he was able to ask himself what in hell he thought he was doing. Sally was sweet and pure and chaste; wasn't that why he loved her? She wasn't a tramp from the street; she wasn't like his sister Freida, who would let any jughead knock her up; she was the woman who would be his wife. He stopped trying to undress her. He touched her breasts again, but gently and with forbearance. He kissed her. They lay there, kissing, petting, touching each other, his excitement and tension mounting until finally he had an ejaculation in his trousers. Sally knew what had happened, and she smiled sympathetically. Strangely, his love for her had not diminished, and he felt none of the disgust with himself he had always experienced when he had sex with one or another of the whores. It was a novel discovery.

"We'll be partners," he said to Sally later, when he was about to leave. "It's not just some money that you're lending me. We're in this together. We'll be in everything together."

. . .

"And what do I do?" Bert asked him. "Do I drop dead or do I cut my throat? Or do I go up to the roof and jump off?"

"Come in with me," Max begged him. "To hell with all that shit about working for me. You don't have to work for me. We been partners for a long time and we can be partners again. I don't want any money from you, Bert. But I need you. You got the kind of class I'll never have. You're a real American, not some kike kid from Henry Street, and if we stick together, we can really set the world on fire."

"Sure, with my looks and your brains," Bert said bitterly.

"That wasn't what I meant. You know that wasn't what I meant."

"You tell me."

"I'm offering you half, half of everything."

"Half of nothing is nothing. You want to be so goddamn generous and be my buddy, so stay with the act a couple of months. We'll find a replacement and break him in."

"Bert, I can't. I'm running all day long. I got a million things to do. I have to track down every piece of moving picture film that exists, damn near, and find out when more will be made, and it takes me two days to find someone'll sell me two hundred folding chairs — which don't exist for sale, only for rent, so I got to get them made."

"Can it. My heart is bleeding for you."

"Bert, I'm leaving the act. That's it."

"Yeah, that's it," Bert said bitterly. "Walk out. Leave me. The hell with me! The hell with everything! You're a buddy, Max, the real thing!"

Meanwhile, Sally was also engaged in a fruitless argument. She had gone home to Brooklyn for Friday night dinner with her parents. The Levines lived on a pleasant tree-lined street in Flatbush in a small yellow frame house with a porch around three sides. While Max had never been to Sally's home and Sally had never been to the flat on Henry Street, she had heard enough about it from Max to have a good notion of what it was like, and she couldn't help contrasting it with the clean and bright respectability of her parents' home. They had come to America a generation before the great tide of Eastern European Jewish immigration, and while a sunny, pretty, almost suburban neighborhood like Flatbush was a world apart from the raucous, teeming, filthy, and noisy East Side ghetto, it was nevertheless sufficiently connected by tribal ties to make Sally shudder on occasion and whisper to herself, "There, but by the grace of my mother and father." Thoughts of this sort undermined her courage. It was not until dinner was finished and they were sitting at the table in a pleasant aftermath of chicken and fish surfeit that Sally unloaded her news — that she was now engaged to one Max Britsky and that she had lent him a thousand dollars for him to go into a business that did not actually exist but which he was going to bring into existence and which would be known as the moving picture business. There it was, the cat out of the bag and standing on four long legs in front of them. She waited. Her mother waited. Both looked at Arthur Levine, and Arthur Levine tried to compose himself.

It was not easy. In a time of large families, they had only one child, whom they adored. She had never been abused, spanked, punished. She was a good girl, as they so often said, and they were very proud of her. But Max Britsky —

"I don't want to try to upset any apple carts," Arthur Levine began, "and your mama and me, we respect a choice you make. But have you thought about it enough? A vaudeville performer, a man from a family you say yourself he never wants you to meet with a twelve-year-old's education. Sally, Sally, think of yourself. You're a beautiful, talented young lady. Sam Goldman's boy, he would get down on his knees to make you a proposal of marriage, and Sam's got his own cloak-and-suit business. Or Jack Kanter, or Richard Cohen — boys who could offer you something. Mrs. Cohen tells Mama all her son wants is a chance to take you out and keep company a little, and he passed the bar. Kanter's a doctor, already a resident. Why should you throw yourself away?"

"I'm not throwing myself away, Papa. You don't know Max. It

wasn't his fault that he had to leave school when he was twelve. It wasn't because he's stupid. He's one of the brightest boys I ever met. In fact, it was a very noble act. I told you how he took care of his mother and his brothers and sisters —"

"You told us," Lillian Levine said shortly. "He's also four years younger than you. What kind of a match is that?"

"You know how hard you worked and saved to put away that money," Sally's father said. "And you give it to him like that. What should I say, Sally? What should I say?"

"You never brought him here. Tell me, Sally, what kind of a boy keeps company and he don't meet the father and mother?"

Sally's eyes misted over. She was at the point of tears, and her father, unable to bear the sight of his daughter weeping, said, "Enough. We got no right to talk until we meet him, so you must bring him here. Then we'll see."

· · ·

In the end, Adolf Schmidt decided not to go to court to void Max as his tenant. After all, he explained to his wife, a seven-year lease was not something you found every day of the week, and the rent was better than the rent Schimmelmeyer paid. In his own mind, Schmidt had faced the possibility that he might even have to lower the rent. The store was too large, and at that time in the development of New York City, a large store was more difficult to rent than a small one, the age of oversized markets being in the future. Overcome with curiosity, Schmidt watched glumly as Max took over the findings store and created what appeared to Schmidt as chaos. The display cases and counters were taken out and loaded onto a huge dray in spite of Schmidt's wails of protest.

"In seven years I'll replace them," Max told him. He had sold the lot for twenty dollars. Then the inside walls were painted a soft gray, the floor dark gray. That was Sally's suggestion. In spite of herself, in spite of her parents' foreboding, she was becoming intrigued with Max's project. If nothing else, she was completely in awe of his energy. He did everything, watched everything, supervised everything. He had to invent a projection booth in which to place the magic lantern device that would throw the moving pictures onto a screen. He sat in her room until two in the morning while Sally made sketch after sketch, until at last they put together a blueprint of what he wanted. When he found that the folding chairs were too light and would be thrown out of line, he devised a method of fastening ten chairs together. He took a train one night for Rochester, New York, disdaining the extra cost of a Pullman berth, and blustered his way into a meeting with George Eastman, who at first reacted with contempt to this skinny, pushy Jew with his ghetto speech. But there was something about Max, an energy, an intensity, that made Eastman listen instead of throwing him out. Max was neither awed nor abashed in the presence of the great inventor and industrialist, and Eastman in turn glimpsed the vastness of Max's dreams. He took time to show Max the newest developments in roll film, and he showed Max a screen, silvered instead of white, that he had been experimenting with.

"I want one," Max said. "What'll it cost me?"

"Won't cost you a nickel. I'll ship you a silvered one and a white one, and see which brings you the best response."

Sitting up all night on the train out of Rochester, Max basked in the afterglow of his meeting with George Eastman. Mr. Eastman might not have known who Max was, but Max knew who Max was, and as he said to Sally the next day, "There I was, little Maxie Britsky, sitting there with one of the biggest men in America and a dyed-in-the-wool Yankee, and he could have tossed me out on my *tush*, but he didn't. He listened to my idea."

"Of course he did!" Sally exclaimed. "He could see that you were just about the brightest thing that ever walked into his office."

"And how could he see that?"

"Well, I see it, and if he's so smart, he could see it. Anyway, if your dream works out, think of all the film he'll sell."

"That occurred to me," Max said.

"Will you have enough money? If you need more, I still have —"

"No, sir," Max said, holding up his hand, palm out. "I am going to make it. We open next week, and I still got eighty-five dollars. I had to pay Sam Snyder his first week's wages and then I had to send him to Philadelphia to look at two other pictures we found out about. One is of a cowboy, one of them badmen types from out West —"

"One of *those*, Max," Sally pleaded. "Try. You can speak correctly when you try."

"Sure, sure. Believe me, I'm trying. You know, a pistol-shooter, he pulls out his gun and shoots."

"Do you see what he's shooting at?"

"No, it's only three minutes. I think he drinks a bottle of booze first. The other picture is a little girl who crawls around the room, and she pulls a tablecloth off a table loaded with junk, and something hits her, I think a piece of fruit, and then she begins to cry and then her mama comes and picks her up. Very cute. Sam says it's supposed to be a real good thing and we can get it very cheap. We're not paying for the films; I just sign notes to pay for them next month, God willing, otherwise I kill myself."

"You shouldn't talk like that. I still have some money."

"Sure, and I got eighty-five dollars, except that fifty is for the sign painter, and I got to pay him tomorrow."

Max could have had a sign for as little as five dollars, but he didn't want to skimp in that area. There was no way he could have anything like the Bijou or any of the valid music halls. No matter how he dressed it, a store was still a store, perhaps a cut above the little synagogues that had established themselves in stores all over the East Side, but still a store. Fortunately, it had double doors opening into the street, inside of which Max built a tiny vestibule, a swinging door into the makeshift theatre, and a glassed-over small counter on the right, behind which he had arranged to station Freida. All his instincts told him that his venture would live or die depending on the honesty of the person who sold the tickets. He could trust Freida. Yet the store was still a store, which prodded Max to invest almost the last of his money in the sign. The sign was forty feet long, stretching the whole length of the storefront, and on it, in bold yellow letters against a crimson background, the legend: MAX BRITSKY'S ORPHEUM.

It was a cold, nasty day toward the end of November, in the year 1899, at twelve o'clock noon, that the sign was lifted into place there on West Broadway. It was an event that went unnoticed in the annals of history. Other things were remembered: the fierce battles of the Boers against the British in South Africa; the births of Charles Laughton and Noel Coward, whose lives would be shaped to a large degree by that sign over Max Britsky's store; and also remembered although unknown to almost all of the folk alive then, the first magnetic recording of sound. But people in motion and action on a cold day are not concerned with history, and the workmen cursed the size and unwieldiness of the sign, and Mr. Schmidt, watching glumly, told Max that his property was being ruined.

"Orpheum," he muttered. "What's an orpheum?"

"You heard of Guttman's Orpheum, you heard of Keith's Orpheum, so that's what an orpheum is."

"You open tomorrow?"

"Tomorrow, you bet."

"Tomorrow it snows."

Schmidt was right. The following morning the snow began, nasty wet flakes that melted when they touched the sidewalk. It was too early in the season for a real snowfall, but when Max looked at the gray skies, he felt his heart sink.

"You still want me there? You still going to open?" Freida asked him.

"You're damn right I am."

Sam Snyder had put together a program of six films, and imitating the style of legitimate theatres, Max had purchased an easel and had the program lettered onto a sheet of Bristol board: MONKEY SHINES, THE ACROBAT, LITTLE ONES, THE HORSE CAR, PUPPIES, and, finally, THE MAGICIAN. *The Magician* was the best thing Max had seen. It ran for almost five minutes, and it featured the internationally famous magician Harvey Eddelson. There was none of the camera tricks, which Sam Snyder was so enthusiastic about and which the film experimenters delighted in. The camera simply fixed on Eddelson, head on, while he went through his assortment of astonishing tricks. All six films added up to a running time of nineteen minutes and thirty-three seconds. Snyder had spliced the films together so that the show would be uninterrupted. It was Sally's suggestion, when she first saw the films, that some sort of title and perhaps a few descriptive words might introduce each of them. She also felt that the man who took the pictures in each case should be given some sort of credit or acknowledgment, as an artist is for a picture or an author for a book. But neither Max nor Snyder considered this to be of any great importance — and, indeed, Snyder admitted that in two instances, he did not know who the photographer was. But they agreed to the title cards, and for *Monkey Shines*, Sally wrote, "Are monkeys smarter than people? Who knows? Watch and see." For *The Acrobat*, she wrote, "Who is this man who flies like a bird? He is the acrobat. Watch and be thrilled." For *Little Ones,* she wrote, "Everyone loves a baby. Nothing is cuter than these little darlings." For *The Horse Car,* she wrote: "Will these soon be as obsolete as dinosaurs? Who knows?" For *Puppies:* "Watch the cuddly darlings. What a pity you can't take one home." And for *The Magician:* "In all the world there is only one Eddelson, the master of illusion."

Max was delighted, and Sally persuaded a friend, an art student, to do the lettering on all the title cards and legends for five dollars. Snyder then took the cards out to New Jersey and had them photographed at Edison's studio. Sally, who had continued to take a dim view of the entire undertaking, came to life when she saw her own words on film.

But it was snowing.

"You're damn right I'm opening," Max said to the assembled Britsky family at breakfast in the kitchen of the flat on Henry Street. "I open if it's another blizzard of eighty-eight."

They hung on his words. Even Sarah had no caustic, undermining comment on the situation. For years she had screamed at Max, blamed him for every misfortune, and in all truth despised him. In some way beyond her comprehension, she held him responsible for her unmarried state, her hopeless future, her poverty — but all this without any kind of insight, and in her mind it expressed itself simply as irritation and anger. Yet today even that anger had cooled. Her son Max owned some kind of theatre, and today was its opening. She deflected her anger and cursed the weather. The other Britskys absorbed excitement and wanted to know whether they could see the moving picture show.

"After school," Max told them, quieting their clamor. "Mama will bring all of you." He placed a dollar in front of his mother. "But you pay for them, Mama. Here's the money. Freida will be at the ticket window, but anyway you pay her. A nickel for yourself and three cents for the kids, except Ruby. Ruby is old enough. He pays full price. The difference is twelve years old. I know Sheila, already she's thirteen, but she don't look thirteen."

Giggling, Freida said, "You're cheating yourself, Max."

"I'm making a joke." He grinned.

"But I know Sheila's thirteen."

"Why should we pay?" Sarah demanded. "I'm your mother. Your mother should pay?"

"Because everyone pays," Max said decisively. "No freeloaders." Excepting, of course, the passes he had handed out at the local police precinct, entitling the captain and the lieutenants to enter free with their families as often as they desired.

He had arranged with Sally for her to have dinner with him and then to accompany him to the evening performance, which ensured a reasonable gap of time between his family's appearance and Sally's appearance. Max, shepherding Freida, got to the store at eleven, an hour before the opening. Sam Snyder was there waiting for him, his normal round, cheery face set and worried, shaking his head at the dismal weather. "This stinks," he said. "This really hits us."

"We'll make it," Max replied with a confidence he hardly felt. "Take your place," he said to Freida.

"It's cold."

"So keep your coat on. I'll tell you something, Sis. If we're not wiped out today, a month from now I'll buy you a fur coat."

"You're kidding."

"So help me — it's a promise." He went into his coat pocket and came up with two rolls of pennies and a bag of nickels, dimes, and quarters. "Here's the change, seven dollars' worth." He did not add that this left him with exactly eighty-five cents as his total worldly wealth.

"You really mean that about the fur coat?" Snyder asked him. "You'd really buy her a fur coat, or are you kidding her?"

"What do you think?"

"I don't know, Mr. Britsky, I just don't know. I never worked for a —" He caught himself.

"For a Jew — that's what you were going to say?"

"Not exactly," Snyder muttered uneasily.

"First of all, you call me Max, I call you Sam. Second, you going to work for a Jew, you face up to it. Either you figure I'm a human being like everyone else or screw the whole thing."

"I didn't mean it that way," Snyder said, his face reddening. He was a large, fat young man, slow-moving and good-natured and, as Max had instinctively felt and would put it later, "smart as hell." He had a round, pleasant face, wide-set baby blue eyes, and a thatch of sandy hair. "Look," he went on, "I think you got something, something big, otherwise I never would have left my job to go to work for you, and I respect you. Sure, there are lots of them that hate Jews, but I ain't one of them, and let me tell you, I'm a Lutheran, and plenty of times when I was a kid, I was a 'lousy Kraut' because my pop came over from old Germany and he spoke with an accent. So how do you feel about Lutherans?"

"I don't know. You're the first one I ever had a conversation with."

"Same here."

"We'll manage." Max grinned. "You married, Sam?"

"I got two kids, and my wife can cook. How about having dinner with us?"

"Someday, sure. And about that fur coat — I don't make promises to kid people. She'll get the fur coat. Stick with me, and I'll make you some promises."

"I'll give it a try," Snyder said, holding out a hand to catch the wet flakes of November snow. "It's letting up."

Max nodded. Snyder was blocking the card that read: GRAND OPENING. Max drew him aside. One or two people had paused in front of the store. It was a weekday. "Maybe you should have opened on a Saturday," Freida said. The Grand Opening card announced: "A new entertainment. MOVING PICTURES. For five cents, enjoy the ultimate in entertainment. A thrilling, marvelous display of science and artistry. An experience you will never forget."

Freida had unwrapped the ticket roll. They were old, unused tickets that Max had purchased from Guttman, who had raised his prices and had no use for the old tickets. There were a thousand tickets on a roll. "It says, Bijou Palace, thirty-five cents," Freida told him worriedly.

"Nobody reads it. If they do, they're getting a bargain. Anyway, we got a better show than the Bijou."

"You should have someone to collect the tickets, Max. Inside, like in the Bijou."

"Forget it. Just tear the ticket in half when you sell it. Keep half of it for our records. You got the cigar box I told you to bring?"

"Right here." She held it up.

"Good, good."

Snyder sighed and went inside to set up his projector. At eleven-forty, Freida sold the first tickets. They were four ladies of the street, their business slack in the early hours, strangers to Max and very excited about the notion of moving pictures. They were followed by a man and a woman — tourists, Max decided; and then Silverman, who had a grocery store across the street and who said to Max, "For a nickel, I can spend half an hour. My wife's at the store. She'll come when I go back."

A carriage with four passengers pulled up by the curb. "What is it?" a man in the carriage shouted to Max.

"Moving pictures."

"What are moving pictures?"

"Like the kinetoscope!"

"Vincent, what's the difference?" a woman in the carriage demanded of the man. "Just get us out of this wretched carriage."

They sent the carriage away and bought four tickets. By now, the wet flakes of snow had slowed almost to a halt, and a small crowd gathered outside of the Britsky Orpheum. At five minutes to twelve, Freida had sold a hundred and eleven tickets. Even Schmidt and his wife appeared, informing Max that as his landlords they should have complimentaries. Max took a dime from his pocket, bought two tickets from Freida, and handed them to Mr. and Mrs. Schmidt.

At noon, Max went inside. He poked his head into the projection booth. "Ready?" he asked Sam Snyder.

"Ready."

"Roll it," Max said exuberantly. Snyder flicked a switch, began to turn the handle, and at the other end of the store, on Mr. Eastman's silver screen, appeared the legend, MAX BRITSKY PRESENTS MOVING PICTURES.

• • •

At four o'clock, precisely, the Britsky family appeared. For years, Sarah had carefully hoarded pennies and an occasional nickel, hiding her fortune in a white ironstone milk pitcher, and in the course of time she had accumulated fifty-three dollars, four and a half dollars of which had gone for material for a new dress, heavy green velvet. Six dollars had gone for a new cloth coat, the first coat she had bought since her husband died, not secondhand but new. She wore all her finery now, including a hat with colored feathers, as she marched up to the ticket window of Max Britsky's Orpheum with all her family behind her, Benny, Esther, Sheila, and Reuben. It was a very fine moment for Sarah. With a straight face, Freida asked, "How many, please?" to which Sarah replied, "Two for grown people and three for children, and I shouldn't have to wait on line," she added.

"Mama, that's good," Freida explained. "It's good business. We been doing wonderful business."

"I'm still his mother."

Inside, Max awaited them. "I saved five seats for you," he whispered.

"In front?"

"No, Mama. It's better not in front. You see better not so close."

Grudgingly, Sarah accepted the seats, certain that Max had given the front seats to more favored people. Then her attention and the attention of the other Britskys was hooked to the screen, and for the next twenty minutes they sat enthralled; when Max suggested that they sit through the show a second time, they accepted eagerly.

Afterward, Sarah dissolved, cast off anger and frustration for the moment, and said to Max almost tenderly, "Darling, it was beautiful, so beautiful I couldn't believe my own eyes."

On Max's part, he couldn't believe his own ears. His mother was being both kind and complimentary. If it had happened before, he could not recall it.

. . .

Sally kept her own counsel. Admittedly, Max had done something no one else had done, at least here in the United States. He had put together a program of moving pictures and established a theatre of sorts in which they could be shown. But until Max picked her up at seven o'clock on the day his theatre opened, she was not at all sure that people would pay money to look at his moving pictures. Aside from the incredible fact that the pictures moved, they held little of interest for Sally, and although Max argued that the bulk of the population of New York — or, indeed, any other of the country's large cities — never went to a theatre or a music hall, Sally wondered whether they would pay money, even as little as a nickel, for what Max had to sell. But when Max came into her room that evening, he was euphoric.

"By six o'clock," he informed Sally, "we took in fifty-two dollars and twenty-four cents. Do you know what that means — daytime on a weekday? It means before we close tonight, we'll hit a hundred and fifty dollars, or close to it. You know, they love it. They go out and come back with their friends. I had to put Ruby in as an usher — that's something I never thought about. I'm paying him five dollars a week, after school. And this is the first day. You know, I didn't even have the brains to put an announcement in the newspaper, except Sammy Snyder knows a guy, he works for the *Tribune*, and Sammy says he'll write a story about us. Sally, I can't take you to dinner tonight. Anyway, how could I eat the way I'm so excited? I got to go back to the theatre. All right, it's only a store — to me it's a theatre. Sally, what does orpheum mean?"

Max was never quiet or contemplative, but Sally had never seen him in this state of excitement, pacing back and forth the length of her small room, refusing her invitation to sit for a moment.

"What do you mean?"

"I mean orpheum, orpheum, what does the word mean?"

"It means a theatre, Max."

"Yeah, of course. Can you meet me there later?"

"You're sure you want to, tonight, Max?"

"Absolutely. I know you seen the show, but I want you to see it with the place filled with people. It makes a difference."

It did make a difference, Sally realized, as she stood with Max next to the projection booth, looking over the packed rows toward the screen. "Only, there's something missing," she whispered to Max.

"What's missing?"

"It's too quiet."

"Quiet? Listen to them laughing."

"I don't mean that. Max, you should have a piano, and the pianist can match the music to the pictures."

He drew her outside, thinking to himself, She's crazy. Still and all, it was Sally, and Sally was smart. He gave her credit as the single person he knew who might be smarter than himself, for if there was one thing Max never doubted, it was his own intelligence. Outside, there was a line in front of the ticket window. Max didn't want anyone standing. As the day had worn on, he improvised his method of operation, instituting Ruby as the usher, instructing him to check for empty seats and report to Freida. Freida complained that she was tired. "I been here all day, Max. I don't even get a chance to pee."

"She peed," Ruby said. "I brought her a sandwich and coffee."

"I paid for it myself," Freida said.

"Take it out of the ticket money. We'll work it out," Max said. "It's the first day."

Freida and Ruby were looking at Sally. So this was Max's school-teacher. "What's so great about her?" Freida asked Ruby afterward. "She's skinny if you like skinny."

Max steered Sally away, walking down the street. "Let's have a cup of coffee."

"That's your sister, isn't it?"

"Yeah, well —"

"She's so pretty. Why didn't you introduce me, Max? The boy is your brother, isn't he?"

"Yeah."

"I don't understand you," Sally said. "Why won't you have me meet anyone in your family?"

"You'll meet them. When I'm ready, you'll meet them." He changed the subject. "Here's a place where we can have coffee. I'm freezing. You know, I forgot my coat. I been walking around in a jacket all day."

"You haven't answered me."

He busied himself with the waiter, explaining to Sally that suddenly he was hungry. He had forgotten to eat lunch. He ordered ham and eggs and a side order of pork and beans. When he was euphoric and defiant, he ate ham. Sarah kept a kosher kitchen. All the annoyance and bitterness Max felt about his mother, denied, suppressed, was momentarily put to rest when he ate ham. In terms of Sarah, it was his act of independence and defiance, although he explained it to himself as proof to Sally that he was as indifferent as she to the rules of Orthodox Judaism. "You see," he said to Sally, "what you said about it being too quiet, I keep thinking about that. What do you mean, a piano player could match the music to the pictures?"

"Well, for example, with the children he could play light, lovely music like Debussy's *Girl with the Flaxen Hair*. With *The Magician*, perhaps something from *The Hall of the Mountain King*."

"What's the *Girl with the Flaxen Hair*?"

"It's just a sweet, lovely piece of music. But there's so much music, so many piano pieces and songs, that a facile pianist could find something to match any kind of a motion picture. But all this doesn't make me forget about your family. I want to meet them, and you must meet my family."

"All right, sure. Just give it time."

"Is it because of where you live, in that terrible flat on Henry Street? Are you ashamed of that place, Max? But you told me all about it. I know."

"You don't know," Max said. "You just don't know."

The next day, Max went over to the Bijou and spoke to Isadore Lubel, who was a fill-in pianist. "What do you get paid here?" Max asked him.

"Four dollars a day — when I work."

"I'll give you five dollars, steady work, no layoffs."

"You got me. For that kind of steady money, Max, I kiss your ass every day."

"Never mind the ass-kissing. Just play good. I got to go rent a piano now, so meet me in two hours at the picture place, and I'll explain to you what kind of thing I expect you to do."

• • •

Five weeks after the opening of Britsky's Orpheum, Max opened his second store on First Avenue, just north of Houston Street. It was a corner two-story building that had been constructed on an empty lot occupied by Hungarian squatters, who lived in tarpaper shacks and grew vegetables in small truck gardens. They gave way to progress, and Max rented two stores, removing the wall that divided them. His experience with Britsky's Orpheum paid off. Sam Snyder enticed two of Mr. Edison's employees to join what was already becoming the Britsky organization. Snyder himself was more valuable as a film scout, hunting down bits and pieces of moving pictures to feed the insatiable appetite of two moving picture theatres.

"You got to understand why I can't pay you back that thousand dollars right now," Max told Sally.

"I'm not asking you for the money, Max."

"Sure, I know that. But I want to pay you back. It means a lot to me to pay you back, but you know, every cent I make is going into the First Avenue place. It's bigger, three hundred and forty seats."

"I don't need the money, Max, but why are you rushing so? You're so young."

"Young! I don't know what the word means. But just give me time and stick with me, kid."

"Max, I want you to come out to Flatbush and meet my family. They'll give me no peace until they meet you, and I want you to be sweet and charming, and I want them to like you."

"You don't know how many things are coming up now, and on top of everything, I got trouble with Clancy."

"Max, you didn't hear a word I said. Who is Clancy?"

"A fat son of a bitch Irish cop from the Houston Street precinct."

"You have no respect for me!" Sally exclaimed. "You use language fit for a saloon!"

"I'm sorry. I swear — I'm sorry, Sally."

"I want you to meet my mother and father. How do I know you won't use language like that?"

"I won't. I'm going a little crazy now. This Captain Clancy, he wants thirty bucks a week — just to have a cop stand around outside the place."

"Why do you need a policeman outside?"

"I don't. But if I don't pay off, they'll run me out of there. You can't sneeze in this town without paying off the cops."

More or less, it was true. "You're asking for blood," Max had said to Captain Clancy.

"Come on, Maxie, me lad, it's a pittance. You'll want to be opening other places in my territory, will you not?"

"I got no plans now."

"But you will, laddie. There's another Jewish lad like you, opened up a ladies' dress place on Rivington Street, and he begrudged us the few lousy dollars for protection, with my lads risking their lives every day to keep the citizens safe. Poor boy. His shop was looted, he was beaten, and, indeed, he'll never be quite the same again."

"So I got that, and I got twenty other things," Max said to Sally. "But I heard you. Sure I heard you. But how about you? Are you sure you want your mother and father to meet me?"

"Of course I do."

Max shrugged. "Good enough."

"When?"

"Right after I open the First Avenue place."

But with all the demands that the second moving picture place made on Max, he still could not evade his family. Now that they were at least in part working for him, they were ubiquitous; and Max's relationship toward them had changed. Sarah had always demanded, but the others had accepted rather meekly. Now the meekness was gone. They all demanded, for Max had evolved into a true source. They wanted a picnic. Other families went on picnics; why not the Britskys? They kept after Max until he surrendered, and one Sunday morning the entire Britsky family set forth for Washington Heights. Since it was December, the unusually warm and sunny day was still quite chilly, and no one with the slightest experience in picnicking would have chosen such a day; but as far as the Britskys were concerned, it would have been a wonderful occasion if snow had been falling.

Of all the Britskys, only Max had been north of Twenty-third Street; the world beyond that was as formless to the Britskys as darkest Africa. For two dollars, Max had hired Shecky Blum to drive them to the Ninth Avenue Elevated line in his old true Fiacre, a one-horse, four-wheel open coach into which all seven of the Britskys were able to squeeze themselves. They sat three on each facing seat, with Benny on the floor between them. Max had purchased reserved seats on the Pullman section of the Elevated, and there they sat and watched the wonders of Manhattan Island rush by, all oblivious to the cold and disapproving stares of the prissy folk who shared the Pullman and were unused to the presence of such loudly vocal creatures as the Britskys. Little did the Britskys care! They had eyes for nothing but the wonders outside as the train roared up Ninth Avenue and onto Columbus Avenue. Max took on the role of tour director, pointing out the green hills and woods of Central Park on the right and glimpses of the majestic Palisades towering over the Hudson River on their left. And then there were the new achievements of this incredible and mind-boggling city called New York — the great apartment houses, the already famous Dakota, and then that improbable building, the vast Museum of Natural History, which would, when completed, dwarf any other museum of its genre in the entire world. And then, to cap everything, the elevated structure soared around the north end of Central Park, so high in the air over the valley that the train appeared — at least to the Britsky children — to be flying with no support; and in response to this, they screamed and screamed in fear and delight.

At the end of the line, at One Hundred and Fifty-fifth Street, they trudged up the hill to the public picnic grounds, deserted in this month of December. It hardly mattered that they were half frozen. There they were finally, out in the country, looking over the great estates sprawled through Harlem Valley and running down to the East River, many of them with their own docks and yachts, the yachts lifted out of the water now for the winter; and on the river, tugs pulling barges into the ship canal, and across the river, the spreading lawns, hedges, trees, and fields of farms and country houses in the Bronx. It was certainly a day to remember.

· · ·

Another day to remember was the day Max finally allowed himself to be persuaded by Sally into a journey to Flatbush. When he confessed to Sally that he had never been to Brooklyn before, she said to him, "Max, how could you be so insular? There's that glorious, wonderful bridge that's like no other bridge in all the world. Do you know that travelers come here from England and France and other places just to look at the bridge and walk across it, and you live a few blocks away from it and you've never taken the trouble to go across it."

"It's a question of time —"

"Time, time, time — you do nothing but talk about time and not having any. You're twenty years old, and you're going to let your life slip by without ever being young."

Whereupon Max surrendered another Sunday and went home with Sally. Sally was so pleased and delighted that she could not help being didactic, and she explained carefully to Max, as they rode along in Shecky Blum's Fiacre, hired for the day, that Flatbush had been an independent township, with an eloquent history of its own, until it was annexed to Brooklyn only a year before. For generations it had been a quiet Dutch town. Indeed, the name, Sally explained, came from the Dutch words *vlacke bos*, which meant wooded flats, and in time, the origin of the name being forgotten, it was corrupted to Flatbush. And it was there, she said, that General Sullivan stood fast with his brave Continentals and prevented the total destruction of the American army over a hundred years before. Max had not the slightest notion who General Sullivan was and only the vaguest sense of what had happened there a hundred years ago. History was hardly his strong point, but he was pleased as punch with the manner in which Shecky Blum hung onto every word of Sally's — to a point where he allowed his horse to fall into a slow walk.

"Come on, Shecky!" Max snapped. "This ain't exactly a school-room."

"That's a smart lady," Shecky said.

Flatbush was prettier than anything Max had expected. Even though it was winter, the great trees, the neat, comfortable houses, the occasional farm that still survived, the dry leaves picked up and swirled by the wind, the delicious scent of wood smoke instead of the stink of the ghetto, and all of this only two hours' drive from Henry Street, combined to give him a dreamlike sense of unreality. He tried to imagine what his life and childhood might have been had he grown up in a bucolic place like this, and he said to Sally, "You're a lucky girl."

He had worn his good blue serge suit, and when they came to the little frame house, painted yellow with white trim, where Sally had been born and had lived most of her life, Max leaped out of the Fiacre and helped Sally down. He was sure he was being watched from a window, and he did not desire the Levines to regard him as an uncouth lout, unworthy of their daughter. He felt out of place, subdued. The small frame house was the most elegant home he had ever set foot in — indeed, the first one-family house he had ever entered. He had to reassess Sally, separate her from the tiny fur-nished room and place her in this new setting. Her mother and father were very ordinary people, shopkeepers; but their substan-tial lower-middle-class respectability placed them well above Max's own chaotic background. His manner was low key, softly polite. Max possessed not only sensitivity but, as Sally had noted, a cha-meleon-like ability to adapt. The Levines had been prepared for some kind of ghetto savage; instead, they found themselves playing host to a slender, good-looking young man who praised Mrs. Levine's cooking and the cigar that Mr. Levine offered him. Max was not a serious smoker. He never bought cigars, but he savored them, and when they were offered to him, he puffed away with professional competence. The smoking took place in the chill of the back porch, since Mrs. Levine would not have her house polluted with cigar fumes, and sitting there, both of them wrapped in overcoats, Mr. Levine explored Max's potential while Sally helped her mother with the dishes. Max explained his position fully: two moving picture places functioning, a third location ready for leasing, and an overwhelming acceptance by the public.

"And you're serious about my daughter?" Mr. Levine asked pointedly. He was not one to mince words where his only child's future was concerned.

"Absolutely. But that don't mean Sally is ready to marry me. She's got a mind of her own."

"She certainly has," her father agreed. "How old are you, Max?"

"I'll be twenty-one in November."

"But since this is only January, you are really only twenty. Sally is already almost four years older. She's a lovely, smart girl, our Sally, and it breaks our heart how she is missing chances. Already, practically all of her girl friends are married. If she remains a single girl waiting for a young fellow like you to make a living, he should be able to afford to care for a wife. But for that, you got to have a living wage. You should forgive me for being direct, Max, but when can you look forward to a living wage?"

"I'll be just as straight with you, Mr. Levine. I love Sally. She is the only girl I ever cared for. But I got no hold on her and she knows that. I got my mother and five brothers and sisters to take care of, so a living wage is not what I need. I need a lot of money, and I'm going to make it."

Which gave Mr. Levine little enough comfort, but after they left that evening, Sally said that they both liked Max and that her mother thought he was a fine, responsible young man. But another matter impressed Max even more than the opinion of Sally's parents, and a few days later he hired Shecky Blum's carriage once again and drove out on the Flatbush Turnpike. He had seen, on his previous visit, a barn with a FOR SALE sign tacked onto it. The barn was in the main shopping area, set in a row of retail stores, an isolated reminder of the time not too long before when the whole area had been farmland. Max prowled through the barn, felt the soundness of its timbers, measured it front to back and side to side, and decided that with a cleaning, a painting, and some modest carpentry, it would hold four hundred folding chairs. Flatbush was not the Lower East Side. Here the admission would be ten cents for adults, five cents for children. Even at less than capacity, Max estimated one hundred and fifty dollars a day and perhaps two hundred and fifty on weekends. He spent the best part of the day dickering with a Mr. Hixby of Hixby and Collins, Real Estate in the New Brooklyn, and finally signed a contract for the barn. He took over an existing mortgage of thirteen hundred dollars and made a cash payment of three hundred and fifty dollars. Thus came into being Britsky's Flatbush.

. . .

The Flatbush moving picture barn was successful almost from the very first day, but it ate into Max's cash reserve. Then, when he had accumulated sufficient funds to clear the debt, Sam Snyder found a small company in Philadelphia that was making ten-minute films. They would choose a subject like trains and show a variety of trains in action from various angles — trains roaring toward the camera, away from the camera, trains on a trestle, engines in a roundhouse; or they would select a zoo and shoot film of many different animals; or they would take up a position in the city and photograph the action at one specific spot. Max joined Sam in Philadelphia and proceeded to option their entire library of seventeen films, with an exclusive first refusal on all additional films they intended to produce. In spite of the fact that Max could schedule the films for exhibition in three theatres, shuffling them in a number of combinations, his hunger for film was never satisfied.

In June, a fourth location was found near Tompkins Square, and thus it was not until October that Max was able to write out a check for one thousand dollars and present it to Sally. He took her to dinner that night wearing a tuxedo he had rented from Wormser's Wedding Specialties on Orchard Street, and he bought her a corsage of pink and violet flowers. Sally wore a dress of mauve crêpe de Chine, her hair piled high on her head, a touch of rouge on her cheeks and lips. Not yet possessed of enough *savoir-faire* to assault Delmonico's, Max nevertheless managed to reserve a table at the Holland House on Fifth Avenue, to which they drove in a hansom cab. Max ordered champagne and, as their main course, filet. He presented Sally with the check for a thousand dollars just before the dessert and proposed marriage at the same time.

"Dear Max, you are the sweetest, most wonderful person."

"I don't want to be wonderful. I just want to be your husband."

"We'll talk about it sometime."

"Now is sometime."

"Max," Sally said gently, "this is a lovely evening. I guess it's one of the nicest evenings of my life. Please don't let's spoil it with an argument."

"You say yes, there's no argument."

"Not tonight. Please, Max."

Hurt, baffled, he went through the rest of the evening with hardly a word. At the door to her room, Sally said, "Please, Max, don't be angry. Will you kiss me good night?"

"For what?" he demanded.

"Max —"

"Good night!" he snorted, turned on his heel, and went down the steps.

[FIVE]

1902

Max at the
Age of Twenty-three

SALLY began to cry.

"Crying doesn't help," her father said. "What are we doing here? Are we your enemies? Or are we two people who love you better than anybody else in the whole world?"

"More than that," her mother said. "Absolutely, darling, more than that."

"But I just don't know that I'm in love with him," Sally whispered. "I don't even know that I like him very much."

"Love. Again comes love."

"Sally darling, sweetheart," Mrs. Levine said, "in the old country marriages were made with the parents, not with the children. Who talked about love? But I'll tell you something, more of those marriages turned out to be good marriages than your love marriages here in America."

"Five years you been keeping company with him," Mr. Levine said, "and now suddenly you decide you don't love him."

"No, no, you don't understand," Sally said tearfully. "Max is such fun to be with — I mean, mostly — but I was never sure that I loved him. And sometimes I hated him, he's so crude and vulgar."

"You gave him a thousand dollars and you weren't sure that you loved him?"

"It was a loan. He paid me back."

"Sally," Mrs. Levine said, "do you know how old you are?"

"I know," Sally said miserably.

"Twenty-seven —"

"I'm not twenty-seven yet."

"Two months and you'll be twenty-seven years old," her father told her. "You know what a girl of twenty-seven is? I got to be very frank with you, my dear child. A girl of twenty-seven years is an old maid already, and God help me that this should happen to a child of mine."

At this, Sally's weeping became uncontrollable. Her mother ran to her and embraced her. "Look what you're doing to the child," she said to her husband.

"She's not a child anymore," Mr. Levine said bleakly.

"You have no heart."

"I got a heart," Mr. Levine said. "Lillian, you'd be surprised how much heart I got, you should see how much there is to be broken, a child of mine should be an old maid."

"Even if I wanted to," Sally sobbed, "I don't know whether he would marry me. I haven't seen him for almost a month."

"You don't know!" Mr. Levine exclaimed. "Only the finest kind of a nice Jewish girl in the world — Tell me —" He began to shout.

"Don't shout, please," Mrs. Levine begged him.

"All right." His voice dropped to a hoarse persuasive whisper. "Just tell me where he finds another girl like you, from a good family who will come into all her mother and father's property, with a job as a schoolteacher?"

"She'd be married if it wasn't for the teaching," Mrs. Levine said, unable to contain herself.

"I can't make him marry me."

"You could call him on the telephone. You could tell him you want to talk."

"And ask him to marry me? Papa!"

"No, not right away. You start to keep company a little but you got to encourage him. He'll ask, believe me, because already I know he's eating out his heart for you."

"I don't know that. Why should he be eating his heart out for me? I'm not nice to him. I correct his speech. I tell him how vulgar he is —"

"Why?"

"Because he is, Papa! Believe me. You tell me to believe you, please believe *me*. If he asks me to marry him and I say yes, then it means I give up all hope. I will die. Yes, if that's what you want me to do, I will die."

"You won't die," Mr. Levine said impatiently. "What kind of talk is that, you'll die? Why should you die? For years you kept company with him. You told me you enjoyed his company."

"That doesn't mean I want to be married to him."

"No? You know what I think, I think you're spoiled. And I'll tell you this, you want to break my heart, your mama's heart? Good. Become a dried-up old maid. No children and no grandchildren —"

Sally's voice failed. She sobbed like a hurt child.

"Leave her alone!" Mrs. Levine cried. "For God's sake, leave her alone! She'll do what we tell her. She's a good girl."

. . .

Max's office was in the Hobart Building, on the south side of Fourteenth Street, between Fifth and Sixth avenues. It was one of the new office buildings designed by that daring young architect, Bradford Lee Gilbert, and built on what he called the steel cage principle. It was ten stories high, and it was serviced by a bank of hydraulic elevators, each of which rode a steel shaft sunk as deep into the ground as the height of the building. The elevators were one of the reasons Max rented offices there. He had read a brochure on the working of the hydraulics, and he became so fascinated that nothing would do but he must have a place in the building. His offices were on the eighth floor. Bert Bellamy rode the elevator to the eighth floor, got off, turned left down the corridor, and found himself facing a large glass door, upon which was lettered in gold leaf: BRITSKY THEATRE CIRCUIT.

"I'll be damned," Bert said. "I will just be goddamned all the way to hell and down the road."

The building had impressed him. The elevators had impressed him, but most of all the gold-leaf lettering had impressed him. There was something about gold-leaf lettering that nothing else matched.

Bert and Max had parted without rancor. For a year after that, they saw each other occasionally, and then two years went by without any contact between them. Then, three days ago, Bert had a message waiting for him in his dressing room. It was a Western Union telegram, asking him to come to Max Britsky's offices in the Hobart Building. Not office but the plural, offices. Understandably, Max could have an office. Offices betokened something else.

Inside, Bert found himself facing a plump, pretty young woman with large brown eyes, a massive pile of brown hair, and too much lip rouge. She sat at a reception desk, upon which was one of the new Underwood typewriters that were the talk of the business community. In fact, only the week before, Bert had worked out a new *shtick* based on the complexity of a typewriter. Along with the young lady and the desk, there were two chairs in the reception room, a coffee table with several copies of the *Saturday Evening Post*, and on the floor a straw rug. In one corner of the room, there was a potted plant.

The young lady behind the desk observed Bert shrewdly, gave him one of her nicer smiles, and guessed that he was Mr. Bellamy.

"Right."

"And Mr. Britsky is expecting you, so just go in through that door." The door said: Private. Bert hesitated. "Go on, go on."

Bert went through. It was a corner room with two windows, a desk, behind which Max sat, two upholstered leather chairs, a rug on the floor, and on the walls, posters with scenes from moving pictures. Max, as skinny and youthful as ever, leaped to his feet when he saw Bert, came around the desk, and shook hands heartily. Bert stared at him speechless, then around the room.

"Feast your eyes," Max said.

"I don't believe it."

"Sometimes, neither do I," Max said.

A door at one side of the room opened, and a short, stout, round-faced young man appeared and said, "Mr. Britsky, I got all the stuff on the public nuisance question — whenever you want to look at it."

"Later, Freddy, later. This is my old buddy, Bert Bellamy." And to Bert, "I want you to meet Freddy Feldman. Freddy is my lawyer."

Freddy and Bert shook hands, and then Freddy excused himself and left the room. Bert simply stared at Max and then burst out, "What in hell do you mean, your lawyer?"

"He works for me, completely. That's his office, next to mine."

"Since when?"

"Since he finished reading law in Meyer Sonberg's law office. Freddy's from the block, from Henry Street. We grew up together, only Freddy's smart, and he stayed in school while I was bumming around with you at the penny arcade. Maybe you don't think I need a lawyer?"

"I never thought about it."

"Think about it, old buddy. I got seventeen movie houses. You think I can keep track of what's going on? No way, never. So I got Freddy and I got Jake Stein, my bookkeeper, and Freddy watches Jake, he shouldn't steal me blind, and also he keeps me out of jail because there's maybe fifty laws you're always breaking one time or another when you run public places, which is what I run."

"It's a damn miracle," Bert said, shaking his head. "I don't know how you did it, but you did it. I'm the schmuck, Max. Don't ever forget that. You asked me, and I said no, bug off."

"We're buddies," Max said. "We started out together when we were just kids —"

"I'm not looking for sympathy!" Bert interrupted angrily. "I said I'm a schmuck, you don't have to tell me, and I'm not looking for a handout."

"Who said you were?"

"You know I been fired."

"I heard."

"All right, I won't starve. The Bijou ain't the only music hall. I got an appointment next week with Carruthers, who's number one with the Keith bunch."

"He's a horse's ass. Screw all that! You know why the Bijou closed down?"

"It was sold, wasn't it?"

"It sure as hell was — and to me, old buddy, to yours truly, Max Britsky. I bought it."

"You? And you fired us?"

"Calm down. Nobody's fired. The acts are laid off. Guttman's out of it, and I got to find a new manager. Now I'll tell you something, Bert, the day of the music hall is over, finished. There's going to be something new, a moving picture theatre with gigs in between the moving pictures, and the first one in New York City is the Bijou. I'm cleaning it up, fixing those lousy old seats, and building a projection booth. I got my eye on two other theatres, one in Brooklyn and another on Second Avenue — real theatres, not converted retail stores — but that has to wait because already I'm going crazy trying to do eleven things at once. And I ain't standing still. I don't go into the Bijou with them lousy little scraps of film I been showing in the stores. Edison is working on films that tell a story. Nothing I seen yet, but it promises to be terrific, and just one of these films will make a program. So what do you think of all that? Tell me."

"What should I think of it? You want me to lick your ass because you got a goddamn money machine and I ain't got a pot to pee in?"

"You're awful mad."

"You fired me out of my job! You want me to kiss you?"

"No, the hell with that." Max sat down behind his desk. "Stop yelling at me and listen."

"All right. I'm listening."

"Sit down!"

Bert dropped onto one of the chairs. "I'm sitting, I'm listening." But inside he was burning up, not thinking of Max, his friend from his childhood, his partner in *shticks*, his companion and confidant, but for the first time, forming in his thoughts, bitterly: This goddamn little Hebe, where the hell does he come off? What am I — his boy, his Sing Hop Toy to kick my ass and then throw me bones?

Max saw it in Bert's face, the twitch of his lips, and said, "All right. So you hate me. Can you forget you hate me for five minutes and listen?"

"I said I'm listening."

"All right. Before the end of this year, I'll have three theatres, not stores but real theatres, and believe me, the Bijou ain't the best of the three. That's only the beginning. I'm offering you a job — run the Bijou, and then, as I add more theatres, you run them too. That means you got to hire the acts, make your pay scales, program the gigs, keep your ticket sellers honest — you got to do the whole *shtick*. I'm up to my neck opening places and trying to run the chain I got and keep the money straight and find films. Sam Snyder takes care of the store shows and the programming, but he's up to his neck too. That's all there is right now, running an enterprise that takes in cash money of at least ten thousand dollars a week, and this is only the beginning, Bert, you hear me, only the beginning.

"The Bijou ain't going to be no cheap nickelodeon. Admission twenty-five cents, fifteen cents for kids. With the gigs and the film, we run a fifty-minute show, eleven to eleven, and we have an intermission to clean the house. I'm going to paint the outside white and gold and give the whole thing class, and someday we're going to have a hundred places like the Bijou and better all over America. And who's running all this — me, Sammy Snyder, and Freddy Feldman. I need you. I'll pay you twice what you made at the Bijou and raise you ten percent every time we add a real theatre to the chain. Moving pictures — it's going to be the biggest thing in the world, believe me. So what do you say?"

"What's to say? I'm dizzy."

"Sure, join the club. We're all dizzy. It's no lead pipe cinch. We work eighteen hours a day, but someday — Well, what do you say?"

"Max, stand up." Max stood up, and Bert went around the desk and embraced him, not freed of his anger but diluting it with guilt.

"The hell with that," Max said. "You want to be loving, go out and get yourself laid. I'll see you at the Bijou, nine o'clock tomorrow morning."

After Bert left, Max went into Feldman's office and said, "Well, Freddy, what do you think of him?"

"Just caught a glimpse of him."

"Give me your impression."

"Good-looking man. He's not Jewish, is he?"

"I'll tell you something, Freddy. North of Rivington Street, the world stops being Jewish. That's always a surprise to me when I think about it, but it's a fact."

"It certainly is, Mr. Britsky."

"Something else, Freddy."

"Yes."

"When Bert comes to work for me —"

"You hired him?"

"Absolutely. Bert is almost as smart as I am. We started together when we were kids. I owe Bert something, and when I owe I pay. That's a principle of mine. Maybe you didn't think I got principles,

Freddy, and while I confess I ain't overloaded, I got two or three. Anyway, what I started to say is that when Bert comes to work here, he will call me Max and I'll call him Bert. So maybe enough Mr. Britsky, and from now on you call me Max."

"Yes, certainly, Mr. Britsky."

"Max."

"Max."

• • •

Sally was a welter of mixed feelings — confusion, fear, excitement, distaste for herself — all of it combined with a strange kind of anticipation. Her father and mother were correct in one thing: every boy she had known or been introduced to in the Flatbush community was now married, and she herself was no longer considered eligible for marriage in the terms structured by the tight Jewish community in which she lived. Twenty-six or twenty-seven, it mattered little; she was already a spinster, one of a whole class of unmarried schoolteachers. She spoke like them, reproduced their mannerisms, and, indeed, had taken on their approach to many things; and in that part of her being, she had always rejected the notion of marrying Max. She had also rejected Max again and again, a rejection which he at first refused to accept. On the other hand, she had never met anyone whom she could successfully compare to Max. Max was exciting; any evening with him promised a surprise. Max was always bursting with himself; and compared to Max, every other man she knew was dull and dreary and only half alive.

Whereby the rejections by Sally and the refusal to accept rejection on the part of Max had become a pattern in their relationship — until finally Max tired of it. Two years before, she appeared to be on the brink of a willingness to accept Max and become his wife, then she moved back from the brink, slowly yet firmly. And now she had not seen or heard from Max for over a month when she took the bit in her teeth, called him, and invited him to her room for a "chafing dish" dinner. The chafing dish fad was sweeping New York at that time. Thousands of young men and women flooded into the city from every state in the Union, and most of them could only find living space in furnished room houses that had no kitchen facilities. The invention of a baked crockery dish held in a metal frame over an alcohol burner was welcomed, and the newspapers were full of recipes to be done in a chafing dish. Sally had decided upon a Welsh rabbit and with it, a bottle of excellent French wine. She had also purchased a small ice-block, which she chipped into pieces to fill the wine cooler. This with candles, a lace tablecloth that her mother had given her, and French pastry to finish the meal was the basis of Sally's plan for entrapment.

And thereby her mixed feelings of fear, excitement, and anticipation. Somehow, this evening, she would maneuver Max into asking her to be his wife, and this time she would seal a bargain. Her parents were right; she had to be married. She was not a white Protestant schoolteacher, like her colleagues; unmarried, she had no place in her world, and if she were to be married, why not Max? Already, he was reasonably rich, he was exciting, he was bright, and he was quite good-looking. What more did she expect? Her romantic dreams? She was too old for romantic dreams.

"My own dream," Max said later that evening, his stomach full of melted cheese, toasted bread, wine, and French pastry, "was that someday we would be married. But the kind of game you were playing with me —" He shook his head.

"You think it was a game?"

"What else? One day you liked me, maybe you loved me, the next day it was no, no, Max, I'm sorry, I can't possibly see you tomorrow; no, for the next few weeks I must be with myself, I have to take stock of myself —"

"Oh, no!" Sally exclaimed. "Did I sound like that?"

"More or less. You're always taking stock of yourself, like you were some kind of dry goods store."

"And that's how you think of me, as a dry goods store?"

"That's not what I meant. You always take what I mean and twist it around."

"Now wait a moment," Sally said. "Did you ever ask me straight out to marry you?"

"Maybe fifty times. You want me to ask you again? Hey, Sally, how about us getting married? I'm twenty-three years old, which means I'm sort of grown up. I draw four hundred dollars a week out of my company, and I have my own hansom cab standing by eight hours a day."

"That's just the way you would ask someone to marry you," Sally said.

"What's the difference? You wouldn't marry me when I didn't have a pot to piss in —"

"That's why!" she shouted. "You think that's so tough and clever — a pot to piss in! Doesn't anything matter to you? Don't you have any standards of politeness or decency? Can't you learn anything? I ask you here and try to make everything as nice and proper as possible, and then you come in here and use language that a stevedore wouldn't use —"

"Sally, I forgot myself."

"— and you spoil everything." She burst into tears, aware that she had blown it beyond repair, ready to run into another room and slam the door behind her; but there was no other room. This was all of it, this one single room that was suddenly chokingly small and intolerable.

Max got up and went over to her and put his arms around her. "Sally, Sally darling, don't cry, please. You're right. Please forgive me. I can understand why you don't want to marry me."

"But I do," she sobbed.

"You do what?" He let go of her and turned her face up to him.

"Don't look at me. I look horrible when I cry."

"What did you say before?"

"I said —" She took a deep breath. "I said I do want to marry you."

"That's what you said?"

"Yes, Max, that's what I said."

*   *   *

Max walked into the precinct house, telling himself, I hate these places. Every time I set foot in one, it means trouble. Since I was a kid, I been paying them. It's no goddamn police station, it's a bank.

Sergeant Carney, sitting behind the desk, nodded at him with a long, doleful face.

"What is it now?" Max asked.

"Your brother Benny."

"So that's where he is. My mother's only tearing out her hair and he's here in jail, right? You got the kid locked up?"

"That's right, Mr. Britsky."

"He's thirteen years old," Max said indignantly.

"You'd better take that up with Captain Clancy."

"Is he all right?"

"Your brother? Full of piss and vinegar, the little bastard."

."You can say that again," Max agreed, and he went up the stairs to Clancy's office. Clancy's two hundred and forty pounds, a balanced mixture of fat and muscle beneath a beet-red face and thinning hair, sat behind a littered desk. He was finishing a sandwich and drinking beer from a tin lunchpail.

"Ah, Max," he said, "me heart goes out to you. You break your ass for that family of yours, and what does the little bastard do but end up in the clink."

"What did he do?" Max asked.

"Not what *he* did, Max. He was enticed, the poor little bastard. The Slunsky twins broke into Cohen's fur place over on Division Street, but we got them now. They're a bad lot, the Slunskys."

"But Benny? Where does he come into it?"

"They gave him a dollar and hired him to be their lookout, and when Officers Delaney and Coogan approached the place, there was this brother of yours hooten and yelling copper, so we collared him along with the Slunskys. Now what am I to do with the little bastard?"

"Let me do it," Max said. "He'll eat standing up for a week."

"But he was nabbed in the commission of a crime, Max."

Max went into his pocket and came up with a roll of bills. "Three hundred and fifty tonight —"

Clancy's pink face remained sad and unresponsive.

"— and a hundred and fifty more tomorrow."

Clancy smiled. "Sure, Max, take the little bastard home and teach him the law."

They brought Benny out to where Max was waiting. Benny's dirty face was streaked with tears, and when he saw Max's expression, he would have gladly turned around and gone back to the holding pen where he had spent the past two hours. Outside the station house, he wailed to Max, "What are you going to do to me? You going to kill me?"

"I'd like to, you miserable little bum."

"Max, I didn't do nothing. They just give me a dollar and tell me to lay chickee."

"If it wasn't your mother would know about it, I'd tan your ass so you wouldn't sit down for a week. Meanwhile, you miserable little shithead, I put five hundred dollars into Clancy's pocket, which is maybe five hundred times more than you're worth, even retail, and you are going to pay it back to me, every cent. So from now on, every day after school, you go to work for me, and maybe when you work off five hundred dollars I'll talk to you again."

• • •

He couldn't stay away from the Bijou. It was one thing to rent a store and fill it with folding chairs and put in a projection booth; it was another thing entirely to have an entire theatre for himself. The *New York Times* paid adequate tribute to this action with a story headlined: "First Moving Picture Theatre Planned by Max Britsky." It was the first time Max had seen his name in print, and although the newspaper story went on to say, "Old veterans of the theatrical business have little faith in the possibility of a theatre surviving on a program of moving pictures," Max's elation was not dampened. He had been interviewed by reporters from both the *Times* and the *Herald*. No, he said, he had no intention of changing the name. The name had nostalgic importance for him since he had once worked as an entertainer in the Bijou. With Mr. Bellamy, he hastened to add, who would now be managing the Bijou. Mr. Bellamy stood in the background, watching, listening, trying to connect this Max Britsky with his old partner. As for the Bijou, it would be called Britsky's Bijou. Max added that he was negotiating for another theatre, the old Garrett Theatre in Brooklyn. It required extensive restoration and repair, but that would be taken care of, and eventually it would be called Britsky's Orpheum. Did they know that orpheum meant a theatre and that it came from a Greek word originally? And here, in Britsky's Bijou, the first moving picture to be shown was a "new and brilliant" work, called *The Automobile Thief*.

Two men, Frank Stanford and Jack Calvin, had opened a place near Plainfield, New Jersey, where moving pictures were being made. Stanford and Calvin were not making the pictures themselves; they ran a booking agency out of Philadelphia. Nor was it believed that the money for the moving pictures came from them, rather that they were fronting either for the Edison interests, the Eastman interests, or possibly the Bell Telephone Company. Sam

Snyder, who had been dealing with them, was unable to pin down the source of their financial backing, but as he pointed out to Max, "It doesn't matter. They're doing the distributing, and we're getting in on the ground floor." Max told Sam to go ahead and sign a rental contract for the film.

Max ran the film for himself and a handful of others in the Bijou a few days before the scheduled opening of the theatre. The silver screen, enormous when compared to the screens in the storefront movie houses, was in itself an exciting visual treat. Max had invited Sally to join him and Ruby and Sam Snyder, Bert Bellamy, Freddy Feldman, and Isadore Lubel, the pianist, who now doubled as music director, not only playing piano himself, but constantly digging up additional pianists for the nickelodeons Max added to his chain. Since Sam Snyder had seen the film several times, he took care of the projection booth. Max put himself and his guests in the first row of the balcony, deciding that would be the best angle from which to view the film.

The film was fourteen minutes in length and would have to be boxed in with short fillers to suit Max's plan. The film opened with a card frame that read: MAX BRITSKY PRESENTS, and then credits for three men involved in the making. There was no credit for acting, scenario, or any technical work and no identification of the roles of the makers. In the first scene, the camera was fixed on a street, and for about half a minute the camera simply photographed the traffic moving by. At first, this was only hansom cabs, carriages, drays, and carts. Then an automobile appeared. The car was recognizable as one of Ransom Eli Olds' curved-dash Oldsmobiles, but instead of being open to the air, it carried a wagon top, and the stick steering bar had been replaced by a wheel. A man and a woman, both of them covered in long dusters, were sitting in the car. The car drew up alongside the curb, and the man got out and went through an exaggerated pantomime of politeness in helping the woman down out of the car. Now two ragged, dirty-faced kids appeared and began to examine the car, touching it here and there. It was plain that they had never seen an automobile before and were intrigued by it, but their curiosity angered the driver, who drove them away and then chased them down the street. The camera turned to follow them as the three, the driver and the two kids, ran away.

Then the camera swung back to the woman, who still stood in

front of the car. She clasped her hands and swayed from side to side, which was obviously intended to indicate an emotional response of some sort, but it was never defined as a response to anything in particular except the fact that her escort was off chasing kids. After the camera had recorded her emotions at some length, it swung back to the driver, who was now returning. Then it swung full around to a policeman, approaching from the other direction. He stopped by the woman, and they carried on a conversation with a great deal of pointing and hand-waving. Then the driver joined the group, and the gesturing went on. Finally the policeman spread his arms and shook his head, as if to indicate that there was nothing more that he could do. Then the lady decided to faint, and the two men knelt over her to revive her. When she was finally revived, she and the driver went off in one direction, the policeman in another direction, leaving the automobile parked by the curb.

Now the camera was inside a room, two painted flats forming a corner. A man sat at a table, eating soup. The two kids stood by the table, talking and gesturing. At first the man paid no attention. Then he responded, rising, picking up a small valise, and following the kids. Then the camera was back at the parked car. It simply fixed on the car for about sixty seconds until the man and the boys appeared. Then the man opened his valise and took out a set of burglar tools.

Sam Snyder called out from the projection booth, "Max, the damn fools who made the picture either didn't know you don't steal a car with burglar tools or they did it for effect. Most of those Olds automobiles don't even have an ignition key. You could just get into it and drive away if you know how to drive one."

"Hell, it don't matter!" Max shouted back.

The theft completed, all three, thief and the two kids, climbed into the car and drove off. At this point the driver appeared, waving his arms, yelling silently, and then running after the car. Then the lady appeared and fainted again. Fainting appeared to be her best point, and even Sally responded to the second faint by bursting into laughter. Then the policeman appeared, with more arm-waving and soundless shouting. Then the policeman ran off after the vanished car. Then the man revived the woman. Then they embraced, apparently to his relief. Then they waited in front of the camera, and then finally the car appeared, the policeman driving, the car thief beside him, hands shackled. Then a great arm-waving of joy and congratulations from the car owner.

After the film had been shown, all seven of the viewers gathered at the Café Coronet on Second Avenue. The Coronet was the regular after-theatre meeting place for Yiddish-speaking actors, writers, and various and sundry theatre people and intellectuals. Regarding himself as very much a man of the theatre, Max had taken to frequenting the place. He enjoyed the atmosphere, which, he had been told, was very much that of a European café; he liked the high-pitched sound of discussion and argument, and he was pleased, having so little education of his own, at being present in a place where intellect was held in high esteem. From his earliest childhood, Yiddish had been a second language for him, and it was the ordinary means of communication between him and his mother; but he had always regarded it with contempt and distaste as less a language than a mark of oppression and misery. But at Café Coronet, Yiddish was the first language at most tables, and here suddenly Max had the marvelous and worldly feeling of having a second language at his command.

Tonight, Eli, the owner, seated them at a round table large enough to contain them comfortably, congratulated Max on the imminent opening of the Bijou, and welcomed Sally, whom he had not seen for some months. In the discussion of the film they had just seen, Sally had been noticeably silent. Max watched her, waiting. After they had given their orders for food, Max said to her, "You didn't like it. I can see that."

"No, it's not that I didn't like it —"

"Why don't you come right out with an opinion for once and say it stinks?"

"It doesn't stink, so why don't you give her a chance to say what she thinks," Sam Snyder suggested.

"Max, you're too nervous about this," Freddy Feldman said. "What we say about the moving picture isn't going to change the audience response."

"What's that supposed to mean?"

"I think," Sally said, "that you'll get a good audience response no matter what I think or what anyone else thinks, and I think that's what Freddy means. No matter what anyone says, it's an advance over the tiny films you've been showing."

"And this *Great Train Robbery* that they're making will be even better," Snyder said.

"Then if that's the case," Max said to Sally, "what are you so sour about?"

"I'm not sour. I've been thinking about it. That's permitted, isn't it?"

"All right. What's wrong with it?"

"If you're going to get angry at me again —"

"Come on, Sally," Snyder said. "Max is nervous. That's understandable. We got a lot of money invested in the Bijou."

"What I'm saying has nothing to do with how it will go at the Bijou, but my feeling is that what we saw tonight is not the product of any real intelligence or talent." And turning to Snyder, "I don't mean the camera operator, Sam, or the other technicians. They seem to know what they're doing. I mean the man who conceived it. He doesn't appear to have the slightest notion of what he was doing. Was he trying to tell a story or present a drama? Had he ever seen a theatrical play or had he ever read a book? And who told the actors how to act? They behaved like demented people, waving their arms and making those incredible faces." Her voice died away. "Well, I didn't mean to be so critical, but you asked me what I felt."

"Sally," Snyder said, "you asked me who conceived this moving picture, and I have to tell you that maybe nobody did. I've seen the way they work up there in Rochester and out at Edison's place and down in Philadelphia too. They don't even write anything down. Someone says, I got an idea, and mostly they don't even use actors, so how can you expect them to act?"

"You mean they don't even try to make a story out of it?" Feldman asked.

"Sure, I've heard talk about that, and there's some fellow says he's going to do Shakespeare's plays on film, but then there are other guys who say that it's absolutely out of the question, because how can you really tell a story without any words —"

"Which brings up a point," Max interrupted. "We had no piano tonight."

"That's absolutely right," Lubel said. "Absolutely."

"I should have never run it without the piano."

"Absolutely," Lubel said. "In those long spaces where you just sit and wait for something to happen — well, you come in there with a theme from the *William Tell Overture* or even with a few bars from *Anitra's Dance* and you get rid of that nervousness when nothing happens, so you can't really judge it without someone putting in a little piano music."

"The trouble is," Snyder said, "that nobody really knows what to do with the moving pictures."

"I can tell you what to do with them," Max said. "You show them and you sell tickets."

"But with *The Great Train Robbery*, I think they're trying to tell a better story. The way they're talking now, they say you got to look for things where it just moves and nobody says anything. That's probably the reason why they made *The Automobile Thief*."

Sally was right about the audience response. The Bijou had a triumphal opening, and no one objected to the construction of the film they saw. Indeed, the *Herald*, taking note of the opening — they had no such thing as a film critic — remarked that *The Automobile Thief* appeared to be a great advance in the making of moving pictures.

* * *

No matter how much money the nickelodeons brought in, Max was so committed to expanding his empire that he was always short of cash; and this time, with Fred Feldman's guidance, he was able to negotiate a line of credit for fifty thousand dollars at no less an institution than the Chase Bank, into whose imposing offices at 177 Broadway Max walked, not with the air of a supplicant but with the easy confidence of a conqueror. As he told Sally afterward, "It was a big moment, but I wouldn't have been surprised if I had a heart attack right there on the spot."

"You don't have heart attacks at twenty-three. But why should you even think that way?"

"Because it's going too good. You know, we got an expression for the uptown Jews, we call them *allrightniks*. For them, everything goes all right. For the Jews like my family, it's only a steady succession of disasters. So how come everything falls into place for me?"

Bert Bellamy put it a bit differently: "What you got to avoid, Max, is the fickle finger of God. It looks for people like you."

But the credit line from the Chase Bank gave Max the opportunity to do what he had been planning for some time, to buy a house for the Britsky family; and since his wedding was scheduled for June, he decided that he might as well purchase two houses as one. The firm where Freddy Feldman had read law, Straus, Cohen and Meyer, a prominent partnership specializing in real estate, had a client who was constructing a block of twelve brownstones on Sixtysixth Street between Central Park West and Columbus Avenue. These houses were wooden constructions in a shell of brick and brownstone, the brownstone being reserved for the front, a style becoming increasingly popular. They had central heating, with half the basement floor given over to the furnace and water heater. The other half, to the rear of the house and frequently opening upon a small garden, contained a large kitchen and pantry. The main floor was divided into two rooms, a parlor at the front and a dining room at the rear, the entrance being up an outside stoop to double doors and a narrow hallway. There were three floors over the main floor, the second and third each containing two large bedrooms and one small bedroom, six rooms entirely, while the top floor was divided into four small rooms for servants. Since the builder had overextended himself, Max was in a position to obtain both houses for a total of twenty-two thousand dollars — a great buy, as Fred Feldman assured him. While Max had some reservations about putting Sally so close to a family which was, to say the least, quite different from her own and which she still had not met as a family, he felt that such closeness might offer some advantages, although at the moment he had not the slightest notion of what those advantages might be.

For himself, the thought of owning such a house filled him with fear and excitement. While it did not compare with the great graystone mansions of the wealthy German-Jewish families, it was nevertheless a dwelling place beyond the wildest dreams of a younger Max, and when he called the whole family together in the kitchen of the cold-water flat on Henry Street to present them with his newest triumph, he expected a response as thrilled and pleased as his own had been.

His three sisters and his two brothers reacted with proper excitement and disbelief. Sarah, however, greeted the news with a dismal stare.

"Mama, ain't you at least a little pleased?" Max begged her. "You should see the place, one room as big as this whole stinking apartment, and no bedbugs and no roaches — everything new, a regular city mansion like the fanciest uptown Jews."

"I'm not an uptown Jew," Sarah said bleakly.

"What does that mean?"

"It means I'm happy enough right here."

"Right here is the worst part of this lousy ghetto. It's a pigsty, a lousy, stinking pigsty."

"So that's what you think of me, I'm living in a pigsty."

"It's got nothing to do with what I think of you. Seven of us, we're cramped together here like sardines. I hate this place."

"I lived my whole life here," Sarah said. "I got my friends here. I raised my family here."

"You'll like it."

"How do I know what I'll like? Did what I like ever mean anything to you? Another son, he cares about his mother. You I see a few minutes in the morning, and that's the end of you."

"A month from now we're going to move," Max said, "and that's it."

"Can you imagine?" Max said to Sally. "I left her there crying her head off. I buy her a mansion, a place she couldn't even dream of living in, and she sits and cries over it."

"I can imagine," Sally said. "Did you ask her?"

"What should I ask her? Since I'm a kid, I took care of her. I fed the family. I kept them alive. Do you think I ever got a word of thanks for it?"

"That's just it, Max. Can't you understand? She's got nothing to give you, and you take away the only role she has, being a mother."

"How do I take it away?"

"Why didn't you take her to see the place before you bought it?"

"She wouldn't know what she was looking at."

"Would I? Why didn't you ask me? Don't I have any say in whether I want to live next door to your family? And how am I to travel every day between Sixty-sixth Street and Clinton Street? I'm afraid to ride on the elevated train every day, and it's such a long walk to the Elevated, and anyway, I can't take care of a house of four floors."

"Oh, Jesus — oh, Jesus, I'm getting it from everywhere. Try to do something good. Anyway, when we're married, you don't go on working."

"Why not?"

"Because it ain't done — O.K., O.K., it *isn't* done. How could I look anybody in the eyes? What do I tell them? My wife works. Is that what I tell them? I can't support my wife. She has to go to work."

"Did it ever occur to you that a woman — yes, even a woman whose husband is a rich man — might *want* to work? Did it ever occur to you that maybe your mother wanted to work? But you took that from her, didn't you? You had to be everything, even when you were twelve years old. She couldn't even be a mother."

"What in hell are you talking about?" Max shouted.

He was becoming agitated. Sally took his arm and squeezed it. "Max, darling, you think I want to humiliate you, but I don't. That's the last thing in the world that I want to do. But I've spent most of my life learning to be a teacher. I think I'm a good teacher."

"You can teach me. You been teaching me. I want you to have kids, my kids. You can teach them. God Almighty, Sally, all my life I dreamed of having a decent place to live, a place where the hall didn't stink of piss and where every morning your sheet wasn't covered with bedbug blood, and now I got it, so don't make me feel lousy about it."

"All right," Sally agreed. "But now I want you to take me to meet your mother. We're being married a month from now, and I've never spoken to your mother."

• • •

"Why can't she come here?" Sarah demanded. "This is my home. She wants to see me, let her come here."

Only the smallest part of Max's conversations with his mother passed his lips; the rest was internal, and now he was thinking, If you ever stopped to see what this place looks like and smells like, with seven of us living on top of each other with the filth and the bugs, you might understand why I don't want her to set foot in this place.

"I raised my children here," Sarah went on.

No, Max said silently, I raised them here. Aloud, he said, "I reserved a table at the Café Coronet. It's the big round table, and we'll all sit there, and we'll have a nice dinner, and she'll be able to meet the family."

"I don't eat in restaurants. They're pig places."

"Café Coronet is a kosher restaurant, Mama," Max explained patiently. "The chef will make whatever you want to eat. It will be a nice change for you, Mama. And please, I gave Freida the money, so go out with her and buy a new dress."

"The way I look, you're ashamed of me!"

"I'm not ashamed of you, please, Mama. I only want you to look pretty."

Sally understood Max's fear and his determination that she should never set foot in the flat on Henry Street. She had worked for years in an East Side school, and she knew Henry Street and Madison and Monroe and Allen streets and Ludlow and Orchard and Hester and all the other crowded, filthy, and stinking canyons that went to make up the ghetto. There were times when she understood Max, and her heart went out to him in pride and compassion. Who else could have done as he had done, and at the age of twelve taken this enormous family and nurtured them and fed them and kept them together all these years? And in that sense she was eager to meet his mother, finally, as well as the remaining Britskys still unknown to her. On the other hand, there was a part of Max that repelled her, an animal-like ferocity that would surface so unexpectedly, an almost insane drive, and a kind of savage, prideful ignorance. At such times, she hated and feared him and at other times she pitied him, but she was never sure that she loved him; the prospect of marriage made her even more ambivalent. And this prospect might have shattered her completely had she seen Max with his secretary the day before the scheduled dinner at Café Coronet.

The secretary's name was Etta Goodman, and Max had hired her a year and a half before the date that had been chosen for his marriage. Miss Goodman was a typewriter, the name used for women with her skill before the more euphemistic term of "secretary" distinguished between the operator and the wonderful new machine that had begun to replace the Palmer method of writing script, taught to millions of children in the schools of the time. Max had purchased the machine. Machines enchanted him, and once he possessed a typewriter (the machine), he had to have a typewriter (the person). Freida recommended Etta Goodman. She had been working at Saxon Fabrics as a bookkeeper for seven dollars a week. Max offered her ten dollars a week the moment she informed him that she had been taking typewriting lessons on Tuesday and Thursday nights, and the speed of his offer was not hindered by her appearance. Etta was five feet two inches in height. She had dark eyes, darker hair, and a shape that reminded Max of a sweet, toothsome, midsummer peach bursting out of its skin. She also thought Max was wonderful, an opinion Freida had primed even prior to Miss Goodman's meeting with him. Nor was she the kind of woman who whined or complained. Not even on this afternoon before the scheduled dinner at the Café Coronet. Instead, it was with a kind of pathos that she observed that Max had not even bought a couch, and the reason for this observation was that she and Max had just completed an act of sexual intercourse on the floor. Max reminded her that they did it not on the floor but on a thick, all-wool rug.

"You're heavy," Etta said, pushing her skirt away from her face. Max never asked her to carry disrobing further than her bloomers, even though the door to the outer reception room and the door to Fred Feldman's office were both locked. But it was only in part a bow to the possibility of interruption; the notion of two naked bodies locked in a transport of passion had occurred to Max as the content of a sexual fantasy, but in his world it was certainly not common practice — or even uncommon practice. Max did remove his own shoes and trousers on such occasions, but he kept his shirt on, which meant that he retained his single-piece underwear, which were known as BVDs.

Now he argued that he only weighed one hundred and thirty-five pounds.

"That's still heavy. My goodness, Max, you'd lay here on top of me all afternoon if I let you."

Max eased back on his knees. "How's that, tootsie?"

"That's better, but the floor is still the floor, Max. You keep telling me that the rug is extra-thick wool, but that don't make it not the floor."

"You know, that's my fault, tootsie, because I should have thought to bring a clean sheet in and then we could spread it over the rug —"

"No!" Etta exclaimed.

"No?"

"No, I don't want a sheet spread over the rug. I want to do it on a bed. Or even on a sofa. A sofa would be better than this. You know, Max, all the times we done it, we always done it on the floor."

"I know," Max agreed unhappily.

"Well?"

"There's no use promising something, because this is the last time."

"What? What last time?"

"No more after today," Max said.

"You mean you're firing me? Why? Don't I work good? Freddy says I'm as good as the regular bookkeeper."

"Calm down. I'm not firing you. Would I fire you? What kind of a louse do you take me for? You ought to apologize."

"Well then, why —" Her eyes were filling with tears of frustration.

"Because I'm getting married."

"Who? That skinny little schoolteacher?"

"That's right."

"Huh! Huh! That's some reason for us not to do it anymore."

Max got up and pulled on his trousers. "For me, it's a reason. I'm not one of those guys who screws around after he's married."

"Max, we never even done it on a bed. Not even once." She began to cry. Max had never seen her weep before.

"Come on, stop that. I made it clear right from the beginning what was the situation between you and me. Anyway, for a kid like you, it's all a happy hunting ground, ain't it? Right here in the office, there's Freddy and Bert, and both of them ain't married. You know something, Sally would chop my head off, the way I'm talking. Freddy and Bert, *not* married, that's what I mean."

"Who cares about what Sally thinks? Anyway, Freddy don't even know which side is up and all he can think of is I could become pregnant, and Bert's always over at the Bijou, and I can't go running over to the Bijou just because Bert points a finger."

It took Max several deep breaths before he was able to say, "I just don't believe this."

"Why?"

"You been fucking both of them! You been fucking Freddy and you been fucking Bert!"

"Please don't use that word, Max. It's a terrible word."

"All the time!"

"I can't stand that word. It makes me feel crawly all over."

"And it don't mean nothing to you!" Max shouted.

"It does so too, it does. I like you better than either of them, Max. You know that."

"No more Max. From now on, you call me Mr. Britsky."

"You're getting married, that's all right. But my having a little fun with Freddy and Bert, that's so terrible —"

"Fucking ain't a little fun."

"It is so."

"That's your trouble. You're debased."

"I am not. Are you firing me now?"

"No, but our intimacy is over," Max said stiffly. "From now on, you call me Mr. Britsky and I call you Miss Goodman."

"Oh." She got to her feet and stared at him for a long moment. Then she shrugged. "All right, Mr. Britsky. Are you going to invite me to the wedding?"

"Absolutely not."

"Why? Just because you're mad at me?"

"I suggest, Miss Goodman," Max said stiffly, "that you return to your duties in the reception room."

* * *

At the Café Coronet the following evening, Sarah put a forkful of *gefilte* fish in her mouth, chewed it thoughtfully, and then swallowed it. Her face remained impassive.

"Your mother makes *gefilte* fish?" she said to Sally.

"Oh, yes, Mrs. Britsky, sometimes."

"What does it mean, sometimes? She don't make it every Friday night?"

"Perhaps she does. I'm not home every Friday night."

"No? Why not?"

"Mama, Sally lives in New York," Max explained. "It's a long trip out to Brooklyn."

"She has a tongue. So let her answer for herself. If you love a mother or a father, you make a long trip. You don't make excuses. My own husband, he passed away, may he rest in peace, leaving me to bring up six children." Sarah took another bite of the fish and chewed it appraisingly. "Your mother puts sugar in her *gefilte* fish?"

"I really don't know."

"She uses carp or she don't?"

"I just don't know," Sally said uneasily. "I never asked her."

"And she never showed you?"

"No, I'm afraid not."

They were all staring at their plates miserably, and Max closed his eyes and fought against the surge of rage that took over his mind; and in his mind and only in his mind, he said to his mother, You fat, stupid lazy bitch, for over five years now you haven't cooked even a kettle of water for tea. You let Freida and Sheila and Esther do the cooking and the cleaning, and that's why we lived in a pigsty, because they were only kids and didn't know how to clean, and you lived on our work and our sweat. But even as a thought it was shattering, and while one part of his mind formed it, another part rejected it with horror, and still another part told him to speak it, and then, following that line of fantasy, he saw his mother shrieking at him, commanding the attention of everyone in the restaurant, shriveling the souls of everyone at the table, and as he told Sally later, "What good would it have done?"

It was a pleasant evening, at least as far as the weather was concerned, and Max and Sally walked across town to her room.

"What good would it have done?"

"I don't know," Sally whispered. The tears started then.

"Please don't cry," Max said. "I love you. I don't know how to say it any better than that. I'm not much, but I love you, and I don't know why you decided to marry me."

"Because you're one of the best persons I ever knew!"

She almost shouted the words, and Max laughed hollowly. "You should know what kind of a great person I am! You think a great person sits there at the table and lets his girl be insulted? I'm some great person."

"I saw those kids," Sally said. "I'm not crying for what your mother said to me. I'm just crying for the whole thing because I don't understand it. Those children are lovely — and they're yours, and they only exist because of you."

"They're not so great. The girls are all right, especially Esther; she's only fifteen but she's going to be a beauty all right, but Benny's a little bum, and Ruby's an oversized *schlemiel* and a *goniff*." He paused as Sally looked at him questioningly. "Thief, a cheap crook. It sounds nasty when I say it, but you might as well know what you're falling into. I got two brothers, Benny and Ruby, and they'd both steal the fillings from my teeth if they could reach inside my mouth. All right, so I'm blowing it out of size, but I want you to know I didn't do so great, and anyway the hell with all that. I'm not putting you into a house next to my mother. I'll sell the house and we'll find another one."

"Don't sell it," Sally said firmly. "I can live with your mother. Just like you, I never thought I could live in a place that nice, right here in the city. I'll manage."

"Then stop crying."

"I've stopped," Sally said, but inside, a tiny flame of fear and resentment arose, and it would not go away. She lacked the courage to flee because it seemed that there was no refuge. She had to be married; she didn't have the strength to bear the curse of spinsterhood. She was lost. There was no alternative to Max Britsky.

• • •

Two weeks before the wedding, Britsky's Orpheum, the first of the storefront theatres that Max had created, was wrecked. The attack took place while the show was in progress, the damage done by six men carrying axes. They shattered the outside windows, smashed the ticket booth, from which the lady ticket seller fled screaming, terrorized the customers and drove them out, smashed the projection booth and the projector, and then systematically destroyed folding chairs until at last, bored with their mayhem, they departed. They spent at least twenty minutes in the place, and although the ticket taker ran to the police precinct, screaming her head off, no police appeared until the wreckers departed.

Awhile later, Max and Ruby and Bert appeared, and Max led the way, glumly, in and out of the wreckage. "Who done it?" he asked Officer Kelly, now forthrightly on the scene, with Officer Murphy to back him up.

"Heaven only knows," Officer Kelly said. "But you'd better see the captain, because when a thing like this begins, Mr. Britsky, it's like a fire, and there's no putting it out."

"I suppose Captain Clancy mentioned that to you."

"It might be he whispered a word in me ear when he heard that his old friend Max Britsky was having a bit of trouble. He even said that me and Paddy here should keep an eye on the place so that nothing that is open to the wind should be stolen."

"Yes, you do that and thank him," Max said. Outside on the sidewalk with Bert and Ruby, Max asked, "What do you think?"

"The Monkey's gang."

"No doubt about it," Bert agreed. "They smash up the place and then Clancy collects. It's going to cost you a lot of big bills, Max."

"Maybe so. But I'm not going to take it lying down. No lousy shithead like Monk Eastman is going to smash up one of my places and just walk away clean."

"You can't fight him," Bert said. "He's too big."

"Bullshit, Bert. We been fighting the big ones ever since we're able to walk."

"It could cost us. He's got three, four hundred bums he can call on. What have we got?"

"I don't know," Ruby said worriedly. "He runs the East Side."

"Both of you think too much and worry too much. Just let me do the thinking and the worrying. I don't need no army, only half a dozen guys. So, Ruby, you get Shecky Blum with his carriage, and then get three or four of the bums you hang out with and tell them I'm paying fifty dollars each for one night's work, and then you meet Bert and me right here at midnight tonight, and meanwhile pick up half a dozen baseball bats."

"They ain't going up against Monk Eastman, Max."

"For fifty bucks they'll go up against anything that breathes. But we don't fight nobody."

"Then what do you need the baseball bats for?"

"To play baseball, stupid. Now get going."

Ruby shook his head unhappily and exchanged glances with Bert Bellamy. It made little sense to them. At that time, Monk Eastman ruled New York's underworld and a good deal of the "overworld" from St. Mark's Place and East Eighth Street south to Fulton Street and east from Lafayette Street. His headquarters was in an old livery stable on Chrystie Street, with a rear exit that gave on the Bowery, square in the center of his domain. It was said that the live ones entered on Chrystie Street and the bodies were trucked out into the Bowery. It was also said that if the need arose, the Monk could call out over a thousand "guns" that would operate according to his leadership; but this was vastly exaggerated, and most of his followers were street bums, winos, and scrapings from the worst *lumpen* elements that lived in shacks and blind doorways down by the docks; in none of his so-called street wars with other gangs, like Kelly's West Side Breakers, were more than a hundred or a hundred and fifty of his followers involved. But this in conjunction with the body of legends that surrounded Monk Eastman was enough to trouble Ruby and Bert enormously, the more so when one remembered that the Monk and Captain Thomas Clancy of the New York City Police — often referred to as the most corrupt police force in the Western world — worked hand in glove together.

Monk Eastman was well protected. He controlled all the gambling and prostitution in his territory, exacting his toll from every faro, poker, and crap game and from every working lady and pimp and madam as well. He also exacted payment from most of the merchants, and he divided his weekly spoils with the various precinct captains in his territory. He was called Monk because of his resemblance to the species. He was only five feet and five inches in height, but he was hugely overmuscled, weighing better than two hundred pounds, his face a mashed mixture of broken nose, missing teeth, tiny pig eyes, and shapeless ears. His only virtue was his love of animals, and his only legitimate enterprise was a pet shop he maintained on Broome Street, where his specialty — and, indeed, special love — was ornamental tropical fish, in tiers of glass cases. There, almost any day, one could find the dreaded Monk Eastman, mooning over his tropical beauties; and it was there, a half-hour past midnight, that Max gathered together his bat-wielding, fifty-dollar hoodlums. "Go to it," he ordered them, but since one and all knew that this silent, locked pet shop was the province of Monk Eastman, no one moved. Shecky Blum said, "Come on, Max, this is the Monk's place. You got to be crazy."

Max grabbed Shecky's bat and yelled, "Stand back!" Then he swung the bat, smashing the lock on the front door. Then he smashed both plate-glass windows and yelled to Shecky, "Get your guys in here and out of here! I don't want nothing left together. It'll take two minutes, and then you all go home and forget you were ever here, and nobody knows any different."

It certainly took no longer than two minutes to reduce the place to a shambles, with fish of every color flopping out their lives on the floor and bewildered dogs barking and Persian cats hissing, and then Shecky and his colleagues piling back into the carriage and galloping off into the night, the entire operation completed before any passerby began to realize what was happening.

Max strolled away, north toward Houston Street. He smoked only occasionally, but tonight he took out a cigar of the best Cuban leaf, nipped off the end, lit it, and puffed with deep satisfaction. He was calmly smoking his cigar when he walked into the precinct house, to be told by Officer Finnigan at the desk, "Now you know well enough, Mr. Britsky, that we'll have no smoking here."

"It's a beautiful cigar, so I will let it go out peacefully. O.K.?"

"And what the hell would you be doing here at this hour of the night?"

"Looking for Captain Clancy."

"At this hour he is home in bed."

"I'll wait for him," Max said. "He'll be here."

"Now what makes you think so?"

"Just an idea."

"Well, it's a hell of a place to spend your time, but if that's your wish, Mr. Britsky, that's your wish."

For the next half-hour, Max sat in the reception hall, watching the parade of petty thieves, drunks, pickpockets, pocket grabbers, disturbers of the peace, and whores who had stepped out of line or out of Monk's protective embrace — and then Monk Eastman himself, followed by Captain Clancy. Monk had a wild light in his eyes, which became even wilder as he cast his glance around the reception hall and let it rest on Max.

"So there you are, you lousy little bastard!" he roared, leaping toward Max. "You fucken, miserable son of a bitch, I'm going to open you up and strangle you with your own guts!" Launching himself as he shouted, he dived toward the bench. Max slid sideways and then dashed toward the desk, where Sergeant Finnigan was observing the proceedings with objective interest. Monk followed, this time producing a revolver, which he fired twice, both shots missing Max and ending up in Sergeant Finnigan's desk. The sight and sound of the revolver in a room full of people brought the policemen into action. They grabbed Monk while Sergeant Finnigan climbed over his desk and worked the revolver out of Monk's hand.

"Now you see what you done," Clancy said to Max, "promoting mayhem and battery here in a police station." He glanced at Monk, who was struggling violently with the three cops who held him. "Can you give me one good reason why I should not let him go and let him pull you to pieces?"

"Upstairs," Max said, "in your office. Lots of reasons."

"Indeed. Well, me lad, you'd better deliver, or you will be the saddest Jew in New York."

"Let me at him!" Monk screamed.

Clancy walked over to Monk and said, "Now shut your yap, Monk. You should know better than to try to murder someone in a police station."

"I'm going to kill him."

"Later, later — and not here. Wouldn't it make an awful stink if you killed him here? Now Sergeant Finnigan is going to put you in a cell for an hour or so until you cool down, and he'll send out for a pitcher of beer, and then you and me will talk." Then Clancy led the way upstairs, Max following him.

In his office, Clancy slammed the door and turned to Max and said angrily, "You are one stupid son of a bitch, Max, going out and smashing up Monk's pet shop. He loves them fish more than you and I love a pretty face, and if he could find a mermaid, he'd be fucking her instead of his scummy whores. You know, he's going to kill you, and I'll be damned if you don't deserve it."

"No, he won't."

"And why not, may I ask?"

"Because you won't let him."

"Jesus, why would I stop him, even if I could?"

"He breathes and pisses and shits because you allow it. He's your boy, Captain, and so help me God, in your place, I'd send him back to his mother. His breath stinks of stupid."

"You're talking very big, boyo, and I ain't a bit sure I like the way you talk. Can you tell me why I shouldn't kick you out of here and let Monk chase you down the street?"

"All right, I'll tell you why. Because you're going to be commissioner of police."

"Oh? And now you got a crystal ball?"

"No."

"But you ain't short on bullshit."

"No, sir. I am going to be a millionaire, and I'm going to break my ass to make you commissioner because we can work together."

Clancy smiled coldly, looking Max up and down without pleasure. "How old are you, Max?"

"Twenty-three."

"You're a punk, a little shithead sheeny, and you're making me police commissioner."

"You know why I smashed up that place," Max said, "not to get revenge on Monk. The hell with Monk. He has the brain of a cockroach, but to get him here and to get you here."

"To get me out of bed in the middle of the night." Clancy rose up and loomed over his desk. "I don't know who smashed up your place, but sure as hell, you smashed up Monk's place, for which I could jail you, if it was not that doing so would deprive Monk of the pleasure of beating you to a bloody pulp. Now get out!"

"Monk put the finger on me," Max said. "One place smashed, and then if I don't pay, a second and a third. I know Monk's price. I pay him a hundred a week to let me operate, and then he cuts you in for a lousy fifty bucks —"

"Get out!"

"— peanuts! I'm ready to pay you five hundred dollars a week, and that's only the beginning."

Clancy was coming around his desk to enforce physically his eviction notice, and now he paused, stared at Max for a long moment, and then motioned to a chair.

"Sit down," Clancy said.

Max sat down, a faint smile lingering at his lips.

Returning to his desk, Clancy rested his chin on his fists and regarded Max with new interest. "If you're pulling me leg, boyo, I'll not wait for Monk to work you over."

Max reached into his pocket, took out a roll of bills, and counted off ten fifty-dollar greenbacks. He laid the money on the desk. "Does this pull your leg, Captain Clancy?"

"Every week?" staring at the money.

"Every week until I up the ante. One year from now, it becomes seven hundred."

Clancy reached for the money and fondled the bills. "What are you buying, Max? I don't promise what I can't deliver."

"All right. I'll spell it out. I want Monk Eastman off my back. I want you to tell him that either he leaves my places alone or you'll put him out of business."

"And you think I can do that?"

"In maybe one night, Captain."

Clancy smiled. "What else?"

"News travels in this town. Vaccarelli hears about Monk, and he's going to start working me on the West Side. I want Vaccarelli to understand that either he leaves me alone or he's out of business."

"That's not my precinct."

"It's Captain O'Grady's territory. You pay off O'Grady. I only want to deal with you."

"Out of my money?" Clancy demanded indignantly.

"Absolutely not. I'll put up the vigorish for O'Grady, but keep it under two hundred a week."

"Monk and Vaccarelli can get mighty ugly."

"So can you," Max said. "Are we in business?"

Clancy took a bottle and two shot glasses out of his desk drawer. He poured and handed one of the glasses to Max. "Drink up, lad. I got me a Jew for a partner."

Max swallowed the whiskey, grimaced, and wiped his mouth. "I'm getting married in a couple of weeks."

"Congratulations."

"I am inviting you to the wedding."

Clancy nodded and refilled the shot glasses.

"And bring the missus."

"I will indeed."

"Do you know Alderman Sweeney?"

"Like I know the sight of me own ugly face." He raised the glass. "Bottoms up."

Max swallowed the rye whiskey. There was an old saw that Jews couldn't drink. Let Clancy beware; he'd match him one for one. "I want you to invite Sweeney and his missus to my wedding."

"And why should he come? Alderman Sweeney's an important man in the life of this city. What the hell difference does it make to him that Max Britsky's getting married?"

"Well, you might tell him that he'll be sharing a table with Mr. Charles F. Murphy."

"What?"

"I thought I said it, Captain Clancy."

"Charlie Murphy?"

"Yes." Max dropped the word coolly. He leaned back and watched Clancy, who now showed signs of agitation.

"Why the hell didn't you say you was a friend of Murphy? What's all this fencing with Monk? Why didn't you just say the word?"

"I clean my own house. I don't come whining for favors. I pay my own way."

"You'll put in a good word with Charlie Murphy? There'll be no more trouble with Monk or Vaccarelli or any other of the dirty hoodlums who infest this fine city. That's a promise."

• • •

Charles F. Murphy had just become the new boss at Tammany Hall, which made him the most politically powerful man in New York. He had taken over from Dick Croker, a brawling, foul-mouthed political hoodlum whose sins had finally caught up with him. Murphy, on the other hand, was a good-looking, ingratiating Irishman who preferred intelligence to brute force and whose soft brogue could be captivating and seductive. Only a week after the executive committee of Tammany had dethroned Croker and voted Murphy into office, a well-dressed young man turned up at Max's office and informed him that Mr. Murphy would like to lunch with Mr. Britsky at Delmonico's new restaurant at Forty-fourth Street and Fifth Avenue — at Mr. Britsky's convenience. Shakily, Max chose a date. It was his first entry into Delmonico's, but he came armed with serious sartorial advice from Bert and financial advice from Fred Feldman.

"Blue serge," Bert said, "nothing else. Blue serge, black shoes, white shirt, and dark striped tie. Just look snotty and knowledge-able and like you consider the waiter to be pure shit."

"The goddamn menu," Max said. "It's supposed to be in French."

"Screw the menu. Just tell the waiter you'll have an *entrecôte* — that's French for a steak and a salad. Steak first, then salad. I'll write it down. Let Murphy order the wine. It's class to order without looking at the menu. If Murphy asks about dessert, tell him you'll have whatever he has."

Fred Feldman, on the other hand, said, "Careful, Max, like you're walking on glass. They say that Murphy wants a piece of everything. Croker wanted to rule the city, but they say that Murphy wants to own it. We're sitting on a gold mine, and word has got to him. There's no way to keep him out, but fight like hell over how much he comes in for."

"We got to give?"

"Or else go to Philadelphia or Boston."

But Murphy's warm greeting and his easy charm as he led Max to a table belied Feldman's warning. He was instantly ingratiating, to Max, to people who recognized him and greeted him as they made their way through the restaurant, to the maître d'hôtel, who knew him well, to the waiters and the busboys. "You're only a lad," he said to Max. "Now what age would you be?"

"Twenty-three."

"Now there's the finest recommendation a man could have. Myself, I was nothing at your age, a poor boy." Bit by bit, he drew Max out, established his background, itemized his family, admired "a kind of guts and love you don't see much these days. And now you're to marry a sweet lassie?"

"Next month," Max said.

"Would I be presuming to ask that myself and my lady be present at the wedding?"

"Well — yes, oh, yes, absolutely. We'd be honored, Mr. Murphy. But it's just a small Jewish wedding out in Flushing."

"There are no small Jewish or small Irish weddings, my lad. It's the size of the heart that measures it. And it's time I showed my face in Flushing. When you're too long away from any part of this populous and wondrous city, you lose touch."

"We'll be happy to have you," Max said, charmed, but still wondering why the lunch had been arranged.

"I been hearing good things about you. They call you the young tycoon. But I had no idea you were this young."

"I've had some luck," Max agreed.

"You call it *masel*, I call it *sechel*," Murphy said, using the Yiddish words for "luck" and "brains." "You got a string of moving picture places all over the city. I trust there'll be more."

"There'll be more," Max agreed, lighting the excellent cigar Murphy had offered him. "We have seventeen storefronts, but in the next five years I plan to replace them with real theatres. Our first real theatre, the Bijou, is operating already. We're renovating two others, one on Fourteenth Street and one on Twenty-third Street, and we bought two lots uptown where someday I'll build, both in Harlem."

Murphy suddenly changed the subject, asking Max abruptly, "What do you know about Tammany Hall, Max?"

"Well, you know, it's like the Democrats with all kinds of influence in the city, but I guess everyone knows that —"

"Trouble is, nobody knows much of anything. Back in the old days, a hundred years ago, when it began, it was Tammany and only Tammany that stood for the people against the rich and the powerful owners who were ready to wipe out everything the revolution brought us. There's many a curse thrown at Tammany, but who remembers that after the American Revolution, the rich and the powerful decided that they'd do here what they have done in England, and make themselves a proper aristocracy. They organized a thing called the Society of the Cincinnati, an organization of the officers of the revolution and of their kids as well. And who was to stand for the people, the foot soldier?

"That's how Tammany came about, the common people against the Cincinnati, and since they named their organization after the fancy aristocrats of old Rome, we decided to name ours after old Chief Tammany of the tribe of Delaware Indians, who was well noted for his wisdom and his love of liberty. We had thirteen trustees to govern our society, one for each of the thirteen original colonies — grand sachems, they were called, after them that ruled the old Indian tribes. And when the dirty schemers tried to undo all the good of the revolution and institute a government based on fear and privilege, who stood beside Jefferson for liberty but Tammany Hall, and you'll hear many a slur cast against the fine and decent name of Aaron Burr because he killed Hamilton in fair fight, but Tammany never turned its back on Burr, and with him we stood for liberty. Sure, every Protestant minister could make a name for himself with an attack on old Willie Tweed, giving him a character that would fit the worst devils in hell and making great stories of how he robbed the city of hundreds of millions of dollars. All you had to do was say 'Boss Tweed,' and the devils were conjured, but you and me, laddie, you as a Jew and myself as a Roman Catholic, we got no illusions about Protestant ministers.

"Well, there it is, a bit about the old organization. I thought it might clarify things in our dealings."

Max listened to this long, rambling story of Tammany Hall with respectful and almost total confusion. Tammany Hall, as everyone knew, ran the city. Tammany Hall owned the police and enforced or failed to enforce the law according to the wishes of whoever led Tammany. In New York, as it was put, one pissed because Tammany raised the toilet seat. Tammany had looted the city, over the past half-century, of enough money to ransom all the kings of Europe, but if one was starving, rest assured that come Thanksgiving or Christmas, Tammany would provide a free dinner; and why not, since Tammany took its tithe from every prostitute, pimp, gambler, and gangster who plied his or her trade in the city. This was common knowledge and Max's knowledge as well, but the rest of it — the talk about Jefferson and Burr and sachems and the Delaware Indians — made no sense whatsoever to Max. Nevertheless, he thanked Murphy for enlightening him and waited for Murphy's demands.

"I have made a few inquiries," Murphy said. "I hear you have taken care of your mother and your brothers and sisters. That's a fine, elegant thing to do, Max, and God will reward you. And you've got a head on your shoulders. This moving picture thing is only beginning."

"I have to agree with you," Max said.

"And as you spread out, every cheap hoodlum is going to try to horn in on you, not to mention them that call themselves legitimate businessmen and are just waiting to cut the throat of a young Jewish lad with more brains than they got."

Max nodded and waited.

"You need Tammany," Murphy said. "You need me."

"What will it cost me?" Max asked slowly.

"Twenty percent of the profit."

"That's too much."

"A year with our cooperation and your profits will double."

"It's too much," Max said stubbornly.

"You name it."

"Five percent," Max said.

"You're pulling my leg," Murphy said without anger. "But I got to respect you. You're a tough cookie, Mr. Britsky. We have just taken over Cappy's Music Hall, up on West Twenty-third Street. Cappy drank and gambled himself into bankruptcy, and we possessed the place for back taxes. You could take title for a hundred dollars and pay the thirty-two hundred in back taxes over the next ten years, and the property's worth a hundred and fifty thousand if it's worth a penny. All very quiet but legal, and that is only an indication, laddie, only an indication of what it will mean to have a friend in the hall. Sixteen percent."

"Seven," Max said.

A half-hour later they shook hands, and Murphy owned eleven percent of Max's operation, with the agreement that Max would take over Cappy's Music Hall and that Murphy would bend the zoning laws to Max's advantage and to the disadvantage of his competitors.

"This is nothing you will regret," Murphy said.

"It will be just a small Jewish wedding in Brooklyn," Max said.

"I would not miss it for the world."

"There's a Captain Clancy over on Houston Street and Alderman Sweeney. I thought I'd invite them. You wouldn't mind sharing a table with them?"

"Delighted," Murphy said.

• • •

Arthur and Lillian Levine had been born in Europe, in Austria. Arthur had been brought to America as a child in 1867. Lillian's parents had come to America three years later, bringing her with them. Since both families had come from the Carpathian Highlands to Vienna a generation before their move to America, they could not properly claim to belong to the genus of German Jew, who belonged to a wave of emigration out of Germany and into America between 1820 and 1860; but then, neither could they identify completely with the great mass of Eastern European Jews who began to pour into New York in the 1870s. They were isolated in a middle ground between the wealthy and respectable German Jews, the "uptown Jews," and the bitterly poor "ghetto Jews" of the Lower East Side, and this isolation caused them to cling to a sort of lower-middle-class propriety as a shipwrecked man might cling to a tiny life raft.

Their respectability had practically replaced their religion. They had established themselves in the fringe German-Jewish community in Flatbush, and sometimes in their dreams they saw Sally married into one of the great German-Jewish financial empires or at least to a German or Viennese doctor or dentist. Max Britsky they had never anticipated, and as the wedding day approached and as Max stubbornly refused to bring them together with his mother, their trepidation increased. It became even greater when Sally informed them that they could not have the wedding ceremony in the Reform temple they belonged to, to be followed by a small party in their home. Max's mother would not set foot in a Reform temple, which she considered to be the abode of the devil himself.

Max did the best he could under these circumstances. He had come to realize that just as his status in the world was changing, so were his domestic needs changing. Suddenly, Sally was a great asset; she had the qualities he was beginning to encounter in certain business associates: restraint, manners, the ability to speak the language properly, and just enough good looks without the opulent sexuality of women he was instinctively drawn to. In other words, in his enlarging lexicon, Sally was a lady, and he was determined that nothing should occur to make her withdraw from the wedding. He bought her a large diamond engagement ring and a gold wedding ring set with tiny rubies, and gave her carte blanche in the furnishing of the brownstone house. He also purchased a double Victoria carriage and engaged Shecky Blum to drive it and take care of the horse, renting horse and groom space in the Sixty-seventh Street stables, west of the elevated structure.

Sally, overwhelmed by this cornucopia, talked her parents into renting Marcus's Lecture and Catering Hall on St. Mark's Place for the wedding. It was not a very large or opulent wedding. The tables at Marcus's held ten people, and each family filled three tables. On Max's side, his family, with Sally and Ruby's girl friend, filled one table; another table seated the people in Max's organization, those he felt should be invited to his wedding. The third table was his Tammany table, as he thought of it, seating Murphy, Clancy, and Sweeney, each with his respective wife, Bert Bellamy and the girl he chose for the occasion, and Sam Snyder and his wife. His wife's name was Alice; a plump, pink-cheeked woman with a mass of pale brown hair piled high on her head and a ready, easy smile. It was the first time Max had met her, and he was taken aback by the uninhibited manner in which she embraced him and kissed him and assured him that she knew all about him, but would find it hard to forgive him if he did not bring his new wife to dinner very soon. The Snyders now had four children, and a fifth was on its way.

"And then, God willing, she'll stop," Sam Snyder said.

"Listen to him." Alice laughed. "Just listen to him."

This assortment of non-Jewish types was regarded with suspicion and hauteur by Sarah, who lorded it over the occasion in an enormous pink silk dress, sewn all over with white imitation pearls.

The thirty people from the Levine side were so many faces to Max, even after he was introduced to them. Nothing, he decided. Schmucks. And as so often happened on such occasions, : two groups kept coldly apart. "They should be grateful," Sarah said, "a boy like Max, who's a millionaire, marrying into a family that's got nothing to show for it."

Max was far from being a millionaire, in spite of Sarah's new-found financial admiration for her son. In fact, his cash reserve, which he had learned to refer to as "a state of liquidity," had practically vanished, the last bite being taken by a dozen cases of champagne, his gift to the wedding. But, as he assured Sally, his incoming cash — another expression he had adopted — was as uninterrupted as the Hudson River.

Marcus's hall had an upstairs and a downstairs, an arrangement which the Levine side of the family accepted with resigned distaste. The rabbi was Orthodox, provided by Max to please his mother. The sixty guests sat on folding chairs with an aisle separating Levine and Britsky. The bride and groom — Sally lovely in white organdy and lace, Max in a tuxedo, this one purchased — standing under a canopy, the rabbi intoning, *"Ha'ray att M'ku' deshet lee' b' ta' ba' at zu k' dat moshe v' ysrael,"* and Max wondering how, in his search for proper moving picture places, he could have missed Marcus's place, and calculating precisely how much he would offer Marcus. A few minutes later, Sally was his wife; he had crushed a glass underfoot, according to the Jewish custom, and he had placed a ring on her finger; then he had kissed the bride. As everyone crowded around to join in the congratulations, Max tried to create in his mind an erotic picture of taking his virgin bride to bed that night. But he had never gone to bed with a virgin, and the prospect was somehow more dismaying than erotic.

The wedding ceremony had taken place upstairs. The tables were set downstairs, a half-circle around a dance floor and a four-piece jazz band. As Max led Sally downstairs, they looked at each other with the sudden alarm of two people who, having known each other a long time, unexpectedly find themselves strangers.

· · ·

Boss Murphy, chief of Tammany Hall, prince and feudal lord of the city of New York, sipped champagne and watched Max and Sally dance a waltz, alone on the floor for this first dance, and he said to Alderman Sweeney, "There, Timothy, is one of the most remarkable men in this city."

"The skinny little Jew?"

"That skinny little Jew, Timothy, has more brains and guts in his little finger than you got in all three hundred pounds of you."

"You're joshing me."

Murphy smiled and patted Sweeney's huge hand. "Indeed I am, Timothy. Indeed I am."

At the Britsky table, watching her son dance, Sarah said to Freida, "Who has such a beautiful son like I have? Didn't I say so, from the day he was born?" Then, dropping her voice to a whisper, "The girl Ruby brought, she's Jewish?"

"I don't know, Mama."

"She don't look Jewish. He should just marry one of them, I'll jump out of the window."

The girl Ruby brought was Kathy Sullivan, whose father was a gripper man on the Broadway cablecar line. She watched Max and Sally dance, thinking to herself that she had become involved with the wrong Britsky. She was a pretty girl with jet black hair, bright blue eyes, and a rosebud complexion. She caught Max's eye as he danced and smiled at him, and he acknowledged the smile and returned it.

"How old is your brother?" she asked Ruby.

"Twenty-three."

Nothing lost, she thought. There were many, many years ahead. Benny was not totally without talent. In the eighth grade at school, one of his teachers had discovered in Benny a gift for drawing, and suddenly Benny found himself able to do something people admired. Now he was drawing Boss Murphy's face on the tablecloth when Sarah reached over and slapped his face. "What are you, a hoodlum, making pictures on the tablecloth?"

Alderman Sweeney stared unenthusiastically at a plate of stuffed derma and stuffed cabbage that had been placed in front of him.

"What is it?" his wife wondered.

"Kishke," Bert Bellamy told her. She was a very attractive, red-haired woman, almost two hundred pounds lighter than her husband and at least fifteen years younger. Seated next to Bert, she had assured him with a gentle pressure of her knee that she was not averse to a further acquaintance if it could be managed. "That's what they call it. It's really very good, beef intestines stuffed with a mixture of flour and fat, much better than it sounds. And the cabbage is stuffed with meat and raisins — very good."

"How do you know so much about Jewish food?"

"Ah, Max and me, we been together since we were kids."

"And how old are you at this minute?"

"About as old as you, Mrs. Sweeney."

"Go on with you! I'm old enough to be your mother," smiling at him and increasing the pressure of her knee.

The Levines took a dim view of the Britsky tables. They watched Bert dance with the flamboyantly red-headed Mrs. Sweeney, and they watched Max's sister Freida dance with Boss Murphy, whom they did not recognize. Told that he was *the* Boss Murphy, they were not impressed. They were readers of *Harper's* magazine and looked upon Tammany as a consortium of thieves and murderers. The strange combination of vulgarity and miscegenation at the Britsky tables puzzled and disturbed them. Introduced to the enormous bulk of Alderman Sweeney, who regarded whatever moved and breathed as both a voter and a constituent, they were at a loss at how to receive his warmth and praise of their daughter, coming from one whom their favorite newspaper regarded as a thief and swindler without peer. They were equally at a loss as they watched Kathy Sullivan, high on champagne, embrace Max and kiss him somewhat more fervently than the occasion demanded.

"I don't like them," Lillian Levine whispered to her husband. "That Sarah Britsky is one of the most dreadful women I have ever

met, and look at the people they invited — Boss Murphy, Alder
man Sweeney, and that man, Clancy, we were introduced to. He'
a policeman, isn't he, and he doesn't even look human. What ha
happened to my poor daughter?"

Her husband comforted her as best he could. Max tried to ge
Mrs. Levine to dance with him, but she protested that she was to
old to dance. Then Sarah Britsky tried to get both of the Levine:
to join in an old-fashioned folk dance that was practically *de rigueu*
at a Jewish wedding. Mrs. Levine fled into the bathroom, where
she burst into tears, but her husband joined in the dance and so did
the Irish contingent, who found the dance almost identical to an old
Irish folk dance. Sally left Max whirling with the dancers and fol
lowed her mother into the bathroom.

"I'm heartbroken," Mrs. Levine said through her tears. "Wha
kind of people are they?"

"Don't cry, Mama," Sally begged her. "They're plain people
It's a wonder that Max and his brothers grew up at all. That's the
miracle of it. His mother is terrible, but I suppose her life has been
terrible."

"And you're going to live in a house next to that woman."

"I'll manage, Mama. Please, don't cry about it."

· · ·

At home that evening, Max and Sally sat in the bedroom of their
brownstone, their bags packed and ready for their honeymoon a
Niagara Falls. Exhausted, filled with an uneasy mixture of cham
pagne, wine, and rye whiskey, more than a little drunk, smelling o
booze and cigar smoke, Max stared at Sally and tried to contem
plate an action as new to him as it would be to Sally, the deflowering
of a virgin lady.

And facing him, sitting on the edge of the bed that she had cho
sen with such delight in its four posts and flounced top, Sally's wa
face stared out of a pile of crumpled organdy. What am I doing
here? she asked herself, and, How can I face this? I'm supposed to
have sexual intercourse now with this man who is my husband
How did it happen? I think I will die if he tries to make love to me
but why do I feel this way? There were times when I almost loved
him, but then it wasn't for the rest of my life. Now it is for the res
of my life, and what will we talk about, what will we say to each

other? And what do I do now? Do I undress? Why doesn't he do something, anything, instead of sitting there like that?

A soft snore answered her question.

"Max!"

No response.

She felt impelled to wake him. Suddenly she felt forsaken. "Max!" she shouted.

No response. She felt her eyes fill with tears. Then she wiped the tears away and went over to Max. "Get up," she said firmly. She put her arms around him, pulled him erect, and half dragged him to the bed. He was not heavy and not much taller than she, and that helped. She pulled off his shoes and then his shirt and his trousers. The sight of his skinny form lying there in his one-piece BVDs set her to laughing. She pulled off his socks, still giggling, standing over the bed in her wedding gown.

She shook him. "Max, Max! This is your wedding night."

A few mumbled words answered her, but his eyes remained closed.

She sat down on the edge of the bed next to him, staring at him. He was really quite handsome, she told herself, and he didn't have an ounce of fat on him. That at least was positive. She made an image in her mind of going to bed with Alderman Sweeney, imagining that huge bulk unclothed, and the thought sent her into another fit of giggling. But now what was she to do? She studied Max again, and then with a boldness she had never dreamed herself to be capable of, she placed a hand over that portion of Max's underwear that covered his sexual organs. She felt the outline of his penis and his testicles, and she felt the increasing excitement within her, and she watched his body respond, mumbled sounds coming through his drunken stupor. Under her hand, his penis began to swell, and suddenly she pulled her hand away. Then, again, she began to giggle. She had drunk three glasses of champagne during the evening, sufficient to hand her the excuse that she was drunk, not like Max, but nevertheless a little drunk.

"That's it. I am drunk."

The self-deception was necessary. She slipped out of the wedding gown after struggling for a few minutes with its fastenings, and then out of the chemise and the wholly unnecessary corset and the oversized bloomers. "Everything, because I am drunk." She had never experienced this kind of heated desire before. Finally, she stood naked, her slender body lovely in the shaded light of the single lamp, her nipples firm on her small breasts, and she said sharply, "Max, wake up!"

He opened his eyes this time and stared at her, and then she put out the light and slipped into bed next to him. He was asleep again. She began to fondle his penis, her excitement increasing as it grew erect, and then, still half asleep, he reached out and put his arms around her.

SIX

1906

—

Max at the
Age of Twenty-seven

THE OFFICES in the Hobart Building had been enlarged, improved, and redecorated. There were three girls who did nothing but work at typewriters, and these young ladies were still called typewriters. There were two bookkeepers who worked under Jake Stein, whose office door now bore the title comptroller, and there was a new receptionist to take the place of Etta Goodman, who was now Max's administrative assistant. The new receptionist was a pretty red-headed young woman, whose name was Della O'Donnell, who was somewhat distantly related to Boss Murphy. Jake Stein insisted that Murphy had asked Max to hire her in order to have a spy boring from within; but Max felt that the amount of boring Della O'Donnell could do was insignificant and that if it were true, Murphy was entitled to have someone inside to report on his share of the business.

For one thing, Max was intrigued with Della O'Donnell. She had the same qualities that Alice Snyder possessed, an easygoing, unflappable good nature and a plump, round warmth that made him wonder how it would feel to be married to such a woman; but the thought of her as Boss Murphy's spy was ridiculous. Yet it was indicative of the workings of Jake Stein's mind. Feldman, who disliked Jake Stein, had mentioned to Max that they might replace him. "He's good," Max protested, to which Feldman replied, "Too good." Max told Feldman that he would think about it, but the more he thought about it, the less possible it became for him to fire someone who had a wife and children, who was brilliant at his work, and who gave no evidence of being the crook that Feldman felt him to be.

The question of Etta Goodman was more bothersome. Her work as administrative assistant was for the most part a combination of the emotional and the physical, although no longer exercised on the floor. In redecorating his office, Max had included a large sofa. The purchase of the sofa and what went with it were a result of Max's sexual relationship to Sally — a weak flame to begin with, which became a flicker and then flickered out. While it flickered, it had produced two children, and after that it more or less ceased; whereupon the affair or exercise, as Max often thought of it, with Etta Goodman was renewed. Max and Etta had been functioning on the sofa when Della buzzed him and informed him, via the newly installed intercom, that two gentlemen wanted to see him. Their names were Frank Stanford and Jack Calvin. While the names were vaguely familiar, Max could not recall them. Since they had no appointment, he told Della that either they could wait or they could state their business and ask for an appointment on another day. Della replied that their business was film production, and Max said that if they wished to see him, they should wait.

Etta watched Max adjust his trousers and button his shirt. "You don't even seem to enjoy it anymore," she said to him.

"I got other things on my mind."

"Sure. Like you said after you married Sally —"

"Stop right there," Max said. "Sally's my wife. That's different. There are women who enjoy this, and then there are women who got different sensibilities, like Sally —"

"Meaning like me, because all I'm good for is to get fucked."

"I don't like that word," Max said, "and most of all not used by a woman, and anyway, I don't know what's the matter with you these days, the way you're losing weight."

"I like myself that way. So what now? You want to fire me? You want to get rid of me?"

"Will you stop that! Who wants to get rid of you? Every time I say something, you start crying I want to get rid of you. Go pull yourself together."

"How would you like it," Etta wailed, "to be kept on hooks all the time, and I never know what you think of me."

"You don't mean hooks. You mean tenterhooks, which Sally says is something they use to stretch cloth —"

"I don't give a damn what Sally says! I'm sick and tired of what Sally says!"

"Come on, come on," Max said gently, putting his arms around her.

"I'm a person, same as Sally."

"Sure, of course you are."

He steered her out of his office through the door that led to Fred Feldman's office. Feldman was not in his office. "Sit down," Max said. "Rest a little. Dry your tears. Then you can go home if you want to."

"I want to be what I'm supposed to be, an administrative assistant."

"I know, and we'll get to that. I promise you."

He returned to his office, asking himself what he was supposed to do with her. He was fond of her. She was not clever — indeed, rather stupid — but that only served to increase his guilt. He couldn't throw anyone out. He was supposed to be hard and tough-minded, according to his reputation in the city's financial circles, but he had just agreed to put his brother Benny on his payroll, and he knew damned well that Benny was a little bum and would never be anything better. His mother received four hundred dollars a week to run the brownstone house, where she lived with Freida and Benny, and she was always crying that it wasn't enough. Fred Feldman had said to him, "I hate to say this, Max, but someone has to. Jake Stein says Ruby's got his hand in the till. It costs us at least a hundred a week." Max shrugged it off. "The hell with it. We can afford it. You want to get technical, Jake's as crooked as Ruby." He was trapped, and poor Etta Goodman was simply another bar on the trap. He had no idea where the trap had come from and how he had gotten into it, but there he was; and now he sat down at his desk, staring at the opposite wall, wondering why he cheated on Sally and tried to understand why being a millionaire at age twenty-seven didn't seem to mean a damn thing. Then the intercom reminded him that Mr. Stanford and Mr. Calvin were still waiting to see him.

"About what?" he demanded of Della.

She took a moment and then told him that they wanted to talk about films. The names stirred his memory again. "All right, send them in," he said to Della.

They were tall, middle-aged men in blue serge and white shirts. Stanford had a long, narrow head, blue eyes, and close-cropped gray hair. Calvin was heavier and round-faced. Stanford took a gold watch out of his vest pocket, contemplated it for a long moment, and then said to Max, "You've kept us waiting for twenty-eight minutes, Mr. Britsky. That's either bad judgment or bad business or plain bad manners."

"Bad manners," Calvin said, looking around him.

"Do I know you gentlemen?" Max asked them, containing his anger. "You had no appointment."

"Not bad manners, bad judgment," Stanford said. "We had an appointment. We made it with your administrative assistant, a Miss Goodman."

"You did?" Max spread his hands. "She never told me. I'm sorry."

"It happens."

"Sit down, please," Max said. "Can I offer you something, a drink?"

They sat down, declining his offer, both of them watching him thoughtfully. Calvin reminded him that years ago, both of them had done business with Sam Snyder. "We had just started making moving pictures," Calvin said.

"Yes, of course. I remember."

"We don't deal directly with Sam anymore, but at this point, we make or control ninety percent of the moving picture material in the country."

"We only make part of it," Stanford explained. "But our distribution organization controls better than ninety percent. In your case, Mr. Britsky, you rent your whole product from us."

"I didn't realize that," Max said. "Sam and Jake Stein, my comptroller, take care of the rentals. Look, I want to apologize for having kept you waiting."

"Nothing to it. Now understand this, Mr. Britsky, we're a bit annoyed at having been kept waiting, but that has nothing to do with our proposition. We represent National Distributors. We own patents on two types of camera."

"I thought Edison —"

"Yes, but we think we can make our patents stand up. Anyway, that is beside the fact of our product. Now in your case, you operate fourteen nickelodeons and seven regular theatres. You also have three new theatres under construction, and you have nine conversions of lecture halls and catering halls. That makes you the largest theatre operator in the moving picture business. Your cash flow is between thirty-five and fifty-five thousand a week."

"What have you got — spies planted here?"

"It's an outside calculation, Mr. Britsky. But we appear to have hit close to the mark."

"All right. Suppose you have. Where does this lead us? What are you here for?"

"To talk business."

"If you're going to talk about rentals and the price we pay you, I'd like to have Sam Snyder and Jake Stein in here, and my lawyer, Fred Feldman."

"Not necessary," Calvin said. "Not yet, Max." He paused to calculate the effect of the first name, the tightening of Max's lips. "Max, you've made yourself into a millionaire with our blood, our quart of blood."

"What in hell are you talking about?"

"The moving pictures."

"I pay for them."

"Not enough. Not nearly enough, Max."

"You mean you're going to raise your price."

"Hold on," Stanford said. "We haven't said anything about raising our price. We're not raising our price. We want something else, and we feel that we're entitled to it."

"What's that?"

"We want a fifty percent interest in your business — half of everything you take out of the theatres and half of the ownership. We'll set up the mechanism that will turn the Britsky theatres into a publicly owned enterprise, and you'll turn over fifty percent of the stock to National Distributors."

Max smiled. "It's a stupid joke."

"We're dead serious."

"It's still a stupid joke."

"Bad manners," Calvin said.

"Don't try to shrug this off," Stanford said. "We're dead serious. If we walk out of here without a deal, we'll yank every motion picture out of your theatres in three days. Your houses will be dead."

Max made no response. He sat facing them, and they sat facing him, and when the silence had stretched as tight as a rubber band, Calvin said to him, "Take a few days and think it over."

"What do I think about?" Max asked him. "How I broke my ass for seven years to build up this circuit and then handed it over to you? You know something — my houses are half empty these days, and you know why? Because your moving pictures stink! Because people are bored to shit watching a horse run around a track or a locomotive rush toward them or a little girl bouncing a ball or some clown driving a cart into a river. You don't have the brains to open a theatre and you don't have the brains to make a decent moving picture. So I'll tell you what you can do. You can both go straight to hell! You want my theatres, you can have them over my dead body."

Calvin spoke first. "You're a snotty little Jew bastard, Britsky. You've just dug your own grave. We'll pick up your whole damn circuit in the bankruptcy proceedings."

Stanford tossed a card on Max's desk. "If you change your mind, call us."

· · ·

In the course of three and a half years as the wife of Max Britsky and mistress of the house on Sixty-sixth Street, Sally had changed. She had given birth to two children: Richard, who was born in 1903, and Marion, born a year and seven months later. She had also furnished the brownstone according to her own taste, which meant a stonewall defense against the taste of Sarah Britsky and Sarah's three daughters, Esther, Sheila, and Freida. In the course of the three and a half years, both Esther and Sheila had married, each to a young man who subsequently became an employee of Max; and Freida, after a period of anger, bitterness, hostility, and jealousy — all directed toward Sally — gave up the struggle and became Sally's friend and confidante, whereupon both of them combined defenses against Sarah's apparent desire to destroy them. Neither Sally nor Freida could understand the source of Sarah's venom, an apparently unremitting revenge against life itself, and after three visits to the house next door, Sally never set foot inside again. Even Max saw the difference between the simple furnishings that Sally had selected and the collection of Victorian grotesques that Sarah and her daughters crammed into their home. The two servants Sarah had employed lived in terror of their mistress. Freida could only say to Sally in explanation, "She's crazy, but she's always been a little crazy."

Freida also said to Sally, once the hostility and jealousy had been overcome, "I know you want to sell the place and move away. But if you do, I'll die. You don't have to go in there. You don't have to talk to her. Max understands. He comes to see her and she abuses him. I don't know why he stands it."

Nor did Sally. In fact, as time went on, she felt she knew less and less about Max. After Marion was born, Sally and Max had not resumed a sex life, which had been intermittent at best. Sally pleaded continuing pains and gynecologic problems — all actually non-existent — and Max accepted her excuses without questioning. Their sex life had never been very satisfactory, and Max's sexual comprehension was still conditioned by the street lore of his childhood, which held that sex was something the man enjoyed and the woman endured — with the exception of certain women, such as Etta Goodman. Indeed, Sally's indifference to sexual enjoyment gave her a certain kind of purity and class in Max's eyes. He liked the notion that his wife was above such things, whereas Sally only knew that her initial fear and repulsion in terms of Max had been overcome in many ways but still persisted where intimacy was suggested. His advances only tensed and tightened her and caused her to take psychological refuge in a rejection of her own feeling and sensation.

There was no one she could turn to for guidance or advice. Her own notions of sex were confused at best, and her inclination to dwell in a romantic world of fantasy only compounded this confusion. Her mother had never discussed such things with her; indeed, it was unthinkable, nor was sex ever a subject of conversation among the lady schoolteachers who had been her only associates for so many years. The only female friend she had now was Freida, but she could hardly discuss her sexual relationship with Max with his sister. Thus she accepted the situation as so many other women of her time accepted it, nor did she feel that she was doomed to unhappiness. She still regarded Max as a man who was both unique and astonishing; she did have a beautiful home, one beyond any expectations she might have entertained; and she had two lovely children. She also had a housekeeper who lived in and a cleaning woman who came in three times a week. She had been provided with a nurse for the children, which gave her all the time to herself that she required. In addition, Freida was there almost every day, utterly devoted to Sally's children, and ready to take care of them if Sally desired a few hours to herself.

On Max's part, his respect for Sally had not lessened. He could not become accustomed to the fact that a woman like Sally had married him, Max Britsky. She was his possession, but a very precious and high-class possession. When on this day, the day he had encountered Stanford and Calvin, he called Sally and told her that there would be a meeting at their house that evening, he also made certain that she would be there.

"Are you sure, Max? I have tickets for a concert tonight, and I was going to take Freida, because I know how you detest concerts."

"Forget the concert. Let Freida find a guy for once. I need you to help me with the meeting tonight."

"What time?" Sally asked. How could she refuse him when he specified that he needed her? That had been his first enticement, long ago.

"Suppose we eat early. I'll tell them to be there at eight o'clock."

At eight P.M., all of them were present in Max's dining room, sipping the tea Sally had poured for them and nibbling pieces of cake — all of them appropriately glum. By now, everyone present, including Sally, knew about the Stanford-Calvin ultimatum and Max's response. Sam Snyder was the oldest of the group, in his mid-thirties now, round and prosperous, vice president of Britsky Theatres, with a wife and five children and a brownstone house on Brooklyn Heights.

Bert Bellamy, head of theatre operations, was still unmarried;

and Max had the feeling that he would never marry. A shell had hardened around Bert, and no man or woman would ever be given the right to penetrate it. Once Max would have unhesitatingly trusted Bert with his life and fortune, but now? Once, long ago, Max felt, they had done everything together — goofed around together, dated together, shared their dreams and secrets, hugged each other after an absence. Not now. Bert encased himself in his three-piece suits, locked himself behind a golden watch chain, wore stiff collars and dark ties, and smiled infrequently.

Fred Feldman, on the other hand, wore his heart on his sleeve, a small, round teddy bear of a man who loved Max and tried to protect him. He understood the strange innocence beneath Max's tough, street-wise shell, a knowledge neither Bellamy nor Stein shared. Stein was a hungry man, hungry eyes, hungry hands — too smart to be a bookkeeper, but too crude to have been much more until Max hired him. He had a narrow hatchet of a face, heavy brows, and a habit of plucking hairs from his nose. Sally detested him, and when he joined the others at the table, Sally prepared to retreat.

"Please stay," Max asked her.

"Can she handle cigar smoke?" Bert wanted to know. Max brought out a humidor, and suddenly it was all very much like a dream, this group of men who worked for him sitting in a wood-paneled dining room around a substantial oak table, lighting twenty-five-cent cigars of the finest Havana leaf while he poured brandy from a cut-glass carafe. Beyond the dream, it made little sense, and even the ominous future spelled out by Stanford and Calvin could not fix it to reality.

"Max?" Sally said.

They were watching him as he stood motionless, the brandy carafe in his hand.

"Thinking," he said.

"I like cigar smoke," Sally said. "Otherwise I'd move out."

"Nobody likes it. You endure it."

Then they fell silent and watched Max, who seated himself gingerly, as if the unsubstantial aspect of reality had infected everything in the house.

He was Max Britsky. The past was very close to him, the past of poverty and indignity and filth and roaches and the stink of urine pervading the tenement on Henry Street, and here he was, the past much more real than this present. He had never really conquered the curse of the inarticulate; he was full of anger and frustration and fear, and he could not verbalize any of it, not even to himself. He was still a lousy little kike. That was how the uptown Jews put it; if your name ended with a *ky*, such as Britsky did, they took the *ky* and made it a designation and a curse, turning it into kike. To the white Protestants who ran things, he was an upstart Jew bastard.

He looked around and there was Sally, standing tentatively at one end of the big table. "For God's sake, sit down!" he snapped at her; and then she sat down, wondering what she had done to make him angry, but Max said apologetically, "Oh, hell. I'm sorry. Those two bastards kicked my belly in."

"Max," Fred Feldman asked, "is there no other source for moving pictures?"

"Sure. They make some here and there. That don't help us. We got over thirty outlets. And if National's pictures stink, which they do, what do you expect from the others?" He turned to Snyder. "Sam, can we make pictures ourselves?"

"Maybe."

"What does maybe mean?"

"It means that those bastards at National can tie us up pretty damn good" — turning to Sally — "if you'll forgive my language, Mrs. Britsky. They're tied in with Edison and Eastman, and once they saw us beginning to buy film and cameras, they'd crack down."

"Not to mention how long it would take," Jake Stein said. "The houses are half empty now. Let them sit empty for a month, and maybe we couldn't survive."

"What do you mean, maybe? Everyone's got a maybe. Could we or couldn't we survive?"

"I don't know, Max. I'd have to sit down with the books and do some very careful figuring. I also need decisions. Who do we keep on payroll and who do we lay off? We got doormen, ushers, janitors, projectionists, ticket sellers — a whole army of people. And it wouldn't be only a month. How long does it take to make a moving picture? We got rentals to meet and maybe taxes."

"I hate to throw cold water on things," Fred Feldman said, "but

I listen to you talking and I think of something else. You asked Jake the wrong question. You ask him how long we can survive if the houses are dark —"

"What's the right question?" Max snapped.

"You should ask him how long we can survive the way things are right now. Five years ago, the movies were so new and improbable that people didn't object to looking at some stupid film that showed a dog standing on his hind legs and begging for food. Anyway, a nickel was not so much to pay, and for a dime a mother could get an hour of relief from three kids, but when you charge twenty-five cents in your theatres, the people want something in return."

"Come on," Max said, "we show better than a dog begging. What about the *Fireman* and *The Great Train Robbery?*"

"How many times can you show *The Great Train Robbery* and expect people to pay for it? The other stuff we show is boring trash. None of it makes any sense. So even if we make moving pictures, if they're the kind of pictures National makes, we're out of business."

"Do you agree with him?" Max asked Snyder.

"Well, I guess so."

"He's right about the attendance figures," Bert Bellamy said. "They keep dropping. It's not so noticeable in the nickelodeons, but in the theatres we're being hit below the belt. We're just about breaking even, and whatever profits show come from the nickelodeons."

"I can't believe it," Max said. "I just can't believe that I hear what you're saying. You're telling me that moving pictures are just a passing fad. No! I don't believe that! Moving pictures are the greatest thing that ever happened in the entertainment industry. You're so damn smart, Fred, tell me something. How come in the uptown theatres where they show Shaw and Shakespeare and stuff like that — and a lot of it ain't Shakespeare but just garbage, from what Sally tells me — their houses are full and they're turning people away?"

"Ask Sally," Fred replied.

They all turned toward Sally, who nodded and said, "Yes, that's so. I tried to get tickets to *Hedda Gabler*, which opened last week, but they're sold out weeks in advance. And it isn't only because

Nazimova is playing Hedda. It's because Ibsen tells a wonderful story about a woman and tries to explain why she does what she does."

"Put it down on Houston Street and it closes in twenty-four hours," Max said.

"I'm not saying that *Hedda Gabler* is the thing for film. I just feel that almost everything you show, even *The Great Train Robbery*, is utterly pointless. You have no story and you never really grip the audience. There's a thing you learn about when you take a drama course. It's called empathy, and it means to make the audience feel and suffer what the actor is feeling and suffering. That's something that exists in every good stage play, but one never feels it in those awful motion pictures."

There was a long moment of silence. Max had never heard Sally assert herself in such terms, and on her part, Sally was overcome with a wave of embarrassment that made her wish she could retreat into invisibility. But Sam Snyder, groping for words, shook one stubby finger at Sally and said, "You're absolutely right, Mrs. Britsky. You need a story. My wife always says the same thing. But in a moving picture, nobody says anything. That's the difference between film and the theatre, and how can you tell a story that will really grab people without words? I was reading that new book of O. Henry's, and he really does it. Great stories, just great, and all about the city here — but words. He couldn't tell any story without words. He calls it *The Four Million* — four million stories to tell right here in New York."

"That ain't what moving pictures are for," Jake Stein said.

Feldman nodded at him. "Suddenly you're an expert on moving pictures."

"I'd like to hear what Sally has to say," Bert Bellamy told them. "At least she's done some thinking about this."

"I'm less of an expert than even Mr. Stein," Sally protested. "At least he knows the business. I only see the pictures."

"I think you know more than any of us," Snyder said. "At least you're in front of the screen, Mrs. Britsky. We're all behind the projector."

"Well, yes, I do think about it a great deal, and I do think there is a way to tell a story with words, even though you can't hear what anyone says. I got my idea from the French moving picture makers, who break up the picture with cards. For example, they will show you a picture of a steel mill, and then they photograph a lettered card which says, 'A steel mill on the banks of the Rhone' — or something.''

"We do the same thing," Max said.

"Yes, sometimes. They use it more. But I was thinking of carrying it one step further. Suppose Mr. Snyder here is a character in a story, and in the story he says to his wife, 'Let's go out for a walk, my dear.' You photograph him saying those words, and as soon as he has completed the statement, you cut the film and insert a card with the words lettered on it."

"Wait a minute," Fred Feldman said. "I lost that somewhere. Would you do it again."

His eyes closed, Snyder had his hands up in front of him. "I'm trying to visualize it. Wouldn't the card have to come before he speaks?"

"Oh, no. After. Mr. Feldman, this way. Watch me, and I say, 'I think it would work.' But you're watching a picture of me without any sound, and then I think you would remember the picture while you read the card."

"But, Sally," Max said, "suppose you could do it that way. Most of the people who buy tickets in our houses can't read."

"Not most of them," Bellamy protested. "And if some kid is there with his mother, he can read her the cards."

"You'd have a racket."

"No, let's not get into that. I want to know how Sally would project that through a whole story," Max said.

"Max, I haven't really thought this whole thing through, and I must confess that I did a good deal of the thinking just sitting here tonight. It would have to be a very simple story, and I don't think we'd have to have cards for everything. Suppose you and I, we were having a terrible fight and screaming at each other —"

"We don't scream at each other," Max interrupted. "I don't want anyone to get that idea."

"I'm just trying to make a point. Of course we don't, but suppose the people in the story do. We could show them screaming and waving their arms. I don't think we'd have to put every word on cards. I'm not sure, but I don't think so."

"How long would such a film have to run?" Sam Snyder asked.

"I don't know. I never gave that any thought."

"If it was a real story," Bellamy said, "you couldn't tell it in much less than an hour, and if this card thing worked — Well, you need time to read. Most people don't read quick."

"Most don't read at all."

"I don't see anything like that," Stein said. "It just sounds crazy, somebody talking and then the words printed out later."

"That's the trouble," said Snyder. "I just can't put the two together, somebody talking and then the words. Suppose somebody pulls a gun and says, 'Hands up!' There's a card. Then the other guy says, 'No, sir, I am not putting my hands up.' Then we need another card, and this first fellow with the gun, he shoots the other man, but when? While we're reading the card?"

"What about that, Sally?" Max asked.

"I think you're making a simple thing needlessly complex. You remember that little picture we had about Baby Lou, four or five years ago. You remember, she falls asleep, and then the dog barks, and they put in a card that said, 'The dog's barking awakens Baby Lou.' Well, all they had to print on that card was 'Bow, wow, wow.' It would be the same. The truth is that people have been reading cards for years, but no one ever thought of using the cards for dialogue." She looked from face to face, and then she got up and said, "Give me a minute, please," and ran from the room.

"What do you think?" Max asked them.

"I'm trying to visualize it," Feldman said.

"It might just work," Snyder said.

"That's one smart lady," Bellamy agreed, "only it's out of the question. It's impossible."

"Why?"

"We got over thirty houses. It would take two, three months to make one moving picture the way Sally thinks it should be made, maybe an hour and a half of film. And to make ten, twenty of them — it would close us down."

Max shook his head. "Schmuck," he said.

"What do you mean, schmuck?"

"By schmuck I mean schmuck, plain, simple English. Maybe what Sally wants to do is crazy, but if we can do it, we don't need no thirty moving pictures. We need one, and then I have the laboratory make me thirty copies. We open every house with the same picture."

"And where do we get an audience for every night and every house with the same picture?"

"From the three and a half, maybe three and three-quarters million people in this city who never saw a moving picture. From all the uptown Yankees who tell us that moving pictures are all right for Jews and micks and Eyetalians and Krauts who can't read anyway, but not for classy blueblood Americans. Because when you come to think about it, Sally's right. We show stupid crap. The moving picture is maybe the greatest invention Edison ever put together, and all we do with it is show them eight-hundred-foot schmuck pieces with magicians making birds and rabbits come and go until you never want to see a bird again, and then a runaway horse or a runaway train or a runaway automobile. I read where *Caesar and Cleopatra* opens last week and they're selling one hundred and fifty standing room for every performance. You tell me, Bert — how much standing room you sold in the Bijou this year?"

"Talk some sense, Max. They're standing for *Caesar and Cleopatra* because it's the newest Shaw play. What do we do — commission Shaw to write for the nickelodeons?"

Sally returned to the room. She held a thin sheaf of cardboards in her hand, and she took a place at one end of the table. "I'm going to try a little experiment," she said. "Please bear with me. It will only take a minute or two."

They turned to face her, waiting expectantly. Then Sally began to speak, but no sound issued from her lips. Her lips moved to form words, but no words issued forth. Then she held up one of the cards she carried. On it, lettered in thick black crayon, was: "I am trying to make a point." After a few seconds, she dropped the card to the floor and again moved her mouth and lips without sound. Then she held up another card which read: "Moving pictures can tell a story." After a few seconds, she dropped the second card and spoke soundlessly again; then the third card: "Do you believe me now?"

They all clapped, and Sam Snyder shouted, "It works! Mrs. Britsky, it absolutely works."

"Maybe," Stein said.

"It works for me," Feldman agreed.

"What do you think?" Max asked Bert.

"I think it could work. It's risky, but it just might work."

· · ·

"You love Bert, don't you?" Sally said to Max. He had just come into their bedroom. Sally sat in front of her dressing table, combing her thick brown hair. She wore a white silk dressing gown that had been a birthday present from Max, who watched her now with caution and disbelief — always with a little caution and a little disbelief. It was not that Sally was beautiful. If anything, as her youth passed, whatever good looks she had had faded rather quickly. She was a small, thin, mousy woman.

"Love him?" Max said. "Maybe. We been together a long time. Bert got me into the act, and maybe that saved my life at the time."

Sally realized that she was a small, thin, mousy woman; she had no illusions. All the more reason for her astonishment when Bert, following her into the pantry ostensibly in search of a piece of ice for his drink, had embraced her from behind, cupping his hands over her small breasts. No man had ever done that to her before, no man except Max, no stranger, and she had no prepared response. She would have screamed, but realized that to scream would produce an endless procession of nasty consequences; and therefore she simply whispered hoarsely, "Please stop. Please don't do that, Bert."

"Why not?"

"Because I don't want you to."

"I think you do."

"I don't, and if you don't take your hands away, I'm going to scream." His whole body was pressing against her then, and she could feel the pressure of his hardening penis.

"You're aching for it. You know that. You get nothing from Max, and don't tell me you're made of stone."

"And you're Max's best friend."

"What does that prove?"

"Don't you have any sense of loyalty — after all he did for you?"

"What the hell has loyalty got to do with it? You're a woman. I'm a man. And just don't ever tell me what Max did for me." He stepped away from her now. "Think about it, Sally, just think about it." And then he turned and left the pantry.

What does one do? she wondered. Does one tell one's husband? Does one pretend it never happened?

"How did he save your life?" she asked Max now.

"He showed me how to steal bread without getting caught."

"Max, I'm serious."

"So am I."

"You don't mean that about stealing bread?"

"Why not?"

"Because you wouldn't steal anything."

"What do you mean, I wouldn't steal? I wouldn't steal ten dollars or a hundred or a thousand. What good would that do me? I'd be stupid to steal. A man who steals is either stupid or desperate."

"But —"

"I know. I said Bert showed me how to steal bread without being caught."

"You're always teasing me and making me feel that I grew up in some insulated place, without knowing anything about the world."

"Didn't you?"

"No! I taught school on Clinton Street. Clinton Street. If you know a worse place than Clinton Street, just name it for me!"

"You're really angry."

"I am!" Sally snapped. "I'm very angry. I ask you a question about Bert and you answer as if I were an idiot."

Max had never seen her this way before, her face white and tense, her lips quivering, her hands trembling. "I wasn't teasing," he said. "I was just a kid and I had seven people to feed — seven — and when we had nothing else to eat, we ate bread. It kept us alive. In those days, the rich people lived uptown around Gramercy Park and Madison Square and Washington Square and Fifth Avenue below Twenty-third Street. Most of them had fresh bread delivered, between five and six in the morning. Bert showed me how to follow the bread wagons. When the bread man went into one of the mews or delivery yards, we'd take a loaf from the wagon. No more than one loaf from a wagon, and mostly they'd never notice it missing and not roust out the cops."

"You stole the bread, you actually stole the bread?"

"Boss Tweed stole over two hundred million dollars from this city. William Henry Vanderbilt boasted that he was the richest man in the world. Murphy says he was too proud to steal anything under a million, but Jay Gould wasn't proud, and he stole anything that wasn't nailed down, and Jim Fisk stole it even if it was nailed down, and Fernando Wood —"

"I know about Fernando Wood. I know about all the others you're ready to name. Does that make stealing right?"

"Goddamn it," Max said slowly, "when you steal to keep from dying of hunger, it's right!" He was angry now. Goddamn her, who the hell was she to lecture him and give herself airs? From the day they met, she had been lecturing him, parading her superior intelligence and manners. He stalked out of the bedroom, slamming the door behind him. Downstairs, he dropped into a chair in the living room and lit a cigar. The darkness suited his mood, but smoking in the darkness was uncomfortable, and he reached out and switched on a lamp. Easy, everything easy these days. No more stinking, sputtering kerosene lamps, no more smelly, dangerous gas jets. Reach out and turn an electric switch, and the light goes on. He was rich. He had only to point to something and it was his, except that now the whole thing had become a house of cards. All their smart talk after dinner didn't add up to a single roll of film. It was so damned easy to talk about something that no one had ever done before, but when he put the reality in front of the fantasy, he saw nothing but disaster. In a week, unless he gave away half of his business, his theatres would be dark.

Sally came into the room and dropped into a chair facing him. "I didn't mean to shout at you," she said.

"That's O.K."

"I guess now you feel that everything we talked about tonight is water down the drain. There's no way you can do it because nobody else did it."

He was amazed at her perception. "Yeah, I guess that's how I feel."

"Nobody else ever did the things Max Britsky did. Wasn't it always that way?"

"Trying to make me feel good?" He grinned at her.

"Why not?"

"What's to feel good about?"

"Beating those bastards, Stanford and Calvin."

"I never heard you swear before."

"It's about time," Sally said.

"Yeah, I guess it is. What makes you think we can beat them?"

"I know you, but they don't know you. They're crazy to put themselves up against Max Britsky. You'll cut them into ribbons."

"You really think so."

"I do."

"Then tell me, where do I start with this moving picture idea of yours?"

"I've been thinking about that. There has to be a story — I mean, written out — so that whenever the cameraman photographs a scene, he will know exactly what it is and so will the actors. And then, I think, each dialogue card must be worked out in advance. I mean, even if they're changed later, they should be ready, otherwise we'd only have confusion and nothing would make much sense."

"Yeah, sure. So where do we find all this? Who does it, if so far nobody ever did it?"

"I'll do it, if you want me to."

"You?"

"Yes, why not?"

"I mean, I was thinking about somebody who writes these plays that are such hits, like Shaw or Ibsen or Wilde?"

"Oscar Wilde is dead, so I don't think he'd be interested."

"All right, so he's dead," Max said petulantly.

"Max, I only mean these men or someone like them might be interested, but they'd want a great deal of money and even with all their reputation, there's no telling that they could do it any more than I could. At least nothing's lost if I try."

"All right, you try, and I'll do the rest some way."

"Put the cigar away and come to bed," Sally told him.

· · ·

Boss Murphy listened glumly to Max's account. "If they were in New York, Max, maybe I could hit them a bit. But National's based in Philadelphia, and as far as Edison's concerned, nobody's got a shoe in with Edison. You really want to fight this?"

Max's impression was that Murphy didn't want to be bothered.

If National took fifty percent, he'd still have his eleven percent or Stanford and Calvin wouldn't operate in New York.

"I'd burn every one of them theatres to the ground before I'd let those bastards have them."

"That's pretty extreme, Max."

"Maybe you're not for me," Max said, studying Murphy shrewdly. "I just don't want you against me."

"What makes you think I'd be against you?"

"You could see it losing eleven percent."

"You could lose eighty-nine percent."

"Oh, no," Max said. "I'm not going to lose."

"All right," Murphy said. "Count on that. I'm not against you. I don't know what Calvin and Stanford got, but you got a barrel of piss and vinegar."

That never occurred to Mr. Alvin Berry, who was in charge of the loan department at the Chase Bank at 177 Broadway. He saw sitting facing him a sober young man in a blue serge suit. Berry kept his own scorecard on his petitioners, and one of his first notations depended on what they were wearing. If the petitioner wore blue serge, as did ninety percent of the stable citizens who earned their living south of Fulton Street, he was already high on the scorecard. A white shirt and a matching cloth collar added to acceptability; and not only was Max properly dressed, but his nails were clean and his hair cropped properly. When the appointment had been set up, Mr. Berry had inquired into the background of Max Britsky, and now he observed with interest the young man who was New York's newest overnight millionaire. Mr. Berry was not surprised that as a millionaire, Max needed cash desperately; he was rather more surprised that this Jew who had murky origins in the East Side ghetto should be well dressed and quite good-looking and well spoken, too. On the other hand, he did not know how tightly and desperately Max was controlling his speech and his grammar.

"As far as collateral is concerned," Max had said, "we operate thirty-three houses. Of course, they're not all theatres in the legitimate sense. Fourteen of them are storefront nickelodeons, and a number of others are converted lecture halls. I mention these simply to point out the extent of our operation. But we do have ten theatres, originally built for theatrical dramatic production. Four of them are mortgaged. Six are owned free and clear." He took out of a briefcase a folder that was stuffed with documents. "Here are all the facts and figures."

Glancing through the folder, Berry asked, "How much are you looking for, Mr. Britsky?"

"I need a half a million."

"Suppose you leave this material with me. We'll let you know."

Berry telephoned Max's office two days later to inform him that the line of credit for five hundred thousand dollars was his. But that was only the beginning. Jake Stein worked out a projection of what it would cost to keep the theatres while they were dark. Stein was a lugubrious man. He regarded himself not simply as an accountant but as the keeper of the flame, a flame that no one else understood and which would be snuffed out if he so much as turned his back. "Max," he said, "it will take every dollar we got. If it wasn't for the bank line, we'd be broke. We got to fire everybody."

"Don't start firing so quick. First thing, I want you to dump the nickelodeons. Sell the chairs and the projectors if you can't sell the leases. But I don't think it'll come to that. National won't give us any film, but if we sell, they'll do business with the buyers. The same thing with the lecture halls. We own three of them. Sell the property. With the rest, sell the leases. The chairs and the projectors go with the sale. We got to realize close to a million."

"Max, you're crazy. You're talking about twenty-three houses. We sell them and what have we got?"

"We got the theatres. The day of the nickelodeon is over. Sure, I know they're opening them all over the place, but it's done. If we don't pull this off, we'll be broke and the hell with it. But if we do, that's the end of the nickelodeon. Who's going to go see a dog jump through a hoop when they can have theatrical entertainment?"

"I still think you're crazy. So we keep the theatres. What do we do, fire everyone? Lock them up?"

"Jake, take it easy," Max said. "Don't be so quick to fire anyone. Let's see how the cash comes in from the nickelodeons. Then we'll know who we got to fire, but maybe nobody. I got to find out how many we need to make a big moving picture, something I don't know where to begin with."

Fred Feldman took another tack. Coming out of hours spent in the law library of his former employer, he informed Max that they had an unshakable action against National Distributors. "Under the Sherman Antitrust Act, it's absolutely clear. There are no loopholes, Max. We got them — in blatant restraint of trade. I think we should sue for ten million dollars."

"You know," Max said, "Sam Snyder can't buy cameras. The word's out, and I think the telephone company's in the deal too."

"Wow! You know what that gives us? That gives us maybe the biggest antitrust action of the year."

"Except that we ain't taking it. Snyder sails for France tomorrow. He can buy all the cameras we need there, and they're better than any cameras we can buy here. He's also bringing twenty thousand feet of film stock back with him. We hired two guys away from Edison, where the pay is lousy, and we'll set up our own laboratory."

"But Max, you got to bring an action against National. We can pin their ears back."

"Freddy," Max said, "what for?"

"They tried to kill us. We return the favor."

"Maybe they done us a favor. I asked Murphy about suing them. He says to go up against people like National and the telephone company and Edison and them cookies up in Rochester, we got as much chance as a snowball in hell. Screw them, Freddy. I got more important things to do."

Among the more important things were two tickets to J. M. Barrie's play *The Admirable Crichton*. It had opened in New York four years earlier, in 1902, to a very good run, and now it was being revived for a limited run of six weeks in the Clarion Theatre on Fourteenth Street. There were plans to tear down the Clarion and erect an apartment house on the site, but Max held an option to buy the old theatre. His option still held for another three months, and during that period the owners took in limited engagements. Crichton was played by Will Fredrickson, a very competent if not great English actor, and the play was directed by a newcomer to the theatre, Gerald Freedman by name. The function of a director in America was still quite recent. While many plays were done with no particular person in charge of the direction, except for the limited participation of the producer, Sally felt that something as untested and complicated as the motion picture they proposed to make required some sort of theatre person to oversee it. Gerald Freedman's parents lived in Flatbush, and they were neighbors of Sally's parents; when Sally's mother heard that she was writing a moving picture, she suggested Freedman as someone who might be helpful. The fact that Freedman was working in a theatre where Max held an option was merely coincidental, but it did help to provide excellent seats.

Sally was uncertain as to what Max's reaction to Barrie's whimsy and satire would be. To her surprise, he loved the play, delighted with the concept of a butler superior to his master, and when they went backstage, he dropped his usual suspicious and cynical approach to shake hands enthusiastically with Gerald Freedman and to insist that he join them for a late supper at Rector's.

Freedman was a year younger than Max, a couple of inches taller, and already balding. He had large, sad brown eyes behind heavy glasses, a long, narrow face, and a prominent nose — a kind of homeliness that was quite attractive and unusual. The revival of the Barrie play was his first important professional job; before it and since his graduation from City College, he had waited tables in the Palm Restaurant on Bleecker Street and had spent all of his spare hours in the theatre, first as a general gofer, then painting scenery, taking small parts when he could get them, and becoming involved in a number of amateur productions at Cooper Union and at the Henry Street Settlement. Thereby his life line had already crossed Max's twice, once on Henry Street and again at the Clarion Theatre; as Max put it, "That's got to mean something, Gerald — Gerry — you don't mind I call you Gerry? You call me Max and Sally is Sally. We're going to be working together a lot, so we won't be formal."

"Of course," Freedman said, "I have to be honest. I'm very excited at the kind of opportunity you're offering me, but I've never made a moving picture of the kind Mrs. Britsky spoke about —"

"Neither did anyone else."

"— or any kind of moving picture. I mean, I have to be truthful. I don't know anything about moving pictures. I have only the vaguest notion of how they are made."

"You went to the nickelodeons?" Max asked him.

"A hundred times, sure."

"Did you see *The Great Train Robbery?*" Sally asked him.

"Oh, yes, yes. Twice."

"Well, if you think of *The Great Train Robbery* as being one incident in a long story that makes some sense, well, that's what we hope to do."

"I still don't see what my role would be."

Max laughed and patted Freedman on the shoulder. Already, at only twenty-seven years, Max was assuming a manner both paternal and feudal. After all, here he was at Rector's, high uptown at Forty-third Street, driven here with his guest in his own carriage, hosting a supper party in what to Max was a restaurant more important if less splendid than Delmonico's. Max did not share in the sense of doom that had overtaken his business associates. When Charley Rector paused at his table to say, "Good to see you, Mr. Britsky, and Mrs. Britsky, lovelier than ever," it was an accolade that he was already taking for granted. He might have had a few hours of doubt after his encounter with Stanford and Calvin, but it had dissipated, and now there were no questions about the ultimate success of their project. He had won this place, sitting here with his wife and young Freedman under the glittering crystal chandeliers, pouring champagne, eating eggs Benedict, taking just a few spoonfuls of the chocolate soufflé he had ordered for dessert, lighting a fine Havana cigar. Let the others have doubts. He knew he would make these moving pictures because he intended to do it, and what he intended, he did.

"When the time comes, Gerry, I'll tell you what your job is."

Not that Max had more than the vaguest idea at that moment. But as he saw it, that was not the important thing. The important thing was to move ahead, to do it.

• • •

The small, cramped, makeshift studio that Edison had built in New Jersey to make his ten-minute films made no sense to Max, but then, neither did he have any clear idea of what a proper moving picture studio should consist of. The Philadelphia operation was being conducted in an old barn, but to Max that was as limited and senseless as Edison's studio. His own thinking was influenced by the legitimate theatres he had taken over and converted into moving picture houses. He admired the backstage height of these old theatres, the way scenery could be pulled up out of sight. He liked the thought of a camera shooting down from thirty or forty feet, although he had never seen such a thing. He was falling into the habit of seeing things with the eye of a camera, squaring off a piece of the reality around him and imagining it on a screen. His distaste for the short subjects shown in the Britsky theatres and nickelodeons had increased over the years, the stupidity and pointlessness becoming something he watched with either indifference or annoyance, and as he sought for a place to make his own films, his excitement at what he proposed to do increased. Day after day, he prowled the streets of Lower Manhattan, rejecting all the suggestions that he might find what he was looking for in New Jersey or in the Bronx. Downtown New York was his home base, his place of sustenance. He had to be there. And finally he found it.

It was an old ice house on Eighteenth Street, between Ninth and Tenth avenues, a building forty feet wide, one hundred feet deep, with a ceiling sixty feet high. The ceiling was the roof of the building, and the inner space was clear except for stairs and landings climbing the rear wall. There was a dray loading platform off the back that opened onto Seventeenth Street. When used as an ice house, the ice would be stacked, the large blocks separated with sawdust, from floor to ceiling, and then sold off for shipping from the top down. Now the place was empty, except for piles of sawdust on the floor. The real estate agent who showed it to Max told him that it could be had for fifteen thousand dollars. The new ice houses had hydraulic elevators; this one was too small and narrow to make the installation worthwhile. "Which makes me wonder," the real estate man said, "what you intend to do with it."

"Make money," Max answered succinctly.

Feldman was dubious as he drew up the papers for the purchase of the ice house. "It's a crazy building, Max. Suppose we have to sell it. Who'll buy it?"

"In five years, the lot it stands on will be worth twice what we paid for the building. Trouble is, Freddy, you worry about things."

"That's what you pay me for."

Sam Snyder, on the other hand, was delighted with the building. He returned from France a few days after the purchase was completed, bringing with him the cameras and the thousands of feet of film stock, filled with excitement and news: namely, that George Melies, the French filmmaker, was planning the same kind of dramatic film production Sally had suggested. Undoubtedly, it was in the air. "The thing is, Max," Sam said, "that the National crowd can't keep our theatres dark. There'll be moving pictures like ours in France and in England too."

As for the ice house, Snyder pointed out that many things had to be done, electric power brought in for super-illumination, fans for ventilation, sets to be built once they knew what the story would be, electricians and carpenters to be hired. "It's easy to talk about," he said to Max, "but when it comes down to doing it, it's one big son of a bitch, and then if those talking cards of Sally's don't work, we can dump the whole thing."

"They'll work," Max assured him.

Meanwhile, Gerry Freedman had become almost a daily visitor at the house on Sixty-sixth Street. Sally had never met anyone quite like him. To some extent, he shared Max's trait of self-confidence, but he brought with it a sensitivity that Max had never exhibited. He seemed to anticipate Sally's thoughts, to know what her response would be even before he made a suggestion. Without his help and encouragement, she certainly would have abandoned the project, dismissing what she had done as absurd and unworthy.

As far as Freedman was concerned, that first night at Rector's found him completely entranced with Sally Britsky. Each to his own taste. Bert Bellamy described Sally as a frightened mouse. Others saw her as an attractive woman. Max accepted the compliments on the subject of Sally's appearance as, in his words, "political horseshit," since most of it came from men connected in one way or another with Tammany. Once, when he used the expression to Murphy, Murphy said, "It has a nicer sound in Irish, my lad. Just blarney." Yet it never entered Max's mind that Gerald Freedman or any other man could fall in love with Sally. Sally was his wife, the mother of his children, even though she had never been very much of a sexual object as far as Max was concerned, and once Richard and Marion had come into the world, Max and Sally's sexual relationship practically ceased. It was two years since Marion Britsky had entered the realm of the living, but Sally still used the aftereffects of birth and nursing as an excuse to refrain from sex.

Max was entirely willing to go along with her, being comfortable in his relationship with Etta Goodman. His horror of venereal disease still persisted from his youth, but in his mind Etta was a nice, clean Jewish girl, and that she might remain that way, he said,

"From here on in, you don't look at another man. Understood?"

"Sure, I understand. So why don't you leave that skinny nothing and marry me?"

"You know I don't like that kind of talk."

"So let me tell you something, Mr. Britsky. Don't think I never looked in a mirror. I'm five times as beautiful as your schoolteacher, and maybe I ain't a schoolteacher, but I'm as smart as she is, so don't you tell me I can't look at another man."

The next time he saw Etta, he presented her with a two-hundred-dollar watch pin to wear on her shirtwaist. But, unmollified, Etta snorted, "She gets a mansion and a carriage. I get a watch pin."

When Sally suggested that they might both be more comfortable in twin beds, Max made no protest, although his mother said in no uncertain terms, "It's absolutely the most disgusting thing. It's a shame to everyone's eyes."

"Sally wants it that way."

"She wants the moon, so go give her the moon."

"She hasn't been able to sleep so well since Marion's birth."

"God forbid she should lose a night's sleep. Your mother could go without sleep for a week, you don't lift a finger. But Sally don't sleep so good, so right away she needs a separate bed."

Yet the last thing in the world Sally would have considered was an act of unfaithfulness, even as a mild flirtation. In her world, such things did not happen. Freedman was a friend, someone she could talk to. There was nothing wrong with having a friend. Max felt the same way. He was pleased that Freedman and Sally got along so well. He was aware that he needed talent like Gerald Freedman's for this new venture he had embarked on. He was more than conscious of his own lack of education, and he did not deceive himself into believing that his glibness and his gift for dissembling substituted for knowledge. There was a whole world apart from himself, the world of theatre and books and art, and this world was shrouded in a kind of darkness that confused and troubled him. Freedman was an asset, just as Sally was an asset, and more to the point, Freedman was a man. Max could not cope with the notion that a woman could deal with complex creative problems, just as he could not even entertain the notion that Sally might be unfaithful to him. For all that he valued Freedman's education and potential skill and taste, he could not imagine Freedman as competition for Sally's affection. Freedman simply did not conform to any of Max's definitions of attractive masculinity.

Freedman and Sally worked together for five weeks. The fact that they had no previous models to compare with and no tradition to guide them gave them a degree of freedom they would not have possessed were they doing a theatrical play, and the fact that neither of them possessed the skill or experience to create a traditional drama did not inhibit them. They were not in competition with Shaw or Ibsen; they were not in competition with anyone, not even with themselves, for they had no real critical faculties, and thus they worked on excitedly yet amiably to the final product.

In those five weeks, Max had accomplished a great deal. The leases on the nickelodeons and the equity in the converted lecture halls had been sold; the purchase of the ice house had gone through, and a crew of carpenters and electricians had been working there under Sam Snyder's direction. The ten legitimate theatres had been closed down, and were being cleaned and refurbished. When they reopened, Max's intention was to charge fifty cents in the orchestra and thirty cents in the balcony, which would result in a cash flow, according to his rough calculations, of at least double the amount the whole chain took in at the time of closing. He had been spending money with a kind of royal abandon, convinced that this throw of the dice must work. And at the end of the five weeks, they gathered at Max's home to hear the results of the efforts of Sally and Gerald Freedman.

Sally slipped into the background. Somewhere, just below her threshold of conscious awareness, she understood that the projection of a woman as a major factor in their scheme might create opposition and resistance; when they were gathered in the living room, she explained that Freedman would outline the camera work, and at the appropriate moments, she would hold up one or another of the stack of dialogue cards that rested in her lap. She had arranged it this way in spite of Freedman's opposition and in spite of the fact that she had done most of the creative work.

"You're going to photograph those cards?" Fred Feldman asked.

"That's our plan, yes." She turned to Snyder. "No problem about that, is there, Sam?"

"None at all. But how long do you figure to hold on each card?"

Sally glanced at Freedman, who explained, "We try to limit a dialogue card to twelve words, except for prepositions and conjunctions and pronouns. Most are less than twelve words —"

Sally read the look on Max's face and said quickly, "Words like 'and,' 'but,' 'I,' 'you,' 'she,' 'he' — we don't count those because we feel they will respond to quick recognition. But even so, we tried to make the dialogue lines very short. It's not always possible."

"I don't know," Max said. "People don't go around talking in two or three words."

"But this isn't real," Freedman said. "I think it works. Now in answer to Sam's question, we worked out the dialogue in two ways. First we would read a card the way you read a book, to yourself. We found we could read the twelve words comfortably in six seconds. Then we mouthed them, because that's the way people read who have learned to read as adults — I mean people of limited education who still struggle with the language — and that takes twice as long, about twelve seconds."

"And I think," Sally added, "that many people will read aloud. I mean, if someone brings his mother or father and they're immigrants and can't read English, wouldn't you think he'd read aloud?"

"Hopefully in a whisper," Freedman said.

"Of course, if we must have more than twelve words, we can increase the card time."

"We'll worry about that later," Max said. "Let's get going."

"Sure, here goes," Freedman agreed. "Our title first. We call this *Jennifer, Child of the Street.*"

"Jennifer? What the hell kind of a name is Jennifer?"

"Well, we shorten it. I mean, in the picture it's Jenny."

"So why shouldn't it be Jenny in the title?"

"Come on, Max," Bert said. "Let him get on with it."

"No reason why it can't be Jenny in the title," Freedman said. "We call her Jenny, in any case. She lives with her mother and father in a cold-water flat downtown. The father's name is Joe Kent, and he's a drunkard and a brute. Sometimes he works as a stevedore down on the docks, but mostly he doesn't work, and the family ekes out its poor existence from the sewing the mother does and from the pencils Jenny sells on the street. The mother, whose name is Alice, is crippled. Of course, this is just background to the story itself —"

"But if it's background," Fred Feldman broke in, "how do you tell it? You don't print it all out on cards, do you?"

"Oh, no. No. We show it in the action. The action is more important than anything else. I'm simply placing Jenny."

Sally held up the first card: "All his money spent on booze, Joe Kent comes home."

"We've established the apartment at this point," Freedman said. "It's our first set. Alice, the mother, sits at her sewing table. Then the card. You see, while most cards are dialogue, we must have a few that are simply exposition. Alice looks up with a smile at first. Then, seeing Joe reeling drunk, her smile fades. She spreads her arms to show hopeless disapproval. He waves an arm and curses her. Then Jenny runs into the room."

Sally held up the second card: "Don't say such things to Mother. You're drunk."

"He turns on Jenny and strikes her. The mother rises with a superhuman effort, then falls to the floor. Jenny gets up from her knees and runs to her mother, then kneeling with her arms around her mother. She confronts her father as he approaches."

Sally held up a card: "Don't touch her."

"Would you know Jenny is speaking?" Bert asked.

"Oh, no doubt of that. We would put the camera directly on Jenny. She speaks the words, then the card. Then we go back to Joe Kent with the camera as he stalks around the room in his fury, knocking furniture around, turning back in anger on his wife and daughter. Then we put the camera on them to show their frightened, hopeless response. Then back on Joe Kent, who turns to them, curses them once more, goes to the cupboard, finds a bottle of hooch, and drains it. Then he flings the bottle against the wall, turns to curse his wife and daughter once again, and exits, slamming the door behind him. Now we move the camera around to another angle to include Alice and Jenny. Alice speaks to her."

Sally held up a card: "He wasn't always this way. He was kind before he became a drunkard."

Freedman looked up from his manuscript. "I must say that once Sally and I got into this, we realized that we could do things we never thought about — I mean moving the camera from place to place. In the next scene, Jenny leaves her home to go to her work of selling pencils. This she must do so that her family may survive.

I would like to show her going down the stairs in the cold-water tenement. Could we do that, Sam?"

"I think we could work it out," Snyder said. "It's just a question of getting enough light in the place."

"And follow her out into the street?"

"Why not?"

He turned back to the manuscript. "I have a lot of details in here," Freedman said, "but the main thing is that this poor, sick child goes out on the street to sell her pencils —"

"Child? What's a child?" Max demanded. "How old is she?"

"Eighteen," Sally said.

"What kind of sickness?" Feldman wanted to know.

"We don't specify. It's not necessary. It could be simple malnutrition, hunger, not enough to eat. Anyway, she's out there on the street, pleading with people to buy her pencils, and they don't. They pass her by, and then suddenly she collapses in a faint."

"You see," Sally put in, "it can be done. We've moved the story to this point with only three dialogue cards and one card of exposition. Do you like it so far, Max?"

"Yeah, I like it so far, but you got to know where it's going. I get the picture all right — the drunken old bum and the mother and this poor kid — but I want to know where it's going."

Freedman nodded. "Yes, of course. We have the scene where she faints, and a crowd gathers. But you know the way a crowd is in New York. They look, but they don't do anything. Now here," he said, tapping the manuscript, "we put in directions about how we think the cameras should be placed, and we keep doing that, but I don't think you want all that because that way we can lose the story. Wouldn't you agree with me, Sally?"

"Absolutely. I think you should just tell the story, and then whenever the proper place comes, I'll hold up the proper dialogue card."

"That makes sense," Max agreed. "I think we're beginning to see how the dialogue cards work, so let's have the story."

"Fine. Now at the same moment, more or less, that Jenny falls down in her faint, a chauffeur-driven limousine automobile comes along, one of those big new cars, and this one belongs to our leading man, whose name is Manfred Van Dyme. He is about twenty-six years old, and he's the only son of a very rich old New York family that goes way back to the Dutch. He's like one of those people Richard Harding Davis writes about, so rich that he doesn't have to work for a living, but all the same a very decent person."

"Not if he's anything like the bankers I deal with," Max said.

"Well, no. He's not in business. He's a gentleman of leisure, and he drifts around in his automobile when he isn't strolling on the avenue. The point is that his car reaches a point opposite Jenny just as she faints."

Sally held up a card: "Pull over, Johnson."

"Johnson's the chauffeur's name. The car pulls over, and Manfred leaps out, pushes through the crowd, and bends over Jenny."

"Why didn't somebody call an ambulance?" Jake Stein wanted to know.

"Jake, it's a story!" Max snapped.

"Well, Manfred sees this beautiful young woman lying there in a faint, and he's touched. He's deeply touched, and he also gazes with anger at those people standing around who haven't enough compassion to do something to help this poor, beautiful young woman. So he picks her up in his arms and carries her to his car. Johnson holds the door open for him, and Manfred places her on a seat and climbs in. Now at this point, Sally and I felt that we could do something that appears to be practical but which we've never seen done. I guess Sam is the one to tell us whether it's possible."

"Name it, Gerry. I'll do my best."

"Well, it's like this, Sam. He picks her up, say, on Fourteenth Street. Now we feel the Van Dyme mansion should be on Fifth Avenue, one of those new graystone houses in the Fifties or in the Sixties. Now he's going to drive her home with him —"

"Home?" Max demanded. "Wait a minute. Maybe I don't know exactly how the classy uptown bluebloods live, but sure as hell there ain't nobody's going to pick up a broad on the street and take her home and present her to Mama and Papa. Not to the papas I've dealt with."

"No, Max," Sally said. "You're getting ahead of us. Manfred's mother and father are away touring Europe. It's the thing with such people. I'm always reading how they're touring the Continent. And you must understand that Manfred's a most unusual man."

"O.K., he's got to be Santa Claus in plain clothes — but why not? I guess every poor kid dreams of something like that."

"Back to your question, Gerry," Snyder reminded him.

"Yes. Well, what we were wondering is whether you could mount a camera on a dray, or on one of those automobile trucks, and then keep photographing Manfred's car as he drives from Fourteenth Street to upper Fifth Avenue. We might need police cooperation, but Max tells me that's no problem. Could we do it?"

"Hey, why nobody ever thought of that, I don't know. Well, sort of. They put a camera on a train and moved along with galloping horses. But this, it's different, isn't it? If we put the camera in front of Manfred's car, then the car would be going right at the audience —"

"If you set up two or three cameras along the way — or even one camera if you moved it," Sally broke in excitedly, "then you'd see the car from one position and then from another."

"Wait a minute!" Max exclaimed. "Why don't you put the camera right in the car with Manfred, next to the chauffeur?"

"Too close."

"No room."

"But you know," Sam Snyder cried, his excitement mounting, "if we could do what Max wants — I mean, even if we have to build some special kind of automobile with a platform or something — it would be spectacular."

They were all caught up in the excitement now, seeing an endless procession of pictures and possibilities between Fourteenth Street and Fifth Avenue. Suddenly, Manfred Van Dyme and Jenny Kent were no longer ridiculous paper figures but realities, pillars of hope for their future. Reinforced with new confidence and authority, Gerald Freedman went on with the story, Sally exhibiting her dialogue cards proudly. "In his magnificent limousine, Manfred carries Jenny to his Fifth Avenue mansion, carries her inside in his arms, and lays her gently in a big fourposter bed. She is very weak. Her eyelids flutter. The servants in the house are aghast. Who is this creature that Manfred brings into this house? Manfred cares nothing for their snide whispering. He summons a doctor, for already he is in love with Jenny. The doctor arrives, examines Jenny, and then informs Manfred that her possibilities for survival are narrow indeed. She appears to be dying."

The dialogue card Sally exhibited read: "Dying! Can this kind of beauty die? Never! You must save her!"

"It is Manfred who makes this speech, and when the doctor spreads his arms and shakes his head in despair, Manfred speaks again, the longest dialogue card in the film: 'No, she will not die! She must not die! Until now, my life has been empty and meaningless. We will spare no cost, no effort, to save her!' "

"You're not letting her die?" Max demanded.

"No. Oh, no. Let me go on.

"Manfred takes up a vigil by Jenny's bedside. She regains her health. Manfred takes her shopping in the best stores, buys her beautiful clothes, a fur coat. Manfred's mother and father are still in Europe. Jenny's father tracks her down, appears at the Fifth Avenue mansion, accuses Manfred of kidnapping his daughter. Jenny weeps, begs her father to go away. But since she is under age, she must go with him. The father returns with a policeman, and he, the policeman, enforces the father's right to Jenny. Manfred watches them depart."

"And he doesn't do a damned thing?" Max exclaimed indignantly.

"What can he do?" Sally said. "The law is with Mr. Kent."

"But life wreaks its vengeance on the cruel, alcoholic Mr. Kent. He is struck down by a team of dray horses and he dies. But Manfred knows nothing of this. His life is empty. His parents return from Europe. Meanwhile, Jenny is once again the sole support of her crippled mother, selling her pencils on the street. And there, again, Manfred sees her. He faces her, begs her to come with him. She refuses. His world is one thing; hers is another. The two cannot mix. But Manfred follows her home. He then sends his lawyer to her, to inform her that a distant relative has died, leaving her a bequest of ten thousand dollars. She accepts the check tearfully. Her mother is sick, her condition worsening, but now Jenny can send her to the hospital. But her mother dies in spite of all efforts to save her. The only mourner at the cemetery, apparently, is Jenny, who stands alone at the grave as her mother is buried."

Sally held up a card: "Alone. All alone in the world. What will I do?"

"And as she stands there," Freedman read, "Manfred appears from where he stood behind a tree. Manfred goes to her. She turns to face him. Manfred speaks."

Sally held up the last of her cards: "No. You have never been alone. I was always beside you. I always will be."

"And that's it," Sally said.

They were touched and moved, and they applauded with a round of enthusiastic hand-clapping. The only one of Max's associates who had a college education was Fred Feldman, and his barely touched on literature or drama. Sally's own normal school training had not included judgmental comparisons of dramatic works, and neither she nor Freedman was particularly gifted in playwriting. They had no tradition against which to measure their work; and out of their moment in history, they all shared a sentimental unwillingness to face the facts of their own existence. The reality of life around them —the filth, the misery, the social cruelty, the hopelessness of so many, the poverty and hunger that they had seen and faced throughout their lives — created no artistic reflection. Their ability to sense sentiment was drowned in sentimentality, out of which came their approval and applause. Sally was so pleased that tears welled into her eyes, and Bert Bellamy said, "Max, you're absolutely right. Something like this — well, we open in every theatre at the same time. We'll turn them away."

Fred Feldman thought the wealthy parents had been neglected. "We ought to see them meet Jenny," he said.

But for Max, it was a question of time above everything else. "We got to move," he told them. "I got theatres sitting empty. Maybe it works or maybe we go down the hole. Either way, we got to move."

•   •   •

Two days later, Max went into his office and found Etta Goodman sitting behind his desk, reading the scenario that Sally and Freedman had written. "Don't move," he said to her. "Just go on sitting there. Only you should have told me you were taking over so we could have an office party to celebrate it."

"Max, I'm not taking over. I just saw this sitting on the desk, and so I sat down here."

"You stick your nose into everything that's on my desk?"

"Only some things." She came around the desk and kissed his cheek. "I like it."

"What?"

"*Jennifer, Child of the Street*, only that's a stupid name."

"Suddenly you're an expert on names."

"It sounds fishy."

"Suppose you let us worry about the name. Now get your ass out of here so I can get some work done."

But instead of leaving the room, Etta moved away from Max until she stopped by his desk, all the while staring at him, and then said almost explosively, "You going to make this into a moving picture?"

"That's right."

"It's wonderful."

"Thanks for your permission. Now beat it."

She didn't move. "Max, all these years you been having sex with me, like I'm a piece of furniture here, and I never asked for nothing and I never got nothing —"

"You got a job! You got paid!"

"What do you mean, I got paid!" she burst out. "I'm no whore. You pay me for having a job here. Maybe I'm not smart, but I try to do whatever work you give me. I do my best. But being a lay — that's free! Sally's got the whole world — the house on Sixty-sixth Street, your kids, a car to drive her around, clothes, jewels, fur coats — and I got *bubkas*. I take care of you, I get fucked by you, I run out to get you coffee and sandwiches, and when you're working late, who goes over to Rosenstein's to tell them what to make you for supper and to bring it to you? Me, me, me, and for what? For what?" She burst into tears, and tears in a woman was something Max could hardly abide. He went to her and put his arms around her.

"Listen, kid. Let me tell you something about that house on Sixty-sixth Street. I sleep there, period. That's all. And the two kids I got, I see them for a few minutes if I'm lucky, and then it's hands off. They got a goddamn German nurse who talks to them in German, because my wife is raising them to be a couple of stinking uptown German Jews. So there it is. Big deal, yes?"

"But what have I got?"

"You got a good job and you got me."

"And in the end, what will I be? A used-up, dried-up old maid."

"No, no, no." Max reassured her. "We'll find you a husband."

"What the hell do you mean, you'll find me a husband?" she exclaimed, pulling back from him.

"You shouldn't be an old maid."

"I don't want no husband. I love you."

"All right, all right. So go dry your eyes and clean up your face."

"No!"

"What the devil has gotten into you, Etta?"

She leaned over the desk and picked up the scenario, thrusting it at Max. "This."

"This? What the hell are you talking about?"

"You're going to make a big moving picture out of this, right?"

"Right."

"So you're going to need someone to play the part of Jennifer, an actress."

"That's right."

"I want it. I want to play the part of Jennifer."

"What!"

"Exactly," Etta said, dropping the script on the desk and suddenly becoming very calm.

"Etta, Etta, this is something I'm spending thousands of dollars on so it should be something. I need an actress."

"I'm an actress."

"Since when?"

"Since two years I been taking classes on Second Avenue over Moshe's dairy restaurant with teachers like Mr. Adler and Mr. Emmelman. So maybe I'll never be a Sarah Bernhardt, but I can act enough for your moving picture if you only give me a chance."

"You're crazy."

"So I'm crazy. Max, why don't you take a look at me? You been sleeping with me for years, but you never look at me."

He looked at her then and realized that what she said was quite true. He had never really looked at her the way one might look at a woman one had never seen before. She was a bit taller than he could have testified to had he been asked, more slender. Perhaps because Sally's breasts were so small, Etta's full breasts had always given him the impression of a person plumper than she was. Her brown hair was thick and rich, her brows straight, her eyes large and dark, her nose small and straight, and her lips full over a rounded chin. "Mr. Fritz Emmelman, my dramatic teacher, thinks I'm beautiful," Etta said.

"Yeah, sure, you're a good-looking kid. Sure. Did I ever say you were a dog? But actress —" Max shook his head. "Nah. You're nuts. Forget it."

"I'm not going to forget it, Max," Etta said, her face tightening. "You know what I think —"

"I don't want to know what you think. I want you to stop being a pain in the ass and get out of here."

"You know, Max, I always used to be afraid of you because I said to myself, if I did something you didn't like, you'd stop loving me and you'd fire me. Well, you know something, I got to realize you don't love me, and it's just convenient for you to have someone in the office to screw whenever you get horny, and you're not going to fire me anyway. And you know why? Because if you fire me, I can go straight to the classy Mrs. Sally Britsky and tell her, 'You know what, your husband, Max, has been screwing me for years, even the night before your wedding, not to mention a week later —' "

"You wouldn't?"

"Maybe I would and maybe I wouldn't," Etta said archly.

"You're not that kind of a bitch. We got too much going between us, Etta. When did I ever threaten to fire you?"

"Maybe this is the first time, but you see, Max, I'm going to tell you what I think whether you want to know about it or not. I think that most girls never get a chance, and sometimes you get one chance in a whole lifetime, and for me this is it. I want that part in your moving picture, and if I don't get it, I don't care what happens."

"But it's not up to me alone," Max protested. "There's this guy, Freedman, who's directing it, and there's Sally, and Sam Snyder —"

"Come on, Max, don't kid me. Nobody around here pees without you say it's all right."

"Yeah. Well, I don't know. Maybe."

• • •

The casting of Etta as Jennifer was done forthrightly, with no tricks, once Max had decided that he had one of two choices: either to give in to her request or hire someone to kill her. Since the second alternative was impossible, not only because he held Etta in great affection, but because he was incapable of doing away with a puppy dog, much less a human being, he decided to give her the part. Once he made this decision, he did not beat about the bush but called Freedman into his office and put it to him straightforwardly.

"You're kidding," Freedman said bewilderedly.

"I'm not kidding, Gerald, and I'm not being funny. I want Etta Goodman to be in this picture playing the part of Jennifer."

"But she's not an actress."

"Who says so?"

"Where has she studied? Where has she played?"

"You know something, Gerald," Max said, "you and me, maybe we'll have a long and profitable association, maybe not. You got more brains than I have and you got education and culture, but one thing you got to learn, or right now we're finished."

Freedman waited.

"A very simple fact. I'm the boss. I take the risk, I put up the money, it's my neck stuck out. You know what's making this picture if it ever gets made, not you and Sally and the actors and Snyder and his crew, but me. You know why it's me? It's me because I want it to be made, and if I didn't want it to be made and put up the money and kick everyone's ass around, it wouldn't get made. And if you think that's a lot of horseshit, just answer me why we're sitting here in the United States of America, with nickelodeons all over the place from California to Kansas to Philadelphia, and there ain't nobody except Max Britsky who gets the idea that maybe instead of the brainless shit that they show in every one of these nickelodeons, there can be a real story maybe an hour and a half long."

Since Freedman had not been at the meeting where Sally had broached the idea, and since Sally then and later took no credit, he did not feel that he could challenge Max's statement. Certainly, it contained the unarguable fact of power.

"And about Miss Goodman," Max went on, "she can't act? Maybe yes, maybe no. That's up to you. You'll get her to act. She's a pretty young lady. Her father," Max added, "is a dear friend. I promised him. It's a promise I can't get out of, so I got to deliver." Max made a mental note to find out whether Etta's father was alive or dead.

"I wish you weren't caught in this," Freedman said understandingly, half believing him.

"But I am, so that's that. Only one thing. Etta Goodman is as glamorous a name as Max Britsky. We got to call her something else. So give me something sounds like the lady is maybe another Duse."

"Another Duse?"

"That's right."

Half jokingly and unaware that he was making film history, Freedman answered, "Feona Amour."

"Feona Amour. What the hell kind of a name is that? Feona? I never met no Feona."

"Well, Feona is English or Welsh — I know it's a name you find in the British Isles — and Amour — well, that's French for love. I just threw both names out. I wasn't being very serious. You know, I haven't met Miss Goodman. Possibly it would be better if I met her, and then I could suggest a name."

"No. Tell you something, I like it. I like the sound. Feona Amour. That's it. She is Feona Amour."

Thus Etta was named and placed among the immortals, but that was only the beginning of the confusion that surrounded the making of The Waif. It was not Freedman but Bert Bellamy who let drop to Sally that Feona Amour was the same Etta Goodman who had been Max's personal assistant, a comfortable euphemism suggested by a slight twitch in Bert's lips. When Sally demanded an explanation from Freedman, he dissembled and informed her that Max had a debt to Etta's father. What resulted was the first rage Sally had ever given in to, screaming at Max, "It's not what you did at the office, but to take my work and give it to her! That is foul, filthy and foul!"

Here was a side of Sally Max had never seen before. Could this be the same shy, gentle, soft-spoken woman he had known and married?

"You loathsome son of a bitch!" she cried.

He had never dreamed that she knew the words. Women didn't swear — unless of course they were floozies.

"You've been sleeping with her," Sally hissed.

"I swear to God I haven't! Sally, on my mother's name, I swear!"

"Your mother!"

"Sally —"

She stalked out of the room into her own private workroom, which adjoined the bedroom. When Max found the courage to follow her a few minutes later, he found her engaged in methodically tearing each copy of the scenario to shreds.

He grabbed her arm. "Don't! Please!"

"Let go of me!" She picked up a pair of scissors on her desk and pointed them threateningly at Max.

"You wouldn't!"

"Oh, I would, I would, I certainly would."

For the following three weeks, Sally did not talk to Max, but she had a number of long, heart-to-heart talks with Freida. It was a time when divorce was still most unusual and when women did not break up a marriage over an act of adultery. Sally had by now lived long enough in Max's world to lose whatever innocence she still might have retained after her marriage, and as Freida assured her, few marriages were any better.

"At least Max isn't a bum," Freida said. "He doesn't beat you up and he's not a drunk and he loves the kids and I think that in his own way he loves you."

Fortunately, the dialogue cards remained, undamaged by Sally's fury. They had been sent to a sign painting company to be hand-lettered, although by the time the picture was finished, most of the dialogue cards had been replaced with new dialogue, written by practically everyone concerned with the making of the film. Also, happily, Max had a copy of the scenario at his office.

Freedman persuaded Eric Sims, who had designed the sets for Gounod's *Faust* at the Metropolitan Opera House, to do the basic interiors for the movie, and while Max howled at his fee of three thousand dollars, he decided finally that the association of so exalted a name as Eric Sims with his project was worth the price. He was spending money now at a rate that numbed him, but like a child, he exulted at the action and confusion inside the old ice house — the carpenters building the sets, the electricians with their wires and cables, the painters and drapery people and carpet people and the procession of actors in and out for the casting. Nothing like this had ever happened to Max in the past. He had transformed storefronts into nickelodeons and lecture halls into moving picture houses, but this thing of making something out of nothing, of a creation out of the whole cloth — this was new and more exciting than anything else he had turned his hand to.

He was constantly frustrated by his lack of knowledge, his lack of judgment in creative matters, his general lack of education, his ignorance of the technology they were using, and to compensate, he bludgeoned those around him and played the boss more and more dictatorially. Yet Max, more than anyone else engaged in the project, had some sort of subconscious realization that what they were doing would be a factor in changing the history of the human race. He could not have phrased it that way, but a sense of the power of those shadows reflected on the silver screen had pervaded his mind for years, had grown and become a part of his being.

But perhaps because he could make no philosophical approach to his life and career, he had no way to take the hardening edges of his personality in hand, to smooth them, and to allow his life to come into focus. So when Bert Bellamy said to him, "What in hell is happening to you, Max? You're becoming a son of a bitch," Max replied, "Maybe it's time."

He had just blown up at Sam Snyder after some test shots showed that the lighting was inadequate. The film had developed dark and muddy, and it meant they would lose three days rewiring, aside from the additional cost. Snyder met the attack by staring at Max blankly and uncomprehendingly.

Sam Snyder was a plump, easygoing man, a family man devoted to his stout wife and his five children, content with his work and with the variety of excellent German dishes his wife produced — and, from the very beginning, the link between Thomas Edison as a source and the driving energy of Max Britsky. Since Max bought the ice house on Eighteenth Street, Snyder had seen his family hardly at all, first making the trip to Europe, then working twelve and fourteen hours a day turning the building into a studio. He was totally devoted to Max and crushed by Max's anger. Bert was witness to the scene, and demanded of Max. "Why? Without Sam, we'd all be dead."

Max went to Sam and apologized. "I don't know what's happening to me," Max told him. "Jesus, Sam, you got to be the best friend I got in the world."

"I thought so."

"You don't hold it against me? You know something, Sam, you could turn around and walk out on me, and all I'd do would be to blow my brains out."

"I wouldn't walk out on you, Max. You know that."

Max made amends with money. He always made amends with money. He raised Snyder's salary to ten thousand a year, a princely sum for the time and enough to drive Jake Stein to tears. "Do you know what we're spending each day?" Stein demanded of Max. "It's all outgoing, and not a dime coming in." Then Max bought an ermine coat for Sally — except that he had to buy two of them. If he bought an ermine coat for Sally and not for his mother, Sarah would give him no peace. Of course, when Sally discovered that he had purchased the same coat for his mother, she refused to wear hers. At the same time, Gerry Freedman was insisting that Sally be consulted on the casting. The battles over that went both ways.

"I don't want her here," Max said. "A wife's a wife. She's got everything in the world. She's got two kids to take care of."

Day by day, Freedman was beginning to realize the enormity of the project he had undertaken. "You don't understand, Mr. Britsky," he told Max. "Mrs. Britsky is very modest, but this is her creation, her story. It's true that I helped her, but she's the one who conceived it, and she can be very helpful." He might have added that Eric Sims, a middle-aged homosexual, had made advances to Freedman which Freedman rejected somewhat crudely, after which Sims would not talk to him. On the other hand, Sims was charmed with Sally.

But Sally was by no means charmed with Max's request that she become a part of the company at the ice house. "With that little whore of yours lording it over things!"

"Come on, come on, Sally. Etta Goodman is not a whore."

"Of course not. She's the daughter of some fine gentleman to whom you have a great obligation. You are a prince, Max."

"Come on, Sally —"

"I spoke to her father."

Max was silent. Etta's father had been dead these five years.

"You know," Max said meekly, "this picture, it ain't —"

"*Isn't*," Sally interrupted. "Oh, why do I bother?"

"Because you like me, at least a little. It isn't only for you and me. There are also the kids. I got ten theatres standing empty. If this don't work, Sally, it's all gone. Everything."

"I want you to tell that little bitch to keep out of my way."

Not only was Sally different, but her language was different. In one short argument, she had used the words "whore" and "bitch." It was incredible. But she was not the only one caught up in the process of change. Etta Goodman died a quick death; Feona Amour stepped into life full blown.

As Feona, Etta had begun the process of being a star, even though no such thing existed. It was not that she possessed any sort of prescience or had any inkling of herself as the founder of a dynasty; it was simply the emergence of her previously crushed spirit as the burgeoning of a monster. It began with the dressmaker who fitted her for costumes, continued with the hairdresser, and came to fruition in the process of casting. Freedman had a large cast to fill within a limited budget. He could make only a very rough estimate of how long it would take to film the story, and since the time was in doubt, he hesitated to try to engage important actors from New York's legitimate theatre. Instead, he turned to the Yiddish Theatre, which was at the height of its glory and which had created on Second Avenue below Fourteenth Street a theatrical center that rivaled the uptown English-speaking theatre. Also, actors in the Yiddish Theatre came out of the Eastern European tradition; not only were they frequently brilliant as thespians, but their emotional level was much higher and their movements more explicit than those of the actors on the New York stage, who were deeply influenced by the British style. Yiddish actors moved their arms, clenched and unclenched their hands, turned their whole bodies into instruments of expression, and since none of the spoken words would be heard, Freedman felt that this specific quality would incur to his advantage. And since they would be silent, engaging in a sort of mime, the fact that they spoke English poorly and often with a heavy accent made no difference.

Feona objected. "They all sound like my grandfather. It's ridiculous. And she" — pointing to Julia Schwartz, who had played in Europe opposite Sarah Bernhardt and who even now, at fifty-five, was one of the great ladies of the Yiddish Theatre — "she is impossible."

Thus a star is born. Freedman pleaded, suffered, connived, and somehow managed. For Sally, it was the breath of life renewed. She realized that since she had given up teaching, her life had been squeezed into a shell of boredom. She was not a housekeeper; she could not exist in caring for two small children; and her increasing bitterness was largely the result of sheer frustration. Working with Freedman in a project that was both creative and fascinating, she found herself. But it was not until they actually began to play the scenes in front of the camera that Sally realized how novel and original their project was. Piece by piece, they worked it out, staring with wonder and excitement at each piece of film that came back from the laboratory. At times the scene was a total disaster, the focus clear in one part and blurred in another, and it would have to be redone. Again, a scene would lack a point of attention. Everyone threw ideas into the hopper, the actors included, and of course Max, whose eye was strangely vivid and clear in terms of what the camera could do. It was his notion to add a second and then a third camera. Sally insisted on a swiveled coupling. Fred Feldman, near-sighted, complained of being unable to make out faces. They tried a new kind of spotlighting, and then they tried moving the camera in on a specific person. Sam Snyder, working on focus, went to New Jersey and consulted with his old pals still working for Edison. They discovered that they needed new lenses, but there was no time to invent and make them. So they improvised.

There were days when the old ice house turned into a battleground, with the actors screaming at Max in Yiddish and Max shouting back in his own kitchen variety of the language, Freedman pleading for peace and Feona waving her arms regally, and Isadore Melchik, the famous Second Avenue tragedian who had been persuaded to play the role of Dr. Anthony Leighton, whispering, "Meshuganas, madmen, I have been given into a den of madmen, with a witless dunce who calls herself Feona." Fortunately, Feona understood no Yiddish — fortunate in this instance, but very unfortunate at other times when the Yiddish Theatre members of the cast joined in opposition to Etta Goodman and Pasquel Massoni. Massoni, a tall, handsome, dark-eyed Italian, had been hired by Freedman to play the part of Manfred Van Dyme since no one in the Yiddish Theatre suited Sally's concept and the few who did in the English-speaking theatre were otherwise engaged. Massoni claimed that he had been one of the leading men in the rather famous Vittorio Repertory Company of Milan, and when they toured the States in 1905, he parted company with them and decided to try his fortunes in the American theatre. Since his English was minimal and since he had survived as a waiter in Dino's Spaghetti Hole on Mott Street, Freedman found his story dubious; but his appearance was so striking, his profile so excellent, his hair so wonderfully curled in black ringlets, that Freedman decided to take a chance. "After all," he said to Sally, "if I can teach Feona to be Jennifer, then I can teach Pasquel to be Manfred Van Dyme." Sally agreed with his choice, Pasquel Massoni being so pleasant to look upon that she was certain his lack of talent and English would be forgiven.

On the other hand, the Yiddish Theatre members of the cast promptly dubbed him the *luksh*, *luksh* being a shortened version of *luckshon*, which in Yiddish means noodle or spaghetti; after watching his first attempts at the role of Manfred, they changed it to the *narisha luksh*, which could be freely translated as noodlehead or fool. He and Feona joined forces as fellow outsiders, and Sally watched gleefully as Feona and Pasquel, whose name had now been changed for program purposes to Warren Heart, each found in the other an object of admiration and affection. They shared an ignorance of Yiddish, which language was used by most of the cast to hurl their imprecations at the leading man and the leading lady, said imprecations being for the most part unprintable. Manfred, who was once Pasquel and became Warren, was easygoing and sensitive; in fact, sensitive to a fault. Pushed too far, he was given to tears. Feona mothered him. Freedman said to Sally, "Does it appear to you as much as to me as a sort of lunatic asylum?"

Sally had just spent a half-hour attempting to teach Yussel Shimkowitz, who was playing the part of the Van Dyme chauffeur, to mouth the words: "Certainly, Mr. Van Dyme. It will be a pleasure."

"What difference will it make," Shimkowitz argued, "if I say it in Yiddish? Who hears me? For eleven weeks I played Falstaff in Yiddish, and I stopped the house. Three times I stopped the house. If I can speak the words of Shakespeare in Yiddish, I can speak the idiot mouthings of an idiot chauffeur."

Fortunately, Sally had less than a nodding acquaintance with the

Yiddish language, but then, no one in the ice house understood Italian. "Very much so," she told Freedman. "But will it really make any difference, Gerry? I mean, how many lip readers will there be in the audience?"

Then the two of them went into a dressing room, closed the door, and while one spoke silently into the mirror, the other tried to read the words. A few minutes later they burst out laughing and fell into each other's arms, still laughing and hugging each other. It was the first moment of abandon or of any kind of joy that Sally could recall experiencing since the day of her marriage. Then they realized what they were doing and drew back and away from each other.

"I'm sorry," Freedman said.

"For what? For laughing?"

"For being in love with you, I guess."

"Is that a joke?"

"Does it sound like one?"

For a long moment Sally stood and stared at him, then she turned and fled from the dressing room. Freedman followed her more slowly, and back on the set, said to her, "I've been thinking about it, Sally, and I don't think it makes so much difference what they say — I mean, even if Manfred says it in Italian."

"What?" Her thoughts were elsewhere. "What do you mean?"

"I mean what we were talking about, the lip reading. Nobody reads lips. Anyway, tomorrow morning we're photographing on Fifth Avenue and the side street. Max has fixed it with Boss Murphy, and they're closing off the avenue and we'll have fifty cops taking care of things. You have to hand it to Max. He does things right."

"Yes, he does," Sally said shortly.

• • •

Fred Feldman pressed Max for a meeting, and Max avoided him. Feldman and Jake Stein discussed the matter, and they went over the books together. Bert Bellamy, together with Ruby Britsky, had arranged the sale of the nine lecture halls that Max had converted into moving picture theatres. Five of the halls had been sold to the Jessup Nickelodeon Company, and there was the regular real estate deduction, with checks made out to Cynthia Collins, agent for the transaction, with an address on William Street. Miss Collins was an attractive woman of about forty or so, and drawing up the papers for the sale, Feldman had no suspicion that Miss Collins was anything other than she claimed to be. However, when he tried to find her a few weeks later to discuss a small change in the contracts, he discovered that she had never occupied the premises at William Street — or, indeed, any other premises that he could find. The commissions had amounted to almost five thousand dollars. Feldman discussed the matter with Jake Stein.

"I know," Stein said.

"What the devil do you mean, you know? What do you know?"

"I spoke to Hymie Brockman. He's in the business, and he knows every real estate broker south of Fourteenth Street. There ain't no Cynthia Collins. There never was no Cynthia Collins."

"What!"

"Just like I say."

"Why didn't you tell me? Why didn't you tell Max?"

"Look, Freddy, I love Max. Even when he's a son of a bitch, which is fairly frequently, I am loving him. He's good to me. My wife had to go up to Keppleman's Mountain House in Sullivan County, and I needed five hundred bucks. Max didn't hesitate. He gives it to me and he still don't let me dock my pay. Ruby's had his hand in the cashboxes for years. He makes a deal with the ticket sellers. They take out two dollars a night — a dollar to Ruby, a dollar to the ticket man. Not much, but it adds up. Then little brother Benny gets in on the graft, just a little bit, here and there. Max knows, but the couple of times I try to talk to him about it, he takes my head off. Now it's possible that Bellamy's in on it, and who's Bert? Only Max's best and oldest friend in the world, since they were kids together working at the penny arcade. So what do we do? We tell Max that his brother and his best friend are crooks?"

"About Bert, we just don't know. You say possibly — that's not good enough. But if Max finds out —" Feldman shook his head.

"How does he find out, Freddy? It's a few thousand lousy dollars. Leave it alone. The way Max is moving these days, he's spending twice that each day. That's what you got to talk to him about. If we don't finish this moving picture in another week, we can all go on vacation."

But to sit down with Max for a meeting was not easy. Feldman and Stein might be worried about money, but Max had his huge toy, the ice house with its sets and lights and cameras and actors. He was happier than he had ever been before, probably happier than he would be again, and when at last Feldman cornered him in one of the dressing rooms, Max said, "Freddy, stop crying. Tomorrow we photograph the cards, and then we paste it all together, and then all we need is ten thousand dollars for the prints, fifty thousand for advertising and *tumeling*, and another five thousand to hire Rector's for the opening night, and to throw the kind of a party this town won't forget. So do we have a lousy sixty-five big ones still in the till, or do I have to go begging?"

"We got about fifty-two thousand, and you don't do the begging. I'll do it, and I'll get it from Chase, where you got your teeth into them already. I'll squeeze another mortgage out of the theatres. But God Almighty, Max, suppose the whole thing fizzles?"

"Then we're all out on our asses, right?"

• • •

They spent the next week, as Max put it, pasting it all together. Sam Snyder, together with a young man named Martin Kellogg, whom he had hired away from Edison, devised a sort of enlarger that magnified the film and enabled them to roll it back and forth as they worked on it. No one in the group — not Sam Snyder or Sally or Freedman or Max — had anticipated the specific difficulties encountered putting the film together. The trained, practiced film editor was far in the future; then they had to invent, guess, and hope.

The consensus was that the entire motion picture should run for one hundred minutes, but they found themselves with one hundred and eighty-three minutes of film, not including the dialogue cards. What to leave in? What to take out? There was a scene of a small, dirty street child weeping. It had little to do with the story and had come about accidentally, and Sally loved it. She wept when it fell to the cutting room floor, the beginning of millions of feet of film, unused, unseen, that would accumulate through the years on the floors of a thousand cutting rooms. There were bitter arguments, screaming confrontations, pleading — as much emotion as had gone into the making of the film itself — but finally it was done, and there had come into existence a feature-length motion picture called *The Waif*, starring Feona Amour and Warren Heart. The supporting cast of Yiddish Theatre actors had also been transmuted into an Anglo-Saxon nomenclature, the list of actors including Thomas Morton, James Spalding, Oswald Smith, Joan Ashley, Alice Henderson, and so forth and so on. But Max bristled at the suggestion that his own name might be changed. "With actors, it is one thing. But Britsky remains Britsky. They don't like it, they can shove it up their ass."

The first screening of *The Waif*, cut and assembled, took place in the ice house on the improvised screen they had used to project their daily takes. The audience consisted of Max, Freida, Ruby, Benny, Sally, Freedman, Feldman, Stein, Snyder, Bellamy, and most of the cast. In spite of the fact that most of them had seen each piece of film many times, they were moved. They wiped their eyes, clapped, cheered, and when it was over, they sat in respectful silence. It was hard to believe that this incredible thing was their creation.

But the silence didn't last. It was shattered by the resonant tones of Julia Schwartz, demanding, "Since when have I become Joan Ashley? After fifty-five years of being Julia Schwartz, with triumphs in Berlin and Paris, not to mention Warsaw, on real stages in real theatres, suddenly I am Joan Ashley?"

"Not to mention Thomas Morton!" Isadore Melchik roared. "It ain't enough that Melchik plays Hamlet, Macbeth, King Lear, not to mention my own translation into Yiddish of George Bernard Shaw's *Caesar and Cleopatra*, in which Melchik plays Julius Caesar, and suddenly I'm Thomas Morton, who don't even exist. Either it's Melchik, or I personally will get an injunction!"

"Please," Max begged them, "please. Don't I know you are great actors? If Shakespeare was alive, he'd go to Second Avenue. I have no doubt about that. And go to anyplace in New York, even with the classiest uptown critics, they will tell you how great Julia Schwartz and Isadore Melchik are. Don't I know that? But the success of this moving picture will be when it plays in every nickelodeon from Maine to Minnesota, and not to mention such places as South Dakota and Oklahoma — which, believe me, will be the end of the nickelodeon and the garbage they show, or maybe not the end but a new era. But what I am saying is in such places they never heard of a Yiddish Theatre, and if you say Second Avenue to them, they don't know what you're talking about, and they see names like

Schwartz or Melchik or Massoni, they also don't know what you're talking about, not to mention how they feel about Jews. So please, please, please regard this as the beginning of a great new career in a hundred Max Britsky films —"

The argument went on, but in the end Max prevailed. But later, Sally said to him, "How is it, Max, that you're not worried about the name of Britsky?"

He stared at her for a long moment before he replied, "I guess I'm used to it." But unspoken, his response was: To hell with them!

• • •

The next day, sitting in his office with Fred Feldman and Jake Stein, Max said to them, "Sometimes you talk and you don't listen to yourself."

"Whatever that's supposed to mean," Feldman agreed.

"I'll tell you what it's supposed to mean. Yesterday when I'm trying to get Melchik to agree to be Thomas Morton, I became passionate. I absolutely outdid myself."

"It was a good argument," Stein agreed.

"Stop agreeing with me. The hell with that. I'm not talking about an argument, but listen. I said to Melchik what a success this picture is, playing in every nickelodeon from Maine to Minnesota or whatever."

"You're very persuasive," Feldman said. "Only it won't be playing in every nickelodeon anywhere except in the ten theatres we got, and maybe not even there if you blow a fortune on a big party at Rector's, like you're planning."

"Stop crying about the money, Freddy. I'll tell you something. You go into a place like the Chase Bank and ask them for twenty, thirty thousand dollars, right away they know you're a bum with your hand out. You come in for half a million, they respect you, and that's what you and Jake are going to do tomorrow, turn up a half a million."

"Max, you're out of your mind."

"Yeah? You don't hear me, like I don't hear myself. I said to Melchik in every nickelodeon from here to Grand Rapids, and you tell me to stop dreaming because we don't have no nickelodeons or theatres in Grand Rapids or anywhere else except here and in Brooklyn. That's just it. We're tossing pennies for gum wrappers, like the kids down on Henry Street. We got something that nobody else in this country has got. We got a ninety-minute moving picture called *The Waif*, and there ain't a moving picture house anywhere in America that wouldn't give both balls to show it, and we sit here tossing pennies into our lousy ten theatres."

"They're not so lousy, those ten theatres," Jake Stein protested. "They're damn good theatres."

"Wake up! Listen to me! I'm not burning our theatres. I'm just saying that there are a thousand other theatres that would give blood to show our moving picture instead of the garbage that National feeds them."

Feldman was staring at him thoughtfully.

"You follow me, Fred?"

"Yeah, but it's big enough to scare the hell out of you, Max."

"Penny business, penny business — I'm sick of that. Where does it say in the Bible that National and Edison and a couple of others got a patent to sell their ten-minute junk and nobody else? Suppose we set up a percentage scheme instead of the kind of rental National uses. Suppose we tell the guy who's got three nickelodeons in Oklahoma City that we'll give him three prints and he gives us fifty percent of the box office take. You're telling me he don't jump at that?"

"Max, Max," Stein said, "you're dreaming, and it's nice to dream, but me, I got to balance the books. At the lab, it costs us five cents a foot for the print, and that comes to a little over four hundred dollars for each print of *The Waif*, and that's twelve hundred dollars in Oklahoma City alone, and you want a thousand prints — four hundred thousand dollars?"

"Something else," Feldman put in. "The only lab we can count on is Tucker's, over in Hoboken, and that's only because we own half the place, and Tucker's takes a week to give us one print if they drop everything else. All the other labs are tied in with National and Edison and Movieland, and there isn't the chance of a snowball in hell that they're going to take work from us. Don't think that the ice house is such a secret, Max. Every newspaper in town's been snooping around the place, and the other operators are just waiting to see what happens. If *The Waif* is a big hit, they'll all start making ninety-minute pictures, now that we've shown them how it can be done."

"Are you listening?" Stein begged him. "Please, Max, are you listening?"

"I'm listening. Not learning, just listening. You want to cry on my shoulder, I'll give you a handkerchief."

"We're trying to be realistic."

"Yeah? Let me tell you what's realistic. Realistic is that nobody does a goddamn thing until somebody else shows them how. I already told Sam that I want the production out at Tucker's doubled and doubled again and then doubled again."

"With what?"

"I gave him a check for twenty thousand dollars. That's to buy the other half. I don't want nobody turning up and telling us we can't use Tucker's. Then I told him to go ahead and hire whatever we need to make it the biggest lab in the country."

"Max," Stein whispered, "you're crazy. You gave him twenty thousand dollars. We ain't got twenty thousand dollars to give him."

"You don't listen to me," Max said. "Tomorrow, you and Freddy here are going to see Mr. Alvin Berry at number One Seventy-seven Broadway, at the Chase Bank, and you are going to hit him for half a million dollars. You are going to hock everything we got — the theatres, *The Waif,* the lab out in Hoboken, and if you got to throw in the two brownstones we got up on Sixty-sixth Street, do that, and give him a pint of blood if he needs it for his stinking Yankee collateral — but you don't walk out of there without five hundred thousand dollars, because while you are doing that, I am hiring two salesmen to start working their way around the country selling *The Waif* and three other pictures —"

"Wait, wait, wait. Please, Max. What three other pictures?"

"You can't tie up a house with one picture. They play it a week, and what then? They go to National, and National says fuck off. You want to do business with Britsky, go do business with Britsky. So what do I tell them — buy our print and go out of business? So this morning I had a meeting with Freedman and Sally, and I told them to start right in with three more pictures."

"What do we use for money?" Stein wailed.

"You know something, Jake, you and Freddy work that out. Because in ten days from now, we are going to open *The Waif.* One theatre first, and then the next day in the others, but first an opening night at the Palace on Twenty-third Street, and it's going to be as classy as a real theatrical opening, and we're going to have the mayor and maybe the governor and whoever else Murphy thinks should be there, and after the opening, where we run the picture just once, I'm going to give a party at Rector's for three hundred people. We got a goose that's going to lay golden eggs like nobody ever dreamed about."

* * *

Richard Britsky was three years old. His sister, Marion, was a year and seven months. Both of them had their father's blue eyes; both of them were healthy, round-faced children. They had a nurse to take care of them, a Mrs. Berger, a German-Jewish widow whom Sarah Britsky hated and who taught the two little children to call Sarah *Omar*, a word Sarah hated; and since Mrs. Berger served as an antidote to her mother-in-law, Sally tolerated her rigidity and took comfort in the fact of her ethnic origin. On the other hand, the situation of the nurse or governess in the brownstone with the two beautifully dressed children was never quite real to Sally. As for Max, he accepted it as a matter of course, a natural development. When he had time for the children, he admired them; playing with them was beyond him; but he insisted that their lives should be the absolute opposite of what his had been.

Freedman played with the children, Sally noted. The nurse was off for the day and Sally had the children, but, as Freedman put it, "Max says we can't lose a day. He's really terribly insistent."

"Yes, Max's world consists of things he wants done yesterday. That's because nobody else is like Max, thank God."

"Well, he is unusual."

"If you keep looking at me like that, Gerry, we won't get much done."

"Which way? Oh, you mean with cow-eyes. But it's not just that, but I saw a painting in the museum and it was so like you, that dress with the stripes —" He took off to catch up with Richard. Marion began to cry. Sally picked her up and rocked her.

"They'll nap soon. Then we can talk."

Richard began to cry. Freedman made faces and stuck out his tongue.

"I know it annoys you if I talk about how I feel about you," Freedman said, "so I'll try not to, and actually —" Richard howled.

"I think they both want a nap," Sally said. "I'm not the best mother in the world or I wouldn't put them into the hands of that dreadful German. But she's so efficient."

They carried the children up to the nursery. The children had stopped crying and were gurgling with laughter. They enjoyed having Gerry around. He sang little songs to them and made faces at them and swung them up and down in his arms. "You should have children," Sally said to him. "You absolutely should be married and have children, you're so good with them."

"Only because they're your children."

"Well, there you go again. You mustn't keep doing that, Gerry." He stood watching, listening, while Sally sang to the children, and when they were asleep, he and Sally tiptoed out of the room.

Sally was very businesslike. "You know what Max is like when he sets his mind to something. He wants to start photography in ten days, and then he wants to start a second picture two weeks after that."

"He wants the moon, doesn't he? He's also a little crazy when it comes to such things. We have to tell him that it can't be done that way."

"Well, perhaps. I'm not sure. You know," Sally said, "the feeling that it's impossible makes it so much more exciting, and last night I lay awake for hours, just thinking about all the marvelous things we can do with that camera. I was thinking about that dreadful *General Slocum* tragedy; it was so heartbreaking, so awful. If we made a moving picture about it —"

"Oh, no, Sally — all that suffering and horror!"

Sally had referred to an incident that had happened four years ago. There was a prosperous, vital community of German immigrants located between Tompkins Square and the East River, just to the north of the sprawling Jewish community. Each year, St. Mark's Lutheran Church, located in the center of their area, organized a Sunday school picnic, and this time, in June of 1904, the community hired an old side-wheeler excursion boat to take the mothers and their children to Locust Grove, on Long Island Sound. Very few men went along; it was for the most part mothers and their children, and 1400 of them were packed into the old boat. Steaming up the East River, the ship caught fire, turned into a blazing inferno, and caused the worst maritime tragedy in the history of the port of New York. Over a thousand women and children died on the *General Slocum*, tearing the heart out of the German community and plunging them into a period of mourning and despair from which they did not emerge for years.

"Oh, yes, yes," Sally agreed. "It was horrible beyond imagination, but isn't that the substance of so many books and plays? I don't mean to repeat what happened on the *General Slocum*, but a film about a ship on fire — it's so close to all of us in the city. I would want to save most of the people."

"I don't know, it's so recent."

"But you suggested the war in Cuba."

"Yes, I guess you're right. I suppose that if you want to excite people, you show them terrible and exciting things. Do you have a story worked out? We could talk about it."

It became the second Max Britsky production, *The Tragedy of the Lucy Gray*.

· · ·

Meanwhile, Max planned the opening of *The Waif*. Fred Feldman worked out a letter as follows: "As a theatre critic, you have perhaps ignored the world of the moving picture, the nickelodeon, the storefront projection booth. Certainly, if you happened to wander into any theatre playing what is euphemistically called a motion picture drama, you found good reason to continue to ignore such places. However, I do believe that we have created a moving picture that breaks all the strictures of the past, that establishes a new arena of entertainment, and that has no precedent. It is the first of its kind and is thereby of historic importance. I am enclosing two tickets for the opening night and with them an invitation for you and your companion to a party at Rector's, to follow the showing of our great motion picture, entitled *The Waif*."

Max signed the letter, which was sent to the theatre critics on the *New York Times*, the *New York Tribune*, the *Sun*, the *Journal*, and the *Herald*. Feldman was dubious about calling it a great motion picture, but Max insisted on inserting the adjective. "We are not hiding lights under any bushels," he said.

Boss Murphy introduced Max to Stephen Allison, who functioned as a sort of link between Tammany Hall and the Social Register, and Allison provided the names of two dozen luminaries who were numbered among the Four Hundred — as the social elite were called, there being, supposedly, only four hundred people worthy of social recognition in the city — and who would almost certainly attend the opening as well as the party to follow. Invitations were also issued to the political elite and to leading people in the Yiddish and English-speaking theatre. Max spent money as if it were going out of style, taking large advertisements in all of the local newspapers to announce the opening at the Palace and then, a day later, the openings at the nine other theatres. He also hired two hundred sandwich-board walkers to parade through the streets of the city. The Palace was sold out days before opening night, and such was the excitement generated that he had to sell advance tickets in the other theatres as well. At that point, every dollar had been exhausted, and Max was borrowing from Bert and Snyder and anyone else he could hit for hard cash. Fortunately, the loan from the Chase Bank came through two days before the opening: half a million dollars to the credit of Max Britsky Productions.

Meanwhile, Max's mother and his three sisters had been running up their own share of the indebtedness — gowns made to order, new shoes, new wraps. Sheila was married to a young man to whom Max had given a job, one Donald Greenway, whom Max had generously termed "Donald the schmuck," and there too the accouterments were charged to Max, as were the trappings of Ruby's wife, the former Kathy Sullivan, whom Sarah avoided like the plague. But Max was indifferent to the expenditure of money. In itself, it had no meaning or lure for him; it was important only as a means to an end. Perhaps his own past made it almost impossible for him to ask what anything cost. In hiring the actors for *The Waif*, he never quibbled about their pay. He gave them what they asked.

And whatever the opening of *The Waif* cost Max, it turned out just as he had planned it. The crowds of onlookers filled Twenty-third Street to the point where the police had to clear a path for the carriages. The gas company had installed special mantles that bathed the street in white light; and one after another, carriages intermixed with automobiles drove up to discharge their elegantly clad occupants. Max himself, in tails that had been made for this occasion, stood at the entrance to the theatre. Most of the people were strangers to him; still, he bathed in the glow of the occasion, and in his mind a process took place that was to repeat itself over and over during the years to come — namely, that this thing, *The Waif*, was his creation, aided and abetted by Sally and Freedman and Snyder and a cast of actors and a crew of cameramen, scenic designers, property men, electricians, carpenters, but only aided and abetted by all such, and mainly and mostly his own creation, Max Britsky presents. "So all of you marching into this theatre, just take note and remember, Max Britsky presents —"

Finally, he entered himself, not to sit down, but to join Sally and Freedman and Snyder, all of them standing behind the last row of the orchestra. At stage left of the old stage — for the Palace had been a great legitimate theatre — a violinist stood by a grand piano, and as the audience finished seating itself, he began to play, accompanied by the pianist, none other than Isadore Lubel, first of Max's piano players, doing a medley arranged by Lubel himself out of *La Belle Helène*, by Offenbach. While it was not quite in the mood to introduce *The Waif*, the fact that Offenbach was Jewish persuaded Max to allow Lubel to have his way. While Max's musical acumen left something to be desired, his sense of style and hype was well developed. He had printed programs for the opening, and it pleased him to have there "Overture by Offenbach, arrangement by Lubel." More to the point, Lubel had found a fiddler who could adapt instantly to the changes of mood, time, and intensity that Lubel performed on the piano.

The film began and ran its course for the following eighty-six minutes. Max, Sally, Freedman, and Snyder stood and watched with the nervous intensity of loving parents. They listened for the nose-blowing and throat-clearing and whispered triumphantly, "Tears. Tears." When it finished, the audience broke into a storm of hand-clapping and shouts of "Bravo! Bravo!" "Go on, Max," Snyder urged him. "Go on up there. They want someone to take a bow. This ain't no nickelodeon audience. These are uptown swells, the same as an opening in a legitimate house."

"Come on," Max said to Sally, taking her arm. "You began it, you done it. Take some credit."

She shrank back, pleading, "No, Max. I couldn't. I just couldn't."

"It's eating candy. Let them see I got a wife."

"No. Please!"

"O.K.," Max agreed, thinking, I got nothing — nothing, and

then he marched down the aisle, vaulted onto the stage, and spread his arms for an end to the cheers.

"Thank you," Max said. "I thank you with all my heart. Tomorrow, *The Waif* opens in all ten of the Britsky theatres. Our second film masterpiece is already in production, and a third one is on the drawing board. Thank you for watching our great effort tonight."

The party at Rector's was no less a success. There was nothing quite like Rector's in America or, as some held, in all the world; and Max's entrée there, into the gates of heaven, as New York measured such things, came out of a meeting with Charley Rector arranged by Boss Murphy. Max Britsky and Charley Rector fell into an instant communion. They harked back to similar beginnings. Charley Rector had driven a horsecar on the Seventh Avenue line, but life smiled on him when he opened a seafood restaurant in Chicago and discovered that by the simple expedient of cooking oysters lightly in real cream with a bit of delicate seasoning, one had a dish that kings could envy. His oyster stew brought him fame and fortune, and he took his money back to New York, where he created the most famous restaurant of the time, Rector's, a long, yellow, two-story building facing Broadway between Forty-third and Forty-fourth streets. On the main floor, in the great spread of mirrors and chandeliers, one hundred tables were set, that the elegant, the famous and infamous, the talented, the rich, and the mighty might dine. Upstairs, on the second floor, those without fame or elegance might have the privilege of dining at Rector's or, on special occasions, the whole of the second floor was given over to private parties, such as Max Britsky's party on the opening night of *The Waif*. That was the case tonight, and Max paid seven thousand dollars for sixty tables of invited guests. Charley Rector's son, George, his round, fat face wreathed in smiles over his huge belly, greeted the guests with the ultimate acknowledgment of belonging, a warm, slightly moist handshake. The accolade was not without significance in the social circle as well as the sporting crowd of New York City. To be known and greeted by the Rectors, father or son, was no small achievement, and for Max a significantly large achievement. Not only was he here, but two full tables that he had placed at the disposal of Sally's family had brought them — Sally's father and mother and aunts and uncles and cousins — to Rector's, a place as far beyond their dreams or aspirations as Delmonico's, more elite than Rector's but less famous and enticing — had brought them here where Max could greet them in his cutaway coat and forgiving smile. He forgave them their early opinion of himself and the other Britskys.

The other Britskys basked in the glow of Max's success: Sarah sitting as dowager queen in yards and yards of white satin and gold stitching, Ruby, Sheila, and Esther married already, Ruby's wife, one-time Kathy Sullivan, greeting Max with a great embrace, a bit more than sisterly, whispering, "Put me in a movie, Max." Quid pro quo. It's in the sound of a voice, the tone, intonation, lilt. Max was hearing it for the first time, but it would thread its way through his life.

He nodded and smiled. "We'll talk about it." Kathy Sullivan Britsky was a lovely, auburn-haired young woman, but queen of the occasion was without doubt Feona Amour. Gone was Etta Goodman, gone forever, and even Max was astonished by the glowing beauty of his star, Feona. Pomp and circumstance do indeed change things, and Max wondered how she could have worked for him all those years without his ever realizing how good-looking she was.

Of course, hairdressers, professional makeup men, and dressmakers made a difference, yet there was no gainsaying the beauty of Etta Goodman. Max turned recent events on their head. Hadn't he always known? Hadn't he chosen her for that reason, for secret talent and beauty no one else could see?

And of course, everyone else was there at Rector's — the cast, Max's associates, the leading lights of Tammany Hall — as well as dozens of others whom Max did not know but who after tonight would recognize the name of Max Britsky and put it together with a river of champagne and dark mountains of caviar. As the lord designer of this ducal lavishness, Max, son of Abe Britsky, spread his arms. Let everyone eat, drink, and be happy, even Pasquel Massoni, who Max considered a total idiot, either as Pasquel or as Warren Heart, but who was quite magnificent in his tails, all six foot one of him, embracing Max with a bone-crushing grasp, "You, my friend, I salute you, maestro. You have enlarged my heart." Which, considering his given name, was not wholly untrue.

Only Sally appeared unable to share properly in the festivities, and she complained to Max of a headache. "This is our big night,

Sally," he said to her. "We are celebrating the greatest night of our lives."

Sally didn't feel triumphant. Her head ached and her stomach churned, and whenever she looked at Max, she found herself asking herself who he was. Who she was also occurred to her, not as an answer but as a fuzzy question. She had been thirsty, and two glasses of champagne contributed to her fuzziness. Caviar did not sit well with her. She tried to be responsive and pleasant to people who told her that she looked just lovely. She did look lovely. She had gone to the Metropolitan Museum of Art and had found the painting that Freedman referred to, a painting of mother and child by Mary Cassatt, and the very real resemblance flattered her. She was at a point in life where she needed flattery desperately, and for this occasion she copied the painting, having a dress made of white silk with vertical stripes of pale blue and aquamarine blue. She looked lovely, and as Max felt, she had class; and while class was not an element that excited him sexually, it did elevate his ego. It made him feel secure in that great, glittering room full of the famous and the infamous and of course the rich. He wanted Sally to laugh, to smile, to be a hostess in terms of the society people present, to let them hear speech eloquent enough to make up for his own less than perfect English. Max always felt the need to be justified. Money justified him and power justified him, but neither acted upon his sensibilities as Sally did. She justified him far more than anything else, and now she was sick and miserable. It was simply a betrayal, and Max said petulantly, "Come on, this is no time to walk out on me. Have some more champagne. It's imported. It's the best that Charley Rector serves, and that makes it just about the best there is."

"I can't drink. You know that, Max. I think it's the champagne that made me ill."

"Well, you can't just sit there that way with people looking at you."

"Please, Max, I want to go home."

"It's just started. This party's going on all night."

"Max, I can't. I'm so miserable."

Finally Max gave in to the inevitable and found Gerry Freedman and said to him, "I hate to do this to you, Gerry, because you're the big man tonight —" He didn't think so. Max was the big man this night, but there was Freedman, talking to the drama critic of *Harper's* magazine, with three beautifully gowned women hanging on to his every word, and Max taking him away from that could have offended Freedman. Max didn't want to offend Freedman. "I'm sorry," he whispered, "but Sally's sick."

"Sick? What is it?"

Max didn't notice Freedman's alarm. "Too much champagne, I guess. Would you take her home, Gerry. Don't worry about the party. It'll go on, and you can get back here —"

"No problem," Freedman said, trying to sound a little disappointed. "Of course I'll take her home."

Out of Rector's, in a hansom cab headed uptown, Sally said, "I don't know how to thank you, Gerry. I've taken you away from that marvelous party, and I feel so stupid and selfish —"

He stopped her short. "Absolutely not! I can't think of anyplace in the world I'd rather be than right here next to you. And as for that party — well, it's a big, damnfool potlatch, and they're welcome to it. I was talking to a writer for *Harper's* when Max found me, but the real critics, those in the daily press, they're at their papers writing — that is, considering that they say anything at all about *The Waif*."

"Oh? But don't you think it was good?"

"I don't know," Freedman confessed. "It was the best we could do, but we're right on top of it. What do we compare it with? Ibsen? Shaw?"

"No, this is something else."

Peering at her in the dim light of the cab, Freedman said, "You look so beautiful. Do you feel all right?"

"Much better. The headache's gone."

He reached over and touched her cheek with his fingertips. Then he put his arm around her shoulders and drew her to him.

"You don't have to come inside," she said. "You can keep the cab and go back with it."

He ignored her and paid off the driver, and she didn't protest. Except for the light in the entranceway, the house was dark and silent, but there were lights burning in the rear rooms, where the children slept. Freedman walked with her as she peered into each room. "They're like angels when they're asleep."

"Aren't we all?"

She put her finger to her lips as they passed the nurse's room. Her bedroom was on the floor below. At the door to her bedroom, she said to Freedman, "Better go back now. You were very kind. Thank you."

He put his arms around her and kissed her. She didn't protest. Silently she pleaded with him to go on as he stood pressed to her, kissing her.

"Let me close the door." He let go of her, and she closed the door and locked it, and then went to the bed and threw back the embroidered coverlet. She went into her dressing room, trembling as she shed her clothes. What was wrong with her? She was a married woman, the mother of two children, a proper matron, but never in her life had she felt such desire. She put on a robe; she was aching with desire, trembling with it. Freedman had turned off the lights. She walked slowly, carefully, in the dark, and then she felt the bed and threw herself onto it and into his arms, her shyness replaced by a tigerlike ferocity, climbing onto him, clenching his bony shoulders until her nails drove into his flesh.

Afterward, their passion spent, she became a little girl lying beside him, whispering baby talk, touching his long, skinny arms, touching his ribs. When he tried to speak, she put her hand over his mouth.

"We don't talk about it, Gerry. It is, that's all. I don't want to talk about it or hear you talk about it."

"Sure. But what time is it?"

She fumbled for the lamp, turned it on, closed her eyes against the bright light, and then opened them to look curiously at his long naked body, thinking of Max's body and comparing the two, and wondering how she could be so objective and callous about it, and wondering also whether she loved Gerry Freedman — or was he like a doctor who came to a sick person with a miraculous medicine?

"How do you feel now?" he asked her.

"Better. I'm trying to understand something. Yes, you asked me the time. It's one o'clock."

"What? I mean, understand what?"

Explosively, like a cry of outraged pain, "I hate him!"

"Who?"

"Max, Max, Max!" She was no longer objective. She was full of self-pity now, and she began to whimper like a hurt child. "He took it all away, everything — my mind, my body, my virginity, my mind — all my mind."

"Sally, Sally," Freedman begged her, "come on. Pull yourself together. Max is no angel. You stopped loving him, but he isn't the devil. It happens."

"I never loved him!" She spat out the words.

"Why did you marry him?"

"Why? Don't you understand why? I'm not strong. Everyone said I had to marry him — Mama, Papa, and Max."

"You don't have to stay married to Max."

"I haven't had, had —"

She couldn't say it, so Freedman supplied it for her. "Intercourse," he said gently.

"Yes, that, not for months and months. And I never will again. Never! Do you believe me?"

"Yes. Of course."

Her mood changed again, abruptly. "Don't you know it's one o'clock in the morning? You must get back to Rector's." She had become calm, practical, realistic, as if the outburst of a moment ago had never occurred. "Now do be sensible, darling, and hurry back to Rector's."

"The hell with it! I don't want to go back there."

"But Max —"

"The hell with Max."

Sally got out of bed and put on her robe. "Now Gerry," she said, "let's be sensible. We're working partners, and I hope that will continue, and the last thing in the world I want is a falling-out between you and Max."

"I've been gone over an hour. What do I tell Max?"

"Max will never notice, not in that crowd. So get dressed and hurry back, and I'll see you tomorrow."

• • •

The following day, the critic of the *New York Times* wrote:

One tends to regard all artistic creations — and *The Waif* is an artistic creation, whatever else it may be — in a comparative sense. We measure Elizabethan plays by Shakespeare, just as we measure our current drama by Shaw, Ibsen, and Chekov. We compare, we look back at the record, and we are highly aware of tradition. Then what is one to say of *The Waif*, that extraordinary moving picture that had its premier at the Palace Theatre last night? There is no question about it being extraordinary; its very singularity underwrites that judgment. It is the first extended treatment of a dramatic theme in the classical sense of the theatre that has been attempted in the new and fascinating medium of moving pictures.

That it opens up countless doors for others cannot be gainsaid. It has in one long and bold step moved film production from technical amusement into the field of drama. Its innovative use of dialogue frames as a substitute for heard speech appears to work, and when refined and learned as a technique may well lead to a whole era of filmed drama. The camera work also opens new horizons. The use of a moving camera on both a dolly and automobiles is both exciting and inventive. Apparently, an entire new art based on the use of the moving picture camera will now explode into being.

Having said all this, one must tip one's cap to producer Max Britsky and applaud his courage and pioneering spirit. At the same time, since *The Waif* is given to us as a work of the dramatic art and set apart from the fragments that have adorned the nickelodeons, and even set apart from such bolder and larger attempts as Edwin S. Porter's *Great Train Robbery*, it must be judged as a work of art. Yet this judgment must be tempered with the understanding that everyone concerned with this production was and is an innovator.

According to our information, the use of dialogue cards was the idea of Sally Britsky, the wife of the producer. I use the word idea rather than invention, since explanatory cards and expository cards have been used in moving pictures before this, but never in so innovative and dramatic a fashion. The story, or scenario, as it might be called, defining each scene as it does, was the creation of Mrs. Britsky and Mr. Gerald Freedman, the director. Now even when one specifies the mawkishness, the adolescent sentimentalism, and the naive characterization of both rich and poor in the moving picture, one cannot dismiss *The Waif* as a worthless drama. It is by no means that. It has vigor, earnestness, and compassion, and so well did it take hold of a not unsophisticated audience that there was hardly a dry eye around me in the theatre.

We must view *The Waif* as a step in the development of American drama, a most important step, and we must deal with what it accomplished and not with what it failed to accomplish. Most important, it provided an evening of emotional entertainment.

The cast was well chosen, and while Mr. Freedman's direction may have been overemphatic, we can accept the fact that acting without speech must develop as a new art. The leading role was played wonderfully well by Miss Feona Amour, a newcomer to the American theatre, whose acting was uninhibited and expressive. She is a delightful person to watch, very beautiful, and I am sure we will see her again. As Jennifer, she was simply adorable.

And while Miss Amour lacks the training and polish of a fine theatrical actress, she almost makes up for it with her ingenuousness. Both she and Warren Heart, her leading man, might be faulted for excessive gestures and posturing, but I am not at all certain that this type of silent drama does not call for such excesses. The other members of the cast were well suited to their supporting roles, particularly Thomas Morton and Joan Ashley.

The other newspapers responded in kind. Indeed, the reception given *The Waif* was beyond anything Max had expected.

[SEVEN]

1912

—

Max at the
Age of Thirty-three

MAX HAD ASKED Clifford Abel, the architect, to join him and Sam Snyder and Fred Feldman for lunch at the Café Coronet on Second Avenue. Clifford Abel, only thirty-seven years old, had already earned a national reputation as an innovator alongside such men as Stanford White and Frank Lloyd Wright, except that he eschewed somberness or granite dignity. As it was said, he built palaces, which was precisely the reason Max had come to him; yet while Abel's experience was widespread, this was his first meal in a Jewish dairy restaurant.

"So we'll find no meat on the menu," Max explained. "You'll try the fish, it's excellent. And why no meat? It ain't like Mr. Upton Sinclair wants we should all be vegetarians. It's a question of the Jewish dietary laws. Myself, I don't pay attention to them, but Jewish restaurants don't want to turn away the Orthodox Jews, who won't eat anything where meat and milk products are mixed. So to sell meat and milk dishes, a restaurant would have to have two kitchens, two cooks, two sets of dishes, and also pots and silver. Much easier to be one or the other. In this case, the Café Coronet is a dairy restaurant."

Abel was not sure that he had followed Max's train of thought, but he nodded agreeably and wondered about fish.

"Not included," Max said.

"You order for me," Abel said. "My tastes are catholic."

"I'm afraid it's only Jewish food," Max said. "I didn't know you were Catholic."

"Only in taste." To Feldman's relief, Abel turned the conversation to the matter at hand, confessing that he had never built a theatre. "It's a very special art, you know. They say acoustics are a science, but I question that. I should think you would have engaged Bill Tuthill. His Carnegie Hall is a miracle of acoustics."

"Because I don't want no Carnegie Hall, and I don't want no Metropolitan Opera House, and I don't want no theatre like fifty theatres we already got. Right now, Mr. Abel, the Britsky chain consists of eighteen theatres here in New York City, eleven in Philadelphia, two in Albany, two in Pittsburgh, six in Boston, two in Atlanta, and seven in Chicago. Makes almost fifty. Most of them were legitimate houses, a few were concert auditoriums, a number of music halls, and a few we built ourselves. But as far as Tuthill is concerned, I don't think he'd know what I'm talking about. It's a question of the movies. Sure, acoustics are important, but that's not my first concern. In fact, I have just about decided that the stage show, the vaudeville act, is a weak sister. It's the old music hall trying to keep pace with progress. Until now, nobody had the guts to do away with vaudeville. Yeah, I know, in the nickelodeons there was no vaudeville, but the day of the nickelodeons is over and now every exhibitor feels that if he don't have five vaudeville acts he can't claim to run a first-class theatre. And why? Because he don't understand the movies. Either he sees the movies as a way to make money — and believe me, it is a way to make money — or else he feels inferior about it. I don't. To me, we're just at the beginning of something that's beyond anybody's imagination, and that's why I want to have this discussion with you. Suppose I order for you cold sweet and sour whitefish? It's better than anything you'll find at Delmonico's or at Rector's."

"It sounds fine," Abel agreed.

Eli himself came over to take their order. Eli was the owner, but for certain old and important customers, only he took the orders. Now he told Max, "My son, Bernard — he's the younger one —he says that in *A Tale of Two Cities*, you left out the most important part. He's studying the book in high school."

"Everyone's a critic," Max explained to Abel. He replied to Eli, "Tell him we'll do a sequel. The French Revolution costs too much, believe me. That was top budget. The whitefish should be perfect."

"It's always perfect."

"You see," Max explained to Abel, "it's involvement. Millions of people who were never involved before. Mr. Synge's play, *The Playboy of the Western World*, just opened. You seen it?"

Abel nodded. "A lovely work."

"My wife dragged me to see it. She thinks it can be a moving picture. I'm not crazy for it. But do you see Eli's boy involved? He don't know it exists. All right, you got to stop me because I can lecture about the movies all day. The main thing is for you to understand what I'm talking about when I say I want a palace. I want a theatre, but I want it to be something new. I think of it as a palace."

"Yes, I suppose there have been some pretty ornate theatres."

"Ornate is not enough. First place, I want it big, at least two thousand seats. Only one balcony, and pitched to the screen, not to the stage. Now Mr. Snyder here, he's our technical expert, and I want you to work with him to get the line of sight. Also, I want a pipe organ, a pipe organ big enough to blow the walls open once you hit it. Instead of a pianist, we'll have an organist, and I hear with an organ you can even reproduce a battle scene if you have to." Turning to Snyder, "That's what you've been telling me, Sam, right?"

"Well, there might have to be some special attachments, but that's the idea, Mr. Abel. Until now, we've had only pianos, and occasionally in the larger theatres a trio, piano, violin, and a drum set. I've been investigating the pipe organ, and I think it can really improve what we're trying to do. Did you see our moving picture *The Stand at Concord Bridge?*"

"No, I'm afraid I don't get to the movies as often as I should," Abel said apologetically.

"We can run it for you. The point is, I have a friend who plays organ at St. Catherine's, and he was demonstrating some of the sounds he can make to suggest a battle. It was very remarkable."

"Oh, I'm sure," Abel agreed. "I've heard some remarkable sounds out of pipe organs, and if I undertake this project for you, I'll certainly have to work with one of the large organ companies —

perhaps in Europe if we can't do it here. However, I'm still not certain of your thoughts about a palace, Mr. Britsky. It's true that some of my buildings have been spoken of as palaces, but that's merely a euphemism from those who feel that ornamentation is sinful."

"All right. This time we'll let them call a palace a palace. I don't feel that class is sinful. I don't want this to look like some nice, quiet theatre. I want it to look like a moving picture palace."

"Well, for example, Mr. Britsky?"

"You seen pictures of the Taj Mahal?"

"Oh, yes. Yes, indeed."

"That's the general idea. Not the towers, not exactly the same, but something a kid looks at, he says to his mama, that's a beautiful palace. And when he goes into it, I want a lobby big enough to hold a thousand people, not the stinking, dark, crowded lobbies they have in the legitimate houses, and I want two huge staircases curving up on either side" — he spread his arms and circled his hands to illustrate — "like this, you know what I mean?" The whitefish arrived, and Max said, "Go ahead, eat. You can starve just sitting there and listening to me. And I'll tell you something else. Inside, when the audience looks up and around them, they should see the points — what do you call them, like towers?"

"Pinnacles."

"Exactly, palace walls and pinnacles, like they're inside the palace looking out, and over the walls, I want them to see the sky, not the real sky, but like on a set, so when the lights go out, the sky is dark with points of light like the stars."

Abel had lost interest in his whitefish. He was staring at Max intently, his gray eyes half closed, and half to himself, he whispered, "In Xanadu did Kubla Khan a stately pleasure dome decree: where Alph, the sacred river, ran through caverns measureless to man down to a sunless sea. So twice five miles of fertile ground with walls and towers were girdled round —"

He caught himself and stopped, and Max grinned and said, "I like that. I certainly like that. You and me, Mr. Abel, I think we think the same way. You want the job?"

"We haven't even discussed cost."

"To hell with the cost. If this works out, I build one of these palaces in every big city in America, and each one different. How do you like that?"

"It's a dream come true. Where will you put this one, the first?"

"I got a lot on Seventh Avenue and Fifty-second Street. It's uptown, but that's where the action's going to be, uptown. So what do you say, Mr. Abel. Do we shake hands?"

"I think we do," Abel said.

• • •

Three floors of the Hobart Building were now given over to Britsky Productions. A year before, the building had gone up for sale, and Max bought it. Yet he hadn't changed his original office. To build a palace for people who desired to spend a few hours watching a moving picture was one thing, but to provide a room like a palace interior for his day-to-day work was another thing entirely. Della O'Donnell, who had come to work for Max eight years ago, and who was some sort of distant relative of Charlie Murphy, boss of Tammany Hall, had been advanced from receptionist to the position of Max's personal secretary. She was the same warm, bosomy, red-headed, overweight, motherly woman about whom Max had his marital fantasies, who had come to adore Max, who had been deserted by an alcoholic husband, and who, being a year older than Max, treated him like her favorite child.

For years Max made no pass at her, treating her with exemplary propriety, firm in his conviction that he would not become involved at the same time with two women who worked for Britsky Productions; this behavior upon Max's part went against everything Della had ever heard about Max Britsky. At the same time, it was combined with a tenderness on Max's part that quite overwhelmed her. For the first time in his life, Max was actually, tenderly, romantically in love. His youthful compulsion toward Sally had been something else, a desperate quest for qualities missing in himself, but never the combination of tenderness and passion he felt toward Della; yet years went by during which time he saw Della daily yet made no movement as a man toward a woman he cares for.

Instead, he approached the matter in another way entirely. Every few months, he raised Della's salary five dollars, an action that drove Jake Stein crazy since he, like others in the office, knew that absolutely nothing serious was happening between Della and Max. On Christmas, Max would send Della a huge basket of delicacies, sensing that anything more personal than food would be odd and inexplicable; finally he learned her birth date and sent her two dozen long-stemmed roses. The day after receiving the roses, Della said to him, very formally, "Could I speak to you alone in your office, Mr. Britsky?"

In Max's office, Della said to him, her voice quavering a bit, "Why are you being so kind to me, Mr. Britsky?"

Max stared at her and tried to think of an appropriate answer.

"I must know," she said, her large blue eyes beginning to mist with tears. "I simply must know, because no one has ever been so kind to me before, and I don't know why, I really don't know why."

Max shook his head. "I don't know what to say, Della. I like you. I guess I love you."

"What!"

"I'm sorry," Max mumbled with a diffidence he had never exhibited before. "Maybe I shouldn't have said that."

"Oh, Mr. Britsky," Della cried, "don't you know how I feel about you?"

"No. How?"

"I think you're wonderful. I think you're the best man I ever met."

"You can't be that crazy," Max said, grinning with pleasure.

"I just didn't dare hope that you'd ever feel that way about me."

"Even when you knew what was going on between me and Etta?"

"I understand that. My goodness, I know how your wife treats you. Sometimes I'd like to shake her, the way she treats you."

"Only it's over," Max said emphatically. "Since Etta became Feona, it has been over, absolutely over. Furthermore, you and me, we'll have dinner tonight, because that's something I been thinking about for years and I'm not waiting any longer."

That way it began. There was no question of seducing Della. She and Max came together without any question or hesitation. She kept on working because, as she explained to Max, she would go out of her mind if she had to sit all day alone, and Max was delighted with a situation where this wonderful, pink-cheeked, redheaded woman could be around him all day; and now, today, Della rose as Max came into his office and whispered, "She's in there."

"Who?"

"Ruby's wife. I didn't want to let her in, but you know how she is."

"I know. What else?"

"A new set of drawings from Mr. Abel. They're on your desk."

"Did you look at them?"

"I just peeked. They're beautiful."

"Not too fancy?"

"I like things fancy. And your wife called. Tonight, she said, you're having dinner with the mayor. You shouldn't forget. Is he nice?"

"Who?"

"The mayor. Mr. Gaynor."

"Jay Gaynor's business is being nice. Mine ain't. Why did you let her in?"

"She's Mr. Ruby's wife. I just don't know how to treat her."

"Treat her like a tramp and you can't go wrong." Then Max went into his office. Kathy was sitting in his desk chair, her back to him and hidden by the high back of the swivel chair.

"Close the door, Max," she said.

"It's closed," Max said tiredly. "What have you got in mind?" Then he noticed her clothes piled neatly on his desk and sighed. "Oh, Jesus, no."

She swiveled the chair, got up, and came around the desk to face him. She was stark naked. She was no longer the beautiful young creature Ruby had married twelve years before, but her figure was still good, her well-shaped breasts high and firm, her hips not too wide.

"What in hell are you up to?" Max demanded angrily.

"What are you up to, brother-in-law? You been eating me with your goddamn eyes for ten years now, and for ten years I been begging you to put me in your pictures. Time's passing too quick. I decided to trade."

"Put on your clothes!" Max snapped.

"Why? You don't want me? I ain't got the goods Etta Goodman had or that tramp O'Donnell out front?"

"Goddamn it, you're my brother's wife!"

"So what? You don't know your brother Ruby? When it comes to offstage fucking, he's got ten to one on me, so don't shed no tears for him." She walked toward Max. He backed away.

"You want to be in one of my movies, is that it?"

"I thought you'd never ask. Come on, Max, I'm as good as anything you ever laid eyes on."

"All right, all right. You talk Ruby into it, and you're in a picture. That's my word. Just put on your clothes."

"You mean that, Max?"

"I swear, absolutely."

She ran to him, flung her arms around him, and kissed him.

"Will you put on your goddamn clothes!"

She clung to him. "You horny little bastard. You got an erection as big as a house."

He pulled loose. "Either get dressed or the deal's off. Now!"

She sighed, shrugged, went to the desk, and began to dress herself. "Here, help me," she said to Max. "Here in back."

Biting his lips, he fastened her stays. "How are the kids?" he managed to say.

"Great. Just great. What kind of a picture, Max?"

"The right kind. Get dressed and get out."

"O.K., but don't screw me, Max. Not that way. I can be a bitch if I have to."

"I bet you can."

When she had left, he said to Della, "You ever let her in here again, ever, I'll —" Words failed him.

"She's Mr. Britsky's wife," Della reminded him.

• • •

It would be difficult to find two men more apparently different than Max Britsky and Sam Snyder. Snyder's parents were immigrants from Thuringia in East Germany, and Snyder himself was a devout Lutheran and an utterly faithful husband whose only vices were cigars and beer. He was slow-spoken, round-faced and had over the years an ample belly that he filled with heavy German food. His sandy hair and childlike blue eyes could give an impression of somewhat stupid innocence, an impression far from the reality; the reality was a mind and outlook unlike Max's, but nevertheless innovative and at times brilliant. It was Sam Snyder who had set up the projection booths, who designed the angles of projection in the theatres, who had devised new and different projectors when National Distributors got an injunction against those already in use in

Max's houses, and who had designed and organized the first studio. It was Sam Snyder who went to France and sat down with Auguste Lumière, and over three bottles of wine and an enormous roast goose, made the deal that gave Max a steady flow of French film stock at the time Eastman Kodak had cut off his supply in collusion with the distribution trust. At the same time, working together with Lumière, Snyder made certain that Lumière's camera was outside of Edison's patents and would not involve Max in a lawsuit — after which he gave Lumière an order for fourteen cameras.

Yet the differences that separated Max and Sam Snyder apparently served as glue to bind them together. Snyder worshiped Max and firmly believed him capable of achieving anything he set out to do; and by 1912, Max's thirty-third year, Snyder was earning four hundred dollars a week, a truly princely sum for a production manager. Max had reached a point where he made no decisions regarding the production of films without first consulting Snyder. When he faced the necessity of producing six feature films a month, it was Snyder who convinced him that it could be done, whereupon they purchased a square block of rotting barns and stables in East Harlem, tore them down, and built on One Hundred and Twenty-seventh Street the first motion picture studio constructed as such. It was also through Snyder's relationship with the Lumières that Max began to buy films from Europe, making the deal just a month before this for the feature *The Queen*, starring the great Sarah Bernhardt. At that point, Max had almost a corner on the better foreign films, and had brought to America over the past few months *Quo Vadis* from Italy and *War and Peace* from Russia.

But it was the casting of Sarah Bernhardt in *The Queen* that set Max and those around him to thinking of what would eventually become the star system, and it was Sam Snyder who pinned it down. With four other film producers, Max had started, three years before, an exchange which allowed each producer to play the films of the others; until National Distributors stepped into the arrangement and let the other exhibitors know that if they dealt with Britsky, they would be cut out of National's product as well as the use of National's projectors, since National had a monopoly on patented projectors, again through arrangements and collusion. When Max ran the Bernhardt film, the other exhibitors made overtures, but only overtures. They lacked the courage to follow through. But independent theatres, still linked to Max, bought the film and showed it to tremendous crowds.

"That's what we need," Max said to Freedman. "We need Bernhardt. With her, we can sell anything."

"Max, we can't have her, and the truth is that the picture's lousy. We make better pictures. I tried using stage stars. It doesn't work."

"Why not?"

"Because they don't know how. They're too low key. As crazy as it sounds, Etta Goodman does it right. She doesn't act, but as Feona, with all her gestures and poses, she gives us what we need."

The night following this exchange with Freedman, Max had dinner at Sam Snyder's house on Thirty-seventh Street, between First and Second avenues. It was an old pre–Civil War red brick house with a wide twenty-four-foot frontage, only three stories high, but with four bedrooms on both the second and third floors, a convenience for a man who had five children. Max felt comfortable in Snyder's house — indeed, more comfortable than in the spotless neatness of his own home. The Snyder house was never neat and never spotless, but it was comfortable, and if Alice Snyder was not the world's best housekeeper, she was a marvelous cook, an art she never left to their single servant. She produced rich German food, kugels and dumplings and six different kinds of sausage and sauerbraten, food that Max loved, and since he never gained weight, food he could eat to the point of satiation.

Sally, who never berated Max for spending an evening away from home, actually appeared to welcome evenings apart from him, especially since so many of her evenings were spent working with Freedman on the endless flow of scenarios. She had little in common with Alice Snyder, a goodhearted buxom country girl out of a Pennsylvania Dutch background who had less than a primary school education and no interest apart from her family, and she was relieved not to have to join Max in his social relationship with Sam Snyder. Max, on the other hand, experienced at Snyder's home a sense of easy comfort and relaxation that he had never known before, not in the flat on Henry Street and not in the elegant brownstone on Sixty-sixth Street. The comfort was increased when one night Snyder invited him to join the family for dinner and Max had to refuse.

"Why not?" Snyder asked. "Is Sally expecting you?"

"As a matter of fact, she ain't. She and Freedman are meeting with two new writers they want to hire, at Rector's. One is a novelist, so they want to impress him. Only —" He stared at Snyder uncertainly. "Well, the truth is, I asked Della to have dinner with me."

"Della O'Donnell?"

"Yeah," Max said truculently.

"Then bring her along. I like Della, and Alice will be crazy about her."

"How do you know that?"

"I know. Trust me."

Snyder was right. Alice and Della were very much alike, both of them balancing small learning with large wisdom, both of them plump just short of stoutness at a time when no premium was placed on a woman's slenderness, both of them soft-spoken, gentle, never challenging the superiority of the male, both of them handsome women. Nor was Della bothered by disorder or by kids. The dinner was a great success, Alice's roasted duck in raisin sauce magnificent, the spring beer dark and heavy, and Max more relaxed and content than Della had ever seen him before. He and Snyder lit long, thick, twenty-five-cent Cuban cigars and filled the dining room with clouds of smoke that neither woman objected to, and Max said dreamily, "If I had five Sarah Bernhardts on my payroll, I'd say *vus felt mere*."

"Which means?" Della asked.

"Which means I got absolutely nothing to worry about except those bas—— excuse me, except Mr. Frank Stanford who runs National, and who's coming to see me next week, I should just live that long."

"What does he want this time?" Snyder asked.

"A pound of flesh, only with all the blood the system holds. You see, Alice," he said to Mrs. Snyder, "this outfit, National Distributors, can't bear that we're alive. First, ten, twelve years ago, they were only a distributing outfit for garbage — you should excuse me, for the eight-hundred-foot films they made which they called moving pictures. At that time they wanted our theatres, and when I told them to go suck an egg, they cut off our product. No more National films for the nickelodeons. Well, you remember, we junked the nickelodeons and made *The Waif*, and I think maybe *The Waif* was the end of the nickelodeons, although not just at once. So once we showed how it could be done, other producers started doing the same thing, and we exchange films because nobody can make enough films to have a new film every week of the year."

Max paused to light his cigar, and Snyder said, "Except maybe we got to."

"Maybe. Who knows. Anyway, like I said, other companies began making films, and each one set up an exchange. Only not National. Those goddamn — you should excuse me, I can't clean up my language and talk about National at the same time."

"The children are asleep," Alice said calmly, "so you just say what you have to, Max, and I am sure that both Della and I will survive it."

"The thing is," Max went on, "that National couldn't make a decent moving picture. With all their money and power and the telephone company behind them and Morgan and the crowd up in Rochester and Edison going along with them — with all that they don't have the brains to make a decent moving picture. So they began buying up the exchanges."

"Except us," Snyder said.

"Except us. That's right, and that's what Stanford and the trust want so hard he can't sleep at night, and next week he comes sucking around for it. He's seen the numbers on the Bernhardt film. Now if I had ten like her —"

"Make them," Sam Snyder said suddenly. "You take a girl like Etta — Etta Goodman," he explained to his wife, "she's now Feona Amour. Well, you take her and spend enough advertising her and put her picture up on the billboards and on the beer coasters in every saloon, and you got something as big as Bernhardt."

"Maybe," Max agreed.

"Max, you got the Welonsky kid, that little Polish girl Gerry named Renee Favour —" Della caught the excitement. "You could do it with her and with Mary Malone."

"It takes time, time." Max shook his head unhappily. "The question is, what do they throw at us this time? This miserable crumb, Stanford," he explained to Alice, "always has a gun in his pocket. Not a real gun, but something to hit us with. He'll come with an injunction claiming that our projectors violate his patents.

He's done that twice. Each time, Sam here, God bless him, he's got to alter the projector to get around the injunction. Same with our cameras. Freddy Feldman could make his bed in the courts, and I hate to tell you what it costs."

"Talking about Feldman," Snyder said, "he's got a cousin Barney, works for the *Tribune*. He did the story about Etta and Pasquel, you remember, Feona loves Warren, or does she? The kid's crazy about movies. You could hire him away and put it in his lap — how to turn them all into Sarah Bernhardts."

"Without learning to act," Della couldn't help saying. "That is something."

"Acting!" Max snorted. "Who needs acting? It's a good idea, Sam. I'll give it a shot."

• • •

"I got to plead with you to come to see me," Max's mother said to him. "You're a millionaire. After all, what kind of use has a millionaire got for an old Jewish lady?"

"Mama, I haven't been avoiding you. I am up to my ears in problems."

"And you live next door. And even now, I wouldn't see you except I got to go and plead with your stuck-up, fancy wife. Please, you should tell Max his mother wants to speak to him. Not anybody. Not somebody dragged in from the street, but his own mother who slaved her heart out for him."

"Mama, Sally's not stuck up. She even said I'm neglecting you."

"Ah-hah, so when she says it it's right, and you come running. Otherwise, I could drop dead. Eat something. I stayed up to the middle of the night baking." She pointed to a dish of cake and cookies resting on a table with a teapot and cups and saucers, the table set in the parlor and covered with a lace cloth. It was a small, round table that stood in front of an enormous velvet-covered sofa. Though his taste was limited, Max recoiled in despair every time he walked into his mother's house. The living room was filled with large, ungainly pieces of furniture set on a garish Persian rug. On marble pedestals there stood a stuffed owl, a stuffed squirrel, and a bronze casting of a young woman in flowing robes. On another table was displayed a collection of sea shells, and on the walls, hanging almost as high as the twelve-foot ceiling, a series of oil paintings that Freida had discovered in the various auction houses she visited.

Max bit into a cookie and praised it, and Sarah said, "See, I would have time to bake if my children were happy."

"So now what, Mama?"

"Your sister Esther, my beautiful Esther with the red hair, she's got two babies, they should starve? That's what you want?"

"What do you mean, that's what I want?"

"With Manny not working, what else?"

"You mean that bum she married has been fired again? I talk Plotkin into giving him the best kind of a selling job a man can have, and he's fired again?"

"What kind of a life does she have with him traveling all the time?"

"At least he's out of the way."

"Manny's a sweet man."

"Yeah."

"I can see the meanness in you. You'll let them starve."

"Mama, I won't let them starve. Only he's such a damn schmuck."

"That's language to use in front of me!"

"I'm sorry, Mama. All right, I'll find something." He got up, ready to leave.

"You'll wait a minute? I got something to say about next door."

"What do you mean, next door?" Max was on his feet. He started to leave, and each step was like pulling a foot out of hot tar.

"Next door is where you live. You got a minute more for your mother?"

"All right."

"So sit down."

"I'll stand. What about where I live?"

"You I don't see going in, but Freedman's in and out of there all the time, except when she ain't there. Instead of raising her children, she's running around."

"She's not running around. She's working."

"She shouldn't be working. She's a lady. Her husband ain't got enough money, she got to be working?"

He left there, his fists clenched so tightly his nails bit into his skin. The following day, at his office, he called Della O'Donnell in and asked her to sit down. "Tell me about your mother, Della," he said to her. "You never said a word about your mother or your father."

"All of a sudden, Max? Just like that? You call me into your office and tell me to tell you about my mother?"

"I got reasons."

"All right. My father was a drunken bum and he used to beat the hell out of my mother. She drank. If she didn't drink, how could she stand it? I was the only kid. I didn't like my father and I don't like to talk about it. I didn't like my mother but I felt sorry for her. My father was a teamster, and one day his horses went crazy and he was dragged to death. I was eleven. A year later, Mama died, and the Murphys sent me off to board at school, at the Good Sisters of the Sacred Heart. Period. You have my life story, Max."

"I shouldn't have bothered you."

He looked so crestfallen that Della went around his desk and kissed him. "I usually don't do it during business hours."

"Why didn't I find you when I was a kid?"

"Maybe you were never a kid, Max."

"Maybe not. Now, darling Della, get out of here and let me think, because in a half-hour I got to talk to that son of a bitch Stanford. Also, send in Freddy and Sam. I need support."

"I think," Feldman said, sitting in Max's office with Snyder and Max, waiting for Stanford to appear, "I think we have to fight him this time — I mean, we have to take him to court under the Sherman Antitrust Act, which National has violated a hundred times. This trust is no different than all the other trusts, and they just march along, figuring that the world is theirs until someone stops them. We have to stop them."

"I don't like it," Max said. "I don't like the courts and I don't trust the courts. National, the telephone company, the Rochester people, Edison — every part of that lousy trust is burning up because a handful of Jews without a dime of capital have put something together that they never even dreamed of. We made this. We created the moving picture, and now that it's here, they tell us to drop dead. Well, screw them!"

"All right. Screw them. But do it my way."

"Hold on, hold on," Snyder said gently. "Max, you remember

when we made *The Waif?* You gambled with everything. You sold the nickelodeons and the halls and put every dime we had into that picture — and it worked. Sure they hate the Jews, but those bastards hate everyone else — the Irish, the Germans, the Polacks, the Italians — the hell with that. We got to stop them, Max. We can't live with it anymore. I can't invent a new projector every time they slap an injunction on us."

"Do you know what it has to cost? Tell him, Freddy."

"It could be half a million before we're through."

"And right now," Max said, "we're shooting four features, two up in Harlem and two in the ice house. Where does the money come from? Suppose it runs to a million, two million?"

"And suppose they slap an injunction on our cameras while we got four pictures going?"

"All right, let's think about it," Feldman said. "Meanwhile, buzz Della in here."

"What for?"

"You'll see. Trust me."

Max pressed the buzzer on his desk and Della came into the room. "Is he here yet?" Max asked.

"Sitting outside and as annoyed as a wet hen. He doesn't like to be kept waiting."

"Let him stew. Now what, Freddy?"

Feldman pointed to the door that led to his office. "I'm going to leave that door open a crack, Della, and I'll put a chair right next to it in my office. After Stanford comes in here, take your pad and go around to my office and sit just outside that door and try to take down every word that's said in here."

Della shook her head. "I don't know, Mr. Feldman. I just don't know if I'm that quick."

"Give it a try. What's important is to get what Stanford says. You can fudge what we say, but get him."

"I'll try."

Frank Stanford, tall, elegant, amiable, gave no sign of the irritation Della had observed. He shook hands with Snyder and Feldman. Max, protected by his desk, did not offer his hand and Stanford did not ask for it. He observed that Max was looking well.

"I got a clear conscience," Max said coldly.

"Hell, Max," Stanford said, "I can't see why you got a chip on your shoulder. You beat the tar out of us on that *Queen* film. We broke our backs to get it, but you got some kind of love affair going with the French.''

"No love affair," Feldman said, trying to ease the tension. "We sell them good films. They sell us their best.''

"Just like that?''

"More or less.''

"We offered them double what you did.''

"Maybe they don't like your ass," Max said. "You're a bunch of tight-ass bastards. Maybe the French don't appreciate that.''

Feldman looked at Max pleadingly, and Stanford said, "That was uncalled for.''

Max shrugged, "Sure. Trouble is, Stanford, that every time you come around, you bring an ax with you.''

"I bring offers. That's the way business works. We would have liked to have *The Queen*. But we can understand how you Jews stick together. We don't hold that against you.''

"What in hell does that mean, the way we stick together?''

"Well, it's no secret Sarah Bernhardt's a Jew lady —''

"And you think that's how we got the picture?" Max said icily.

"Now, hold on," Stanford said, spreading his arms. "Let's not have unpleasantness. I came here to make you an offer. We want your moving pictures. We'll buy them or rent them, whatever you wish, and we'll open our stock to you. But we want the European films and we want the European market. You bow out of that, and we'll open our doors to you.''

Max burst out laughing.

"I don't find it amusing.''

"Go fuck yourself," Max said.

"I expected that. You never got your face out of the gutter, did you, Britsky? All right, we have put up with you — now you're finished. We are going to wipe you out. We'll smother you with injunctions. We'll make it impossible for you to buy film stock if we have to buy half of France, and we'll lock every film you try to import into Customs. And we can do it. We have the money and the connections, and if you think you can buck a trust the size of ours, you're out of your mind. We got the telephone company behind us, and we got the whole Rochester crowd locked into this. We'll tie up every camera you got in your studios. You're a two-bit little East Side Jew, Britsky, and too big for your boots. If you think that you alone, out of every producer in America, can buck the trust, you are crazy. You're finished!" With that, he turned on his heel and strode to the door, flung it open, and then slammed it behind him.

Silence after he left. Then Feldman grinned tentatively. Snyder looked at him. The smile was catching. Max burst out laughing and through his laughter managed to say, "He never changes. That dumb son of a bitch never changes."

"Della!" Feldman called out. "Come in, Della — come on in!"

Watching Feldman, Max continued to gurgle. By now, Feldman's intent was obvious, and Max could have embraced and kissed the chubby little lawyer. It had never occurred to him that they had picked up his own style or even that he had a style of his own; but Snyder also followed Feldman's reasoning, and he watched with pleasure as Della entered, waving her notebook.

"Got it all?"

"Every word."

Max bounced around the desk and kissed her cheek. Feldman said to her, "Type up the whole thing, three carbons. Then take out that last remark of Mr. Britsky's — you know what I mean?"

"Indeed I do, Mr. Feldman."

"Good. Now, put this down as a heading: Meeting at the Britsky offices in the Hobart Building, April 11, 1912. Present, Max Britsky, president, Britsky Productions; Samuel Snyder, vice president, and Frederick Feldman, corporation counsel. Testimony taken by Della O'Donnell —"

"But he didn't know I was there, Mr. Feldman."

"Doesn't change anything. You make the three carbons, bring the original and two carbons here, and send in Jake to notarize them. Give the third carbon to Millie, and have her make copies. I want three dozen copies."

Della left, and the three men sat in silence, looking at each other. Then Max went to a cabinet and produced a bottle of Old Overholt and three shot glasses. He poured the drinks and said, "You used to be my conscience, Freddy. Honest Fred. Would you believe it?" he asked Snyder.

"Nope."

"Here's to Stanford, poor bastard," Max said. They drank. "You know what I'm going to do, Fred? I'm going to take an ad in the *Tribune*, and I'm going to print the whole thing. Is that legal?"

"Why not? If the *Tribune* runs it."

"If they don't, the *Post* will. Maybe not the *Times*, but the *Post* will. What's your play for the end of Mr. Stanford?"

"I don't hate him as much as you do, Max. I'm after the trust. Stanford's only an errand boy. Clyde Hillering is the president of National, and these notes will go out to him today, notarized, with a covering letter that we are bringing suit against the trust for twenty million dollars. That's a nice round sum. Restraint of trade and violation of the antitrust act."

"What about Rochester?" Snyder asked.

"They'll get copies, and Mr. Edison too. I wasn't thinking of the advertisement, Max, but of getting a copy to each paper and let them run it as news. Of course, nobody may take it either way because they'll be afraid of slander."

"I know Hillering," Snyder said. "He'll break Stanford's back."

"Unless —" Max began.

"Unless what?"

"They're both vicious bastards."

"I have a feeling," Feldman said, "that today is the beginning of the end of the trust. When word of this gets out, all the independents are going to turn brave. The lawsuit will go on for years, but the shock value is what counts. And in the end, we win, believe me, Max."

The *Tribune* printed Max's advertisement the following day, and it became a news item in every other newspaper in New York as well as in three or four hundred that were not in New York. Theodore Roosevelt took time out from organizing the Bull Moose party for the coming presidential election to send the following telegram to Max Britsky: GREETINGS AND SALUTATIONS FROM AN OLD TRUST-BUSTER STOP GO GET THEM MAX STOP AND WHEN I AM ELECTED PRESIDENT AGAIN THE GOVERNMENT WILL JOIN YOU IN KICKING THE PANTS OFF NATIONAL AND THE TELEPHONE COMPANY TOO STOP BULLY FOR YOU. Max took ads in the *Times* and the *Tribune* and ran Roosevelt's telegram in large type; then he made his first political contribution, sending a check for five thousand dollars to the local organizing committee of the Bull Moose party.

A few days later, Snyder informed Max that he had heard, via the film grapevine, that National had fired Stanford.

"You know, I feel sorry for the dumb bastard."

"You're crazy," Snyder told him.

"Yeah, maybe."

And then Dan Silverman, the largest film producer and theatre owner in Boston, telephoned Max the following day.

"What can I do for you?" Max asked him.

"Max, I got brave. I told the trust to fuck off and pulled my films. But now I'm out on a limb. I need moving pictures. I got thirty-two houses with appetites for movies like a horse for oats."

"Are you offering me an exchange?"

"You got to let me in. I'm out on a limb."

"I'll have Freddy draw up the papers. Meanwhile, I got twenty-four features in my library since you walked out on me for the trust. How many do you want?"

"All of them. Every moving picture you got that we didn't show."

Roosevelt came to New York to make a speech in Cooper Union. He asked to have Max Britsky on the dais with him, and he embraced Max in front of a packed hall of cheering Bull Moose supporters. The following day, Abe Cohen in St. Louis and Frank Immelman in Chicago broke with the trust and joined Max's film exchange. Feldman was walking on air. Max invited Feldman and his wife, Leah, a shy little woman, to dinner at his Sixty-sixth Street house. All through the evening, she never spoke except to say "Please" or "Thank you" or "Excuse me." Sam Snyder and his wife, Alice, were also at the table, since the dinner was in the way of a victory celebration, but Alice was quiet and uneasy. She could live with Max's inclusion of Della O'Donnell at the Snyder dinner table, but two women in relation to Max were more than she could handle. Nor was she fond of Sally, who was very formal and very reserved.

Feldman was not a good drinker. He had too much wine, and he proposed a garbled toast to the "two great men of our time, Teddy and Max!"

"Oh, I wouldn't compare Teddy to Max," Sally said.

Snyder sensed the sarcasm and hostility, but Max, who also had too much to drink, spread his arms and said, "There's a lady respects her husband. But you got to give Teddy credit where credit's due."

When Max handed Snyder a long Cuban cigar and started to light one himself, Sally said sharply, "I think you might wait until the women are out of the room."

. . .

When Frank Stanford telephoned Bert Bellamy and asked Bellamy to join him for lunch, Bellamy agreed: not out of any sense of disloyalty to Max, but because Bellamy was a man who felt that the world changes. He was less aware of how much he himself had changed, for he still preserved somewhere in his mind a shadow of the relationship that had once existed between himself and Max. But it was very much of a shadow. In the old days, he had accepted the fact that Max was shrewd and very often damn clever. He could afford this generosity: he was taller than Max, better looking than Max, and just as wealthy as Max. Now Max was a millionaire and he, Bert Bellamy, was Max's employee. It made a difference, and there was no question but that those around the industry were aware of the fact that it made a difference. Sally was aware of it. Fred Feldman was aware of it, and so was Frank Stanford — which was why he came to Bert.

Like Max, Stanford had spent most of his adult years in the moving picture business, and he knew the burgeoning industry from top to bottom. Stanford was a tall, good-looking man, well over six feet, with graying hair and pale blue eyes. He said to Bellamy, "You and I can talk to each other and understand each other, Bert, a lot better than I can do talking to Max. Maybe you think I'm anti-Semitic. That's a lot of horseshit. If I lose my temper and call someone a Jew, well, it's just calling a spade a spade, and I just can't remember how damn sensitive those people are."

"They're sensitive, all right," Bert agreed.

"Now that statement Max picked up and made such a big thing with — Hell, you get excited and you talk. I had no idea what I said was being taken down."

Bert nodded and waited.

"It looks like hell in print."

"It does."

"I can understand why I became the whipping boy for the trust. They had to have someone to lay it on, but I've been out of work for three months now, and I got this Jew-baiting thing hung around my neck like a goddamn sack of cement. You know me long enough. I may be a son of a bitch, but I'm no Jew-baiter. I been working with Jews for years, and if Max thinks there are no Jews in the trust, he's wrong."

Bert nodded. He anticipated what was coming and wondered how Stanford would put it.

"I need a job. Desperately. I want you to ask Max to give me a break. I hear his exchange is growing every day, and I'm a damn good film salesman. He knows that."

"What makes you think that Max, of all people, would give you a job?"

"You get that feeling about Max. He'd kill you at the drop of a hat, but he doesn't hold grudges. All I want you to do is to put a word in and get Max to talk to me. Do it, and I'll remember it, Bert."

Bert shrugged. "I don't know, Frank. Max is a funny guy, and there's no telling what he'll do. But I'll give it a try."

A week later, Della came into Max's office and said, "You will never believe who is outside and says he has an appointment with you."

"Frank Stanford."

"Himself."

"Send him in," Max said. When Stanford had entered the room, Max walked around, closed the door behind him, and told him to sit down. "Don't cry about it," Max said. "I hate to see anyone ass-licking, so don't tell me you're sorry. Those shitheads at the trust dumped on you because someone has to take the fall, and now no one will hire you. Bert laid that out for me. Can you think of one reason why I should give you a job?"

"I can think of one," Stanford said. "It was my stupidity that gave you your opening to go in after National, and now they're falling to pieces, even without your lawsuit."

"That's a good reason. But who hires someone for stupid?"

"I'm not stupid, Max. You know that. I was running errands."

"Yeah. All right. See Bert. He runs the theatre section."

"Just like that?"

"Yeah, just like that."

"I don't know how to thank you —"

"Forget it, forget it."

Afterward, Della asked him why, and Max told her, "I don't know, kid. It's a lousy world, and when you start sliding down — Ah, hell, Frank's no worse than any of us. He was just on the other side. He was their son of a bitch. Now he's our son of a bitch. We can use him."

· · ·

It had to happen sooner or later. People get careless. They were shooting four pictures at a time, two in the ice house and two in the big studio in Harlem. Sally and Freedman often worked until midnight, and Max spent more and more evenings at Della's tiny flat on East Twenty-third Street. It reminded him of the room Sally had had on Tenth Street. How strange it was that the time of his meeting and falling in love with Sally had become so distant as to belong to another life. He wasn't in love with Della. He never thought of Della in terms of being in love, nor had it occurred to him that since he had first gone to bed with Della, he had gone to bed with no one else — not his wife, not any of the pretty little kids who were always hanging around the entrance to both studios, pleading to work in movies for two dollars a day and ready to crawl into bed with anyone who gave them the opportunity. Max wasn't introspective; he did what he felt the need to do without any great self-examination; and it was enough that with Della he felt comfortable. For one thing, Della was an inch shorter than Max, Sally in heels was an inch taller; it made a difference. For another, Della cherished him and mothered him and never corrected his speech.

Thus with both of them falling into two separate existences and becoming increasingly casual about it, it had to happen that Max would walk into his house unexpectedly and find Sally in Freedman's arms, the two of them engaging in a deep and passionate kiss. It was before the era of Sigmund Freud's pervasiveness, and if anyone had told Max that they were caught in that posture because they wanted to be caught, he would have said that the whole notion was insane. For Max, it was purely an accident.

Sally and Freedman, aware of Max's presence, pulled back from each other; and then the three of them stood in a tableau for a few seconds. No one said a word. Sally and Freedman stared at Max. Max looked through them. Then Max walked between them and they stepped back to let him pass. The incident had taken place in the vestibule of the brownstone. Max went past them into the living room, where he remained standing and heard the outside door close. He stood with his hands in his pockets, facing the wall. Sally entered the room.

"I'm sorry it had to happen like this," Sally said.

"Yeah." A long moment of silence.

"For God's sake, aren't you going to say anything?"

"What's to say? I could tell you not to shit on your own doorstep, but that's done. What do you want to do? You want to marry that pisspot?"

"No!"

"Then go to bed!"

From that point on, Sally and Max had separate rooms. Max never mentioned the incident again, nor did he have any real sense of what he himself felt. He had not had intercourse with Sally for a number of years, and while he had never suspected her of having strong and unsatisfied appetites, he could hardly blame her. But no concept of equal rights had ever entered his head, and if he did not feel any sense of a betrayal on the part of Sally, he did feel an invasion of property rights on the part of Freedman. He was also disappointed in himself. He should have been enraged. He should have, as he thought of it, kicked the shit out of Freedman, whom he had always held in a certain degree of contempt. But he wasn't enraged, and he had no desire to beat up Freedman. In fact, he was relieved, and the fact that he was relieved provoked him. As for Freedman, Max couldn't even fire him, since the four films in production were all more or less under Freedman's control if not his direction.

What irritated Max more than anything else was the fact that Freedman never came around to apologize or explain — if such things can be explained — but instead acted as if nothing of consequence had taken place. Freedman had changed, but the change in him over the years had been so gradual that Max had never become specifically aware of it. Freedman was developing a national and, to some degree, international reputation. When he directed *The Raiders*, a Civil War film shot almost entirely out of doors on

Long Island, critical articles were written about him as well as about the film. In interviews Freedman made no mention of Sam Snyder and his innovations in terms of laying tracks for a moving camera and his use of new lenses for close-ups, nor of the photographers, nor of a brilliant young writer, Jo Stefenson by name, who had written the scenario and who had offered a way to substitute action for most of the dialogue cards. The picture was embraced by Freedman as his own work, his total creation. He was no longer uncertain of himself. For the Long Island work, he had donned riding breeches and leather puttees, and though he never mounted a horse, he liked the gesture of emphasizing his orders with a quirt, which he slapped against his open palm. He also had a young man who kept pace with him, carrying a megaphone and a jug of hot coffee. He was by no means unconscious of his role-acting. When he had started as a film director, there had been no such creature. He felt it incumbent upon him to define the animal, and this he did.

So he's screwing my wife, Max said to himself. I ought to break the bastard's ass or fire him or both.

But he did neither. He just didn't care. There were three new young directors working for him under Freedman's guidance, and four months later, feeling that these new men could carry on perfectly well, Max called Freedman into his office and said, "I think you're an overpriced shithead, Gerry, and a second-rate son of a bitch."

"Why don't you just fire me, Max, and not indulge your gutter beginnings?"

"I've outgrown them, Gerry. Otherwise, I'd kick the shit out of you. Sure, you're fired."

A week later, Freedman went to work for Sunrise Productions in New Jersey, and about six weeks after that, Max read that Gerald Freedman and Sunrise's bright new star, Monica Legrange, were to be married. He felt sorry for Sally. She was suddenly older and very tired-looking. For weeks, she had been working on a scenario based on *David Copperfield*. It was the first scenario she had undertaken entirely by herself, and Max promised her that it would be the most important production they had ever mounted. Any anger he might have felt toward Sally had turned into enormous guilt, and he bought her a magnificent ermine wrap.

She thanked him lackadaisically.

"You shouldn't have told Mama we were sleeping in separate rooms."

"She asked me. She keeps coming in here when we're away."

"She likes to see the kids."

"It's still my house. She comes in and prowls through it. She talks to the servants."

"She so upset about the separate rooms," Max explained.

Sally snorted. "That one!" She flung the fur wrap across the room. "I'm upset too. Tell her that!"

* * *

"You have no reason to feel guilty," Della said to him. "She did the same thing."

Max stopped pacing in Della's living room to turn and stare at her. Della was sitting in a Morris chair, knitting calmly. Della's apartment lacked the color and charm Sally had given to her place; it was solidly comfortable, with comfortable, unimaginative furniture, with a picture of the Virgin with the Child on one wall and, facing it, a crocheted sampler that asked the viewer to speak a small prayer and bless our happy home. The windows had lace curtains, and in the bedroom, over Della's bed, there was a crucifix and the figure of Christ. All of this made Max somewhat uneasy, especially the act of sexual intercourse under the crucifix. To Max, Della's Catholicism was totally confusing. She was delighted to have him for a lover, and without question, she loved him; but she made it plain that if he divorced Sally, she could never marry him, nor was she certain that she could carry on the affair with a divorced man.

Not that Max had ever seriously raised the question of divorce. He was incapable of contemplating a divorce from Sally any more than he could contemplate a divorce from Britsky Productions. Each was a major achievement of his life, each the living proof that the poverty and hopelessness that had surrounded his childhood could be overcome. In all truth, Max would never actually be separated from his childhood; the skinny little kid who had been saddled with the responsibility for the survival of a family of seven human souls lived inside of him as a constant companion; and it was as much this skinny little kid as it was the adult Max who turned to stare at Della.

"What do you mean, she did the same thing? What do you mean by that? You'd better explain yourself."

Della stopped knitting and looked at Max in surprise.

"Just tell me what you mean," he said.

"You're angry at me."

"You made a statement," Max said.

"All I said was for you not to feel guilty, Max. You seem to suffer in so many ways, and I just don't know why."

"Never mind my suffering. You said she did the same thing."

"Oh —"

"Come on!"

"Well, you told me you found her kissing Gerry passionately. She's been having an affair with him, Max. It's been going on for years and years. Everybody knows; I was sure you knew."

He struggled to breathe, gasping, and then, getting hold of himself, fairly shouted, "That's a damned lie!"

"Max —" Della said weakly.

"A goddamn lie! Everyone knows? Who knows? You just tell me who knows, and how come you know so much?"

Della put down her knitting and spread her arms hopelessly. "Max, darling, what can I say?"

"You said enough. Now I goddamn well want to know who says my wife is fucking Freedman."

Della shook her head.

"So what is it then? Some fancy plan to get me to divorce my wife? And don't talk to me about any even Steven. A man's got a right to get laid if he wants to. Not a woman! No, sir! Not a woman!" And he walked out, slamming the door of the apartment behind him.

After that, at the office, Max treated Della with cold formality. It was Mrs. O'Donnell now. Sam Snyder invited both of them for dinner. Max made his excuses, but Della came, and after dinner she sat with Alice Snyder and had a good cry.

"I didn't mean it that way," Della told Alice. "I thought he knew. Everybody else knew, so it just makes plain common sense that I should think he knew."

"Plain common sense doesn't count with Max Britsky."

"It's two weeks now, and he treats me like I'm not there. I love him. I really love him."

"Then if that's the case," Alice said to her, "you're a real dumb-bell. I don't like to talk this way, but it's time someone spoke to you without mincing words. You're a beautiful young woman, Della —"

"Hah! That's to laugh. Young — I'm thirty-four."

"It doesn't show. You should marry some fine young man and have children, a family. You can still do that. Instead, you've thrown the last six years away on Max Britsky. He'll never leave Sally."

"Alice," Della said through her tears, "I'm married. And he's a no-good drunken bum and walked out on me, and he's living with some tramp in Yonkers, so I can never get married again."

"Oh, I didn't know."

Unexpectedly, a week later, Max asked Della to have dinner with him. She accepted with the same quick delight that had marked her first response to his advances. He took her to Luchow's on Four-teenth Street, where they dined on bratwurst and lentils and dump-lings, washing it all down with sweet dark beer. Della wondered how Max could remain so thin while she gained weight constantly. "I'll soon look like one of those fat old Irish ladies, and then you won't want to look at me."

"You're beautiful, and you'll always be beautiful."

Tears came to Della's eyes. "You were so mad at me. You said such awful things to me. I didn't think you'd ever want to see me again."

"You know how I feel about Sally."

"Sure. I know, Max."

"So we won't ever talk about those things again, right?"

"Right, Max."

That night, with his head pillowed on her abundant bosom, with the warm smell of her body surrounding him, Max was as much at peace as ever in his life.

. . .

The opening of the Britsky Xanadu was a New York City event of great importance, from the architectural as well as from other points of view, rising as the first of those great and improbable temples to the glory of the moving picture that were built between 1912 and 1929. When work began on the actual construction, Max obtained a copy of the Coleridge poem and read it over and over, finally deciding to name the theatre the Britsky Xanadu. Sally was thunderstruck, and told Max flatly that the juxtaposition of the two words was absolutely ridiculous.

"So I'll be ridiculous," Max said, shrugging.

"It makes no sense. No one will know how to pronounce the name."

"According to Abel, it's pronounced Zanadu, but suppose they say Exanadu — what difference does it make? Since this Coleridge fellow who wrote the poem has been dead for a long time, he can't tell nobody how to pronounce it, which I wish was the case with the rest of the English language."

"It's just too bad that I try to improve your speech. I still say it's ridiculous."

Max sighed. "Then I'll be ridiculous. It's not a new position for me, is it? I don't know why you should resent it."

"And just what does that mean?" Sally snapped.

"What does it mean? It's a question of being ridiculous. I'm used to being ridiculous. It seems that everyone in New York knows that Freedman is fucking my wife except me. So I'm ridiculous."

"You love that word, don't you?" She was shouting. "You use it over me like a club! Well, it's true! True! True! Look at yourself! You're a cheap, vulgar, East Side hoodlum! That's what you are and that's what you'll always be!"

Max couldn't understand why he felt relieved. He was very calm. A strange woman was shouting at him. "Why did you marry this hoodlum?" he asked almost gently.

She began to cry then. Like a little girl, she whispered, "Papa wanted me to, Mama wanted me to."

"Yes, I suppose so." Then he walked out and left her.

Yet the problem of the name still remained, and Max decided that he would present the question to Clifford Abel and abide by his decision. Increasingly, he had come to depend on Abel in matters of taste. It was part of the rapport and mutual admiration that had grown up between them.

"Maybe I'm crazy," Max said, "but I want to call it Xanadu. Certain people say it's ridiculous."

Clifford Abel thought it was unusual, but not ridiculous. "In fact," he said to Max, "it has a certain kind of validity. Like Kubla Khan, you decreed it."

Della wanted to call it the Palladian, having read somewhere that a great theatre by that name had been built in London, and while Max liked the sound of the word, Abel pointed out to him that it had a rather historic connection with the Classical style. The theatre they were building was as distant from the Classical style as architecture could get. Max insisted that somewhere in the lobby should be a prominent line of ornamental writing in large letters: "In Xanadu did Kubla Khan a stately pleasure dome decree." Abel liked the idea, and Barney Enfield, who was Fred Feldman's cousin and who had worked for the *Tribune* and had been hired away by Max, thought it was absolutely fantastic. After Sam Snyder had suggested having their own publicity person to turn their movie actresses into Sarah Bernhardts, or at least the equivalent in terms of fame, Max had sought out Barney Enfield, spoken to him and hired him. Enfield leaped on the comparison between Max and Kubla Khan. It was good publicity, and he felt that the term "pleasure dome" was both artistic and useful.

On occasion, by no means frequently, Max would spend time with his children. That was where his mental picture of pinnacles had come from. Max was never very easy with his children. Marion was now seven years old and Richard was eight and a half. Their German nanny regarded Max as an uncouth interloper and Max in turn found his children so different and alien that no easy approach was possible. However, alone with them at rare moments, he took to reading to them from their illustrated storybooks. Max had never seen such books, and though he was not a very good reader, he was enchanted by the illustrations. It was the pictures of palaces, lacy fairy buildings, many-towered, that took his fancy, and he had brought one of the books to Abel.

Many people sneered at the enthusiasms that were founded in Max's lack of sophistication and education. Clifford Abel did not. He was intrigued by Max's bursts of excitement and by the unfettered nature of his ideas; and he explained rather regretfully that a New York City street could not approximate the rocky pinnacles upon which the story illustrations were constructed.

"But," Max insisted, "we can have the towers, Cliff. Suppose just in front, two towers coming up on either side of the entrance, and then behind it a dome. I want it to be like something they never saw before in a theatre. Different, the way the movies are different."

"I suppose it could be done."

"And inside, the feeling you're inside a dream."

"Maybe."

When Max finally chose the drawing that would become the Britsky Xanadu, Barney Enfield had it printed in the *Tribune* with a long background story regarding its genesis. He kept the interest going all through the fourteen months of excavating and building, and during those months, there was hardly a day when Max wasn't on the site, as eager and interested and excited as a kid with a new toy.

The unpleasant interlude between Max and Della O'Donnell had been forgotten by Max and forgiven by Della. She understood Max far better than he understood himself — his fears and doubts and his desperate constructs that were so far from reality. She had never known anyone as tender and loving toward her as Max was, nor had he ever received such unquestioning devotion; yet he was incapable of wholly admitting to himself that for the first and only time in his life, he was truly in love with a woman who loved him. He could accept the fact that Della had become a necessity and that he couldn't live without her, that the only moments of peace and security and comfort he knew took place in her company; but at the same time he relegated her to a place outside his world. In his world, or rather in the eyes of the world as he fancied it, he was Sally's faithful husband and Sally was his faithful wife, and the incongruous nature of all this hardly disturbed him.

During the building of his beloved toy, the Britsky Xanadu, it was frequently Della who accompanied him as he prowled among the scaffolding and hoists and workmen. She wore heavy shoes on such occasions and would hike up her skirts to reveal plaid woollen stockings, and with her flaming red hair and abundant bosom, she brought joy to the workingmen on the construction, grinning at their hoots and whistles. After a time, they came to know her. They were a wonderful assortment of people — the masons Italian, the laborers and ironworkers Irish, the plasterers Jewish, and the carpenters Yankees; and when Della missed a few days, they would welcome her with bitter complaints for her absence. Max always watched her with pride and delight. The only women he had ever known who were as outgoing and as uninhibited as Della were the whores of his youth, but with Della it was neither hostility nor enticement, but just the simple warmth of her nature.

The excavating had begun during the summer of 1912, and by the following January, the shell of the structure had been completed and an army of craftsmen were at work on the interior. They were designing the interior walls, not the actual walls of the theatre but a sort of reverse cornice cut out of thin wood and mounted high on the theatre walls but about six inches away from the supporting walls, the wood cut to give the illusion of parapets. Behind these thin walls, a sky would be painted with rheostat lights to complete the illusion. Abel had worked this out to satisfy Max's wish that the people in the theatre should feel that they actually were in a palace, and having mounted the first section of this wall, he wanted Max to see it. As excited as a kid — since Abel at first had doubted that this could be done — Max stopped by Della's desk and said, "Come on, baby. We're going to step into a Jewish palace on Seventh Avenue."

Della shook her head. "I'd love to, Max. But I have a rotten headache. I think I'll go home."

"I got my car downstairs. We'll drive you home first. Unless —" He touched her brow. "No, I thought maybe I'd talk you into it. But you're hot. I think you got a fever."

"No, no, I'm all right. You really want me to go with you?"

"Only if you feel all right."

"I'll go. If I faint, you'll take me home, won't you, Max?"

"Absolutely."

She didn't complain of her headache again. On the way out, they picked up Sam Snyder. Clifford Abel was waiting for them at the theatre. The ceiling had been given a prime coat of sky blue, and at Abel's urging, the electricians had installed a single bank of lights, enough to illuminate about ten feet of the false wall. Abel sat them on crates so that they could look up, and then slowly he raised the power of the rheostat. The illusion was excellent, a true sense of the sun rising behind the crenelated wall, and Della clapped her hands in delight.

"Max, it's wonderful! Absolutely wonderful!"

Not for a moment did it occur to Della that Clifford Abel had anything to do with the effect. As far as she was concerned, it was Max who did things, who made the world turn, who sheltered her and protected her.

"It is quite wonderful," Abel agreed. "Odd thing is, no one ever thought of it before; that is, turning the inside into the outside. It's a marvelous illusion."

"And you're a genius," Max said generously.

"Oh, no, no. It was your idea, Max. Although I must say that the stars in the sky are my notion. There are eight hundred tiny sockets set into the ceiling. When it's all complete and the ceiling is a much deeper shade of blue, then as you turn the sunset rheostat down, you can also control the starlight with a second rheostat. I didn't just set in the sockets at random. We followed a midsummer star map, midsummer being the time most people look at the sky. Just consider it, Miss O'Donnell," he said to Della, "here you are, sitting in the theatre and waiting for the moving picture to begin —"

"The organ's playing," Max interrupted. "The fifth biggest pipe organ in New York."

"Oh, yes," Abel agreed, "the organ playing, and now the light in the theatre begins to fade. You look up, and suddenly you're not in a theatre anymore but in a walled palace, and beyond the walls you see the last rays of the setting sun. There, look," pointing to the ceiling as he turned down the rheostat. "And across the ceiling, when we get the lights in, the summer night sky appears, just faint bits of light at first, but then twinkling brighter in all the major constellations, the Big Dipper, the Little Dipper, the North Star —"

Della's eyes were wet. "It will be the most beautiful place on earth."

"I hope so," Max said.

Driving back to Twenty-third Street, Della curled up against Max. When he touched her face, her cheeks were as hot as fire and wet with tears, and when Max wanted to know why she was crying, Della said, "It was so beautiful, Max. It was just so absolutely beautiful, except that Sally was there, and she didn't want me to see it."

"Sally. No, she wasn't there."

"Up behind the wall. She was looking over the wall."

Max carried her up the stairs to her flat. He didn't know where his strength came from, but he managed, just as he managed to undress her and put her to bed with a quilt and a heavy blanket over her. He thanked God that he had insisted, the year before, that she have a telephone installed, and when he left her to call the doctor, she was huddled under the covers, shivering.

Dr. Traub was a small, fat man who mumbled. He examined Della and mumbled that it was pneumonia. Then he mumbled that she ought to go to the hospital.

"I want the best, the best there is," Max said.

Dr. Traub was already on the telephone; when he finished, he told Max that he had ordered the ambulance.

"The best hospital —"

"All right, Mr. Britsky. Don't be nervous. I'm sending her to Mt. Sinai. That's my hospital. It's as good as any hospital."

"Look," Max said, "money is no object. You can hire the best doctors in the world. I want her cured."

"Money won't help. She has pneumonia. We'll do the best we can. Tell me, Mr. Britsky, this is a relative? She don't look Jewish."

"This is my secretary and business associate."

Dr. Traub nodded and said no more. Since he was the Britsky family doctor, there was no need for him to pursue his inquiries. "When the ambulance comes," he said, "we'll wrap her in a blanket. You can bring it back. You're going to the hospital?"

Max nodded.

"Do you know where it is?"

"On a Hundredth Street and Fifth?"

"That's right."

After the ambulance arrived and Della had been carried away, Max went downstairs to where his car was waiting. Shecky Blum had made the transition from carriage to limousine seven years ago, and by now he felt comfortable and superior in the driver's seat of Max's new Buick. When he reached Mt. Sinai Hospital, he asked Max, "What do I do now?"

"You don't do a damn thing. You sit right here."

"Mrs. Britsky wanted the car this afternoon."

"I told you what to do. You sit here!"

Dr. Traub met him in the corridor. "You have a very sick lady there, Mr. Britsky. We're doing our best, except that for pneumonia the best is practically nothing."

"I want to see her."

"Sure, sure. In a minute," Dr. Traub said. "Tell me first, she's not Jewish, is she?"

"What the hell is the difference?"

"The difference is, Mr. Britsky, that I got to talk frankly. Has she got a family? Also, is she a Catholic?"

"Goddamn it —"

Dr. Traub stopped mumbling. "Hold on! Just hold on, Mr. Britsky! I'm saying something very important. If that woman is a Catholic, she must have a priest. This is a Jewish hospital, so we don't have a priest in attendance, but if Miss O'Donnell should die without the last rites, that could be a terrible thing in the eyes of her family. That's why I say her family must be notified and we must have a priest — if she's Catholic."

"She's Catholic, but she's not going to die! You hear me, Doc, she is not going to die."

"That's in the hands of God, and with pneumonia He doesn't do too well. Maybe she has a fifty percent chance of pulling out of this, and I wouldn't even bet on that. I'm being very blunt, but her temperature is already one hundred and five degrees. Dr. Solomon is with her now, and he's our best man with lung infections, but I don't know what he can do."

"Can I please see her now?"

"All right. But don't delay what I told you."

Max's mind was a jumble of confused thoughts and tearing sensations, facing what he felt for Della O'Donnell and yet unable to face it, tempted to get down on his knees and plead with her to live and not to desert him, yet unable to do anything but stand by the bed with the tears running down his cheeks, the two doctors watching him curiously before they stepped out of the room.

Della opened her eyes and saw him and whispered something. He bent close to hear it. "Please don't cry," Della said, and the effort to speak brought on a fit of coughing, a froth of dark brown sputum coming out of her mouth. A nurse came into the room and wiped Della's face.

"Where are the doctors?" Max demanded. "Why ain't they here?"

"They can't help," the nurse said. She had a basin of cold water and she wet cloths, using them to cool Della. "We're doing what we can."

Della's eyes were closed now. She appeared to be breathing a little more easily. Max left the room and went to the floor desk and picked up the telephone. When a nurse tried to stop him, explaining that visitors had to use the telephone in the main lobby, he took a ten-dollar bill out of his pocket, threw it at her, and said, "I'm using this phone, lady."

He called Tammany Hall, to be informed that Boss Charles Murphy was at City Hall, where the mayor was handing the keys to the city to the new President-elect, Mr. Woodrow Wilson.

"Well, you damn well get over there and find him!" Max shouted. "You tell him that this is Max Britsky, and I'm up at Mt. Sinai Hospital up on One Hundredth Street, and that it's a matter of life and death that he get up here and bring a priest with him!"

"A what?"

"A priest, goddamn you! A priest!"

It was nine o'clock that night before Murphy reached Mt. Sinai, and by then Della had passed through delirium and had sunk into a coma. Max came out of her room to greet Murphy, and Murphy introduced the tall, heavyset man he had brought with him as Bishop Brady.

"We need a priest," Max said.

"Sure, I'm a priest," the bishop told him.

Overcome with emotion, Max spoke with effort: "I think she's near the end."

"Then we'll waste no time," the bishop said, leading the way into the room. Dr. Solomon was there, bending over the bed. He straightened up, nodded at Brady, and said, "Quickly, please."

The bishop administered the last rites. Shivering, bent over, his face twisted with grief, Max watched and listened. When the doctor drew the sheet over Della's face, Murphy put his arm around Max's shoulders and led him from the room.

Bishop Brady joined them in the visitors' waiting room. Past visiting hours, the three men had the room to themselves. Murphy took a flask out of his pocket and handed it to Max. "Take a good shot. You need it."

Max drank and handed back the flask.

"Sorry I couldn't come earlier, Max, but there I was with the President. You can't just walk out. Still, we got here in time, poor child."

"May her soul be blessed," Brady said. "I knew her only moments, but I could see the mark of goodness and innocence upon her face. God will forgive her and receive her."

Max had never wept before, and he hardly realized now that tears were still sliding down his cheeks. He wondered what Della had to be forgiven for. In the six years that she had been his secretary and his mistress, he had never heard a word of anger or seen an act of petulance or hostility.

"She has no family, poor child," Murphy said, "only me and my wife."

"I'll take care of it," Max said. "Whatever the funeral costs, whatever you need."

Brady was watching Max with interest. "You must have loved the woman with all your heart," he said.

I never told her that, Max thought. I never told her that I loved her. Why didn't I tell her? He rubbed his eyes and felt the wetness of his cheeks, went into his pocket for a handkerchief and found two tickets there. He looked at them curiously, then handed them to Murphy. "Tomorrow night — maybe you can use them. George M. Cohan's new show, *Broadway Jones*. She liked George M. Cohan." He stood up suddenly. "Oh, shit! What a stupid, fucked-up, senseless world!"

[EIGHT]

1914

Max at the Age of Thirty-five

NATALIE LOVE, who had been born Alexa Vasovich twenty-three years before, stretched lazily, yawned, and smiled at Max. When she smiled like that, she reminded him of Della O'Donnell, and when anything reminded him of Della, a stab of pain went through him. There were other ways in which Alexa reminded him of Della. She had the same fair skin, blue eyes, and rounded limbs. Her hair was different, corn silk, and she was not quite as plump as Della had been, which prompted Max to remind her not to gain any more weight.

"Max, I'm not fat, am I?" She kicked off the covers and displayed her naked and very lovely figure.

"Cover yourself. I don't want you catching cold."

"Always worrying about someone catching cold."

"Never mind." He lit his cigar. "Cover yourself."

"It's warm as toast in here."

"Never mind. Cover yourself."

"All right." She sighed. "Now what do you think my papa would have said? All them years he worked down by the docks, breaking his back for a lousy six, seven dollars a week until he killed himself under a chain that broke his back, and here's his little Alexa, a movie star making three hundred dollars a week. And fucking Mr. Max Britsky," she added.

"Alexa, I don't like to hear that kind of language from a lady."

"Fucking?"

"That's right."

"But you say it all the time."

"For a man it's all right. Not for a lady. I never knew about your father. What was he, a stevedore?"

"What else for a Polack? The docks or the slaughterhouses. He hated the slaughterhouses." She stared at Max thoughtfully. "You like me, Max, really, truly?"

"What do you think I made you a star for — for kicks? Two years ago, when we were shooting *Slave Girl*, I seen this kid with the yellow hair, and I ask Hook Mason who's that pretty little kid? He tells me it's some dumb Polack he's hired on for three dollars a day. I don't like that. I don't like it when someone says dumb Polack or stupid Hunky or lousy mick, because that same son of a bitch is going to turn around the next minute and call me a lousy Jew bastard, and that's going to make me beat the shit out of him. The truth is, I'm getting too old for street fighting. So I said to Mason, one more crack like that and you can go to Philadelphia and make pictures for National. So Mason starts licking my ass and telling me he didn't know I was interested in you."

"And you were, weren't you, Max?"

"No. Good God, Alexa, I never seen you before. Sure, I got interested. I made you a star, didn't I? I pay you three hundred dollars a week. And I like you. What I pay you has nothing to do with me screwing you. I never went to bed in my life with a woman I didn't care for. I got nothing but contempt for men who do that."

"I heard that Biograph pays Mary Pickford eight hundred dollars a week —"

"What else did you hear?" Max interrupted. "I hear the angels sing better than the chorus at the Metropolitan Opera House. You're learning, cookie, but you ain't no Mary Pickford. Not yet, and believe me, you're a lot luckier to be with Britsky Productions than with Biograph. They never made a picture could compare with ours."

"Max, I'm not going with Biograph. You know that."

"I know it and my lawyer knows it."

Alexa began to cry.

"Why are you crying? What did I say?"

"Lawyers, that's what you said. You think I'd walk out on you, so you throw lawyers right in my face."

"Honey, honey, I look at things the way they are. That's the name of Max Britsky. People go around saying Max Britsky's a son of a bitch. Maybe yes, maybe no. I got to look after Max Britsky because nobody else is going to. You don't know what I'm talking about, do you? Let me explain. For years, Vitagraph and Biograph kept the names of their actors secret so the actors shouldn't have no handle on them to push up their pay. Mary Pickford had to squeeze blood to break through that. I never did that. I made my actors famous, because the more famous they got, the more people packed into my houses to look at them. I got nine Clifford Abel theatres around this country, and every one's a palace like no king ever had a chance to live in, and I'm packing them in. All right, you're telling me Mary Pickford makes eight hundred a week. You know I do business with the Chase Bank down at One Seventy-seven Broadway. Berry down there manages the bank, and they pay him forty a week less than I pay you. But I'll tell you something else. Mary Pickford makes eight hundred — you got eight hundred and fifty, starts next week."

"Max —"

"Think about it."

"Max, you don't mean that. You're kidding me, aren't you?"

"Nope. I'm not kidding you. I go back to the office now and I talk to Jake Stein, my comptroller. He says to me, Max, you're crazy. I say to him, Yeah, crazy like a fox. Then I call in Barney Enfield, and I tell Barney, We got the highest paid movie star in the United States of America. No, in the world, because the French pay peanuts, and now with this schmuck war starting in Europe, even peanuts they won't pay. So Britsky Productions has Natalie Love, who's not only more beautiful than Pickford or Gish, and more talented and sexy, but paid more. That's the whole *emmes* with Americans — more pay and you got to be better. With that kind of thing, Barney begins feeding stories to the newspapers and the magazines, and we get maybe fifty new photographs of you, and I sign Oscar Bitterman, who just has a new hit play opening on Forty-second Street, to write a scenario so that Barney can tell them that the most expensive star in America stars in the most expensive picture. So I got a couple of million dollars of publicity and maybe fifty million dollars of new business, and all it cost me is five hundred and fifty dollars a week to a young lady, and I couldn't think of a better place to put it —"

Alexa leaped out of bed, flung her arms around Max, and covered his face with kisses. "Oh, Maxie, I love you, I love you, I love you."

He disentangled himself and agreed. "For that price, why not?"

"Tomorrow, Max?"

"Tomorrow, honey, I'll be sitting in a double bedroom suite, on my way to Chicago and from there to Los Angeles, and there maybe making the biggest decision of my life. Who knows?"

• • •

He had thought about it on and off, but it only began to take shape as a real possibility when he had lunch with Irving Lunberg in Café Coronet two weeks before. Lunberg was a small producer, a man who made half a dozen moving pictures a year and who depended entirely upon Max for his distribution. He made his pictures in a place called Hollywood, a district in Los Angeles County, where he had set up a studio in an old barn on a road called Gower Street. Lunberg had been pushing during the past twelve months for Max to buy him out, a move which Max resisted. Lunberg, to Max's way of thinking, made third-rate films, and since the man came with the company, Max had no desire to own either. On the other hand, he liked Lunberg and took him to lunch whenever he was in New York.

On this day, it was pouring, the third day of uninhibited rainfall, and when Max mentioned that a crew working on an outdoor film had been sitting on its hands for three days, Lunberg observed that it couldn't happen in Hollywood.

"Why, it don't rain there?"

Lunberg was a fat, bald little man with fluttering eyelids that gave him an appearance of constant excitement. His hands shook, which added to the impression; and evidently Jewish food had not yet made its appearance in Hollywood, for he ordered a bewildering assortment of blintzes, sour cream, potato pancakes, and a pasta-buckwheat concoction known as *kasha-varanashkas.* On the side, he ordered bagels and cream cheese. "An empty stomach makes me nervous," he explained to Max.

"I can see that. About the rain?"

"Sure, it rains. It has to rain, but it rains intelligently, so you can put together a schedule of shooting that won't drive you into the poorhouse, like this," he said, pointing outside.

"Tell me how it does that."

"All right. From April until November, you can be *pretty* sure it won't rain and it won't cloud up. From May until October, you can be *absolutely* sure it won't rain. You got sunshine like you never seen — clear, pure, beautiful light. Max, have some," pushing the platter of potato pancakes toward Max.

"I'm not hungry. Tell me more."

"They're not like my mama used to make."

"What?"

"The potato *latkes*."

"You were talking about Hollywood."

"Like I said, sweet air, clean, none of the soot, like you have here, hills covered with cactus and that kind of stuff, plenty of room. It's like nobody ever been there except the oil companies, and already they found some oil in my back yard, would you believe it, right there on Gower Street. You ever read books by Zane Grey?"

"I don't read much. I know the name. My wife was talking about him."

"Oh? Yeah, sure. How is Sally?"

"I guess she's fine. We're getting divorced, Irving."

"No. Gee, I'm sorry to hear that."

"Let's get back to Hollywood and this Zane Grey writer."

"Yeah. Sure. Well, I read a couple of his books — he writes books about the West, with lots of cowboys and gunmen, you know, the Buffalo Bill kind of stuff — and I put together a scenario. I wouldn't say I stole it from Mr. Grey, because if he sees it he'll never recognize that it had anything to do with his book. There's this Mexican ranch down in the southern part of Los Angeles County, and we took the cameras down there with our cowboy actor, who ain't really a cowboy but comes from Pittsburgh, a Hunky named Frank Lutzman, except that we call him Don Durango. We shot a pretty good picture, Max, and I think you'll like it. But also, I think there's going to be a real craze for these cowboy pictures."

"Why?"

"Because everyone's looking for cowboy stars."

"They didn't have to go to Hollywood to make *The Great Train Robbery*."

"Max, this is different," Lunberg said. "You got space and hills and scenery like you never dreamed."

"When can we see it?" Max asked him.

"This afternoon. I got it with me at the hotel."

The Western film that Lunberg had made and which was not exactly a steal from Zane Grey was the final argument that convinced Max that Los Angeles had to be seen and seriously considered as a place to make moving pictures. The Lunberg film was not very good, but it was the first thing of its kind that Max had ever seen, the first Western film shot, not on Long Island or in the piny wastes of South Jersey, but actually in the West. The splendid, chaparral-covered mountains, the expanse of land and sky, the marvelously skilled Mexican *vaqueros* — all of this combined to fill Max with a strange, romantic longing as well as a sense of what good pictures made in this background could mean at the box office. As he said to Alexa, he might well be facing the most important decision of his life.

That morning, he went from her apartment to his office in the Hobart Building, where Fred Feldman awaited him. Feldman said, "I got good news and bad news. Which do you want first?"

"We'll take the good news."

"Is Sam in the building?"

"Could be."

"Then call him in and Bert Bellamy as well. I want to make it in the form of an announcement. Take out the bottle of schnapps you keep in your desk, Max, and line up four glasses."

Max smiled as he listened to Feldman. The lawyer was even smaller than Max, which made it even easier for Max to like him. He was short and prematurely bald and fat, and he got stouter each year, and right now he was so excited that he had to restrain himself to keep from hopping and dancing. Max buzzed his secretary — a new girl, Josie Levy, in her middle twenties and needle-nosed and efficient — and asked her to find Snyder and Bellamy. When they entered Max's office, he had finished filling four shot glasses with Golden Wedding Rye Whiskey.

"Drink up," he said.

"What are we drinking to?"

"Felix Chapman."

"And who the hell is Felix Chapman?"

"Nobody except a federal judge," Feldman said smugly. "Just a little old judge in the Federal District Court, Southern District of New York, who decided a case. And you know what he decided?"

Feldman gulped down his glassful, choked, swallowed, took a deep breath, and managed to say, "Come on now, drink up!"

"All right, to his honor," Max said.

"And since you don't know what his honor decided, let me tell you. First of all, he decided that National is in violation of the Sherman Antitrust Act, the Clayton Act, and one or two other laws, not to mention conspiracy to fix prices, conspiracy in restraint of trade, and conspiracy to eliminate competition, and if that ain't a bundle, what is? My friends, the trust is finished, done, castrated. And who did it? Nobody but Max Britsky Productions."

They all clapped hands while Max stood up and took a bow. "I almost feel sorry for the poor bastards," Max said, "but what the hell! They never made a good picture, and for schmucks, they had a nice long run for their money. As soon as this gets out, every little cockroach who stayed under their thumb will be asking to be let into our film exchange."

"And we'll let them in," Bert agreed, grinning. "Oh, maybe we'll make them kiss ass a little, but we shall take them in. Freddy, pour. And this time, I make the toast. Max and me, we go back a long, long way — a long, long way to a place called Rowdy Smith's penny arcade. Right, Max?"

"Absolutely. Poor old bastard, I suppose he's been dead these many years."

"And that is where it all began," Bert said, "turning the handles on the kinetoscopes, so my toast is to old Rowdy Smith, bless his Irish heart."

"I drink to that," Max said.

"But with all this," Snyder wondered, "do we still go to California? A few days from now, we'll have more business than we know what to do with."

"All the more reason to go — except that you got to hang in here, Bert. The distribution is your baby, and you got to sit on it.

If we settle on something out there in the West, you'll have plenty of sunshine in the years to come. Meanwhile, someone has to deal with those poor, liberated producers."

Feldman remained in Max's office after the other two had left, and he said to Max somewhat tentatively, "How about it, Max? Do you realize what you're putting in Bert's hands?"

"Will you once and for all get off that! What the hell gives with you and Bert? Bert is like a brother — yeah, a damn sight more than those two worthless crumbs I call my brothers."

"All right, all right," Feldman said quickly. "Don't bite my nose off. I only asked a question."

"Then stop asking that question. Now, before you said we have good news and bad news. Suppose we get to the bad news."

"Sally."

"I thought so. Tell me what she wants."

"A million dollars."

"You're kidding."

"I wish I were kidding, Max, but I'm not. She wants a million dollars, and she wants the house on Sixty-sixth Street."

"I figured on that. She can have it."

"She knows we're off to the Coast, and she knows that if you go, your mother will go, and she wants the right to buy your mother's house for five thousand dollars."

"It's worth four times that, but she can have it. The million I don't understand. She wasn't like that. She was never that crazy for money."

"She is now. And she wants custody of the kids and she wants alimony of twenty thousand a year."

"On top of the million dollars?"

"That's right, Max."

"That's crazy. I don't have a million dollars. You know that, Freddy. I don't have a damn thing. Jake Stein pays my bills, and each month he gives me the cash left over from my pay, you know, seven or eight hundred bucks. I don't even have a bank account."

"Max!"

"What's the matter? You think I'm conning you. You're my lawyer."

"Max, who owns Britsky Productions?"

"Me. Who else?"

"Exactly. And Max Britsky Productions is the biggest theatre owner and the biggest moving picture production company not only in America but in the whole world right at this minute — that's right, bigger than Biograph or any of the others — and do you know how many millions of dollars that adds up to?"

"So what? Do I sell my company?"

"Maybe."

"Then you're out of your fucken mind!" Max exploded.

"Will you listen?"

"If you got something to say, I'll listen. But don't tell me maybe I'll sell this company, because if that's the way you're thinking, you can get to hell out of here."

"Will you calm down and listen to me? I been working for you twelve years and I haven't sold you out yet, so maybe you can accept the fact that I got a little loyalty and I try to do what is in your best interest. But sometimes I wonder whether you really know what Max Britsky Productions represents, because you still run it like that candy store on Clinton Street where you hung out when you were a kid."

"That's bullshit, Freddy. There's nobody knows this company like I do. It's my life."

"Yeah, you know it and you don't know it. Just let me run down what you got. There are nine large moving picture theatres that we built and own outright. There are seven hundred and twenty-one others that we either own or lease. We own this building, the Hobart Building. We got three studios, the ice house downtown, the studio in Harlem, and the studio we bought last year in Fort Lee. Right now, we have four pictures shooting, and the past twelve months, we turned out thirty-one features and God knows how many short subjects. There are more than three thousand people on the payroll, and trying to get some kind of a figure together with Jake on what we're worth — you know, it's got to be better than seven or eight million in pure equity, leaving out mortgages, and maybe a hell of a lot better than that."

"I still don't have any million dollars to pay off Sally. What do we have in cash right now?"

"About a hundred and sixty thousand. But I'm not thinking that way, Max. What I'm thinking is what Alvin Berry down at the Chase Bank has been talking about. We should put out a stock issue and turn this into a public corporation."

"No! Goddamn it, no! I built this company. I'm not going to give it away."

"You're not giving it away. Whatever happens, you retain fifty-one percent of the stock, so you have control. You own it. And we can pay off Sally with five percent of the stock, which will be worth a damn sight more than a million in a very short time, if not now. Berry had his economist put together a graph on our earnings. We have been doubling them every two years and tripling our net worth. There's never been anything like this, Max, and all the big boys, the old school, high-powered *goyim*, the Rockefellers and the Morgans and the Lamonts and the Carnegies, are eating their hearts out. With all their banks and steel mills and oil wells, they've never seen the kind of a money machine the moving picture business is, and they thought they could move in with the trust and eat us up, and now they found they can't and they never will. But this isn't something you can continue to keep in your back pocket."

"I can't figure Sally. She ain't that kind of a person. Ain't — you hear me, ain't. Last time we spoke, she says to me, 'Max, your language is rotten, and you forgot everything I ever taught you, and you forgot because bad English is your weapon against me,' and she's right. She is absolutely right. She's the smartest dame I ever knew, but not money crazy. She never was money crazy."

"Well, she's insecure and she's frightened, but believe me, Max, if this comes to a dirty court fight, she can take you for a lot more than a million. I don't want that to happen. And let me tell you something else. You got people like Sam Snyder and Bert Bellamy, not to mention myself, and we been with you for years, and there's nothing in the world means as much to us as this business, I mean outside of family —"

"What the hell is it?" Max demanded. "Don't I pay enough? Sam Snyder makes forty thousand a year. There's no other business in this country pays an executive that kind of money, and you know it. And you —"

"Max, Max, I'm not saying we're underpaid, but we got wives and kids. You own Britsky. I get a heart attack and drop dead, my wife's got nothing. I never thought it would come down to my saying it, but we deserve a part of this business. Are you going to deny that we do?"

"Does Sam Snyder feel like you do? And what about Bert? Does he feel I been giving him the short end of the stick?"

"Sam wouldn't say so if it meant his life, but you know the way Sam Snyder feels about you. He thinks you're the greatest guy on earth. And where the hell would we be if it hadn't been for Sam? As far as Bert is concerned, I can't say, but I think maybe he does feel that way."

"You figure you can talk to me like that and get away with it, right, Freddy?"

"What are you going to do, fire me? Go ahead! You know damn well I can do better on the outside with my own practice than with what you pay. Nobody else talks to you. It's about time someone did."

"Take it easy. Don't get sore."

"No? Maybe it's time I got sore. If you had hired one of those big downtown *goyisha* firms to fight this trust case, it would have cost you half a million, but I did it on salary with two law clerk kids helping me and working eighteen hours a day and Leah and the kids not seeing me for weeks at a time, and you screwing your head off with every piece of ass we cast in a picture —"

"Shut up! You hear me, shut up! Who the fuck do you think you are to talk to me like that?"

"I'll tell you who. Your ex-lawyer!"

Feldman swung around to stride out of the room, but Max bounded from behind his desk and caught Feldman before he reached the door. He grabbed Feldman's arm and swung him around, and when Feldman snorted, "Let go of me!" Max replied, "You dumb son of a bitch, where are you going? You're like a brother to me. You think you're going to walk out on me? Like hell you are — if I got to beat the shit out of you to keep you here." He embraced the fat little man in a bear hug that made Feldman wince with pain. When Max let go of him, Feldman burst out laughing and Max joined in.

"All right, all right," Max said. "Sit down and we'll talk. But just let me tell you something, Freddy. In all the years I had something going with Della, I never touched another woman. Now I got what they call a biological need and that's all. Is Sally going to let me see the kids?"

"Sure, we can arrange that. But with Sally living here, if you settle out on the West Coast — Well, it's a long train ride."

"I don't know. The kids are like strangers anyway. I don't know why, except that it was never real living with Sally in that brownstone. Well, I'll manage."

Feldman shook his head uneasily. "I got to talk to you about Ruby and Benny, and I hate to."

"Why? You talk to me about everything else. You even tell me what a bastard I am. Look, do it — and if Sally will settle for five percent of the stock, give it to her, and take the same thing for you and Sam and Bert. Now what about Ruby and Benny?"

"I told you before, Max, and I hate to go through it again. They're stealing from you."

"What can they steal? Peanuts. They skim a little and it makes them feel like big men. The hell with it! What does Jake Stein think?"

"I told him to check it out. He says it's nothing to worry about. He says he knows about it, and he does a little fancy bookkeeping to cover it. Sometimes I feel he does a little fancy bookkeeping on his own."

"All right. If it begins to hurt, I'll read them a riot act. I'd throw them out, but it would break Mama's heart."

· · ·

The thought of leaving New York City for a fuzzy destination somewhere out west was not an easy one for Max to deal with. He had never been to California, and if he thought about it at all, he thought of it as a bleak and inhospitable desert. New York City, on the other hand, was more than a geographical place; it was his roots, his origin, his language, his security.

Like Max, the city was flexing its muscle, expanding and living with boundless energy. In the Woolworth Building, it had just raised up the tallest manmade structure in the world. Its new, expanding subway gave you the longest, cheapest ride in the nation for five cents, and its great bridges had taken their place as one of the wonders of the world. Max had never felt diminished by the city; it was his place, his world, and elsewhere was so vague as to be practically nonexistent. Elsewhere, a war was being fought and millions of men were in motion, killing, destroying, ravishing. Far more important, in Max's world, was the emergence of a young man named Charlie Chaplin, who had just finished a film called *Making a Living*, in which he was supported by an interesting actress named Marie Dressler. But elsewhere was also California, and standing in Grand Central Station, still brand new, its great arched expanse making it without a doubt one of the most grandiose railroad stations in the world, Max felt a shiver of fear, a sense that perhaps the glory was behind him and over. Not that he shaped his thoughts in such terms, but he was sensitive enough to know that things have a beginning and an end, and California was too vague, too uncertain, to add up to a valid continuation. Sam Snyder had come back from checking through their bags, and he joined Max and Fred Feldman.

"All set," he told Max. "We got only ten minutes before train time, so we might as well get on."

"Cheer up," Feldman said to Max. "I always wanted to go to California. You know, we might enjoy it."

"Hollywood," Max muttered. "What in hell kind of a name is that?"

"It's a town, Max. It doesn't have to be Hollywood. There's plenty of room to put down a studio, from what I hear."

Sitting in their compartment, the train plunging north along the eastern bank of the Hudson River, Max began to mutter again, and finally, almost angrily, he announced that he was going into the club car to smoke a cigar and that he would see them for dinner.

"Freddy, what's gotten into him?" Sam Snyder asked after Max had left.

"It's been getting into him for a long time. Since Della died."

"That's over a year now."

"I guess it's not a question of time. Something happened to him. And the women — it's like a drug. He has to screw every good-looking dame who works for us. I worry about that, because sooner or later we're going to get a big, fat paternity suit."

"Funny thing is," Snyder said, "that he never looked at another woman, including Sally, while Della was alive. It must have been five or six years then. He used to bring Della to dinner at our house, and he was just as relaxed and happy as any man you ever saw. Not that we ever did anything special. My Alice is a great cook. I got to admit that. She does the best German food on this side of the ocean — good, heavy stuff, which is why I got this belly of mine. We'd just sit and eat and drink beer, and then Della and Alice would go into the parlor and Max and I would sit at the table and smoke a cigar and talk about the business. Mostly the technical side, I guess. I remember when I was working on some substitute for those damn mercury vapor tubes we had to use for lighting. They made everyone look sick. We had to paint the faces — what was I saying, Freddy?"

"About Max coming to your house."

"It got to be a regular thing. Every Wednesday night. You know, the kids were crazy about him. He used to bring them presents until Alice had to beg him to stop because he was spoiling them, and he'd get down on the floor and play with them, but from all I hear, he could never get close to his own kids."

"That's right. He says they're like strangers to him."

"I don't know, unless Sally has been feeding them stuff about Max."

"I don't think Sally would do that," Feldman said.

"Maybe not. But she knew what was going on, and a couple of times when she had some excuse to pin him down, she called our house. Maybe she hired a detective to follow him, but she knew."

"Why didn't he divorce her and marry Della? She's divorcing him now. Why didn't he do it while Della was still alive?"

"Didn't you know? First place, Della was married. She was a Catholic, so she couldn't get a divorce from the bum she was married to. You know, I was talking to Steve Maguire a couple of years ago, I think it was about six months before Della died, and Steve said that Boss Murphy had enough influence in the Vatican to have Della's marriage annulled, and that it would only cost two thousand dollars. But when I told Max about it, he said it was no use and that he just couldn't face his mother if he left Sally to marry Della."

"That one — My God, people are strange. Well, he's doing it now."

"Not him. Sally's doing it."

• • •

While this went on in Max's suite, Max was in the club car, where he had selected an excellent twenty-five-cent Cuban cigar and ordered a rye highball. A dollar tip had engraved his name with the porter, and when the man handed him his highball and said, "Just tell me if you need anything else, Mr. Britsky," a woman sitting facing Max regarded him with interest. Max had noticed her and guessed that she was either a buyer or someone in show business, since single women traveling first class who were not in those professions usually avoided the club cars. The woman was in her early forties, attractively but quietly dressed, and with less makeup than one would expect from someone in show business. She had even features, dark eyes and hair, and a good figure — attractive but hardly beautiful. After a few minutes of observation, the woman glanced around the car. It was not crowded, and the half-dozen men in the car were not watching her or Max, a lack of attention she evidently welcomed. She's coming over here, Max thought, and she's not used to this kind of thing. Then she rose and stepped across to the chair next to him and said without apology, "I heard your name, Mr. Britsky, and I only saw that name in one other place, so even if this is most unwomanly — well. It's such an unusual name. At least you must be his cousin."

"Whose cousin?"

"Max Britsky's. All right, I'm a buyer for Altman's in New York. My name is Frances Button, and I buy shoes. So you see some things are predestined."

"Max Britsky."

"I thought so. Shoes and purses. I do a lot of traveling in New England and west to Chicago, and I fill most of the lonely hours with the movies. I am a confirmed fan and addict, and I've come to look for Max Britsky Productions. That *is* you?"

"That's right. Britsky in person. Can I buy you a drink?"

"I'll have a sherry, yes, if you don't mind."

Max motioned for the porter and gave him the order. "What did you mean by predestined?" he asked, turning to the lady beside him.

"Not you and me, Mr. Britsky." She burst out laughing. "Oh, no. My name. Frances Button, buyer in shoes. Button — shoes. My maiden name was Smith, but of all people, I had to go and marry Oscar Button. Fortunately, that ended some years ago, amicably and without issue, mostly because I didn't ask for alimony, which I didn't because the bum couldn't have paid any. And what do I need him for? I make a good living — for a woman, a damn good living."

The porter set down her glass of sherry and Max paid him.

"Are you traveling with your wife, Mr. Britsky?"

"No. With two associates."

"Gentlemen, of course."

"Possibly."

"Possibly? Oh, you do have a sense of humor. You know, I love trains. Some of the most interesting people I ever met I meet on trains. Of course, I never met an important moving picture producer before, but you know, all sorts of interesting people. I'm sure you have arrangements for dinner with your friends, but after dinner —"

"What happens after dinner?"

"The car behind the diner. Room D."

"Why?" Max wondered.

"Why not? A few laughs, a few drinks. What else is there, Mr. Britsky?"

"I don't know, just like I don't know you. You don't want to go to bed with me, Mrs. Button. I might just have a social disease."

"There's no need to be nasty."

"No, I'm sorry. I'm really sorry."

"No," she whispered, "you're not sorry at all. You're a disgusting, nasty, little Jew." With that, she rose and left the car. Max relit his cigar, which had gone out.

· · ·

The three men were in the double bedroom, relaxed in their shirtsleeves and suspenders, their shoes off, their feet stretched out, drinking beer and smoking cigars and staring through the window at the Arizona arroyos and canyons that crisscrossed under the Santa Fe tracks. The wonderful, jagged formations of red and black and yellow stone, the deep, terrifying cuts in the earth, and the growths of cactus and mesquite were like nothing any of them had seen before. Neither Snyder nor Feldman had ever been west of

Chicago. As for Max, he had once done a two-day stint in Denver with Bert Bellamy, but his memories were of a dreary and uninspiring town that sat on a large and uninspiring prairie. None of it was like this. This changed his mood, elevated and excited him, and drove away the depression that had gripped him since leaving New York. It was a landscape he had never dreamed of, for him a wonderland, a dreamland, and above all a moving picture land; and as he stared at the landscape through the window, he experienced a marvelous sense of completeness, an emptiness that was almost exalting and unlike anything he had ever experienced before. He wanted nothing. Here he was, in the small cubicle of the railroad suite, with good beer and a good cigar and with two old friends closer to him than anyone else in the world, and there was absolutely nothing in the world that frustrated him or pricked at his desire.

"When I was a kid," Sam Snyder remembered, "Pop took me to see Buffalo Bill's Wild West Show. It was just about the greatest day of my life. I shook hands with him. Can you believe that? I actually shook hands with Buffalo Bill Cody, himself, in the flesh. I'll never forget that. He was dressed in buckskin, white-fringed buckskin, absolutely beautiful. And he wore two pearl-handled sixguns."

"From what I hear," Max said, "those guns were loaded with buckshot, which is how he managed to never miss."

"I hate to believe that."

"Closest I ever got to one of those fellers," Feldman said, "was when I was reading law in old Meyer Sonberg's office. A guy walks in and becomes our client by the name of Bat Masterson. Heard of him?"

"Who hasn't?" Snyder said.

"He was one of them western hoodlums, like Billy the Kid," Max said.

"Oh, no. No, sir. Billy the Kid was a hoodlum. Bat Masterson was a sheriff or something in one of them little towns we passed yesterday, I think it was Dodge City. Well, he became a newspaper writer in some western city — maybe Chicago, I don't exactly remember — and someone made a deal to tell his story in a book and then cheated him on the deal. I don't remember the details, but he needed a New York lawyer and someone sent him to Sonberg, and Sonberg called me in and said to me, 'Freddy, I want you to meet one of the great ones.' And then we shook hands. Nice feller."

There was a long moment of silence while Max puffed on his cigar and stared at the rose and pink and purple landscape, and then Snyder said, "Shook hands with Sitting Bull. He was part of that same show. I got his picture on a postcard with his signature. I keep meaning to frame it for the kids, and I keep forgetting."

"How come he could write?"

"I think just his signature. They showed him how to do that. You know, I heard that when Buffalo Bill made the deal with him to join the Wild West Show with some of his braves, Sitting Bull said that instead of payment in money, he'd settle for the concession on postcards of himself. He sold them for twenty-five cents each."

"That's a good head for business," Max agreed, "but I'm not sure I want that in the scenario."

"What scenario?"

"I been dreaming it while you two are talking. *The Adventures of Buffalo Bill* — the first really great moving picture about the West. But great, not like the schlock Lunberg makes with his Mexican cowboys. Real cowboys, hundreds of them. Whole tribes of Indians."

"I don't know if there are any whole tribes of Indians left, Max," Feldman said.

"We'll find them."

"Buffaloes," Snyder said. "Where do we find buffaloes?"

"We'll find them. And if we can't find them, we'll use cows and dress them up. Who knows the difference between a cow and a buffalo?"

"A lot of people, I'm afraid," Feldman said gently.

"All right, so we'll find real ones. And someone to play Buffalo Bill. Hey, is he still alive?"

"Come on," Snyder said.

"Wait a minute, wait a minute," Feldman told them. "Come to think of it, he is. I read a piece in the *Tribune* about him just last week. I think something about him putting together a new show."

"I'll be damned."

"Max," Snyder said, "maybe Fred can work out some kind of

agreement. I'll bet he'd be excited. Maybe we could work him into it."

"Anyway, Custer's dead," Max said. "I been thinking about Custer's last stand. You know, with something like that, you could just about do away with the dialogue cards — just let people watch it as it happens."

"I know what you mean," Snyder agreed. "I know what you mean."

•　•　•

It was a strange and somewhat wonderful few days in Max's life, and though he was to take that train ride across the continent again and again in the years to come, it never had the same quality or worked the same magic as the first time. That evening, when Snyder and Feldman decided that their bedtime had come, Max left them and went into the club car. The thought of sleep was impossible; he was totally alive. It was as if he had been born adult the day before, and he grudged the surrender of a moment of the feeling. It was almost midnight, and Max was alone. Before they closed the bar, the porter had mixed him a tall rye whiskey and water, and Max lit a cigar to taste with it. The cold, sweet taste of the diluted whiskey joined with the cigar smoke to add to his feeling of loose, unharassed contentment. He felt young and strong and part of some natural flux of existence — feelings he could neither articulate nor hope to communicate. The thought occurred to him that Sally, the old Sally, the Sally he once knew so long ago, might understand how he felt; but that Sally was gone.

He had been sitting in the club car for about a half-hour or so when the train ground to a stop, and the club car porter came in to ask him whether he would like a breath of fresh air since the train would be there for twenty minutes.

"Where are we?"

"In the Mojave Desert, Mr. Britsky. We change engines and take on water here."

"Desert, really? Yes, sure, I'd like that."

"Then you better get your hat and coat, Mr. Britsky. It's cold out there."

Max found his coat and got off the train. The air was icy cold, so cold that he thrust his hands into his pockets, but clean and sweet with a strange scent that he had never experienced before. When he looked up at the sky, he again experienced something new and improbable, a sky that fairly blazed with starlight. He was relieved that he had left his cigar in the ashtray in the smoking car. There was a purity here that amazed and frightened him; you didn't smoke cigars, you didn't speak, and you even moved carefully, as if any untoward movement or sound would shatter what was here. He walked slowly down the long line of dark and silent cars to where the great locomotive discharged its pent-up pressure in clouds of steam. A trainman, walking by with an oil can, nodded at him. The silence had been broken, and in the distance a train whistle shrieked its warning. Max stood between the tracks as an eastbound freight, taking advantage of the passenger train's dalliance on a siding, thundered by, car after car, without end and seemingly forever.

Later, back in the club car, lighting his cigar once again, he felt a warm sense of security, and a little later, he went to his room, crawled into the berth, and fell asleep almost instantly, rocked by the clanging, bouncing motion of the train.

· · · ·

Fred Feldman had a relative by the name of Stanley Meyer, a first cousin once or twice removed — Feldman was not precisely certain of the nature of the relationship — who had moved to Los Angeles some years before. The move had been occasioned by his wife's health, and once there, Stanley Meyer had gone into the real estate business, which, as he had written to Feldman, "happens to be a business in which even a moron cannot escape success." Feldman explained to Max that Meyer was hardly a moron, but a very shrewd operator who knew the Los Angeles area very well indeed. Meyer was waiting for them when the train pulled into the Santa Fe depot, a tall, thin, solemn-faced man who bore not even a vague resemblance to his eastern cousin.

After they were introduced and their luggage collected, and after Meyer had begged them not to judge Los Angeles by the tacky train depot, he told them that he had made reservations for the party at the Alexandria Hotel, at Fifth and Spring streets. "It's an excellent hotel," he told them, "and it's centrally located. I managed to snare their only three-bedroom suite, so you'll be comfortable. I've set aside the whole week to work with you, but if we don't find something this week, I'll cancel everything for next week as well. We want you out here in Los Angeles, Mr. Britsky. Mack Sennett's Keystone Company is already out here, and both Biograph and Mr. Lasky are very seriously considering moving their entire enterprises out. As yet it's only a small thing, but I have a notion that we may well outpace New York in time — that is, as a moving picture center."

"We'll see," Max said. "If I got nothing else, I got an open mind, and believe me, I'm not complaining about the sunshine and the warm weather."

Meyer's car, parked outside the station, was a hundred-horsepower Pierce Arrow 66, a large, powerful open-top touring car with, as Meyer informed them, an 825-cubic-inch engine. "It's a damn monster, but you need it out here. Some places there are roads that are called roads and other places there are cart tracks called roads. And you want a car that stands high, because when it rains out here, it rains like hell. You notice I carry four spare tires."

"It's beautiful," Max said. "Do they sell them out here?"

"They certainly do."

"Order one for me," Max said.

Meyer nodded with new respect.

Riding from the Santa Fe station to the hotel, Max was openmouthed with delight. The shabby jerry-built houses, most of them not much better than shacks, the abandoned oil derricks standing everywhere, the unpaved streets, the huge, clanging, interurban cars grinding by on the railroad tracks that divided the roads — all these bothered him not at all. He was enchanted with the hills all about them, with the lush semitropical vegetation, with the profusion of roses climbing over old fences, with the blue sky and the sweet smell of the air.

"Just yesterday," Meyer explained, "we were an oil field, maybe the richest in America. Then, as we used to say, you couldn't see your nose for the derricks. But now the oil is running out, and maybe we can replace it with a city. Not everywhere, but in some places you can still count ten derricks for every city block."

That afternoon, after the three travelers had bathed and put away an excellent lunch in the Alexandria's grandiose dining room beneath an amazing display of stained-glass windows, they gathered around a table in their suite. Meyer spread out a large map of Los Angeles County.

"I brought this big map of the county," he told them, "because you can get awful damn confused without it. This is a hell of a big place, and I think someone once said that the county is bigger than the state of Rhode Island. Maybe so. Anyway, Freddy here wrote to me asking about Lunberg's operation. He has an old barn out in a suburb called Hollywood. It's a sleepy little town with not much of anything to recommend it."

"Isn't Lasky out there?" Max asked.

"Right. Like Lunberg, he rented himself a barn on Vine Street, which is one of the dirt roads that come down out of the Hollywood Hills. But Lasky's thing is tentative. I understand he rented space to shoot a few pictures, but he keeps his operation in the East. Freddy doesn't think that's what you had in mind, Mr. Britsky, is it?"

"No," Max said decisively. "Absolutely not. I like to keep my operation in one place. Already, it's too spread out. We got our corporate headquarters in the Hobart Building on Fourteenth Street, which I own. Not Fourteenth Street, I should live so long, but the building. Also, we got studios on Eighteenth Street, up in Harlem, and over in Jersey. If I make another studio here in California, I'll go crazy. So if you sell me on this, Stanley, I'll move the whole kit and kaboodle out here. That's the way I operate. I don't do things maybe I do them. I do them."

"Good. I'm glad to be clear on that, because it will save us lots of time. I told you before that Lasky and Biograph were considering a move out here, but for the time being, they rent whatever shack or barn they can put their equipment in. You don't want that kind of thing?"

"No way, Stanley. Sam Snyder here heads up our technical operation. Sam, tell him how we function."

"You see," Snyder said, "we're a little different from the others. We got over seven hundred theatres around the country, and we got to feed them constantly. We run a film exchange, in which we exchange our films with other companies, but Max wouldn't sleep if he was at the mercy of other picture makers. So we got to manufacture our basic product. Which means that we got to keep a minimum of six companies going all the time. That's a minimum. More often, we can have as many as twenty companies working —"

"And at the rate we open theatres, that ain't enough," Max put in.

"Right. So what do we need if we come out here? All the way out here on the train, Mr. Britsky and I and Mr. Feldman here have been discussing the cowboy and Indian pictures that Mr. Britsky feels are going to be the biggest thing in the business. So we got to have space. I suggested to Mr. Britsky that we build a western town, like some of those we seen from the train, and he agrees. We feel that we need a basic plant of at least a hundred acres. We have to put up stages, dressing rooms, offices, shops for our carpenters and our plasterers and costumers, and we need some kind of warehouse arrangement to store sets in. We need other things, like for example generators for our lighting and a good water supply. How cold does it get out here?"

"Well, never very cold. Most days in the winter months, December, January, February, and March, range between seventy and ninety degrees. Nighttime, it can go down to forty, but that's unusual. Mostly, winter nights are forty-five to sixty degrees. Summer — which means April to November — is a few degrees warmer, day and night. Even during the rainy season, you get mostly some sunshine each day and sometimes weeks of sun between the rains. In May and June, you get some foggy mornings, but it almost always clears by noon."

"And you think you can find us what we need?" Max wanted to know.

"Oh, no question. Not in Hollywood. Hollywood has too many streets and houses. They've been nasty as hell with your friend Lunberg. Did you know that no bank in Hollywood would do business with him — or with Lasky, either. Not because their credit isn't good, but because they don't like New York Jews. Would you believe it? The banks wouldn't take their money. Anyway it's a lousy little nothing of a small town, and I don't think it's right for what you want, Mr. Britsky.

"Now there's a feller name of Harry Culver, and he has an enormous piece of property that he's trying to sell off and subdivide. He calls the property Culver City, and if you look at the map, it's right here, just north of El Segundo and Inglewood. He was in to see me yesterday, because Lunberg told him you'd be coming out here. Now the trouble with Harry Culver is that he wants to hang on to the mineral rights; he thinks there's some enormous pool of oil somewhere under his property. He doesn't know where, and I don't think that after investing all the money you're talking about, you'd want them putting up derricks and drilling on your property. Anyway, he wants more than I think the land is worth, almost a thousand dollars an acre, and while we could knock down that price, I just don't think it's the right place."

"Why?" Max asked.

"Landscape. You just couldn't have the kind of spread and scenery you want out there on Harry Culver's property. Now here, going north, we got Santa Monica and Beverly Hills. Neither of them offers the space or scenery you need."

"What about down there in the south?" Snyder asked.

"Right through here, oil fields and tank farms. Over at Palos Verdes, hills and subdivisions. Inland, it's flat and mostly pretty miserable country. I'm just laying it out now. Tomorrow, we can drive through those places, because I don't want you to feel that I'm pushing you into some area out of self-interest. I know that if you bring your business out here, there's going to be hundreds of people wanting homes and property, so if I deal with you right at this point, I got a lot of business coming my way."

"Makes sense," Max agreed. "You must have given this a lot of thought, Stanley. What's your idea?"

"All right. Now right here, there's a range of hills they call the Santa Monica Mountains, and inland here, they call them the Hollywood Hills. They're not really mountains, because none of them are much more than a thousand feet high, but they come up sharp and they look impressive. Now here, to the north of these hills, is an area called the San Fernando Valley. Most of it is flat or easily rolling, and practically none of it is subdivided, and the land is cheap. You can pick it up for two, three hundred dollars an acre, and up north for less than that. You got plenty of open space, and here, here and here" — pointing to the eastern, western, and northern rims of the valley — "you got just the most spectacular mountain scenery you'll see anywhere in the West. You travel west toward the Malibu canyon, and you'll see some of the loveliest ranchland in California — cheap. You been talking about cowboys and Indians. Well, you can pick up a ranch of five, six hundred acres just for peanuts, and if you want some desert scenery that beats anything you ever dreamed of, you got Death Valley just a hoot and a holler away, a day's drive. You got all that, and still you can come up through the Cahuenga Pass and be in downtown Los Angeles in an hour and a half or so. Now my suggestion would be the eastern edge of the valley, where you got both a nice flat space and the foothills of the San Gabriel Mountains practically in your back yard. So there it is, and tomorrow we can begin to look at it.''

The following morning, with the three men loaded into his big Pierce Arrow Tourister, well armed with cold drinks, beer, and sandwiches, Meyer warned them, "Don't be put off by our local roads. It's true that most of them are no better than cart tracks, but just remember that twenty years ago this city practically wasn't here. Now it's growing like no other place in these here United States. If you build a studio, the city will build roads to connect you. Might cost a dollar or two in smearing, but what doesn't. From what I hear about Tammany Hall, you're no stranger to a little vigorish.''

"It's been known to happen," Max agreed.

"I'm trying to be truthful," Meyer said.

"Nobody ever made a buck out of the truth. Just show us.''

He showed them for the next four hours. They labored north on a dirt road to the village of Hollywood, then they turned west onto Hollywood Boulevard, another dirt road between an avenue of broad-branched pecan trees. They turned south at Fairfax, down into the Wilshire Valley, where there were few houses, but many sweeping barley and wheat fields, many of them gone to seed and weeds, their only crop a veritable forest of oil derricks. A broad dirt road to the west was euphemistically titled Wilshire Boulevard, mostly oil-surfaced gravel, with here and there short stretches that appeared to be asphalt pavement. The farmers who owned the fields that surrounded the oil derricks, taking a river of black gold out of the ground, had given up farming and with it irrigation, and most of the fields were brown and lifeless. The farmhouses that one could see from Wilshire Boulevard were decaying, as were the roadside sheds where once produce had been loaded for shipping; only here and there, a newly installed gasoline station bespoke prosperity.

"It looks pretty lousy," Meyer admitted, "but a feller called Burt Green has an idea that may change things. Right here, where we are now, used to be the Rancho Rodeo Las Aguas, and Green put together an outfit called the Rodeo Land and Water Company and bought up the entire old Spanish land grant, and they named the place Beverly Hills."

"Who's Beverly?" Feldman asked. "His wife?"

"That's the funniest part of it. You know, President Taft used to take his holidays at a place in Massachusetts called Beverly Farms. For some reason, Green picked up the name, and since the tract includes those hills to the north, he named it Beverly Hills. I was at a dinner a few weeks ago that Green put together for a group of real estate brokers, and he fed us like pashas and spent an hour and a half telling us what he intended to do with this tract. He wants to incorporate it as an independent city, even though it's mostly surrounded by the city of Los Angeles, but he can do it if he can build the population to five hundred people, and he thinks he can do that in the next few months. Then he plans to subdivide into streets and lots and turn the place into one of the fanciest towns in America. He's selling full-acre lots for fifteen hundred dollars and half-acres for a thousand, and it might be an interesting investment if you locate here. Not for the studio, of course, but for homes."

They continued westward, the road becoming worse, the few houses even less prepossessing, what was euphemistically called Wilshire Boulevard becoming Orange Boulevard, the oil derricks increasing, the tart smell of raw oil filling the air. As they approached the sea, the air became sweeter, and at Santa Monica, they paused to change a tire at the edge of a high palisade-type bluff. It was quite pleasant here, cottages already fronting the road that ran along the top of the bluff. Meyer, pointing to the marshy wetlands below them, said, "When we clean that up, maybe another year, we'll have one of the finest beaches in the country. What you got to realize is that this town is boiling. Come back in twelve months and you won't recognize it."

They ate their sandwiches and drank their beer at Santa Monica, and then, swinging southward, they made their way back to the hotel. Meyer arranged to pick them up again bright and early the following morning.

Before dinner, Max spent an hour on the telephone, speaking to New York, and at the dinner table he announced, "I telephoned

Cliff Abel. I told him to get his ass out here, so I'll be here for another week, and I guess both of you will be here too — a week at least, maybe more."

"Do you think he's the man for it?" Snyder wondered.

"Aren't you moving a bit fast?" Feldman wondered. "This is a strange place, Max, and to tell you the truth, it kind of gives me the creeps. What do we know about it? We're a million miles from anywhere."

"You're right. We don't know a damn thing about this place, but I can smell it. It's crazy as hell, but it's right. It's right for making moving pictures. We can't go on cooped up back there downtown and up in Harlem, and every time it snows and rains we got to pull our cameras out of the streets and with the goddamn telephone company and Edison every *Montag* and *Dunnershtick* slapping an injunction at us for some piece of equipment Sam here puts together, and we're ready to film and none of the cast can get there on account of the weather. This place is new and open. It makes sense for us even if it makes no sense any other way."

Feldman looked at Snyder, who nodded and said, "Max is right. I know how you must feel, Freddy, because you got all that family back in New York. Me and Alice, we're from Milwaukee, so it's no great shakes for us to pick up the kids and move out here. But Max is right. We got to get out of New York. Maybe someday Eastman will come up with film that lets us shoot pictures out of doors without sunlight, but right now we're going crazy trying to meet our schedule."

"You got to understand, Freddy," Max said gently, "what a moving picture is. I'm only just beginning to understand it myself. It moves. The writers keep giving us wonderful scenarios we can't shoot because we got to stay indoors. If we stay in New York, Lasky and Ince and Biograph and even a bum like Lunberg are going to make us look like bums. No, sir. Absolutely not. As soon as we decide with Meyer where to start building, I'm leaving Sam here with you and I'm going back to start things moving. I'm going to have a company shooting out here next month, so you might as well accept it. You got to find lodging and all the rest. Meanwhile, Cliff Abel starts building the studio."

"Max, that's crazy," Feldman protested. "You can't move so

quickly. We got three studios back east, not to mention the Hobart Building and the theatres. You don't liquidate something like that overnight."

"Who says anything about liquidating? We'll keep the studios and keep making pictures there. Bert Bellamy can run the operation there. But meanwhile, we'll build one big studio here, one studio big enough to take care of everything, a place where we can shoot twenty-five, thirty pictures at one time."

"I give up," Feldman said hopelessly.

The following morning, Meyer loaded them into his big Pierce Arrow again, and like the canny salesman he was, having shown them the dismal oil fields and tank farms of West Hollywood and West Los Angeles, drove them north through the Cahuenga Pass into the San Fernando Valley. "It's not like we're that far out of town," he explained to them, pointing to one of the big red interurban cars that was careening through the pass alongside them. "These cars will put you in downtown Los Angeles in half an hour. A great transportation system. But also, we'll have a paved road into the valley by the first of the year."

Max stared, fascinated, as they swept down into the valley. This was as close to a Garden of Eden as he had ever come — the air as sweet as honey, orange groves, pecan and pear and peach groves, as far as the eye could see — no oil derricks here — but a valley fruitful and lovely and succulent, ringed with high and splendid mountains, unspoiled and marvelous. No doubt, this was why he had come here. This was the place.

"I can get you a hundred acres for twenty-five thousand dollars," Meyer told him.

"Three hundred acres," Max said. "I want three hundred acres," thinking of the only poem he knew by heart:

> In Xanadu did Kubla Khan
> A stately pleasure dome decree;
> Where Alph, the sacred river, ran
> Through caverns measureless to man
> Down to a sunless sea.
> So twice five miles of fertile ground
> With walls and towers were girdled round.

And here were gardens bright with sinuous rills,
Where blossomed many an incense-bearing tree,
And here were forests ancient as the hills,
Enfolding sunny spots of greenery.

* * *

"Mama," Max said, "it's not a wild place filled with Indians. No-body walks up to you and shoots you. Believe me, I swear to you."

"Freida was crying her eyes out. You realize that? Or maybe you're too busy running around with *shiksas* to remember you got a sister, she's thirty-four years old and she ain't married. What will she find out there, cowboys?"

"We should be that lucky."

"Yeah? That's a way to talk?" Sarah began to weep. "Kill me. Then you got no responsibilities."

"Mama, don't cry. Please. I can't stand it when you cry."

"All my life I slaved my heart out for my children. I worked my fingers to the bone. And what do I get —" She submerged herself in her tears.

"Mama, please."

"First," she sobbed, "you pull me out of my home in Henry Street and drag me uptown, I don't know a soul. So now I make myself a little life here, now I got two married daughters and my sons are married, with grandchildren, what a woman dreams about, and you tell me I should leave this and be killed by Indians."

"There are no Indians in California, Mama. I swear to you."

"What then? Wild Buffalo Bills?"

"It's a place like any other place."

"What does Sally think about all this?"

"I don't know."

"What do you mean, you don't know?"

"Nobody told you?" Max said uncertainly.

"What should they tell me?"

"Sally and me, we're separated. We're going to be divorced."

"What!"

"Don't get excited, Mama," Max begged her.

"Oh? Sure, I shouldn't get excited. Only my home is taken away from me and my grandchildren are taken away from me, and I shouldn't get excited."

"Mama, I'm not taking away your home. You can live here with Freida, if she wants to, only she told me she wants to go to California. Ruby and Benny are both going to California. I gave that bum Esther is married to a job mismanaging the Bijou, but Sheila's husband seems to like the idea of moving to California —"

"So I should stay here!" Sarah snapped. "Then you're rid of me, and I'm left with that cold-fish stuck-up wife of yours, thinks she's better than anybody in the world. So why bother? Kill me! Throw me out in the street to die from the cold! That's better."

"Mama, nobody's getting rid of you. I told you, I bought this lot in Beverly Hills, and Clifford Abel's designing a house for us. It's a seven-bedroom house, with plenty of room for you and for Freida. And there's no hurry, because the house won't be ready for another six months at least, and maybe a year."

Actually, it was a year and a half before Max's Beverly Hills home was completed, and during most of that time, Max lived in a tiny cottage that had been part of the three-hundred-acre tract he purchased in the San Fernando Valley. During that time, he made five two-way train trips between Los Angeles and New York, but it was after his return from his first trip to Los Angeles that he spoke to his mother and Sally. Even though his mother's house and Sally's house stood side by side — his own living quarters having been transferred to a suite at the Waldorf-Astoria — he could not take the few steps from Sarah's house to Sally's. The door was barred to him, and Sally's response to his voice on the telephone was to slam the receiver down on its cradle. Finally, after several discussions with Fred Feldman, Sally agreed to see him, and for the first time in months he went up the steps of the brownstone that had once been his home. The date had been made for two o'clock in the afternoon, when the children were still in school, but Max had every intention of prolonging the visit until they returned. It could not be said that he actually missed his son and daughter. Richard and Marion were far too much strangers for him to feel any real pangs of separation, but he had a gnawing sense of duty combined with guilt.

Sally answered the door herself. She was wearing a white, lace-trimmed blouse of cambric and an ankle-length gray skirt of fine, thin wool. Her hair was drawn back and held by a ribbon at the nape of her neck, and there was just the faintest touch of rouge on her face and lips. Except that her face had become somewhat more severe, her mouth tightened and held in place by tiny lines at the corners, she looked no different than she had when Max married her twelve years before. She had gained little if any weight, her figure trim and tight; yet, looking at her now, Max could not find any response in himself, any emotional quiver that would explain to him why he had been so compulsively driven to her years before.

Sally, on the other hand, did give evidence of an emotional response; she regarded Max coldly, almost with loathing, and told him evenly that she had set aside a half-hour for his visit, which would mean that he would not see his children after all. He didn't contest that immediately, but simply nodded and went into the house.

Seated stiffly in the parlor, Sally said without preamble, "I suppose you've come to talk about the settlement. I have agreed to Feldman's proposal about the stock for myself and twenty thousand dollars a year support as well as this property and your mother's house. But I also want five percent of the company stock for each of the children."

"Why?" Max was taken aback by this. "When I die, the kids get everything."

"When you die is a long time off, and with that wolf-pack family of yours, they'll fight for every penny. Also, God only knows what low creature you'll be living with then."

"I don't understand," Max said tiredly. "I don't want to fight with you, Sally. I just don't understand why you hate me so much."

"Hate is not the word. I despise you."

"Yeah. I don't know as many words as you. I still don't know why you hate me. What did I ever do to you?"

"Aside from making me the laughingstock of this city, aside from going to bed with every actress you employ —"

"That's crazy. What do you mean, every actress I employ? That's a lot of crap and you know it."

"I love your elegant English. Are you going to deny that you had an affair with Della O'Donnell and were practically living with her all those years while we were still married? And that slut, Etta Goodman. And Alexa — that bitch you call Natalie Love. Oh, why go on?"

"Because there's no place to go. So I did it. Why in hell don't you ask yourself why? Going to bed with you was like going to bed with a goddamn iceberg, and since the kids came, your high-class cunt is locked as tight as the vault at the Chase Bank!"

Sally leaped to her feet and snapped, "I won't have that kind of filthy talk in my house! I think you should get out!"

"Damn it, Sally, what did I do to you? Why do you hate me?"

Sally stared at him, her face quivering with rage. "You had better go, Mr. Britsky. I don't want you here." Her voice shook, and she appeared to be fighting to get the words out. "I don't want you here at all. You disgust me. You're a dirty, nasty little man, and you disgust me."

Sighing, Max rose and said, "I'm sorry, Sally. I didn't want anything like this to happen. Sometimes I think I'm going nuts because I just don't know what happened. We loved each other, didn't we?"

"Oh, no!" she shouted. "No! Love? You can't love anything except your wretched moving pictures — and you wouldn't have those if I hadn't shown you how to make them. I'll tell you what happened. You beat me down. You forced me to marry you — dirty little Max Britsky from Henry Street, who lived like an animal with his family of animals — and I threw away my life and now I have nothing. Nothing."

He left, and he didn't get to see his children after all, and when he had dinner that evening with Fred Feldman, the session with Sally became something that he could not deal with at all.

"You did see her?" Feldman asked.

"Oh, yeah. I saw her."

"Did she raise the question of the children's stock?"

"Yes."

"How did it go, I mean the meeting?"

"O.K."

"She was friendly?"

"Well, not exactly friendly."

"Oh?" Feldman shook his head. "That's too bad. I was hoping the two of you might hit it off, at least for an hour or so."

"Freddy, are you crazy?"

"Yeah, well, that's the way it goes. I tried to convince her that one five-percent piece of the stock would be worth about five million in a year or two."

"Did she believe you?"

"I don't think so. But I did get her agreement to put the kids' stock — providing you agree — into an irrevocable trust, with the voting right retained by you until the kids are thirty. And that's not such a bad idea, Max. You know, you're still a young man, and you could marry again and have more children, and well, well, this protects Sally and her kids."

"Do I look like a schmuck who puts his hand in the gearbox twice?"

"Well, that's up to you. But we got to work out something about the kids, visitation rights. If you're living in Los Angeles and Sally remains here, well, it won't be easy."

"I hardly know the kids. They're like strangers to me. I don't even know what I feel for them, and they look at me funny."

"What do you mean, funny?"

"Like I'm some kind of animal, I don't know. I guess Sally tells them things about me. I tried to kiss Marion last time I saw her. She pulled away. God knows what kind of an animal those kids think I am!"

"Max, you have legal rights."

"I got no rights, Freddy. None. What do I do, tell the kids I'm not a murderer and that it's legal for them to believe it? Ah, the hell with it. Give her whatever she wants and get it over with."

· · ·

If Max had possessed the word "quintessential" in his vocabulary, he would have termed Clifford Abel the quintessential *goy*. Where Max was short, Abel was six feet and two inches; where Max was dark, Abel had a shock of blond hair and pale skin; and where Max was tightly knit, Abel had a big-boned and fleshless frame. Only their eyes were alike, bright blue, and kindred dreams united them. Abel loved Max. In his mind, Abel clothed Max in a high jeweled turban and silken robes, one who came out of the East, with many beasts of burden carrying fragrant spices, wondrous bales of cloth, and priceless jewels.

Max, on the other hand, thought of Abel in some such terms as the duke of Milan had once considered Leonardo. In terms of business — buying and selling and pricing — Clifford Abel was witless, and it fell to Max to set his wages and fees. But as an artist, Max had supreme confidence in him, assuring him that once his building projects were over, he and no one else would be the art director of the Britsky studio, instead of the young Yale and Carnegie Institute graduates that Max hired and fired and cursed out endlessly.

Clifford Abel understood Max. When Max brought him out to Southern California to look at the three-hundred-acre tract of land in the San Fernando Valley, Abel licked his lips in delight. Where there were only orange trees and pecan trees and weeds, Max said, "Right here, the gates. Large enough. Twelve feet wide."

"Twenty feet wide," Abel said.

"Wood?"

"Cast iron," Abel said.

"Absolutely. Maybe seven feet high?"

"Ten feet high."

"And on top, the name," Max said.

"Polished cast brass letters."

They understood each other. Given his own preference, Abel would have called the studio Xanadu, but Max, leading the way for those more timid than he, Lasky and Zukor and Laemmle and Warner and Mayer, would have none of the ambiguous. The studio would be called the Max Britsky Studio. There was a barn behind the cottage where Max took up his California residence, and with a few renovations and the introduction of electricity, Clifford Abel turned the barn into his studio. He hired two bright young draftsmen from San Francisco, and he sat with Max for hours, poring over the drawings. Max wanted a fifteen-foot-high brick wall to surround the entire three hundred acres; but Abel convinced him that even the wealth generated by Britsky Productions could not easily afford six or seven miles of masonry wall. Prices had changed since the time of Kubla Khan, and they compromised with the inclusion of about twelve acres with the wall and the rest with a nine-foot-high chain-link fence. New York had demonstrated to Max the kind of spectator insanity that surrounded the making of moving pictures, and while by his lights the San Fernando Valley was still an undiscovered wilderness or Garden of Eden — depending upon how one regarded it — he was all too aware of the speed with which cities grew and changed. There would be two large gates into the studio, each well guarded, and inside Abel would construct six stages, each with five thousand square feet of floor space, each capable of holding four good-sized sets. In addition, Max suggested a city street, and Abel felt that it might well be done in the Potemkin manner.

"Which means what?" Max demanded.

"Well, this Potemkin was a sort of administrator for Catherine the Great, the empress of Russia at that time, about a hundred and fifty years ago, and I suppose he wanted her to feel that she ruled over something a bit better than the real thing. So when she traveled, he had pretty little villages constructed along her route, but since it would have been too expensive to build the real thing, he only built the fronts — sort of outdoor sets."

"Wonderful. Absolutely wonderful."

"We might have a little country village too —"

"Yeah, but if you do that, Cliff, make the houses real. We start bringing out actors and technicians, and where do we put them?"

"Do you know what it's going to cost you, Max?"

"Don't worry about money. Freddy's turning us into a public corporation, and we'll have more money than we know what to do with. Anyway, the banks are breaking down the door wanting to lend me money. With this crazy war going on in Europe, we got the kind of prosperity nobody ever dreamed about. So you just build, and let me worry about paying for it."

By the spring of 1915, Clifford Abel's plans had evolved sufficiently for him to receive bids from the contractors, and by the beginning of May of that year, ground was broken for the Max Britsky Studio.

[NINE]

1923

Max at the Age of Forty-four

THERE WERE SOME FACETS of a changing world that Max observed and were of great importance to him, and there were other things that he dismissed. The Great War in Europe was a madness beyond his comprehension, and the fact that his youngest brother, Benny, had enlisted once America joined the Allies and was actually shipped over to France did not serve to upgrade his opinion of either Benny or the war. And since Benny returned from Europe unwounded and more intolerable than ever, Max gave no points to the benefits of army life.

It was easier to block out the war as a piece of lunacy totally apart from him than it was to escape the local insanity called Prohibition. Yet unlike war, the Volstead Act could be tempered by money, and a few financial adjustments renewed the studio's access to the best imported liquor.

In the area of wardrobe, Max eschewed the changes. A Southern California style of dress was coming into being — the Hollywood style, as it was called — but Max never accepted the validity of sport clothes. And with reason.

He possessed no personal historical antecedents for either sport clothes or leisure clothes. His first purchase of a suit that did not come from a ragpicker's bundle or from a sidewalk dealer of secondhand clothes had been a three-piece outfit of blue serge. He had paid four dollars for it at Barney Schlochter's Haberdashery on Canal Street. His most recent acquisition of blue serge had been made to order by Mort Singleton, whose tailoring shop on Vine Street in Hollywood was the most exclusive in Los Angeles, and the price had been a hundred and ninety-five dollars. Aside from the fact that both the cloth and the fit were better, it was not very different from Max's first suit. Max was not terribly interested in clothes. He owned two dozen suits, but they were all of either blue serge or dark gray worsted, and he wore them with black shoes, white shirts, and ties whose diagonal stripes were always of various shades of blue and gray. He also wore Homburg hats. He had purchased his first Homburg in imitation of Boss Murphy, and since then he had seen no reason to change to any other kind of headgear.

Whereupon this day in 1923, walking slowly along the sidewalk that paralleled Santa Monica Beach, he was dressed in a blue serge vested suit and he wore a Homburg. It was about half-past five in the afternoon, and he had driven from the studio to the point where Sunset Boulevard embarks on the Pacific Ocean, and then he had parked his car and begun his slow, lonely walk along the beach. He liked this part of the beach better than the section to the south, where his contemporary tycoons were building their great beach houses. Here it was still untouched and unspoiled. Max had no lust for a monumental personal house, for the strange castles his colleagues had built on Sunset Boulevard, in Beverly Hills, and on the beach. He had built a large and substantial house for his mother, Freida, and himself; but he rarely slept there. He preferred the small cottage on the studio property.

Clifford Abel had remodeled the cottage to Max's specifications, and he had decorated it to his own taste. The bottom floor contained Max's office, a receptionist's desk at the entrance, and a small office for Max's secretary. Since the cottage was a sort of modified Spanish Colonial stucco building, Abel had decided to do it in a simple, almost severe Spanish Colonial style: the floors tiled, the walls white, the furniture ordered in Guadalajara from friends of Abel's who operated a small furniture factory there. There were three baths in the building, and on the second floor, two rather large bedrooms. Max loved the building. In a way, it was his first real home, the first place that was entirely his, to his taste and not shared by another. He had thought of dividing the second bedroom in half so that his children might use it if and when they visited him, but then he decided that a studio lot was hardly a place for them. But they came only once and stayed in his mother's house, and they hated it, playing the role of two surly, silent kids, hating their grandmother, their Aunt Freida, and perhaps Max as well. It was no use for Freida to whisper to Max that Sally had poisoned them against the family; Max suffered as he had never suffered over anything before. Marion was twelve and Richard was almost fourteen when they came to spend two summer months with their father. They were beautiful, healthy, blue-eyed children, and they made Max more miserable than he had ever been before in all his life. They were bright kids, and they mimicked Max's English, his ghetto inability to pronounce a *t* or an *ng* properly, his use of "ain't," his misuse of pronouns; but it was done subtly, as were their other hostilities, without ever creating a situation that Max could pick up on. Not that he had any desire to confront them or discipline them. For all Max's comprehension of them, these two children might have come from another planet. Sally had been sending them, for the past three years, to an exclusive private school on New York's Upper East Side.

After two painful weeks in the house in Beverly Hills, which included an unpleasant scene with their grandmother, the two children decided that they wished to return to New York. Max did not protest, but called Sally, made the arrangements, and sent the children back along with a treasure trove of expensive presents. The following year, Sally informed Max that the children were protesting the visitation, whereupon he relinquished it without argument. So the problem of an extra bedroom in his studio cottage never had to be faced.

Other things had to be faced, and one of his necessities in facing other things was to be with himself. He would have said, if anyone had asked him why and if he had been capable of articulating the answer, that all his life had become a dream and the only way he could awaken, at least for a moment or two, was to be alone, preferably by the sea. There, with the soft, cool wind blowing in from the water, he could achieve a kind of sanity. He walked with his hands in his pockets, his black Homburg tilted back, his head thrust forward, a small, forlorn figure meticulously dressed.

Tonight, as he walked, Max became conscious of being followed. The person following him kept about forty feet behind him. When Max walked, the person, the shadow, walked; when Max stopped, the shadow stopped, and when finally Max stopped, turned around, and faced this person following him, the person following stopped as well, and the two of them stood there in the early twilight, confronting each other.

The person following him was a girl of about twenty years. She had straight blond hair cut in a bob, large blue eyes, and a wide, pretty face. She was quite thin, wearing a plain blue cotton dress and sandals, and she stood her ground with a sort of pathetic defiance; she was like enough to a thousand other girls Max saw each day in the streets of Los Angeles to be their sister.

Max walked up to her. She stood her ground.

"Following a strange man can get a girl like you into a lot of trouble," Max said.

"You're not a strange man."

"Oh? We've been introduced?"

"No."

"So how is it I'm not a strange man?" Max asked her.

"You're Max Britsky — or I think you are. Are you?"

"Is that why you're following me? Because I'm Max Britsky?"

"Yes."

"So you figure you follow Max Britsky, maybe you can meet him?"

"Yes."

"And then you ask him for a job."

"It ain't just asking you for a job, Mr. Britsky. You are Mr. Britsky?" with just a shadow of a doubt in her voice.

"Maybe it's somebody looks like me."

"Nobody looks like you, Mr. Britsky."

"Nice, nice. That's the way to make friends."

"Oh, no," she begged him. "I didn't mean it that way. I didn't mean it that way at all. You're a very nice-looking man, Mr. Britsky. It's just the way you dress, with that funny hat. I seen it in pictures. Nobody else out here wears a funny hat like yours. I don't mean a funny hat, I mean —"

"Take it easy," Max said. "What's your name?"

"Are you Mr. Britsky?" she asked pleadingly.

"Yes. You want two hats like this in one place?"

"I'm an actress."

"Like I didn't know," Max said. "I'm surprised, honey. Like I didn't know that every kid with blond hair and blue eyes who wins a high school beauty contest, or maybe they just tell her she's beautiful, and off she goes to Hollywood like ten thousand other kids, so it's a big surprise to me you're an actress. My advice is, stop being an actress and go home." Delivered of that, Max turned to continue his walk. "And don't follow me. It makes me nervous."

"Please." She plucked at his sleeve, then tightened her grip on it. "Please, Mr. Britsky."

"Please what?" Max demanded, pulling away.

"Anything you want, Mr. Britsky. I'll go to bed with you. I'll do anything you want me to do. Anything."

Max turned and stared at her curiously. "Anything?"

"Yes, please."

"For what?"

"To give me a part — any part. I must. I can't go on like this. Please —" She began to cry.

"Oh, God," Max said. "I hate to see a woman cry. Maybe I'm not Max Britsky after all. I'm not too sure myself."

"You're making fun of me."

Max gave her his handkerchief and said, "Come on, dry your eyes and stop the crying. What's your name?"

"Gertrude. Gertrude Meyerson." She dried her eyes and handed the handkerchief back to Max.

"Where are you from, Gertrude?"

"Milwaukee."

"How old are you?"

"Twenty."

"Yeah. Well, now you tell me where you live, and I got my car here and I'll take you home, and don't go stopping people on the street and telling them you'll go to bed with them. Maybe it's not Max Britsky. Maybe it's someone who'll cut your pretty little throat for that gold chain you got around your neck."

"It ain't gold. It's just imitation."

"*Mazeltov!* It ain't gold."

"And you can't take me home."

"Why?"

"I ain't got a home. I had a job waiting tables and I lost it because I wouldn't go to bed with the ape who owned the place, and then my landlady threw me out. I spent last night on the beach. I got my bag there on the beach."

"So him you won't go to bed with, but with Max Britsky —"

"I'm an actress."

"So, for a part, it's different?"

"Yes."

"And I suppose you think I never got such an interesting offer before?"

She stared at him for a long moment, then she pressed her palms against her cheeks and closed her eyes. For a few seconds she stood like that; then her hands dropped and she turned and began to walk away. She had taken a dozen steps when Max called after her, "Gertrude!"

She paused and turned.

"Gertrude," Max said, "go get your bag from the beach." She approached Max as if she were walking on glass. "I'm going to take you to dinner, and after dinner, I'll give you a card that'll let you in to see the casting director, Britsky Studio, and maybe he'll hire you for something and maybe he won't, and for this I should have my head examined. Also, I don't go to bed with little girls who follow me on the beach. That's your first lesson, you want to stay around Max Britsky."

"You're kidding."

"No, I'm not kidding."

"You'll wait here?"

"Absolutely."

Her face changed and her body changed, as if a bottle of youth had been poured into her, and she raced down the beach, looking backward every few steps to see whether Max was still there. Her bag was an old AEF knapsack, and she plucked it from the sand and raced back to Max.

"That's it?" Max asked her. "All your worldly possessions?"

"That's it."

"And suppose you don't see me to follow, and suppose my head ain't like a bowl of oatmeal tonight, what then?"

"I don't know. Something comes up. Someone pays me five bucks to go to bed with them if I'm lucky."

"You done that before?"

"Once or twice. Sure, I could lie to you. What would you do if you were that hungry, Mr. Britsky?"

"Same thing."

"You still going to buy me dinner?"

"Think I should dump you because you got laid for a few bucks? My goodness, Gertrude, I would have to dump maybe seventy-five percent of the ladies I know, and that's a low percentage. At least you were hungry."

They reached the car, a long, sleek, open-top Packard twin six, painted silver and black. Gertrude stared at the car in silent admiration.

"Throw your bag in back."

"It's beautiful."

"It cost beautiful. Time was, I could have lived five years on what that piece of tin cost me. Get in."

They had turned away from the beach, the Packard groaning in low gear as it climbed Sunset Boulevard up to Pacific Palisades, when she asked him where they were going to eat. "I keep thinking about it. I guess that's because I'm so hungry."

"How hungry? If you're actually starving, we can stop and get you a sandwich. Otherwise, you can wait and we'll have dinner with a king. Come to think of it, that won't be until maybe nine o'clock tonight. So maybe we'll have a sandwich."

Max parked alongside a small stand in Pacific Palisades, where a sign advertised FIRST-RATE NACHOS AND TACOS. "These are the best, north of the border. Believe me." The proprietor, a small man who walked with a limp, greeted Max enthusiastically.

"Glad to see you, Mr. Britsky. Long time. How are you feeling?"

"*Bueno, bueno*, can't complain, Pedro. This here's Gertrude. She's hungry, so make her a couple of fat *nachos*. Beer. You like beer, kid?" he asked Gertrude.

"Sure."

"Best Mexican beer there is, which is maybe the best in the world. I'll have a beer, too, Pedro."

Max put down a ten-dollar bill when the food came and told Pedro to keep the change. Gertrude wolfed down the two *nachos* and accepted a third.

"They want to move me out, Mr. Britsky," Pedro said.

"What?"

"They got a chamber of commerce now. Pacific Palisades is becoming a classy place. A little while ago, it wasn't even here, but now they don't want no cheap Mexican hotdog stands lousing up the scenery."

"You need a lawyer, give me a call, Pedro. I'll put Freddy on it."

Back in the car, she asked him, "You eat there a lot, Mr. Britsky? A place like that?"

"The food's good, ain't it?"

"Sure, but you're Max Britsky."

"Whatever he is now, girlie, little Pedro Sanchez, he used to be my *vaquero* foreman. In case you don't know, *vaquero* is the Mexican word for cowboy, only they're a damn sight better than cowboys. When we make a cowboy picture, we use them, and Pedro used to recruit them for me and then boss them until he took a bad fall with his horse and broke a hip. I put him into that stand because he can't ride no more, and I tell you this, kid, you ate better there than you'll eat with the king tonight."

"What king? You mean a real king?"

"Absolutely."

"You're kidding."

"Nope. This is the real thing, just like the Cinderella stories I turn out in my dream factory. One minute you're on your ass on Santa Monica Beach, and the next you got a belly full of *nachos* and you're on your way to have dinner with King Alfonso the Thirteenth. How about that, kid, thirteen Alfonsos, and this one, number thirteen, he's king of Spain."

"You're kidding, Mr. Britsky. I'm not that dumb."

"Who is? On the other hand, I'm not even exactly sure where Spain is. It connects with France, right?"

"I think so."

"You graduated high school, Gertrude?"

"Oh, sure."

"Funny thing, I can give you a rundown of the Spanish market. We do business with a Dom Francisco Sergova. He's got thirty-three theatres, or whatever goes for theatres in Spain, and if Jake Stein was here, he could tell you what the theatres grossed last year.

But that's all I know about Spain except that they laid it heavy on Mexico until Mexico threw them out."

Puzzled, Gertrude asked Max whether he was taking her home.

"I'm taking you to dinner, kid. That's our arrangement. We're going to Pickfair, which is the classy home of Mary Pickford and Douglas Fairbanks over in Beverly Hills. I'm invited there tonight to meet Alfonso, the king of Spain. I couldn't care less, except when you turned up on the beach, I decided to exercise what Clifford Abel calls my Haroun El Rashid complex and to bring you along."

"I don't understand anything you're saying, Mr. Britsky. You said you were going to get me into the studio to see the casting director."

"That's a promise."

"You're not taking me to Mary Pickford's house?"

"Why not?"

"Oh, no! No. It's a joke."

"Yeah, I agree with you. It's a kind of Jewish joke, but that's where we're going, to have dinner with Mary Pickford and Douglas Fairbanks and King Alfonso of Spain, who kicked us all out of there in fourteen ninety-two — did you know that? — and now he's here, and he doesn't mind if the industry's practically all Jewish. He's a very liberal character, this king, especially when it comes to eating in classy places like Pickfair, and he don't even mind if maybe Fairbanks is Jewish, which I've heard said, but for myself I never asked him."

"Mr. Britsky," Gertrude wailed, "I really don't know what you're talking about, but you can't take me to Douglas Fairbanks' house the way I'm dressed. Just look at me!"

"You look pretty good."

"This is my only dress."

"Nobody's going to ask you for the others."

"I'm wearing sandals."

"They'll think it's very stylish. Believe me, darling, the people you'll find where we're going are too stupid to know what's stylish and what isn't, and that includes the king, believe me, and even if you come in a paper bag, they got to kiss Max Britsky's ass." He glanced at her. "You're better looking than most of them. Right away, they'll make you a discovery. Max Britsky's new discovery.

Goldwyn and Mayer and Lasky, they'll hear about it before they go to sleep tonight, and they got to believe that if you're my discovery, you ought to be their discovery, and maybe you won't turn up at Britsky Studio tomorrow. Maybe you'll have a real offer, because the world I live in is a sort of lunatic asylum. Also, about the way you're dressed, it don't matter. I have seen Tom Mix turn up stinking of manure with three days' beard, and I've seen girls there with practically nothing on, so what does it matter?"

As they turned north from Sunset Boulevard into Benedict Canyon, Gertrude's pleading simmered down to a final whisper, "Please let me out, Mr. Britsky."

"You're ready for any kind of unnatural act with Britsky, but Mary Pickford is scary. Why not? You been out here how long?"

"Two years."

"All right." He stopped the car. "You want to get into this lunacy, you come with me. You want to get out, all right. But for God's sake, go back to Milwaukee."

"I'll go with you," she whispered.

"Good." He started the car. "I'm not taking you to any drunken brawl. It won't be a Fatty Arbuckle party. They don't have orgies at Pickfair. Actually, they don't serve liquor, not even wine. The worst can happen, Fairbanks, he gets down under the table and bites the ankle of some of the ladies."

"You're kidding."

There was a police car flashing its lights at the junction of Benedict Canyon and Summit Drive, and two private guards with rifles blocked the narrow dirt road that led up the hill to Pickfair, the home of America's sweetheart and America's super-athlete star. One of the guards peered into the car, and then waved him ahead. "They'll park it for you at the top of the road, Mr. Britsky."

"So now you got my name confirmed," he said to Gertrude as he drove up the narrow dirt road. "This place up here, it used to be a kind of a hunting lodge, when you went hunting in Beverly Hills, and now it's an institution to put money into. If it wasn't for Pickfair, what would they do with their money? A few years ago, Mary Pickford was making twenty-five dollars a week at Biograph in New York. Nobody knew her name. They used to call her the kid with the curls. Fairbanks used to be a guy, name of Ullman, a stage actor and pretty awful. He's better when you don't hear him talk. Both of them teamed up with Zukor, and now they gross better than two million a year between them. Don't agonize. In a year or two maybe you'll do as well or maybe you'll be back in Milwaukee. I had a girl, Alexa Vasovich, who I named Natalie Love. She could have been the greatest of them all, but she was crazy for chocolate creams. She gained fifty pounds, poor kid."

Running off at the mouth, Max thought as he parked the car. You pick up some poor kid at the beach, and you have to impress her with all you know about the business. She'll do anything — degrade herself, humiliate herself, and probably let herself be whipped, or put out for hire, or any other variety of sickness or viciousness or brutality — only give her a part in a movie, any part. My God, he had to ask himself, what happened? Did I make this? That's giving myself too much credit, too much credit.

He parked the car, guided by the flashing lights of the red-jacketed attendants. "Gladys Smith," he said as he helped Gertrude out of the car.

"What's that?"

"Mary Pickford's name. We can't leave you Gertrude Meyerson."

They were being guided and greeted into the house. Gertrude was staring at the golden curls of America's sweetheart. Fairbanks embraced Max. "Max, Max, it's always a pleasure to welcome you here. And who is this enchanting creature?" He greeted Gertrude and kissed her. If Mary Pickford noticed the dirt on Gertrude's feet in the worn sandals and asked herself who was this slut in the three-dollar dress Max Britsky picked up somewhere and brought to her house, inserting her among the silks and minks and sables, a skinny little blond kid shivering in blue cotton — if indeed she thought that, she gave no sign of it. She was glazed and animated at the same time. The dark little man who was Alfonso, king of Spain, descendant of the grandees and the conquerors — Cortés and Pizarro and Ferdinand and Isabella and Torquemada — then appeared, honored to be invited to a renovated hunting lodge in a city that had not existed ten years before. He bowed back to those who bowed before him, mumbling his delight. He was honored to be introduced to another small man whose name was Chaplin, Charlie Chaplin, "Oh, yes, yes," the king said in very broken English, "I see your picture." He returned to Spanish to say that he had seen

The Kid. Wonderful, wonderful, wonderful! Such is the accolade of royalty. Tom Mix towered over the little king. Hoot Gibson stood next to Tom Mix, and as a backdrop to these two large, masculine ranch hands, the sparkling colored lights of Pickfair illuminated the smooth lawns and the splendid semitropical plantings. Did the little king recall that once all of California had belonged to his ancestors? Max said to him in Spanish, "This is Tom Mix and this is Hoot Gibson. They are the famous Western actors. *En español, vaquero. Comprende usted?*" His face lit up. The crowd around them applauded. Extraordinary! Max speaks Spanish. Actually, it was very little and poorly, only what he had picked up.

The enormous table was set for sixteen, seven on each side and one at each end. Host and hostess took the ends, the king sitting gratefully next to Mary Pickford, his interpreter next to him. The king was very democratic. Everyone remarked at how democratic the king was. They whispered to him. They whispered that everyone said he was being very democratic. He nodded his own approval. He was delighted with all the beautiful women. At every other place at the table, a beautiful woman was seated, and all of them were smiling at his majesty.

Fairbanks made a fuss over Gertrude. His exaggerated movements made him appear either a graceful dancer or a ridiculous actor, depending on what one approached with, either reverence or mockery. Max had neither. He observed without judgment. Somehow, the theme and passion of his life had created this and so much more, but why and how was not for him to decide. Fairbanks kissed Gertrude's hand. Her nails were dirty, and as she looked at her hands, her gaze directed there by Fairbanks's gesture, her whole body winced with an agony that Max understood very well indeed. Fairbanks winked at Max, the wink indicating the actor's approval for what a sly old devil Max was. At the table, Max was seated on one side of Gertrude, and on the other side, a tall, handsome actor, recently imported from England. He had been offered to Max, but his height turned Max off. He was six feet and two inches. Max accepted people who were reasonably tall, but six feet was a sort of limit — and the man was also a *womanizer*. The word was used then, and defining it, Max said that the Englishman would fuck the squirrels in the park if he could catch them. Max never moralized on sexual matters, but he had contempt for a man who went to bed with a woman he didn't care for deeply. Now the English actor introduced himself to Gertrude by sliding his hand across her thigh toward her cleft, and when she whispered a plea to Max, he pointed out that she who would sit in the seats of the mighty and the beautiful accepted certain risks. Then he leaned across her, whispering to the English actor, "Listen, you fucken Limey, you touch this kid again and I'll blacklist you in every studio on the Coast." He smiled as he said it, and the actor pleaded instantly that it was inadvertent, done without malice or motive. "Of course, you shithead," Max whispered, smiling again.

A large, stout Frenchman, white hair and white mustache, introduced as the Comte de Poicte and utterly without a word of English, was seated opposite the king. "I think," Max whispered to Gertrude, "that he gets the dribble glass. I could be mistaken, but — No, he's got to be the mark."

"Who is he, and what's the dribble glass?"

"He's a Frog count. Doug collects them. Anything with a title, look," pointing on the tablecloth, "up there, the little guy, Charlie Chaplin." Max glanced at the count. Chaplin nodded. "He agrees with me. Watch." A uniformed footman was pouring the wine. All eyes of those who knew were on the count, and then Tom Mix rose and drawled a toast to their host. "It ain't wine," Max whispered. "Grape juice in a wine bottle. Watch now." They drank. The king of Spain grimaced at the sweet gop in his glass, but the Comte de Poicte never tasted it. As he raised his glass, the grape juice poured through a slit onto his waistcoat. Great laughter, while he stood at the table, dumbfounded.

"How could they do that?" Gertrude asked.

"Learn, kid, learn. You want to join the tribe in the jungle, so learn."

Another uniformed footman wiped the grape juice from the count's clothes. He sat down, smiling foolishly. There was no interpreter, no one who spoke French. No one explained how he had gotten there. The meal went on under an unwavering din of talk. "Most of them," Max explained to Gertrude, "get tanked up before they come to a dinner at Pickfair. They come here drunk and they keep reserves out in their cars. It's a kind of an idiot game."

She couldn't forget the dribble glass. "Is that poor man a real count?"

"I guess so. You'd be amazed how many of these schmucks with titles come here, and it's their big moment to get invited to Pickfair. Now take it easy. You're going to get your ankle bitten."

"What?"

Max nodded at the head of the table. Douglas Fairbanks had disappeared, and the inner circle of Pickfairians, up and down the table, paused in their consumption of mounds of strawberry ice cream topped with Alpine slopes of whipped cream laced with heavy syrup and maraschino cherries to await the heady result of Fairbanks's humor.

"He's under the table," Max whispered into Gertrude's ear.

She screamed, and the inner circle burst into convulsive laughter.

* * *

Later, in Max's car, Gertrude Meyerson was weeping and she wanted to know where Max was taking her.

"I would take you home, but you tell me you got no home, so I'll give you a place to sleep tonight. Why are you crying? Does it hurt where he bit you?"

"No. It didn't even break the skin."

"So what's the tears? It ain't every kid from Milwaukee gets bitten by a great movie star."

"I don't know."

"What don't you know?"

"I don't know why I'm crying, except that I feel crazy and I got no home and no money and I don't want to think how terrible those people are, because maybe that's the right way."

"What right way?"

"I don't even know what I mean. I don't even know why I'm frightened, because I don't think I'm frightened of you. I don't know why I'm crying."

"Don't you feel lucky?" Max asked her. "After two years of breaking your heart, you got a chance to be in the movies."

"Have I? Really?"

"I told you."

"I'll try to stop crying."

Then she sat quietly while he guided the car over the pass and down into the San Fernando Valley and along the palm-lined dirt road that led to the studio. He had planted the palms himself along this approach road, four hundred of them, lining what would one day be a broad avenue. Palm trees fascinated him. Max was not a reader. In all his life he had never read a real novel, and the readers used as textbooks during his first years of schooling were only a dim memory. He had read many scenarios, but this was an act of discipline, performed without pleasure. Without any background of reading and with his religious education truncated at a very early age, Max had only the vaguest notions of a place where Jews had once originated. Yet he connected it with palms and the dry dust of desertland. He loved palms and century plants and Morocco ivy and the marvelous variety of cactus plants obtainable in Southern California, while Southern California itself became a strange love-hate place. During the nine years he had been here in Southern California, Los Angeles had changed from a sleepy backwash of a village into a place that urbanized itself overnight, growing with explosive force. After his purchase of three hundred acres in the valley, studio after studio appeared, each producer purchasing a large tract of land — in Culver City, in West Los Angeles and Hollywood, and in the San Fernando Valley — and with the studios came surfaced roads and houses and thousands of people to operate the studios, and more thousands of working people and merchants to build the houses and sell the goods that the people in the studios required, and the raw, dry tracts that Harry Culver and Burt Green had cornered and euphemistically titled Culver City and Beverly Hills had each in turn, in the space of a few years, become an actual city, Culver City a sprawling mélange around three film studios, and Beverly Hills, the residential paradise of the new industry that threw up stars and directors and producers with the speed of mushrooms after a rain, most of them paid more than most tycoons of American industry had ever dreamed of earning.

And when Gertrude Meyerson, staring ahead of her down at the stygian darkness of the San Fernando Valley, had asked Max where they were going, he told her, "To my studio."

"The Max Britsky Studio?"

"So they tell me."

"And you live there, Mr. Britsky?"

"Sometimes. I'll have a place for you to sleep, so tomorrow you won't need a pass after all. You'll be inside, and I'll call Melvin

Dubberman, who's our casting director, and lo and behold, you're in movies. Meanwhile, I'm glad you stopped crying."

At the studio gates, an armed, uniformed guard flashed his light into the car, recognized Max, nodded, and then opened the gates. Vaguely, in the headlights, Gertrude could make out the studio street, the towering stages and the bulk of other buildings, and then, a bit farther on, a sleepy village street, and then a white cottage, where Max parked his car. A switch on the porch flicked on the lights, and then Max led the way into his reception room.

"In there," he told her, "is my private office. You become a big star, I'll see you in my private office. Meanwhile, we go upstairs." He led the way up a staircase at one side of the entry, past the eighteenth-century Spanish Colonial furniture, past a needlepoint rug on the floor and a subdued striped wallpaper that followed the staircase to the second floor. There were two bedrooms on the second floor, each opening off the small landing, each with its own bath. Max's bedroom had a hooked rug with a large turkey design on the tile floor, a toile wallpaper, a rather heavy post and ball bed, and two early eighteen-hundreds chests of drawers. The other room was furnished more lightly, a delicate fourposter with a canopy, another needlepoint rug, and a wallpaper of pastel pink and yellow stripes. Max watched Gertrude's face as he turned on a lamp in this room. The tears and depression had given way to delight.

"It's so pretty," she said.

"Yeah, so they tell me."

"And you live here, Mr. Britsky, all alone out here?"

"Actually, I live in Beverly Hills, my mother's house. The way it works out, I mostly live here. It's convenient. I don't have to drive to work. I'll find you a pair of my pajamas, and in the bathroom there's toothbrush, cream — whatever you need." She was still standing where he had left her when he returned with a pair of pajamas. Then he left, closing her door behind him. He closed the door to his own bedroom and opened the window, letting in the cool night air. He loved the smell of night-blooming jasmine and had ordered a large stand of it to be planted outside his cottage. Then he undressed, brushed his teeth, put on his own pajamas, and got into bed. He selected a Cuban cigar, clipped the end, lit it, and lay back on two pillows, drawing the rich smoke softly and lovingly. He was amused by his experience with Gertrude Meyerson.

His studio had just finished a very expensive film titled *The Caliph*. It was the story of a Middle Eastern potentate, a caliph of the Middle Ages, who donned the garb of a simple peasant and went among his people, having all sorts of violent and acrobatic adventures along the way. Like so many people with no training in or real knowledge of history, Max believed in the validity of his studio's childish recreations, and to some extent he saw himself as the caliph. On the other hand, he had had no intention whatsoever of attending the dinner party at Pickfair. He possessed an intuitive sense of what was gross, tasteless, stupidly vulgar, and while he tended not to be judgmental of the stars and directors who had finally emerged from his nickelodeons to become the culture heroes and the popular kings and queens of the twentieth century, he avoided when possible their celebratory rites. He was not too given to the curse of loneliness, and he still dined at least twice a week at the dinner table of Sam Snyder, filling his stomach with heavy German food and sweet, dark beer. The few evenings he spent alone in his cottage, which was actually a part of the standing sets at the Britsky lot, he enjoyed. Sally had never permitted him to smoke in bed, and when he smoked in the Beverly Hills house, Sarah denounced his action with her customary fury, none of it tempered by age. This tiny cottage was actually his first home, the first home that was wholly his and in which his word was absolute law. Now and then he had been tempted to build or buy a home of his own in Beverly Hills, but with second thoughts, he discarded the notion. He had not married again, and he saw no need for a great empty house. Through the years, he told himself that someday he would find another woman who was at least a good deal like Della O'Donnell, but as the years passed, Della became increasingly wonderful in his memory and her replacement increasingly unlikely.

But perhaps it was the aphrodisiac of power that prevented him from ever again finding a Della O'Donnell, particularly that aphrodisiac that surrounds a moving picture tycoon. The dry fields of West Los Angeles, spotted with hundreds of oil derricks, had given way to a city that became a magnet for beautiful young women from all over America and indeed, the world. They poured into Los Angeles with the dream of becoming stars in this incredible new phenomenon called moving pictures, and such was their hunger and their frustration that they would have sold their souls to the devil if success came with the contract. In the center of this, as the reigning lord of the Max Britsky Studio and the thousand or so theatres that it serviced, Max had at the flick of his finger the sexual services of any one of a thousand beautiful women. In all truth, he went to bed with very few. His fellow tycoons outdid him, but whatever happened in this strange new world of Hollywood took on legendary proportions, and since Max was always at the center of the legend, the truth was submerged in the myth.

Gertrude Meyerson believed the myth and pursued it, and knocked timidly at the door to Max's room.

"Come in."

Max was a small man, but she was smaller in his pajamas. The sleeves covered her hands; the trousers were rolled up. She walked in barefoot. She stood by Max's bed, staring at him.

"Smoke bother you?"

"No. My father smoked cigars."

"He's dead?"

She nodded.

"Sit down."

She sat on the edge of the bed and asked timidly, "Why don't you think I'm attractive?" She had washed the cheap, badly done makeup from her face. It was a broad, open face, pale and sad, the blue eyes widely set, the mouth full and well shaped.

"You're a nice-looking girl. You came from a farm, didn't you?"

"It's near Milwaukee."

"You never studied acting."

"No."

"Just come here and do it."

"Because I can," she cried. "I know I can."

"Sure."

"Let me come to bed with you," she said flatly. She had no artfulness, no tricks, not even an intuitive sense of feminine enticement.

"You know, kid," Max said to her, "my own daughter, Marion, she's just about your age. Some men like that. It makes them feel young. I look at you and think about how I don't see my own kid since maybe eight years ago. That stinks like hell, don't it? So I screw a little farmgirl who don't know which side is up, and that makes me feel better? I got to have shit in my blood to think like that."

Tears welled into her pale blue eyes.

"That kind of language you're not used to," Max said. "My mother used to say my mouth should be washed out with soap. Brown horse soap. Listen, kid, you're not an actress. That's something I know. You're sweet-looking, but you don't look the way they want girls to look right now."

She began to cry.

"Don't do that, please. I'll tell you what I'm going to do. Tomorrow, I'll find you a job. Can you type?"

She shook her head.

"What can you do? Can you sew?"

She nodded.

"All right. I'll put you in the wardrobe department. We'll start you at thirty-five dollars a week, which is very good money, believe me. We got half a dozen rooming houses over here on Ventura Boulevard, and I'll find you a room in one of them, clean and decent, and you get breakfast and supper for fifteen dollars a week. Then we got a coach on the lot here, he has a class in the afternoon three times a week. You go to his class, and maybe you learn something, because even if most actors are brainless schmucks, still, it's not something you get born with. You got to learn."

The tears were pouring down her cheeks now.

"Please, stop crying."

"Why are you being so nice to me?" she managed through her sobs.

"Because I'm a schmuck. Now stop the goddamn crying and get out of here."

"And you don't want me?"

"Jesus, Gertrude," he snapped, "tonight I don't want to get laid — not by you, not by the queen of Sheba. Now get the hell out of here and go to sleep."

It was remarkable how lighthearted he felt after she had left the room. He got out of bed, found a bottle of imported sherry in a commode, poured a small glass, and then went back to bed, lying propped up on his pillows, smoking his cigar, and sipping the sherry. There was no sharing a cigar; it was a foul, filthy thing to everyone except the man who happened to be smoking it; and the brief presence in the room of the wide-eyed girl from the beach served to underline the fact. Max felt better than he had felt in a long time. The sherry was sweet and pleasant. He had a serious and reliable bootlegger who did business only on the Britsky lot, and in return for the concession he brought in the very best. There were two scenarios on his night table that were waiting to be read, but Max was in no mood for reading tonight. He was full of a poignant sadness, content and discontent at once, thinking of the little blond farmgirl asleep in the next room, half regretful that he had not taken her to bed, but at the same time placing Sally in bed with him in his fantasy, the Sally of long, long ago.

* * *

Max slept late the following morning, and when he had shaved and dressed and glanced in the room next door, he discovered that Gertrude had left. But she had taken pains to put the bed together neatly. He went downstairs. The studio was already alive and working, and his secretary was at her desk in the reception room of the cottage.

"Did you —" he began.

"Yes, Mr. Britsky. She came down about fifteen minutes ago. She said she wanted to look around outside."

"She comes back, tell her I'm in the commissary, having breakfast. Tell her to go into the VIP room and ask for my table."

He stepped out into the hard, brilliant California sunshine. This was his domain, his world, his creation, this vast cluster of buildings, stage shops, castles of papier-mâché, desert hovels and suburban streets, cranes, cameras, and generators. And on the streets of this great enclosure called the Max Britsky Studio, hundreds of men and women — Indians, cowboys, gamblers, exotic dancers out of the Arabian nights, British hussars, grips, carpenters, cameramen, electricians, writers, directors — and standing entranced, bewildered, a small blond girl named Gertrude Meyerson.

Gently, Max tapped her arm. "Come on, kid, I'll buy you some breakfast and then we'll find you a job."

[TEN]

1927

—

Max at the
Age of Forty-eight

THE DAY STARTED with a writer. He was a young writer, twenty-eight or twenty-nine years old, a graduate of Syracuse University — Syracuse, out of Max's frame of reference, vaguely indicative of the ancient world, of the chariot racetrack on the back lot. Max asked him where the college was, and he replied that it was in upstate New York. The writer had an air of poorly concealed superiority, the patience one exercises in conversation with the ignorant, the uneducated, the culturally deficient; but Max was familiar with the attitude and did not resent it. The writer, whose name was Dudley Langham, had published a novel and two short stories in the *Atlantic*, and he had also done a skit for one of Ziegfeld's reviews. He had come to Los Angeles because he felt, as he told Max, that the film was the art form with the greatest potential, and Fulton Hazig, Max's studio editor, had taken him on with a salary of two hundred a week. "He's pretty snotty and wet behind the ears," Hazig told Max, "but at least he can write his own name and spell it correctly — which, considering the level of writing we get out here, is something."

Max had read his first scenario and asked to talk to the man, a long-legged gangling man, heavy glasses, tweeds.

"Personally," Max said to him, "I write my own name, but not so good, so I don't try to pretend to be a critic. Everybody else is a critic, so I figure the society can operate without me joining it. For criticism, I hired Mr. Hazig. That's his business."

"But I want very much to know what you think about it."

"Ah-hah, that's criticism. I say it stinks, that's criticism. I say it's wonderful, also criticism. All I can say is I like it or I don't like it. I don't like it. I'll tell you why. For me, a movie should do one of two things. Either the hero, which can be either a man or a woman, is somebody you like so much, you're ready to die if he dies and bleed when he bleeds, or it should be somebody you hate so much you'd like to kill him yourself, you could only get into the screen. This here"—tapping Langham's scenario — "this don't do it to me. I don't love and I don't hate. You come right down to it, I'd rather play the Victrola."

"Aren't you applying your own subjective judgments, Mr. Britsky? You pose a very simplistic approach to literature."

That took nerve, Max admitted to himself. Mayer or Zukor would have booted Langham right out of the room. "Only it ain't literature," Max said, not unkindly. People like Langham always loused up Max's grammar. In spite of himself, he couldn't control it. It was his defense. "Maybe it ain't even drama, the way it's done in the theatre. You see, boychik, movies are something else, stories told in pictures. Think about that — stories told in pictures. Try it again."

He handed Langham the script, opened the door to his office, and ushered the young man out before Langham could think of an appropriate retort. Then he called Hazig and shouted at him, "Don't send me no more of your goddam geniuses with their scripts!"

"Langham?"

"That's the shithead's name. Yes."

"He's got something, Max, and you have a gift for putting your finger on it."

Max softened.

"Did you talk to him?"

"I talked to him."

"Did you tell him what was wrong? I tried, but I couldn't get through to him."

"I told him," Max said.

"Thanks."

Max put down the phone, grinning and shaking his head. Fulton

Hazig handled him with great skill, and Max appreciated anyone who handled him with great skill. Out in the reception room, Sam Snyder was waiting for him. At least Sam didn't have to handle him. They let each other know exactly what was on their minds, and now Sam said to him, "I don't want you to blow up at Mike Benson. He's a brilliant engineer, and he's been working sixteen hours a day on this."

"I don't blow at him," Max snorted. "If I get pissed off, it's because this should have been done twenty years ago, right at the beginning. If Edison cared one stinking bit for art instead of his goddamn machines all his life, he would have done it."

"Max, you're too damn high strung. You lose your temper at the drop of a hat. You never were that way." Snyder never lost his temper. Through the years he had become heavier, his belly larger, his tangled hair snow white. Now he bought his dark sweet beer by the case from a brewery in Seattle. Alongside of him, Max seemed to contract, to become smaller and skinnier, regardless of how much beer he consumed.

"You're right," Max said.

They started off down the studio street toward the Sound Shop. The Sound Shop was a laboratory of sorts that Max had set up five years ago in an attempt to conquer his pet hate, the dialogue card. As the years passed, his distaste for the device of breaking a film again and again with dialogue cards and for the lip motion that produced no sound had increased, finally reaching a point where he decided that if *he* didn't solve the problem, no one would. Whereupon he built a sound laboratory on the studio ground and staffed it with a research staff of sound engineers. At this point, early in 1927, they were very close to success, almost at the point of embarking on a feature film to be developed with dialogue cards replaced by the actor's speech. The screenplay — for it had to be a play rather than a scenario — had been written. A number of actors who could actually act had been hired, and one of the large stages on the lot had been soundproofed.

His bitterness worn fuzzy by time, Max had been persuaded by his colleagues to rehire Gerald Freedman, who during the past dozen years had directed a series of films hailed by the critics as artistic triumphs. Max had his own opinion of just how triumphant these films were, but he appreciated Freedman's reputation, and he succumbed to Barney Enfield's pleadings that this venture into talking pictures be encased with every publicity gimmick that could be bought or invented. Enfield, no longer a single, lone flack but chief of a public relations and advertising section of Britsky Productions that employed eighteen men and women, sensed the gigantic revolution in the whole world of entertainment that the talking pictures would produce, perhaps more so even than Max, and he insisted that when the first talking picture was made, it be launched with more fanfare than any opening in the history of film. Max agreed. Sometime in the past decade, this thing spawned out of the kinetoscopes and the nickelodeons had changed from a storefront entertainment for illiterate immigrants into an art form, generating a whole new order of critics; and Max sensed that the talking picture would complete the transition.

And now Max said to Sam Snyder, "You're right. I'm nervous as a cat, Sam, because I got to be first. It was my idea, and by now I put over a million dollars into it, and now every goddamn studio out here is trying to get in there with a talking picture device, only there ain't no device and what we got is not a device. That's what Freddy keeps telling me. We don't have a device and we can't patent it, so either we get in there first or we'll be entirely up shit creek."

They were walking along the studio street toward the sound laboratory, part of the eddying population of what Max called his dream factory, Max as always in proper dark gray, white shirt and striped tie, and Sam Snyder in the blue jeans and work shirt he donned each morning on reaching the studio, a great ring of keys and a flashlight hanging from his belt, still with no real title, but nevertheless the man who operated the mechanisms of this vast enterprise, with its own security force, fire department, electric generating plant, water supply, garbage collection, plaster casting shop, carpentry shop, machine shop, auto pool, warehouse, garment factory, art studios, paint shops, and, of course, fake streets, castles, cities, suburbs, stages, and offices. And still, calm and unhurried as he said to Max, "Come off it. We are not up shit creek, and you know it. No one can beat us, Max. We got five hundred theatres wired for sound already. It will take at least a year for any other studio to catch up with us, so why don't you just relax and let it happen."

"You think we got it? I paid Mike Benson fifty grand to come in and make it work."

"It's money well spent. He's damn good. What about Jake Stein?"

"What about him?"

"They took him to the hospital yesterday. His wife says they can't operate. The cancer's too far gone. I think he's dying, Max."

"Yeah, poor bastard. I feel guilty as hell. I never liked him."

"We ought to go to the hospital."

"I hate hospitals. God Almighty, I hate hospitals."

"Yeah. Still, he's been with us a long time. What's to feel guilty about?"

"I'll tell you what. All these years I never said two words to the man that wasn't business, never went to his house, and last week, when I heard he was sick, someone tells me he's still on the payroll for three hundred a week. Never asked for a raise, never asked for a nickel for himself, worked himself out like a goddamn slave — what the hell for? I don't ask for anything like that."

Snyder shrugged. "We'll talk to his wife. See what she needs."

They were at the sound laboratory now, a square, gray, windowless stucco building, much like the shooting stages that lined the studio streets, only smaller; and inside, out of the bright, eternal sunshine into the cavelike darkness of the entry, they stood blinking while Mike Benson greeted them. He was a pudgy, moon-faced, middle-aged man who, like so many other important sound experts, had gotten his early training with Edison. He had been waiting for them, and he shook hands eagerly.

"This time." He nodded. "This time, absolutely. We're set up. The others are here."

The sound lab had a small viewing room, three rows of six seats. Freedman was there with his assistant director and the screenplay author, Eugene Cape, three Broadway hits and the best writing reputation in the legitimate theatre world, Fred Feldman, Bert Bellamy, Barney Enfield, Clifford Abel, who was designing the film, and Max's brother Ruby. Max and Snyder took their places in the last row. Ruby sat down next to Max, and said to him nervously, "What's this about Jake going to the hospital?"

"So I'm told. I think he's dying."

"Dying? What the devil do you mean, dying?"

"He has cancer and he's dying," Max said flatly. "It happens.

You want to talk about it, we'll talk later. Now I got to watch this."

"I don't understand this? Why didn't I know?"

"You want to weep over Jake, I can understand," Max said not unkindly. "Maybe somebody ought to cry over him. But not now."

"I just want to know what this is about him dying?"

"Not now!" Max said with annoyance.

Ruby rose and stalked out of the room, saying as he left, "I got to call him, I mean the hospital."

"Since when is he that close to Jake?" Snyder wondered.

"He's always been chummy with Jake," Bert Bellamy said.

"Shall we wait for him?" Benson asked Max.

"No, go ahead."

"Whatever you say." Benson rose and faced them. "There could be a hitch when we change records. I hope not, but it is just possible. It isn't that we don't understand the problem and how to overcome it. It's just that we had to build every component for the slow-turning mechanism, and some parts need further testing. So if we go out of sync, bear with us."

"No, sir," Max said. "I've seen it out of sync fifty times. Like hell I'll bear with you."

Benson sighed and nodded as he went into the control room. Snyder glanced at Max.

"So it ain't nice. That son of a bitch is paid to do it, not to make excuses," Max said. "You ever known me to ask anyone to bear with me?"

Snyder smiled. "There you got me, Max."

The lights went off, and the identifying numbers flashed onto the screen. Then the film ran blank for a few seconds, and then the picture of an attractive young woman appeared, standing on a stage fitted with four platforms of varying heights. There was also a set of drums on the stage, several folding chairs and a small table.

The young woman smiled and nodded, and said, "This is sync test number forty-seven. My name is Sandra Johnson. I am a member of the Metropolitan Opera Company in New York, and I have been brought out here at the suggestion of Mr. Benson, not because I'm any great shakes as a singer, but because I have both a high range and a middle range. We're also old friends — can I say that, Mike? — pardon me. Now to business. I'll start with a simple song, Stephen Foster's 'Jeannie with the Light Brown Hair.' "

Max, listening open-mouthed, his gaze glued to the woman's lips, looking for the almost inevitable out-of-sync gap, failed to find even an indication, and he whooped with delight. "Benson, you ugly son of a bitch, you done it!"

"Wait for the transition," Benson's voice pleaded through the woman's song.

After "Jeannie," Sandra Johnson sang an aria from *La Traviata* and then a light patter song from Gilbert and Sullivan. As she sang, she moved, going from one platform to the next, running a few steps, then standing still. Next, a radio sound man came on, spreading his equipment on the table. "I'll do a succession of sounds," he explained, "aiming for recognition. First the sound, then I name it."

"Do you hear a slight undersound?" Sam Snyder whispered to Max. "A scratch sound?"

"It damn well don't matter! Goddamn it, Sam, you technicians want to be God. We got a talking picture."

"That was a door closing," the sound man said. A telephone began to ring. "I'm sure I don't have to identify that."

Bert Bellamy had reached for the control phone next to him. "I'll be damned!" he shouted. "Did you see that, Max? I actually reached for the damn telephone. I actually thought it was ringing."

"I don't believe it," Max said softly. "I had the same damn reaction. I just don't believe it."

The sound man gathered up his equipment and then scattered some nutshells in front of him. "You have to walk for this one," he said, and then he walked across the crackling shells and off the screen. An enormous black man appeared on the screen. His name was Art Jones; and he had a small role in a jungle film they were doing at the other end of the lot. He was vaguely familiar to Max.

"My name is Art Jones," he said. "I'm not a professional singer, but I do my thing in church ever since I been a little kid. Main reason for me being here is I'm a basso profundo. I'm a going to sing an old spiritual called 'Go Down Moses,' and Mr. Benson say to give it all I got. So here goes."

The voice blasted into the small viewing room, filling it with an almost physical presence of sound: "When Israel was in Egypt land —"

The tremendous voice continued. Benson came out of the control room and slid into the seat next to Max. "A little bit of under-noise," he admitted. "Can't help it with this low range and extreme volume. We'd never allow such volume in a theatre, and I can cut back to practically eliminate the undersound. Have you been look-ing for the transition?"

"When is it coming?" Max wanted to know.

"Coming? My dear Max, it came. And not in a silent interval, either. We shifted records while Art was talking."

"No."

"Scout's honor."

There were tears in Max's eyes. "Benson, you bastard." He threw his arms around Benson and kissed his cheek.

The others, having overheard, were applauding. The black man finished singing, and four couples appeared on the screen, all of them talking and shouting at once, eight voices assaulting the abil-ity of the records to pick up and clarify. It worked, but no one was paying much attention at this point. They crowded around Max and Benson.

"This is historic," Bert Bellamy said. "This is goddamn historic. Max, do you know what this means?"

Max wasn't sure he knew, although he had gone over this in his mind at least a hundred times. Perhaps better than the others, he at least sensed that the world would never be the same, that a new, somewhat frightening genie had popped out of its bottle and would never be contained again. Most assuredly, life could be displayed and reflected in pictures, but the human condition was sound. All of his life, he had worked with half of a thing; now it was completed and whole; and now what?

"I'll tell you what," Barney Enfield crowed. "This has got to be the biggest newsbreak in the history of the business. We hold a press conference and bring out our four biggest stars to back Max up. Get everyone — press, wire services —"

"Barney, this is sound," Freedman said. "Do you know what your four biggest stars sound like?"

"I'm not sure about the press conference. Maybe we ought to sit on it."

"You can't sit on it. The technicians know. The studio knows. How can you sit on it?"

"What do you think, Max?"

"I think we start making the picture and we let the world know. What's to hide?"

"Shoot the works?" Enfield asked him.

"We're all shouting," Max said, pointing to the screen, "and they're shouting back at us. I'm trying to make some sense out of it. Sure, shoot the works. Only, I'm thinking about the piano players. We fire five hundred piano players. I hate to do that."

They broke out into laughter. Big joke, but Max hadn't meant it as a joke, not at all.

• • •

Sam Snyder changed into city clothes. They decided that the very least they could do in terms of Jake Stein, like him or not, was to pay a visit to the hospital. He was dying. It cast a damper over their triumph and sobered them. Stein, like a handful of others, had been there at the beginning. On their way to the hospital in downtown Los Angeles, they drove through the deep cleft of Cahuenga, the sides wet and green with a burst of rainfall, the air sweet as honey, the blue sky speckled with a handful of fluffy white clouds, so rare in the California sky. The intensely high and low moments tugged at their emotions; they were both quiet and thoughtful and turned inward.

In Hollywood, they stopped for lunch at a tiny place called Leon's East Coast Deli. They made a matzo ball soup that reminded Max of his mother's cooking but tasted better. Sarah was never a good cook. Snyder liked their heavy pot roast and potatoes. There were no German restaurants in Los Angeles. "Why don't you use one of the studio drivers?" Snyder asked Max as he parked his big Cadillac in the muddy lot behind Leon's.

"I like to drive. I had a driver back east, Shecky Blum, remember him, Sam?"

Snyder shook his head.

"Big tough guy. Good with his fists. He started with a carriage — horse and carriage. My God, the world changes. We behaved like a bunch of hoodlums. Settled things with ax handles. You remember those days."

"I'd rather forget them."

"I tried to get Shecky to come out here. Offered him good money too, and I told him he could bring his wife out and I'd find a house for them, but he wouldn't budge. He said if he ever left the East Side of New York, he'd just curl up and die."

"People feel funny about a place. How many years we been out here, Max?"

"Twelve, thirteen."

"I'm still not used to it. I look around at the damn palm trees and mesquite, and I wonder where I am."

"Yeah."

"Trouble is," Snyder said tentatively, "you never got over Della." He was uneasy talking to Max about Della, but he felt he had to. "You can't live out your life alone in that damn cottage on the lot. There's more to life than the lot and this business."

"You tell me what."

"What I mean to say," Snyder getting at it uneasily, "what I mean to say is that you can't live without a woman. I know you that well, and we been together a long time, so I want to get this off my chest, and out here, my gracious, there are maybe more beautiful dames than in any other such given space in the whole world —"

"Drop it, Sam," Max said. "Just drop it."

"Are you sore?" Snyder wanted to know.

"Sam, when did I get sore at you?"

"Maybe it would do you good if you did. Anyway, I sure felt good about the sound. It wasn't only that the damn thing finally worked, but I haven't seen you enjoy anything so much in months."

"Yeah, and you know what else I could enjoy? Some of Alice's cooking. So invite me around."

"Last three times I invited you —"

"Screw the last three times."

"O.K., O.K. Tonight."

When they reached the hospital that afternoon, they were told that Jake Stein had passed away two hours earlier. His family had been there and left.

• • •

Jake Stein's funeral took place the following day, and after the funeral, Max went back to the lot, spent two restless hours in his office, and then walked across to the back lot, where the Battle of the Argonne Forest had been revived. The picture was tentatively titled *Inferno*, and its schematic was woven around a single day with an American rifle company in the war to end all wars. Max disliked war films. The enormous, monstrous horror of World War I affected him deeply, but the complex of causes was beyond his understanding, and until now the Britsky Studio had made no important war films, only a number of comedies about the army and the recruits. Max had let himself be talked into the very large expenditure that *Inferno* required because Anthony Clark, their very best scenario writer, had put together a scenario that required almost no dialogue cards. The story and the narrative were contained in the pictures, and to Max, this was a close to perfect use of the medium, and even though he disliked the content, he was so eager to see how far one could go in a moving picture without words that he decided to make the film.

Today, it was not difficult for him, despite the blazing California sunshine, to imagine himself actually in a place where this lunatic action had happened. The gentle breeze carried the scent of gunpowder to him as the charges that simulated artillery fire were exploded; and walking up to the camera positions, climbing the twelve-foot-high wooden platform that held the cameras for this scene, he found himself looking down into a muddy trench where a line of actors dressed in doughboy uniforms crouched with their bayoneted rifles. Package charges of black gunpowder had been laid out in a complex pattern in front of the trench, and as Max approached the camera platform, the explosions moved toward the trench, simulating a German advance. Two more camera platforms gave different angles, and as Max stood watching, a line of advancing German soldiers appeared through the smoke and flung dirt of the explosions. Shouting into his megaphone, Gifford Brown, the director, screamed, "Will you goddamn motherfuckers get shot! Seven, four, nine, sixteen, twenty-two, you are dead! Do you hear me! Dead! Dead! Dead!"

The five numbers indicated threw up their arms, staggered, and died. Brown reached out and an assistant handed him a clipboard, and from it he read: "Ten, twelve, fourteen, three! You stupid bastards!"

More Germans fell before the gunfire of the men in the trench and the fragments of bursting shells. Brown thrust the clipboard to his assistant. "My voice is gone. Get those bastards out of the trench into the counterattack!"

The scene went on. Max stood at the end of the platform, out of the way, a small, skinny man in a dark blue worsted suit. The director and the assistant director raged, the charges exploded, the doughboys climbed out of the trench into the counterattack, and finally the director waved his arms and shouted for them to cut.

"Set it up for the close pan on the dead!" he shouted into the megaphone. "I want the dead in position. Take five, that's all." And to his assistant, "Check those fuckers! I want them filthy dirty and bloody. Also, Pete worked out something for limbs torn off. I want at least three of them." He turned and saw Max for the first time. "Hello, Mr. Britsky. Didn't know you were here. I'm sorry about the confusion, but the goddamn extras are the dregs. Stupid shitkickers right out of the farms. They can't look alive and they can't look dead."

"They try," Max said softly. "They don't work much. They got a hard time staying alive, just staying alive."

"Yeah, I suppose so. You excuse me, Mr. Britsky? This is a complicated shot."

Max nodded and left the platform. He walked slowly away from the quiet that now fell over the Western Front, thinking to himself, We dream bad dreams and good dreams, only when you're in the business of dreams and you get older, the bad dreams make you uneasy. Still, people buy tickets, and that's what matters.

· · ·

Sarah called him at the studio. "For a half-hour I tried to call you," she said. Time had not dimmed her eye or lessened the timbre of her voice. "So you know what they tell me? Tell me, do you know what they tell me?"

"No, Mama, I don't know," Max said.

"They tell me, you should believe it, Mr. Britsky ain't taking calls. No calls. I should drop dead, I should have a heart attack right here talking on the telephone, I should, God forbid, have cancer, it don't matter, because Mr. Britsky is taking no calls!"

"Mama, did you tell them who you were?"

"You know what she tells me, this *shiksa* you got on the telephone? She tells me, 'Save it, sister, I heard that before.' "

"Mama, I'm so sorry. She's probably a new girl."

"Tell her —"

"Mama, please," Max begged her, "we got sixteen telephone operators here on the lot. Forget it. I'm talking to you now. Believe me, I'll post a notice for the operators that if you call, to put you through, no matter what."

"All right. I'll try to forget I'm nobody here in this *fabissena* place. I only called to tell you something important, that's all."

"So tell me, Mama."

"Your son and daughter are here."

"What?"

"Ah-hah. Now you're interested."

"For God's sake, Mama, what are you talking about? Are you telling me that Richard and Marion are there, at your house?"

"That's right. And believe me, friendly they're not. I tell you, it's God's curse gave me such grandchildren. Not even a kiss, and they call me Mrs. Britsky."

"Where are they staying?"

"At the Beverly Hills Hotel. Where else? After all, your wife is a rich woman — a millionaire, they tell me — not like your mother and your sisters, God forbid they should be comfortable."

"But they're at your house now?"

"What then?"

"Mama, please. Ask them to wait there. I'll send a limousine for them."

Then he was nervous as a cat, pacing back and forth, and then out to the reception room, where he told his secretary, "I want the table set for three for lunch in the private dining room. No one else in there today. I want to be alone there with my kids."

Miss Shelly Greene, his secretary, middle-aged and spinsterish, said, "Why, Mr. Britsky, I didn't know you had children."

He hardly knew himself. He had not seen either of them for eight, or was it nine, years. On their birthdays and every Christmas he sent them presents, but somehow Sally had managed to make their visits to California less and less frequent and finally to halt them entirely. Max tried to remember how old they were now. Richard would be twenty-four, or was it twenty-five? Marion would be a year or a year and a half younger, not children anymore, and what would they be like? How do you talk to them? Sally had always been too clever for him. Whenever he went East and tried to make contact, the children would be spoken for elsewhere; and then when they became their own masters, the decision was theirs. "They don't want to come and I can't force them," Sally would tell him. "They're not children anymore."

In 1915, Sally had remarried. She was forty years old, but still slender and attractive, and, as her mother would have put it, she returned to her own, marrying the widower Felix Upperman, fifty-five years old and father of three children. The Uppermans were a German-Jewish family that had settled in New York in the eighteen-twenties; they controlled the Upperman-Lutze Bank and owned, some said, at least five percent of the best real estate in the city. Sally sold the two brownstones on West Sixty-sixth Street and moved into her new husband's graystone mansion on East Seventy-ninth Street. It was by no means a marriage of financial opportunism on Sally's part, for her share of stock in Britsky Productions had already appreciated to over two million dollars, not to mention her other holdings.

As befitting her new position in New York City society, Sally sent her children off to the best private schools, Richard to Phillips Academy in Andover, Massachusetts, and Marion to Miss Spence's school in Manhattan. Richard went on to Harvard and Marion to Wellesley; and thus both of his children entered into worlds unknown to Max and beyond any experience that would enable him to construct these worlds in his imagination. Their coming so unexpectedly and unannounced to Los Angeles was an almost frightening shock to him, and the shock was compounded by the fact that they went, not to the studio, but to the house in Beverly Hills. Well, that was indeed his legal residential address, but by now, after his years working with Clifford Abel, Max had come to distinguish between the monstrosities performed by Beverly Hills decorators and good taste — a sense that he could add to his inborn instinct for what was right and what was wrong, what was beautiful and what was ugly; and the thought that his two children, these two strange and well-educated and well-bred products of New York society, should come to him after all these years via the gateway of

Sarah Britsky's huge Beverly Hills palace was almost more than he could bear. Now that the limousine had gone off to pick them up, he nervously anticipated their coming to the lot. Well, regardless of how classy they were, the lot would impress them. This vast institution for the making of moving pictures, the largest and most productive studio lot in the entire world, impressed everyone — kings, presidents, prime ministers, tycoons — they were all impressed with Britsky Productions.

On the other hand, where should he meet them? Should he wait at the gate, where every strange car entering the lot was halted by an armed guard? No, he decided, that would be gauche. The limousine would bring them to his office in the cottage, best to leave it that way. His office was simply and beautifully furnished, and the cottage itself was modest, important without shouting its importance. But having decided on that, he was nervous as a cat, going to the window constantly to see whether the limousine had passed through the gates. And when finally it did appear, he leaped away from the window, unable to face the thought that they might see him peering out.

He forced himself to sit quietly at his desk. The seconds ticked away, and then Miss Greene's voice came over the intercom: "Mr. Britsky, your son and daughter are here." She knew who he had been waiting for so nervously, yet her designation of them irritated him. The old fool! Why couldn't she have said Richard and Marion Britsky are here.

Should he sit or stand? "Send them in, of course." Then he stood up quickly and came around his desk.

His first impression was of their height. Richard was easily six feet, perhaps an inch more, and the girl was quite tall too, perhaps five feet and eight inches in her heels. They were both of light complexion, and both of them had Max's blue eyes. The boy was good-looking in what Max thought of as a *goyisha* manner, his head narrow, his nose thin and straight, and the girl was sternly handsome, too thin for Max's taste, too flat-chested. But most of all, Max's impression was of their height. They loomed over him, and in one of those flashes of third-person perspective that people occasionally have, Max saw himself as they saw him, a small, skinny, balding Jewish man, his face wrinkled, his nose hawklike, a reasonably ugly middle-aged man; and with the insight came a flash of recognition and remembrance of his beloved Della O'Donnell, who had said to him once, "You know, Max, you look like Saint Paul." "And who was Saint Paul?" "Silly, he was a disciple of Jesus." "And suddenly you know what he looked like?" "Everyone does, because it's written down." But, he felt, it would not occur to these two children of his, not even that dubious honor, although perhaps they might know about Saint Paul. Max's mother always insisted that German Jews were not Jews at all.

"Hello, sir," Richard said.

Neither of them smiled. Max smiled. What should he do? Embrace them? That was conceivable yet inconceivable. He held out his hand, and each took it in turn. Perhaps they were shy. It would be only natural for them to be shy with this father whom they hardly remembered.

"I'm glad you're here," Max said quickly. He couldn't say any of the important things that he felt — his pleasure at their physical beauty, as rewarding as it was intimidating, his longing for them, his fantasies of closeness and love in which they participated, his hunger for them mixed with his bitterness at their unwillingness to see him or accept him — none of these things could be said, none of the profound, only the inane.

"I made arrangements for lunch," Max said. "It's after twelve already. You'll have lunch with me?"

They nodded. They were as ill at ease as he.

"I'm so happy you came here. It was thoughtful of you." He was listening to every word he spoke. God, let me talk grammatically, he prayed. "After lunch, I would like to take you around the lot by myself. It's very interesting. Would that be all right?"

"That would be nice," Marion said. She had a deep, rich voice.

"Where are you staying?"

"At the Beverly Hills Hotel," Richard said.

"The studio keeps a suite there. Sometimes, I stay there myself." Now why had he said that? They'd think he used it as a one-night stand, which he had. Hurriedly, he went on. "You can have the suite as long as you want to stay. It has two bedrooms. It won't cost you a cent." Again, the wrong thing to say. They were Uppermans. They had been formally adopted by Felix Upperman years ago, and as wealthy as Max was, the Uppermans were wealthier. What posible difference could a rent-free suite at the Beverly Hills Hotel make to them?

"Thank you," Richard said, "but, you know, we're checked in nd unpacked and all that, and we're only staying a day or two."

"Yeah. Sure. Of course. Why don't we go to lunch now."

They nodded their agreement, and Max led them outside into he hot sunshine. Max pointed to the electric cart parked outside he cottage. "We use that if it's any distance. After all, you can go hree miles from here and you're still on studio property. That, we all the back lot. But the executive dining room ain't far." He had lipped. He caught himself on the point of amending it to "isn't ar." That would only make it worse. "That building over there. The building is called the commissary, a cafeteria set-up where we an feed three hundred people at a sitting. You see, here it —" He aught himself this time. "Well, it's not like New York. No restau-ants in walking distance. For the executives, the stars, the direc-ors, we have a special dining room with service, but the food is ust as good in the cafeteria, believe me, and there's also a small lining room if we want to discuss with privacy while we eat." He lanced at his son and daughter. Why couldn't they comment? Why ouldn't they at least say that it was impressive? That goddamn fat ig of a Felix Upperman had nothing like this in his Nassau Street kyscraper. He didn't dispense food without making a cent of profit ut of it so that his workers could eat decently.

The studio street was thronged in the lunch break. Though he ad seen it a thousand times, Max never tired of the parade of cos-umed actors — the cowboys and Indians and doughboys and Ger-nan officers and Pilgrim Fathers with their big bell-nosed guns and retty girls in long skirts and short skirts and tights and bangles — ut as far as Max was able to tell, it made no impression on his son nd daughter. They reacted as if every street in New York was opulated in the same manner, never exclaiming in delight or as-onishment. At least, Max thought, the fact that so many people ent out of their way to say, "Hello, Max" or "Hello, Mr. Britsky" ust impress them; and then Max saw Sam Snyder and called him, Sam! Hey, Sam, over here!"

Richard and Marion saw a burly, white-haired man approach, his eavy paunch protruding over his belt. He wore a grease-stained blue work shirt and old jeans and, around his waist, a tool belt with hammer, screwdriver, and pliers thrust into it. He came over grin ning, his hand thrust out. "You're Max's kids. Shelly told me," he explained to Max. "By golly, I wouldn't recognize you. Last time saw you, you were a couple of little shavers. Now — cast them both, Max. Leading man and leading lady."

There was no way Max could stop Sam Snyder. He was genu inely delighted to see these two handsome people. Max said quickly "This is my friend and associate Sam Snyder. This is my son, Rich ard, and my daughter, Marion."

Richard took Snyder's dirty hand tentatively. Marion's hands re mained at her side.

"Truth is," Max said, "that Sam Snyder here really runs the lot He makes it function. Anything happens to him, I close down."

"Bull, bull, bull," Snyder said good-humoredly. "I'm an exalted handyman. I spent the morning trying to talk our main generato, out of breaking down and quitting on us."

"And?" Max asked him.

"It promised. But sooner or later we'll have to replace it. That' a big one, Max."

"What can we do? You see," he explained to Richard and Mar ion, "we generate our own power because we use as much electric ity as a small city. It pays us in the long run, but there's just abou nothing in the world costs as much as a generator. We'll talk abou it, Sam."

At lunch, Richard and Marion opened up. Neither of them pinned his or her heart on his or her sleeve, but they did convey a certain amount of information. Marion was engaged to be married to on Peter Cogsall, who was the son of the Cogsall who was president of the Merchantman Bank of New York, not quite as big as Chase o Morgan, but not too much smaller. Richard had just taken his ba exam, Since Upperman-Lutze was a private banking and invest ment house, he would probably find a proper niche there.

"And if they don't find it for you," Max said, trying to put ou what he had been thinking lightly, offhandedly, "you might find here. My old friend Freddy Feldman heads up our legal depart ment, but it's not just a legal department. We put out maybe thousand contracts a year, not to mention bad debts, collections and a hundred other things. Fred has six young lawyers in his department. We could sure use someone in the family."

Richard smiled. He was very polite and well bred, Max realized, concerned less with an unwillingness to hurt his father than with whatever was the proper and gentlemanly response.

Perhaps a bit more sensitive, Marion explained, "We have always been so very curious about Hollywood. I mean, who isn't? And we had heard so much about this marvelous studio, we had to see it." As an afterthought, "And to see you, of course."

"You are a legendary figure," Richard added.

"Legendary? No, hardly." He wanted to ease their awkwardness, they were such healthy, beautiful people. Why shouldn't he be proud of them and take pleasure in them? They were his kids, he told himself, but they couldn't call him Father or Dad or Papa. "Call me Max," he said gently. "After all, you're both grown up."

"Sure."

"How is your mother?"

"Very well," Marion said.

"She sends you her best," Richard said.

"Did she? That's nice. Thank her. Do you like California?" for want of anything else to say. They did not make conversation easy.

"Well, we haven't been here long enough —"

"I can't believe the palm trees," Richard said. "Everything's like a movie set. You expect it to come down if you look the other way. The weather's nice."

"Yes, the weather's nice," Max agreed. "Would you like to meet some of the names out here — stars, big directors? John Gilbert, Mary Pickford, Garbo, Crawford — I could arrange a little dinner tomorrow night or a party, if you'd prefer?"

"I think we'll be leaving tomorrow," Richard said. "We've been trying to get out here for months, but it was so hard to find a time when we'd both be free."

"Of course. I understand," Max said. "But this afternoon you're my guests. I've canceled all my appointments, and I would like to show you what we have here. After all, someday it will be yours."

Richard and Marion stared at Max in amazement.

"Didn't that ever occur to you?" Max asked them.

"But, well, you have brothers and sisters," Richard said. "And it's a public corporation. I know Mother has large stock holdings —"

"You're my children, my only children. Sure, it's a public corporation, but I hold fifty-one percent of the stock. My brothers and sisters got enough, believe me. None of them will starve. But this stays with my own blood. Well, I ain't dead yet. We'll talk about it later."

Their attitude changed after that, and they became more pleasant. Yes, of course they wanted to see the studio.

"We'll take an electric cart," Max said. "After four o'clock, it cools off, but now it's too hot to walk for miles. Myself, I like to walk. It's the only exercise I get. Golf —" He shrugged. "My colleagues who played golf had a little difficulty, since most of them are Jewish. The golf clubs around here are very exclusive when it comes to Jews, which is not so different from anyplace else, is it? So we bought land and built our own club, of which I am one of the founding fathers. But I don't play golf, and mostly I live my life right here. I can't think of myself without the lot."

They sat on either side of him in the little electric cart. "I don't like to bore you," he said, "but I want to tell you about this place. Of course, what we have here is like the tip of an iceberg, but a very important tip. It supplies our outlets, more than a thousand movie houses all over the United States. That movie house property alone is worth over thirty million dollars, and just the land here at the lot is worth another ten million. But it's hard to add up a net worth. We got a weekly payroll of almost three hundred thousand dollars. Glenda Lane, our hottest star right now, gets six thousand dollars a week, much more than I take for a salary, believe me. They figured out once we got over ninety-three different professions practicing right here on the lot. Whatever you need — barbers, hairdressers, seamstresses, doctors, nurses, shoemakers, riding instructors, masons, carpenters — here, this is the carpentry shop. We'll get out for a moment."

It was an enormous shed, like a small lumberyard, one side of it open to the studio street. It was stocked as well as a lumberyard, with the addition of worktables, power saws, lathes, power jigs, sanding machines, and of course the men to operate them.

"We can build anything that can be built of wood right here,"

Max told them. "And you'd be surprised how much iron and steel and stone can be built out of wood."

They went on, past the great racks holding the flats of a thousand dead sets, pausing to watch World War I in progress, pausing again to see three elephants and a troop of Gurkhas marching through an India cane thicket, spending a few minutes in a viewing room to look at dailies, prowling through a warehouse filled with French, English, and American antiques. "Most of them real," Max told them, "almost three million dollars right here."

It was not a bad afternoon. Unfortunately, Richard and Marion appeared to have no innate warmth. They did the best they could to appear interested and friendly, but Max couldn't help thinking of gentile acquaintances who bent over backward to be pleasant simply because he was Jewish. He did not press them to see him again the following day, and since they didn't suggest dinner this evening, he made no mention of it. He tried not to feel relieved when they were back in the limousine and on their way to the Beverly Hills Hotel.

When he reached his cottage, Shelly Greene was powdering her nose in preparation for leaving. She was a gaunt, long-faced woman, unhappily misplaced in this welter of feminine beauty, usually unsmiling. After Della died, Max could not bear a secretary who was either attractive or inclined toward an emotional relationship; but that day he had the feeling that Miss Greene had glanced at him with something akin to compassion. When she said good-night, she added, "I hope it was a pleasant afternoon with your children, Mr. Britsky. They certainly are a handsome young man and young woman."

Max thanked her. She left, and Max went into his office and sat down behind his desk. I would like to cry, he said to himself. I wish I could cry.

A voice called out, "Are you in there, Max?"

"It's possible."

Sam Snyder poked his head through the door and said, "I thought you'd like to look at the dailies."

"Also possible."

As they walked across to the viewing room, Snyder wondered how the afternoon had been.

"Lousy. They came here encased in ice, two sharp young eastern aristocrats to see what their ignorant Jew father had put together here in this vulgar shithole called Hollywood."

"Come on, Max. They both seemed to be pleasant kids."

"They turned pleasant when I mentioned that I had nobody else to leave the company to."

"You're being hard on them."

"Why not? You know, Felix Upperman adopted them. Richard Upperman. Marion Upperman. A better name than Britsky. He mentioned that he might run for Congress."

"Who? Upperman?"

"No, Richard. Well, why not? He's probably no dumber than the others in there."

"A lot smarter, if you ask me."

They watched the dailies. There was a battle scene, the soldiers going over the lip of the trench and then being mowed down by machine-gun fire. Brown, the director, had evidently been fascinated with this bit of action, for there were apparently an endless number of takes. After the second take, Max got up and walked out. Snyder followed him.

"I hate that damn movie," Max said.

"It's going to be a big art thing, Max. That's what everyone says."

"Screw the art stuff. For me, a picture should make people feel it's worth something to be alive. God knows, it ain't worth a hell of a lot when they come out of the movie house, and this guy, Brown, he's got a thing with death. I don't know why I don't like directors. I never did, and now we got this shithead Freedman back on the lot."

"One picture."

"You think he's some kind of goddamn genius, Sam?"

"Who knows? That's what they say."

"I can't sleep, thinking about that sound movie. Just think — the first moving picture with sound in the whole goddamn world. You know, all the time these newspaper guys, they say to me, how come in the industry every advance it comes from either the French or the British? Well, that's bullshit, and you know it."

"I certainly do," Snyder agreed.

"How many of them you worked out yourself, Sam — the trolley, the arcs, the zoom — Who put a camera on a cherry-picker? You, not no Frenchman or Limey, and this talking picture's going to put them right on their asses, and we are at least a year ahead of anyone."

"We certainly are."

"You bet your sweet patootie. All right, now I got to go have dinner in my mother's house and have indigestion and explain to her about why her grandchildren are the way they are, which I don't understand any better than she does. And tomorrow, Sam, keep the afternoon free because we got to get over to Jake Stein's house."

"Come on, Max, I'm loaded tomorrow afternoon. What's so important about getting over to Jake Stein's house? The poor bastard's dead, and I never met any of his family."

"Me too. I never been to his house. But they're sitting *shiva*, which is like a Jewish wake, and I want to get there. There's something funny about him being on the payroll for three hundred a week right up to his death."

"It's more than he was worth."

"Because you don't like him," Max said. "He was a damn good bookkeeper. Anyway, you and me, we represent the company. We got to at least look in and say we're sorry."

"I said it at the funeral."

"So we'll say it again."

. . .

Max knew vaguely that Jake Stein lived in Westwood Village, a thinly populated suburb of Los Angeles, whose only claim to fame was the fact that the new campus of the University of California was being constructed there. That part of Westwood to the north of Sunset Boulevard was called Bel Air by enterprising real estate promoters, but Max had never known anyone actually living in those low wooded hills, and his visit to Jake Stein's home was his first venture into the neighborhood. He had heard something to the effect of Stein buying sixteen acres there, but he was not prepared for the seven-foot-high cement-block wall that surrounded the sixteen acres, nor was he prepared for the imposing iron gates to what lay beyond the wall. The gates were open, and beyond the lawns and plantings inside, at the end of a curving graveled driveway, there loomed a stucco-covered architectural monstrosity that was a cross between a Mediterranean chateau and an English country house.

"I'll be damned," Sam Snyder said.

"Pool, pool house, two tennis courts, and a lawn like a golf course — all on three hundred a week."

"Max, Freddy's been telling you for years that Jake steals."

"In this business, everybody steals a little."

"I don't and you don't, and this ain't a little."

"I suppose not," Max admitted. "You do it on three hundred a week, the gardener takes most of it. The whole thing makes no sense. He wasn't exactly hiding. We didn't come here, but other people did."

"I think he only finished building this place last year."

"Why the hell didn't he raise his wages?" Max wondered. "He could have had double what he was getting, and I wouldn't have complained."

"He didn't know that. He knew you didn't like him, and maybe he figured that if he asked for a raise, you'd dump him. Then he'd have to take his hand out of the till."

"Miserable son of a bitch," Max said. "All right, no use cussing out the dead. Let's meet the next of kin and get it over with."

The two men parked their car, walked up to the house, and paid their respects to the relatives. Stein had left behind him a wet-faced, overweight wife, a daughter and two sons, and various less-affected relatives ranging from two sisters, a brother, and a withered mother whose mind was mostly gone, to cousins, first and second. Apparently, his move to the West had brought his sisters and his cousins and his aunts trailing after him. Now they were all gathered together around a huge dining room table that groaned under its weight of food. One of Stein's sons, Herbert by name, whom Max had met only once before but who nevertheless addressed him by his first name, said, "Max, I want you to do something about this. Pop had some little tramp he kept over in the Hollywood Hills, and I understand he dumped a fortune in jewels and furs on her, and I think that belongs to us."

"Oh? You do?"

"Absolutely."

"And how do you know this?"

"I dated a friend of hers."

"It belongs to you, sonny, go ask her for it. Certainly, your father was a remarkable man to be able to dump a fortune on some floozie and still be able to pay his gardener."

"What's that supposed to mean?"

"Think about it, sonny."

Back in the car, Max said to Snyder, "What makes me sick at heart is that they're all Jewish."

"So what? You want a race of angels with no bastards? You want me to apologize for the kaiser? That's bullshit, Max, and you know it."

"Sure it's bullshit, and I still feel sick. That snotnose son of his — should go recover what his father laid on some little whore."

"Yeah. Max, how much could he steal?"

"That's an interesting question."

"Wouldn't we feel it?"

"Do you know what our cash flow is, Sam? Four, five, six million a week, just in America — maybe as much foreign. You could steal enough to buy the British crown jewels every *Montag* and *Dunnerchtick,* and we'd never feel it providing somebody as smart as Jake Stein sits on top of the books and manipulates them."

Snyder brooded over that. They were halfway back to the studio before he asked Max, "What do we do?"

"I don't know."

"We got to do something."

"Yeah, we sure as hell got to do something. Personally, I'd like to dig Jake Stein up and beat the shit out of him, dead or not, but that don't help. I think tonight we should sit down with Freddy and work something out."

"Can't it wait? Alice's sister and her husband just arrived, first time in California, and they're expecting me for dinner tonight."

"It can't wait, Sam. It's like a stick of dynamite waiting to go off — if what I'm thinking is real."

• • •

"What you're thinking is real," Feldman told Max soberly. "This kind of thing is the worst thing that can happen in a business."

"Just hold on," Sam Snyder said. "I know the condition of this company as well as you do, and the condition is good. In fact, it's better than good. There isn't a business in America has a cash flow better than ours. Our receivables are heavier than our credit line. Our cash on hand is good, and as far as Jake is concerned, the son of a bitch is dead. If we want restitution, we can sue his heirs. I don't know, is that legal? Well, we don't need it. We can write off everything Jake took."

They were sitting in the private dining room in the commissary. The studio had closed down. The kitchen workers and the waiters and busboys had gone home, and only the guards were left, at the gates and patrolling the lot. Max and Snyder had lit cigars, and watching them through the murky haze, Feldman speculated that just breathing in their smoke all those years should have hooked him to nicotine.

"So what are you and Max in such a sweat over?" Snyder went on. "I say, write it off and the hell with it."

"You don't write something like this off until you know what it is," Feldman said gloomily, "and then you don't just write it off. You been around long enough to know that, Sam. We're a public corporation. We'd have to call a meeting of the board and present them with the facts and figures, and then it's up to them what kind of action they intend to take, and negligence and lousy management are bad enough, but there could be more than that."

"What do you mean, more?"

"No matter what happens, we got to have an audit right away, and God only knows what we'll turn up. Jake couldn't be in this alone."

"Why not?"

"Because you can't do it all with the books, not in this business. You have to have someone on the road, someone who deals with the theatre managers and with certain people on the lot. Jake couldn't do that. For one thing, he was a little worm who nobody would play games with, and for another, he knew the books but he didn't really know a damn thing about how pictures are made."

"Ruby," Max said hopelessly. "He's talking about my son of a bitch brother."

"Come on, Ruby? Ruby's a —"

"Go ahead, say it. Ruby's a cheap tin horn sport. Ruby's a nickel drifter. Who'd ever believe that Jake Stein, little Jake Stein, would keep some tramp in a house in the Hollywood Hills and shower jewels on her? One thing you got to say about Ruby — he's got more class than Jake Stein. And something else you can be sure of, if Ruby's got his hand in the till, my brother Benny's right in there with him."

"Max, you don't know that," Snyder protested.

"Don't be kind to me, Sam. We been together too long to bullshit each other. We got us some real trouble, and the question is, what do we do?"

"Whatever we do," Feldman said, "we have to move very quickly. For the moment, Joe Klepper has taken over Jake's job. He's young and ambitious, and if he wasn't in this with Jake, it won't take him long to find Jake's tracks. There are five other men and women in the accounting department who might be in this or who might smell it out. If anyone else blows this open, our position will be untenable. We have to do it ourselves. As far as Ruby is concerned, I've warned you for years, Max, that he has sticky fingers; but we don't know yet that he's guilty, or Benny or anyone else."

"How do we find out?"

"It's two weeks before the board meets, and I think that gives us enough time. My wife's cousin, Arnie Greenberg, has gone into business here in L.A. His partner is Mike Hendon, a local boy. They're both certified public accountants, and they're young and honest and trustworthy. I think we should hire them immediately, pay them a fat bonus to drop everything else and work on this day and night. They'll do an audit that only we have access to. It can't possibly take in everything in that time, but it may well point in the main directions."

"At least we won't be blowing off in the dark," Snyder said.

"Max?"

Max nodded tiredly. "Yeah, I suppose so."

The others left, and Max walked back to his cottage. Fritzie Cooper, with whom he had a date that evening, was waiting for him. Max never dated his stars. For one thing, he felt great distaste for the stories about his contemporaries in the other film companies, of them browbeating poor, defenseless, and innocent stars into bed with them. While he had yet to find a defenseless and innocent star, the stories left a bad taste in his mouth. And for another, stars were simply too skinny. Fritzie Cooper was a round and pleasant one hundred and thirty-five pounds, a good-natured, easygoing woman from Findlay, Ohio, who tired of the smell of oil wells and small-town morality and betook herself and her high school acting ability to Hollywood. Max discovered her waiting counter in a hash joint on Hollywood Boulevard and gave her a job as a contract supporting actress. There was no question of a quid pro quo, and it was not until a month or so after she had come to work on the lot that Max encountered her and asked her to have dinner with him. After that, he took her to dinner and bed perhaps once a week. Max had always found it difficult to believe that women could like him for himself. When he looked into the mirror, he saw a thin, worried Jewish face with a receding hairline; but looking into a mirror he never saw his warmth, his generosity, or his pleasure in women. And in turn, women enjoyed him. Fritzie was only twenty-five years old, and Max was only two years short of fifty, but she mothered him. Most of the women Max took to mothered him.

It was a warm evening, the area lying under the benign heat of the Santa Ana desert wind, and they dined in the garden at the Beverly Hills Hotel. Max was glum, and Fritzie said to him at least five times, "Come on, Maxie. Cheer up, old chap." She had been dating some of the British actors who had swarmed into Hollywood and, chameleon-like, she mimicked them without being aware that she was doing so. Looking at her round, pink-cheeked face and her blond curls, Max grinned in spite of himself, and she in turn began to laugh in real delight. He was quite aware of the absurdity. But then, from the very beginning, his world had been totally absurd.

"Why don't you get it off your chest, old dear, and tell me all about it."

Max thrust a finger at her. "Right out of *Sanderson's Girl.*"

"How did you know?"

"Sweetie, I own the studio. I read the scripts. I see the movies."

"Oh, Max, you must think I'm very stupid."

"I think you're delightful."

"Do you? Truly? Then I want a big fat New York steak with french-fried onions and french-fried potatoes."

"You shall have it."

In some strange way, Max realized, it all made sense — or as much sense as most things.

· · ·

Feldman had aged. He had shrunk, or perhaps his width made him appear smaller, his width and his little belly protruding against the tight vest of his three-piece suit and his fringe of gray hair around his mostly bald skull. After all, a quarter of a century had gone by since Max had first said to him, "How about it, Freddy. You want to be my lawyer?"

"Well, I'd have to take that up with my employers."

"What employers? You mean Meyer Sonberg and his brother? You got more brains in your little finger than both of them put together. They're loser lawyers, crumb bums, ambulance chasers —"

"Come on, Max."

"You remember back on Henry Street, them tough Irish kids from St. Mark's Place used to come around looking for trouble, and we used to beat the shit out of each other. Only, when they caught you alone, you talked them out of it. I'll never forget that. Well, I want a lawyer in my company, somone who can talk the bad guys out of it."

Twenty-five years ago; still Max remembered that first time. Perhaps Feldman remembered it too, looking around Max's office, then telling him, "Send Shelly home."

"Why? It's only four-thirty."

"You don't need her anymore today. I don't want anyone outside who might overhear us. Let her cut the telephone and go home."

Max stared at Feldman for a long moment. Then he went to the door and told Shelly Greene to call the studio switchboard and tell them no more calls and then go home.

"I'm not taking any chances," Feldman said. "I don't want to be overheard. Not that this won't come out, but I want it to come out straight and properly, not as gossip."

"If you don't think having Greenberg and his partner all over the place, demanding every record and checkbook we own and pulling out the ledgers from ten years back — Well, if you don't think that has everyone gossiping and speculating, and three days ago they bring in five young snotnoses who act like they own the lot —"

"I told them to, Max. I told them time was running out and they should bring me whatever they had."

"From all this hush-hush crap, they brought you something."

"Yes."

"All right. Don't sit there like some half-assed judge. What have you got?"

"We'll start with Jake Stein. They've only gone back seven years. In that time, it appears — mind you, *appears,* because this still is not a regular no-holds-barred audit — that he stole close to five million dollars. Now understand me, this is Jake Stein as captain of the swindle. From what Greenberg and his men can come up with, two other men are directly involved and a number of others are indirectly involved."

"Who are they? Ruby and Benny."

"That's right."

"I suspected those two bastards were skimming the theatres for years, but how can you get that out of an audit of the studio books?"

"That's what frightens me, Max. We can't. What we get is another side of it, cardboard companies that don't exist, acting as suppliers. For example, an outfit called Creative Market Research, market analysis and consulting. We've paid them three thousand dollars a month for seven years. Ruby has the authority to sign checks regarding distribution. It's a laundry outfit, pure and simple. Take another type of thing. A film is budgeted. The director is in there for fifty thousand. He kicks back ten thousand to Ruby."

"You got proof of that?"

"Ralph Leone — five pictures, five kickbacks, fifty thousand to Ruby. Ruby has been billing Jake Stein for years — consultant, unit manager, production manager."

"And Benny?" Max asked icily.

"Benny. Why in hell must I give this to you?"

"Because I'm telling you to."

"All right. You know with every picture we make on location, there's a cash slush fund, three to five hundred dollars a day. It bribes the cops, pays for background homes, and pays the releases from background people we want to use —"

"You telling me something I don't know?" Max demanded angrily.

"O.K. The unit manager dispenses it. Sam Snyder's been talking to a couple of unit managers. They both pay off Benny, which probably means that every unit manager working outside the lot is paying Benny fifty dollars a day. Nice money — and, goddamn it,

Max, they all think you're in on it, that you're skimming the company."

"That little bastard. What else?"

"You want me to go on? It's sickening. There are four office workers who don't exist, two guards, two carpenters — Jake Stein was a genius. And we haven't even touched distribution, where Ruby is king shit."

Max's cheeks were quivering. He closed his eyes and shook his head. "My own flesh and blood."

"Easy, Max, please," Feldman pleaded. "We got to handle this."

"How? How? Just tell me how in hell we handle this?"

"All right. The board of directors meets in three days. You have to explain that Stein's death and Stein's house instigated our action. Then you make full disclosure of everything we have, everything, and then I'll make a motion that we postpone any decisive action on the board's part until a complete audit is made, and I'll suggest that we bring in a firm of prestigious San Francisco accountants to do the audit. It will probably take them a couple of weeks, and that will give us some breathing space."

"For what?"

"At this moment, I just don't know. I want to read some law and consult some colleagues."

"And what happens to those two shithead brothers of mine?"

"I don't know."

"Do they go to jail?"

"Max, I just don't know. Give me a chance to think and inquire."

•   •   •

Ruby was three inches taller than Max, and with his even, sunburned features, his dark, curly hair, and his tight body, he appeared a good deal less than his forty-four years, and one and another of the many girls that slid in and out of his life had remarked that he really couldn't be Max's brother, they looked so different. Ruby was a valid Hollywood product. There were only two topics of conversation in his life, sex and movies. His areas of interest were somewhat broader. He played golf and tennis, and he enjoyed being in the company of the stars. His name had been linked to half a dozen lady stars, and in this linkage there was some truth and some puffery.

Max found him on the tennis court behind their Beverly Hills house, meticulously clad in white flannels and white short-sleeved shirt and in the company of three giggling blondes. Ruby, who had one divorced wife in New York and another in Los Angeles, contented himself with a suite of rooms in the Beverly Hills Hotel as his own residence; at the same time he felt free to use the huge house that Max had built for Sarah and Freida, the forlorn unmarried sister. Nominally, it was Max's residence, but he almost never slept there. Benny, who headed up the New York office, still in the old Hobart Building on Fourteenth Street, preferred a hotel to Sarah's Beverly Hills house, since a hotel gave him full opportunity to use the female facilities his brother Ruby so generously supplied. Ruby had built the tennis court himself. "Didn't cost you a nickel," he explained to Max, and Sarah found that the sight of her two younger sons playing this strange game behind her house was curiously satisfying. Even in the most bitter days of poverty on Henry Street, Sarah had never been given to self-denial, and it was absolutely astonishing how easily she fell into the life of Beverly Hills. At age seventy-one, she was still healthy and vigorous and determined to take full political advantage of her role as Max Britsky's mother. And as ever, Ruby was her staff and delight.

For a few minutes, Max watched her staff and delight returning a tennis ball to his blond opponent, and then he walked onto the court and said to Ruby, "Tell the girls to go home. I want to talk to you."

"Just like that?"

"Just like that."

"For Christ's sake, Max, you could at least ask me decently."

"Why? You're so fucken decent, I got to ask you decently?"

Ruby faced Max for a moment; then he sighed and called out, "O.K., girls. Pack it up and go home. I got business to talk with my brother."

"Well, who drives us? You want us to walk home?"

Ruby handed one of them a twenty-dollar bill. "Call a cab. Use the phone inside. Now, blow."

Each of them made certain to pass Max slowly, and each of them said, "Good-bye, Mr. Britsky" to Max, not to Ruby.

"Tootsies, sweet little tootsies," Ruby said, looking after them.

Max's response to this was to deliver a stinging slap across Ruby's face.

"What the hell's the matter with you!" Ruby cried. "Are you crazy?"

"Don't raise a hand to me, you shithead!" Max yelled as Ruby's hand came up. "Just try it, and I'll beat the shit out of you!"

Ruby's arms dropped to his sides. "Max," he whimpered, "what the hell is going on?"

"I'll tell you what's going on. Jake Stein died and we ran an audit."

Ruby's jaw dropped. Speechless now, he stared at Max.

"Tell me what we found, little brother."

"All right! All right!" bravado beginning to return after the initial shock. "So we skimmed a little here and there. Everyone does it. It's in the nature of the industry."

"You lousy little creep. I pay you eight hundred a week and expenses, and I pay that for a schmuck who couldn't pull down fifty a week on the open market, and you tell me you skim a little here and there. A little? How many millions add up to a little? I took care of you from the time you were pissing in your diapers. I fed you. I put clothes on your back, and this is the way you pay me back? What did you do, work it out with Benny, the two of you making a fancy little syndicate of crime?"

"Come on, Max. We didn't wreck the company. So we took a little cream off the milk. There's plenty left."

"You're right. You're absolutely right."

"So why all the —" Max had turned on his heel to walk away, and Ruby said, "Wait a minute."

"For what?"

"A minute ago, you were ready to take my head off."

"Yeah."

"So?"

"Well, it's done. No use of my getting so excited about it. The way I figure, maybe you and Benny, you'll be lucky and you'll pull down the same cell. Then you'll have all those years to think about it and decide whether or not it's a crime to take a little cream from the milk."

"Jesus, what are you talking about?"

"Jail, brother — j-a-i-l. That's what happens when you becom a crook and you get caught, and sure as hell, that's going to happe to you."

"Max, you're kidding!"

"Oh? We'll see."

"Max, you're crazy. You can't put Benny and me in jail. We'r your brothers."

"That's right. You're both my brothers."

. . .

Max's board of directors, like many other boards, reflected not onl his company but a number of other institutions closely allied wit' it. Max was chairman of the board and also president of Britsk Productions. Sam Snyder was vice president of Britsky and also member of the board. Fred Feldman, the third member of th board, was secretary of Britsky Productions, and Bert Bellamy an Clifford Abel were both members. Abel was the art director at th lot and Bellamy was vice president in charge of distribution. Sally chiefly as a part of her settlement with Max and her very substantia stock holdings, was also a member of the board, but since her di vorce from Max, she had not attended any of the meetings. Outsid the company, there were three more members of the board, to ad up to a total of nine: Kurt Avanti, a vice president of the Bank c America, Julius Holms, a vice president of the Chase Bank, an Royce Byron, one of the many vice presidents of the telephon company.

The years had brought an air and appearance of distinguishe prosperity to Bert Bellamy. He had thickened without becomin fat; his abundant hair had gone from corn silk to white, and he wor a pince-nez with quiet authority. Clifford Abel had changed least c all; he had retained his youthful delight and excitement in ever new aspect of Britsky Productions. Avanti, half Italian, half Ger man, was properly aloof and suspicious, as befitting a banker wh represented one of the largest banks in the world; and while Juliu Holms had known Max since the old New York days, he too wa highly conscious of the forces he represented. Tall, skinny, dour Royce Byron always gave the impression of the Greek in the cam of the barbarians. In the old days, the telephone company ha backed the trust and had been soundly drubbed by Britsky, but time had brought both new patents and new cooperation.

Max had suggested to Feldman that as secretary of the corporation, he was best suited to present the facts, aware at the same time that Feldman was more charming and amiable than he could pretend to be. No one in his right mind could think of Freddy Feldman in terms of malfeasance, and Feldman's rather transparent treatment of everything in legal terms even helped a bit. When he had finished, Avanti stated, "For the moment, I am simply expressing normal shock and surprise. I would like to address a few questions to our president and chairman."

The others nodded their agreement. Each of them had something to say, but each deferred to Avanti. The people working in the company had some indication of what Feldman would say. To the three outsiders, it was a total and shocking surprise.

Max rose and nodded. "I'll answer any questions. Our decision is complete disclosure."

"Whose decision would that be?"

"Mr. Feldman and myself. We discussed the first findings."

"When did you or Mr. Feldman discover these shortages?"

"It was not a matter of discovering shortages," Max said. "After Jacob Stein's death, Mr. Snyder and I paid a condolence call on his family at Mr. Stein's home, which is located in a very fine section of Los Angeles called Bel Air. As a matter of fact, neither I nor any other officers of the company had social relations with Mr. Stein, so it was our first visit to his home. Prior to that, I had been informed that Mr. Stein had not asked for a raise in wages for the past twelve years. He was being paid three hundred dollars a week, a very low wage for a man of his caliber and intelligence."

This drew bitter laughs from around the table where the board members sat.

"A crook, but a smart one," Max went on. "He was not liked in the firm, and we feel that he must have felt that if he asked for more money, it would give us an excuse to let him go. He did not want that, and since he supervised the payroll, no one commented."

"Still, you must have known. How could it escape you?"

"We're a very large organization, Mr. Avanti. A lot escapes me. But when we saw the Stein home, we realized there had to be a discrepancy between what he was paid and what he spent."

"You and Mr. Snyder?"

"Yes."

"And your next step was to take it up with Mr. Feldman?"

"He's our attorney."

"Of course."

Then Holms, of the Chase Bank, asked, "Can you make any estimate of what the final figure will be?"

"At this point, no. I wouldn't dare to."

Royce Byron asked Bert, "Mr. Bellamy, how would you assess the financial condition of Britsky Productions?"

"We're in no danger, absolutely not. In a rough way, I can assure you that our cash flow is sufficient to service our credit line, pay our current expenses, and provide for continuing operations. Our profit for the year nineteen twenty-seven will probably be the largest in our history."

"I'm relieved to hear that, quite relieved. I think I speak for most of us when I say that these revelations have been shocking almost beyond belief. The magnitude of the sums embezzled is almost without equal in the annals of modern business —"

Max leaped to his feet and said, "Now hold on, Mr. Byron. I don't want to make little of this; it's just too damn big. But I lived through the days of Gould and Vanderbilt. At least here the stockholders were robbed, not the public, and since I'm the largest stockholder, I took most of that beating."

"You can't complain. You took it from your family."

"That's below the belt!" Sam Snyder roared.

"This gets us nowhere," Avanti said, "nowhere at all. And until we know the facts, we have no course of action. If the board so wishes, I will be responsible for bringing in our own accountants. I think we should give them at least a full month to do the audit. Can I make this as a motion?"

"So move," Feldman said. "Are there any demurs?"

There was none, and the motion was carried. They agreed to meet again in thirty days. "And I think," Holms said, "that we should make every effort to have Mrs. Upperman present. I think that for the record we should have a meeting of the entire board."

"I will try," Feldman agreed.

"You understand, Max," Avanti said to him before he left, "that none of this is directed against you personally. Some of the finest people I know have some colorful families, perhaps myself included. It takes a few generations to sort ourselves out, and there the Yankees have the jump on us. For myself, I feel that your management of this company has been nothing short of brilliant."

"It's a nothing fuss in a teapot," Clifford Abel said. "I'd let them steal the whole bloody lot if we could come out of it with one great film. Who gives a damn?"

Julius Holms shook hands warmly with Max before he and Avanti left. Clifford Abel followed them. Bert Bellamy mumbled a few words and walked out with Royce Byron.

"He didn't have to leave with Byron," Max said to Snyder and Feldman. "That was deliberate as hell."

"Sure it was deliberate," Feldman agreed. "Don't be a muttonhead, Max. Bellamy and Byron have been waiting for an opening for years, and I'm not a damn bit sure that our two banking boys are going to be either with us or neutral."

"Bert Bellamy — My God, Bert Bellamy, he was like a brother to me."

"So was Ruby."

"Come on, we're still alive and kicking," Sam Snyder said. He looked stiff and uncomfortable in his blue serge suit. He was natural and himself only in a workingman's jeans, his cotton shirt rolled up over his muscular arms, his belly slopping over his tool belt. This way, he couldn't breathe with his vest buttoned, and now he pulled off his jacket and vest. "Nine of us on the board. With Holms and Avanti, we got our majority if worse comes to worse. And maybe Sally will turn up. You can't tell me a woman lives with a man all those years and doesn't feel something for him."

Max grinned for the first time since the meeting had begun. "Sammy, you know what you know about women? Alice. That's what you know about women."

"What's the matter? Alice ain't a woman?"

"A jewel. The way God screwed me most was arranging for you to marry her instead of me."

"Max, you never even met her until after we were married for years."

"I know, I know. The point is what Sally feels for me. I'll tell you what Sally feels for me. She'd cut my throat, but she wouldn't stand there and watch me bleed, because she don't like the sight of blood."

"Come on."

"Look," Feldman told them, "to speculate on this is a waste of time. What matters is that Max owns fifty-one percent of the stock. I don't know what kind of a ploy Bert and Byron think they're hatching. You got the votes. They maybe can push you right to the edge, but right there on the edge, you stand up and tell them to go to hell."

"Come on, Freddy, this is Max you're talking to."

"What do you want me to say?" Feldman demanded almost belligerently. "There are times when you're so goddamn smart you don't need a lawyer."

"Freddy, Freddy," Max said, going over and putting an arm around the lawyer. "Is this a time for you to get testy about me? You know what I'm talking about as well as I do. You know damn well what kind of a ploy Bert and Byron are hatching."

"Tell me."

"Will Ruby and Benny go to jail?"

Feldman did not reply.

"Now, you tell me."

"Only if the board votes to indict, to bring criminal charges."

"Ah-hah! And for that, we don't need even a majority. One member of the board could do it. Am I right?"

"Yes."

"And then I can take my fifty-one percent and shove it. Yes?"

"If the board decided to move against your wishes."

"Who were you telling not to be a muttonhead?"

"Max, do you know what you just did?" Feldman said angrily. "You put forward a series of suppositions with which I could not disagree; then you leaped to a conclusion which has no validity at all. The truth is, we don't know what's going to happen. We haven't even raised the question of Ruby making some sort of restitution —"

"And Benny. Why leave out Benny? You know, Freddy, Ruby couldn't even make restitution for today's breakfast. He borrows from my mother for his poker games. You'd have to run down every floozie in Hollywood to begin to put together restitution, and then if you got two cents on the dollar, it would be a miracle. A crook don't buy bonds or stock or put money in the bank. He blows it. Ah, what the hell! Let's go have dinner."

* * *

Max heard that Benny was in Los Angeles, but as far as Max could determine he did not come near the studio. Unlike Ruby, who had gone through two wives and two divorces, Benny had remained married to a wife who had given him three children and great leeway. Benny was the tallest of the three Britsky boys, six feet and two inches and red-headed and very much in demand with the ladies. He had explained to Max in great detail once that when it came to the art of screwing, Ruby was a schmuck. "You stay married," Benny had said, "so no matter what happens, you don't get involved. And what does it cost — a mink every other year, a convertible every other year? Cheap at the price. My Stella, I could screw every girl in the Vanities and send her picture postcards of me doing it, and as long as she has her mink and her house in Great Neck and her personal pool and tennis court, she don't complain." Max's defense against Benny was to turn him off; he saw Benny when he had to without hearing him or actually seeing him, and it never occurred to Max to tabulate the cost of the minks and convertibles and the showgirls that Benny used to support the speakeasies and the fancy hotels.

So when Max heard that Benny was in Los Angeles, he made no effort to confront him. What for? As far as he was concerned, he would be happy never to confront either brother as long as he lived. Letters had gone out to every theatre manager, suggesting that criminal action would be taken if there was any improper diversion of funds, and every production manager on the lot had been notified of the ongoing audit. There was no question that Benny knew exactly what was going on, and whatever he was not aware of, Ruby would supply. After three days, Sam Snyder informed Max that Benny had returned to New York and that he would be at the Hobart Building if Max wished to talk to him.

"How come you're telling me this?"

"The kid called me to find out how you felt about him," Snyder said.

"And what did you tell him?"

"Max, it's family. I can't get mixed up in it. I told him to call you and ask you."

"You know damn well how I feel. I should have beaten the shit out of both of them when they were still kids. I should have taught them the law. I was derelict, derelict."

"Yeah, when you were twelve years old."

"I was never twelve years old."

"He asked me whether you'd let them send him to the can."

"Can I stop them?"

But the question Max asked himself was whether he wanted to. He was hurt. He had been hurt before, but never this way. It was one thing to peddle theatre passes to whores so that his family could eat. It was another thing entirely to take care of all six in a style they had never dreamed of, to provide well-paying jobs not only for his brothers but for the deadbeat husbands of two of his sisters, to provide a goddamn Beverly Hills mansion that his mother and poor spinster Freida could live in, not to mention Ruby when he wasn't shacked up at the hotel, and handing Freida a thousand dollars every week for her and Sarah to run the house with — and on top of that, those two bums took him for maybe two, three, maybe four million dollars. He didn't give a damn about the money. When in his whole life had he ever given a damn about money? If they had asked — But to steal it, to make a *putze*, a high-grade schmuck out of him in front of his friends and the board of directors and the studio people and the world; and already he felt that every time he walked down the studio street, a hundred faces turned after he passed, whispering, "There he is, the horse's ass who was taken like nobody else was taken since Grant took Richmond."

The telephone broke into his reverie, and Shelly Greene informed him that his mother wished to speak to him.

"Tell her I'm not here."

He went back to the question. Did he want Ruby and Benny in jail?

The following day, Shelly Greene said to him, "You can't keep avoiding her forever, Mr. Britsky. It's only noon now, and she's called five times."

"You'll live through that, Shelly."

"I don't know what to tell her anymore, Mr. Britsky."

"Tell her I'm dead."

"I can't do that. You know I can't do that."

"All right. Tell her I'll be over this afternoon, about four."

She saw the look on his face, and she said as gently as she could, "Well, it's not a funeral, Mr. Britsky. It's your mother."

"No, sweetheart," he said. "It's a funeral."

His sister Freida greeted him at the house in Beverly Hills, as if it actually were a funeral. Her face was swollen, her eyes red, and with a salty handkerchief she was wiping away additional tears. Max had always had a special feeling about Freida. Life had not been good to her. The two other Britsky girls, Sheila and Esther, were married with children of their own. It did not matter to Freida that the men Sheila and Esther had married were, in Max's eyes, deadbeats and bums who could not have earned carfare without his help, without him to make them theatre managers. None of that meant anything to Freida. Her womb was barren and her heart was barren; and she could never shake off the belief that God was punishing her for her abortion in spite of Max's insistence that God had better things to do with His time than worry about Freida Britsky's abortion. Max showered her with gifts, with money. He found jobs for her on the lot, even though she was not very good at anything, and he even found men to introduce her to. But her plump, juicy, youthful attractiveness had turned into fat, and every match Max found for her went sour.

Now, when he asked her where Mama was, she weepingly replied, "In bed. What then? You want her to be dancing with joy? Only her two sons are going to prison like common thieves, but you want her to be dancing for joy."

"Will you cut that crap out, Freida," Max said with annoyance.

"Sure, sure. What's it to you, my beautiful brother Benny goes to jail like a common criminal?"

"Your beautiful brother Benny and your beautiful brother Ruby are both miserable, conniving shitpots. Jail is too good for them."

She burst into tears again, and Max put his arms around her and told her, "It's all right, baby. Don't you worry about it."

"Go talk to Mama. She's waiting for you."

Sarah Britsky was seventy-one years old, but as the poet remarked, time had not withered her charms. After some initial protest and sulking, Sarah Britsky had taken to Beverly Hills like a fish to water. If Max had been a philosopher, he might have speculated upon the fact that his mother possessed the essential nature and qualities of those women who live in palaces; but since he had other things on his mind, he was simply content that she was content in the huge nine-bedroom neo–Louisana plantation house. Facing the competition of other elderly worthies on the newly created Beverly Hills scene, she took eager advantage of all the good things that flowed there from every corner of the nation — the expensive hairdressers, the couturières, the masseuses, the makeup experts, the furriers — all the little bits of sparkling water thrown off by that fountain of youth called money. She took for her own bedroom the largest bedroom in the house, fourteen by twenty-two feet, with two huge walk-in closets that offered at least two or three years of shopping, and it was in this room, in her bed, wearing a pink and blue silk and satin and lace bedjacket that had cost almost two hundred dollars, that Sarah received her son. Her hair, dyed light auburn, was marcelled tightly; her cheeks were touched up with rouge and her lips painted with lipstick. The silk and lace bedspread was folded back, and Sarah was propped on three pillows. The room had thick white carpeting, blue silk for wallpaper, a chaise, and two bedroom armchairs.

Seeing his mother this way made Max somewhat sick to his stomach, but what to do? You don't tell your mother she looks like a hideous old crow, and do what he might, he could never overcome a very deep-seated fear of Sarah.

"Come over and give your mother a kiss, Maxie darling," she said, dabbing at her eyes, not wiping, which would ruin her eye makeup.

Max kissed her, feeling that he was plunging into a choking miasma of strong perfume.

"Sit down, Max."

He sat down in one of the small white wicker armchairs.

"I should be dying here, right here on my bed, you'd lift a finger to help me?"

"What?"

"Who hears a mother's cry? The world goes on. Who hears? Who cares?"

"Mama, what on God's earth are you talking about?"

"See? I talk, but you don't hear me."

"Mama, I hear you. Of course I hear you. I didn't know you were sick. You only had to say a word to my secretary about being sick and I'd be right over here."

"You know what kind of sickness I got? My heart is broken."

There was a long silence after that, and finally Max said, "Well, nobody dies from a broken heart."

"Ha! That's something to say to your mother."

"Mama, what do you want?"

"I want your brothers, my two beautiful sons, they should not go to prison. That's what I want."

"Mama —" Max stopped. She was staring at him with that same grim look of power she had exercised when he was a little boy. He dropped his gaze and said, "Mama, your two beautiful sons are crooks, thieves. When crooks are caught stealing, they go to prison. This is not something that I do or anyone else does. It's the law of the land."

"What is stealing? So they took a few dollars. It's family. Family. From strangers they weren't taking."

"Not a few dollars, Mama," Max said slowly. "A few million dollars."

"So? So? Are you starving? Is your company going into bankruptcy because of this? I look out the window, I see you drive up in a Cadillac limousine with a chauffeur yet. For you the whole world — you sit like a king out there in the valley — but for your brothers nothing. Don't think I don't know. Don't think Sarah Britsky is such a fool. Sam Snyder you make into a millionaire and put on the board of directors, and he's not even Jewish — a *goy*, like Bellamy, who was nothing but a cheap entertainer in a music hall. And Feldman, whose father owned a candy store on Division Street, and you make them into millionaires and they sit on the board of directors. Oh, don't think I don't understand, because Ruby and Benny tell me everything, but for your brothers, for your own flesh and blood, nothing, not one share of stock —"

He interrupted her. "That's not true. You have stock in the company. Freida has stock in the company."

"So I'm a liar?"

"Mama, I didn't call you a liar."

"And you gave stock to Ruby and Benny, so I'm a liar."

"Mama, Mama — why do you have to twist my words? I didn't give no stock to Ruby or Benny. I gave them good jobs in the company."

"And now, because they had to take a few dollars from you, you must kill them. You must send them to prison and kill them. Kill me, instead, because the day my children go to prison, I die. I die. That's all."

"Mama, I can't help them. They did it and they got to pay for it."

"Ruby says it's up to you."

"It's not up to me."

"Ruby says it is. He says you got chips to trade. I believe him. If you do this to my children, Max, I take sleeping pills, so you can live with that. You kill your brothers, you kill your mother too. I won't live to see my boys go to prison." She began to sob, and through her tears she whimpered, "That I should have to endure this. After all my suffering, that I should have to go through this."

• • •

That evening, Max had dinner at Sam Snyder's house. Alice cooked weisswurst with lentils and sauerkraut and fried apples. Snyder had found a place in San Francisco where they made good fresh German sausage, and he had a shipment sent to him each week. Both men stuffed themselves with the food, washing it down with the dark, sweet German beer Max loved so much. For the hundredth time, Alice wondered why, when they both ate the same amount of food, Max remained as skinny as a rail while Snyder's stomach grew larger and larger. Alice had finally put her foot down on the matter of smoking in the house, so after dinner, the two men took their cigars out onto the terrace. It was one of those occasional Santa Ana nights, when the desert wind turns the otherwise chilly Los Angeles evening warm and balmy, and the two men stretched out comfortably on lounge chairs. The scent of night-blooming jasmine mingled with the sweet smell of good cigars, and faintly, from a house nearby, there came the sound of a Victrola playing "Barney Google."

"You know," Max said to Snyder, "this is as good as I ever felt, except maybe when Della was alive, but I've given up dreaming that I'll find somebody else just like Della, and right now I'm pretty happy, and all it takes to buy a fine Cuban cigar is fifty cents."

"Alice's cooking helps."

"You can say that again."

"Yeah, but I got to sound a sour note. Sally is coming to the board meeting."

"How do you know that?"

"Freddy told me. He was trying to locate you this afternoon, and when he finally tracked you down to your mother's house, you had left." Snyder was watching Max thoughtfully. "I just don't understand it, Max. The woman was in love with you."

"Who?"

"Sally. Who else?"

"What makes you think so?" Max demanded almost angrily.

"All right, all right. Don't bite my head off."

"Come on, Sam, forget it. The day I start hitting on you, it's time to leave the human race. Sure, everyone thinks Sally was in love with me and we had some beautiful thing going until I screwed it up by leaving her for Della — that is, everyone believes it except Sally and me. No, Sally never loved me, and I don't think I ever loved her very much. When I was a kid, she was everything I wasn't. To me, she had class and brains. Hell, she was a schoolteacher. I never saw a Jewish schoolteacher before I met Sally. Do you know how many Jewish schoolteachers there were in the nineties? Zilch. And I was a crazy kid who had to get what he wanted, especially when she didn't want me. She thinks she married me because her mother and father pushed her into it once they realized that I was on my way to make a few bucks and that their daughter might turn out to be an old maid. No, sir. She married me because I made the other boys she went out with look like shitheads, and that's what she never forgave me for. I spent a lifetime trying to figure it out. She'd do something like putting together that first big picture of ours, and then she'd turn on me like a wildcat. You want to know why she hates me? She hates me because she married me, because she did something she can never forgive herself for."

Max lit his cigar, which had gone cold. Snyder shook his head.

"Doesn't make much sense to you, does it?" Max asked.

"Not much, no. I seen too many ladies go crazy about you."

"It didn't make much sense to me at first, but I been living with t a long time. Maybe I figured it right, maybe not. I tell myself I was good to her, but Sally thinks I was a son of a bitch. Who knows?

Maybe she's right. I tried to be good to my mother, but that doesn't cut much ice either."

"How does your mother feel about all this?"

"She says that if Ruby and Benny go to the slammer, she's going to kill herself."

"You believe that?"

"My mother?" Max shook his head. "Not a chance. If she killed herself, who'd be here to torment me?"

"You got something there."

"Sam, tell me, what do I do? You know as well as I do what's going to happen at that meeting. They're going to come up with three, four million dollars that can be pinned onto Ruby and Benny. Freddy tells me they're going back twelve years. Thank God, they can't trace the cash those two *momzers* skimmed."

"Maybe it won't be that much, maybe only a million or so. Remember that most of it went through Jake Stein, so it won't be easy to pin it on Ruby."

"Don't change a thing. You know why Sally's coming out here?"

"Sort of."

"That goddamn husband of hers is ass to ass with every big bank in New York. You can be damn sure he's been talking to the people at the Chase. It's one thing to be a classy uptown Jew like Felix and it's something else to be a vulgar Henry Street kike like Max Britsky. As for the telephone company, I been a bone in their throat ever since we busted the trust. Sally'll be out here because her five percent of my stock is worth better than ten million at today's prices, but that ain't enough for those greedy bastards. They want the whole pie — they want the company — and this is the chance they been waiting for. They'll tell me, either you hand it over or we prosecute your brothers. Sam, what do I do?"

"You really think that's it?"

"I know that's it."

"They can't ask you to hand over the company. That puts them in Jake's class."

"Right. They'll simply ask me to make restitution."

"Can you?"

"I don't know. I don't know what they're cooking. I don't know how much they'll come up with. Feldman says that without question, Ruby and Benny entered into a conspiracy with Jake Stein.

Under the law, that could make Ruby and Benny responsible for the entire sum, which might be eight, nine, ten million. How in hell could I come up with ten million?"

"Max, my stock is worth three million. I'll sell it tomorrow if you need it to keep control."

"Sam, I love you, but that ain't the way it works. I'd dump the whole package before I touch a share of your stock or Freddy's or Cliff's. Anyway, if I know those shrewd bastards, they took it into consideration. You wouldn't have to give me the stock. The voting rights would be enough. But they know that, and they won't leave such loopholes. The choice is up to me. I tell them to go fuck themselves, and I hold on to the company, and Ruby and Benny go to jail, and we see the biggest scandal this town has seen since Fatty Arbuckle."

Fred Feldman confirmed Max's thinking. "You might as well know," he told Max, "that Upperman checked into the Beverly Hills Hotel with Sally. I slipped the bell captain a five-spot to let me know when, and I added another five to it for him to make some notes about who the Uppermans hobnob with. Last night, they had a long, talky dinner with someone who fits the description of Bert Bellamy. My guess is that Bellamy's payoff will be your job, president of Britsky Productions."

"So they're burying me before they hang me. How do they know what I've decided? I don't know myself."

"My guess is that Sally has assured them you won't let Ruby and Benny take it."

"What does Sally think? That I'm decent? If she does, it's the first time."

"What do you think?"

"I don't know."

"Come on, Max, you must know. You've had almost a month to think about this."

"Does the conspiracy thing hold? Are you sure of it?"

"Look, Max," Feldman said quietly, as if to make the point even more strongly, "the conspiracy factor is not something they created to hit us with. There was a conspiracy to defraud. The embezzlement could not have occurred as it did without the connivance of each of the three conspirators. We weren't certain of that at the beginning. We are now. Stein controlled the books, but he was in a sense a prisoner of his office. He needed an outside man on the lot and he needed an outside man in the theatres. So the fraud was an almost classical conspiracy. One of the conspirators died, but the law does not divide responsibility for the fruits of the crime. Ruby and Benny are responsible for the whole thing. And by the way, have you seen Ruby lately?"

"No, and I don't want to."

"Well, he was in to see me. I wasn't going to tell you this, but he broke down and cried like a baby. He begged me to use my influence on you to get him off the hook."

Max shrugged. "All right. Use it."

"I have no intentions of doing so, and I told him so. Anyway, I know you too well to imagine that anything I might say would make a difference."

· · ·

The board meeting was scheduled to take place on the lot, in the VIP dining room. Max had arranged passes for the four off-lot members, sending Sally's pass to the hotel and arranging for a studio limousine to be there to pick her up. He was still in his office on the afternoon of the meeting when his telephone rang. It was Pat Maguire, the guard at the west gate, and he said, "The limo is here with Mrs. Upperman. Shall I let it through?"

"Pat, she's got a pass, hasn't she? So what in hell are you calling me for?"

"I'm sorry, Mr. Britsky. I should have known better. Sure, she's got a pass, but her husband's name ain't on it."

"Wait a minute, wait a minute. Are you telling me her husband's with her?"

"Yeah."

"Mr. Felix Upperman?"

"That's what he calls himself."

"Mr. Felix Upperman. Pat, you were absolutely right to call me. Mrs. Upperman goes through. Mr. Upperman does not. He can stand at the gate and wait until Mrs. Upperman is through with her meeting or you can phone for a taxi to take him back to his hotel."

"You don't want the limo to take him back, Mr. Britsky? I mean, I've never heard you tell me to call a taxi for anyone —"

"Pat, the limousine functions on studio business. I can't imagine any studio business that brings Mr. Upperman here."

"But Mr. Britsky, sometimes it can be an hour before a taxi comes."

"So it can," Max agreed. "Sometimes an hour, sometimes even more."

Max put down the telephone and smiled for the first time in days. "Little things," he said aloud. "Sometimes, they're more important than the big things."

Then he walked over to the VIP dining room. Feldman and Avanti and Sally were there, and as he entered, Sally turned on him in fury. "You malignant bastard!" she cried. "To humiliate a man whose boots you aren't fit to wipe!"

Max spread his arms. "Sally, Sally, I didn't know he'd take it so hard. After all, he understands the confidentiality of a meeting like this."

"He didn't come here for the meeting. All he wished was to walk around the lot and look at it —"

"Now that he's taking over."

"He's never been in a studio before."

"Poor man. But won't he have time enough for that?"

Sally pulled herself together. "The West Coast hasn't improved you. I don't know why I should have thought that it would. You're the same old deplorable little delinquent from Henry Street." And with that, she turned on her heel, walked to the other end of the long table, and seated herself. For Max, the amazing thing was how little she had changed. Like Sarah, she adapted well to the advantages of wealth. She wore a stockinette Chanel dress with satin collar and cuffs, a knit scarf loosely carried, a diamond of at least four karats, and a pearl necklace. Her marcelled hair displayed spit curls and showed no gray. She had always been slender, and though she had aged well and changed little, Max could not connect her with the Sally he had known years ago; and it occurred to him that if he saw her on the street, he might well have walked by without recognizing her.

Feldman and Avanti had watched Sally's outburst in bewilderment, and now Max felt ashamed of his tawdry little triumph. He walked over to Sally and said, "If you want me to, I'll have them admit your husband. He can have the freedom of the lot."

"Go to hell," Sally said to him.

There was a telephone on a small side table. Max picked it up and asked for the gate. "Pat," he said, "is Mr. Upperman still there?"

"Yes, sir, waiting for his cab."

"Admit him to the lot or tell him he can have the limousine take him back to his hotel, whichever he prefers. Give the cabby a five-spot for his trouble if you can stop him, and remind me that you laid it out."

He put down the telephone, and Sally said to him, "And aren't you the big, gracious host."

"I do my best."

The room was filling up. The last to arrive was Frank Humboldt, from the San Francisco firm of Humboldt, Lee and Morrison, certified public accountants. Mr. Humboldt carried a briefcase, and out of it he took nine bound folders, one for each of the board members.

"These reports," Feldman told them, "contain all the information pertinent to the reason for this extraordinary meeting, namely the embezzlement of monies over a period of twelve years. I have examined this statement together with Mr. Avanti, and we are both satisfied that it presents a fair and reasonably complete picture. Mr. Humboldt will remain in the next room, available for any questions we may wish to address to him, but both Mr. Britsky and Mr. Avanti join with me in feeling that this meeting should be absolutely confidential and limited to the nine members of our board of directors. Since the subject we entertain here is of a most serious nature, I suggest that the board members take the next half-hour to examine the auditor's statement, after which we will open the floor to discussion."

Max went through his copy of the audit. The embezzlements added up to something over seven million dollars, and he was somewhat relieved that the auditors had ignored the untraceable cash thefts, not even alluding to the possibility that they had taken place. That they had taken place, Max had no doubt, but there was no way to trace them. He was fascinated by the number of dummy companies Stein and Ruby had created: a billboard rental company, three different advertising agencies, two travel agents through which to launder the cost of several hundred European trips that had never taken place, a costume company, a lumber supply house, and an industrial cleaning company. Max himself had opened up the kickback question. The dealers they bought automobiles and trucks from kicked back to Stein. When Max had threatened to cut them off, they opened up and laid it on Stein, but that at least was not in the audit. Nevertheless, that and much more would be in the audit if criminal charges were filed and subpoenas were issued for the records of Stein, Ruby, and Benny.

How much more would it amount to? Max wondered. Three million, four million — he shook his head in wonder at the amount of money generated by this instrument he had created, turning the pages until he had skimmed through the whole sorry report.

When the half-hour had passed, Feldman rose and said, "Mr. Britsky has asked Mr. Avanti to chair this meeting, since he feels that he himself has too vested an interest to act objectively. As with our last meeting, I felt it best not to have a stenographer present. I will take notes. I'm a bit rusty, but I did learn shorthand when I was a law clerk."

Avanti then accepted the gavel from Max, called the meeting to order, took the roll call, and noted for the record that all nine members of the board of directors were present.

"Mr. Britsky has requested that he be allowed a few remarks before I open the floor to a general discussion. Does anyone object?"

There were no objections, and Max rose and said, "Britsky Productions went public about twelve and a half years ago. Since then, everyone in this room has profited. We put out our stock at ten dollars a share. Today it is selling at four times that. We paid dividends the first year we were public, and we never missed a dividend after that. Now we've discovered a huge embezzlement going back almost to the day we went public. If Stein was still alive and my two brothers were not even involved, I would still say to you, let us eat this ourselves. Nothing is gained by public prosecution. A scandal is provoked, and God knows, this industry has suffered enough scandal. I would put it another way. For a company to take that kind of embezzlement and not even know it is a sign of great financial health. So I move that we adopt the new accounting procedure suggested by Mr. Humboldt and put this matter to rest. Of course, Reuben Britsky and Benjamin Britsky have been fired. They will not work for Britsky Productions again."

Without asking for the floor, Byron said, "No reflection on the financial health, but a reflection on management. You can underline that."

"I think we should proceed orderly," Avanti said, tapping with his gavel. "We accomplish nothing by shouting or abuse."

Both Sally and Snyder were asking for the floor. Out of deference to her sex, Avanti recognized Sally, who spoke without looking at Max.

"I do not understand Mr. Britsky's suggestion," she said, appearing to be genuinely puzzled. "Is it conceivable that if a man robs your house, you tell him to go in peace and keep his loot simply because public prosecution would involve you? Can Mr. Britsky be so unaware of criminal procedure in America that he does not realize that all prosecution of crime is a public matter? And that this system could not work without the public's involvement? And I'm afraid I must mention the moral issues involved. If we should cover up this enormous crime, are we not then joining in a criminal conspiracy, becoming part of it ourselves?"

"I have to speak to this point," Feldman said. "We have to clear it up immediately."

"I'll give you the floor after Mr. Feldman," Avanti said to Snyder.

"About the point Mrs. Upperman raises," Feldman said. "There is no question of conspiracy if we should choose not to prosecute Mr. Britsky's brothers. That is our right. In fact, there are legal precedents where this right has been called into question, but never overturned, and there have been thousands of incidents of precisely this nature where no prosecution occurred —"

"But not of this magnitude," Julius Holms interrupted.

"Possibly not, but that makes absolutely no difference. We have the right to prosecute or to refrain from prosecution. Any suggestion to the contrary is ridiculous. Suppose a wife empties her husband's pants pocket of cash while he sleeps. Is he obligated to prosecute her?"

"A swift kick in the tail would be more helpful," Clifford Abel said, breaking the tension and provoking the only smiles that punctuated the meeting.

Avanti recognized Sam Snyder.

"I'm different from all the rest of you in one thing," Snyder said. "I've been with Max from the very beginning. I set up his first projector. I adjusted his first camera. I watched him through the years, starting with nothing and building this company into one of the giants of America. I'm a plain workingman, and I spend a good part of my days bawling out the dunderheads who are supposed to keep the machinery of this business functioning. But I know one thing." He paused and directed a stubby finger at Max. "If it takes seven million dollars to give that man some peace of mind, it's cheap at the price. What in hell do you want him to do? Sell his brothers? Sure they're crooks! But they're his flesh and blood, and you don't deliver your own flesh and blood to the hangman. That's the way he feels and that's the way I feel!"

"Hear! Hear!" Royce Byron exclaimed. "I'm sure Al Capone has a brother."

"That's a dirty shot!" Abel told him.

Max looked around the table, face to face. Clifford Abel was a little drunk. Understandable. He couldn't have faced it otherwise. Big Sam Snyder sat and stifled his desire to punch out every one of the New York sons of bitches, including the well-dressed Mrs. Upperman. What had he done to her? Max wondered. How had he generated such cold, malignant hatred? Even when he laid all the guilt upon himself, accepting the fact that he had forced her into a loveless marriage, which was by no means true, a union with a Lower East Side hoodlum, less than true, it could not account for her hatred. He had never been cruel to her; he had never struck her, never humiliated her. He had given her wealth and what social position he could offer, and eventually she had married a man who had given her the rest, entrée into the top society of New York City. Well, one more very large one in a list of things Max could never understand. Bert Bellamy was more transparent, more relaxed, than anyone else at the table, the prince regent ready to step onto the throne. How many hours they must have spent working this out, every step of it, every detail. When had he lost Bert Bellamy as a friend, as an ally? Did it go all the way back to when he had taken him out of the cheap music hall circuit, hired him, and put him on the first step to becoming a millionaire? Now Bert was a man of parts, white and silver hair over pince-nez, a three-piece suit made at long distance by his tailor in London, distinguished, apart from the nasty bickering going on here at the table. Leave the bickering to others. Bert would speak in his own good time. It came from giving, and with the giving a reduction in size. He had reduced Bert Bellamy. I gave you what you couldn't earn on your own, what you never had the brains to create on your own. Drunken Cliff Abel, Sam Snyder near to tears, fat little Freddy Feldman — we all created; we made something where there was nothing, but you took the way Ruby and Benny took. That was their revenge and this is your revenge. Sort of understanding it made things a little easier for Max, but nothing to write home about.

Sally smiled thinly. "The James boys were brothers." Max heard her if no one else did. Royce Byron was snarling at Clifford Abel.

"Dear man," Abel said, "I look upon you as an elephant's asshole. One is interested in the trunk and the tusks, but only maggots investigate the other end."

"I will not sit here and endure this!" Byron said.

Avanti hammered his gavel.

"Asshole," Abel hissed. "If you walk out, your Machiavellian majority is up shit creek. But don't let me keep you, dear man."

"Do I have to listen to this loathsome homosexual?" he asked Feldman pleadingly.

Feldman shouted, "For God's sake, Cliff, you're only making matters worse!"

"Could they be worse?"

"Come on, Cliff, shut up," Snyder told him.

Leaping into a moment of silence, Avanti said, "I think we can all remember that we are adults — and that includes you, Mr. Abel. This is probably the most important board of directors meeting in the history of our company. Let us treat it as such." He pointed his gavel at Bert Bellamy. "I think Mr. Bellamy would like the floor."

Now it was his own good time. Bert rose to his feet slowly, his face grave but not stripped of compassion by any means, and he said gently, "I can understand Max's feelings. To ask a man to condemn his own brothers is more than obscene. It's un-Christian and vile —" So there it was at last, slipped in gently like the sharpest, most slender dagger, the sheep separated from the goats, the designation pinned on this skinny little Jew who had the effrontery to challenge them to mercy. "— and I, for one, would never dream of asking Max to take action against his brothers." He paused and looked from face to face. "Nevertheless, some justice must be served. So does our society function. As Max suggested, we should put this matter to rest, put it in the past, let it die here behind these closed doors, and, if Mr. Feldman agrees to the legality of such a thing, destroy the minutes of this meeting."

Again he paused. Julius Holms cried, "Hear! Hear!" Max smiled bitterly. Sharp, sharp, old buddy, he said to himself. You always did the routines better than I did, especially when we played the high-class gigs, and this is the classiest of all.

"Nevertheless," Bert continued, "as I said before, some justice must be served. We have no desire to put Reuben and Benjamin Britsky behind bars, and we will not, but they must make restitution. There can be no quibbling on that score." He looked around the table again, nodded, and resumed his seat.

"I would like to know, Bert," Feldman said, "how many members of the board concur in your statement? I say this because it sounded to me less like a suggestion than like a decision."

"I have consulted legal opinion on my own. I have been assured that any single member of this board — indeed, any stockholder — could bring charges against the Britsky brothers."

"Quite true. I have been explicit on this matter in my discussions with Mr. Britsky. But since I am keeping the record of this meeting, I would like to poll the members. May I make a motion to that effect, Mr. Avanti?"

"A motion is on the floor."

"I second it," Snyder said.

"I would rather not put this to a vote," Avanti said. "If anyone objects to Mr. Feldman polling the board, would he raise his hand?"

No hand was raised, and Feldman began, "Mr. Britsky?"

"No."

"Mr. Avanti?"

Hesitation. "This is my first knowledge of this suggestion. Could I wait?"

"Mr. Holms?"

"I think yes. I would want to expand on that opinion."

"Mr. Abel?"

"Oh, no, Freddy. The suggestion is sheer nonsense. You know that."

"Mrs. Upperman?"

"Yes."

"Mr. Byron?"

"Yes."

"Mr. Snyder?"

"Of course not, Freddy."

"And for the record," Feldman said, "I would oppose it too."

Max asked for the floor. "I said no as to Bert's suggestion. I am very much aware of the compassion he expressed, and it's exactly what I would have expected from a dear old friend," refraining from adding: who happens to be the slimiest son of a bitch I ever broke bread with. "But the truth is that restitution for seven million dollars, well —" Max spread his arms and shook his head. "My brothers don't have a nickel. They're worthless, penniless bums. Benny is a poker player and a big man with low ladies. Ruby has dropped at least a million at the crap tables in Reno. It adds up to nothing. They can't make restitution."

"But you can," Sally said.

"Thank you, my dear."

"I think," said Feldman, "that restitution is out of the question. We can take the time to run an audit of Ruby and Benny, but it won't change a thing. If we sold them down to their underwear, we might generate a few hundred dollars, and that's it. For my part, I simply do not see the necessity for restitution. We have a large, healthy, powerful company. Every other studio out here — Fox, Metro, Columbia, Warner's — every one of them has dropped millions on bad films, bad decisions. It's in the nature of the business. The cash flows must be generated with a degree of risk. We don't make automobiles. We make moving pictures. It may appear incredible to say that seven million dollars is of no consequence, but if you will examine the balance sheets of this company, you will realize that is the case. It is of no consequence. Therefore, I make a motion that this board, in the light of Mr. Britsky's years of dedication to this company, vote not to prefer any criminal charges against Reuben and Benjamin Britsky."

"Second!" Abel cried.

"Before there's any vote," Royce Byron said, "I wish to remind the board that such a vote is not binding. As a stockholder, I have the right to prefer criminal charges."

"Is that your intent?" Avanti asked.

"It certainly is — unless restitution is made."

"We've been through that. There's no way restitution can be made."

"There certainly is."

The sheep from the goats, Max thought. He liked Avanti. He was glad Avanti was not a part of it. Who was it, then — Bert, Sally, Byron, and most likely Holms? That would be it. They must have planned it step by step — not Bert now, not his old buddy, but Royce Byron, New York, Wall Street, the telephone company — all the standard stock villains. Bert had to come out smelling like a rose. He was the only one who could step into the driver's seat.

"Then enlighten us, Mr. Byron," Avanti said.

"I'll be happy to. The person most interested in keeping the Britsky brothers out of prison, the person who has the most to gain by it, is Mr. Britsky, our president. Mr. Feldman assures us that the corporation has not been damaged. I wonder whether, if that assurance were offered to the stockholders, they would agree with him. Myself, I do feel damaged, both morally and financially. So I say that if the miscreants are not to be punished and pay their debt to society, if not to our company, restitution must be made, and since it cannot be made by the culprits, then the interested party, Mr. Max Britsky, must make it."

A hubbub broke out, a half-dozen people speaking at once, Avanti pounding his gavel, and Max sitting back in his chair and watching the board members and listening to their angry words almost with detachment. Finally restoring a semblance of order, Avanti asked for a vote on the motion, regardless of whether it was binding.

Max, Snyder, Abel, and Feldman voted for the motion to drop the matter and take no criminal proceedings against the Britskys.

Bert, Sally, Holms, and Byron voted against the motion.

Avanti did not vote, and when Feldman asked him to please make his preference known, he explained that since his bank had extended a large credit line to Britsky Productions, it would hardly be proper for him to vote — certainly not without consultation with his home office. Therefore, he must abstain. "And," he added, "I can say that in a matter of this nature, I am almost certain that San Francisco would advise me to abstain."

"But, you see," Byron said, "the vote is only a formality. There is no way for Mr. Britsky to avoid the question."

"It does come to me," Max agreed. "Let me put my cards on the table, gentlemen. Britsky Productions pays me a wage of two thousand dollars a week. That's comfortable, but a number of our stars earn much more. I also charge some expenses to the lot — a studio car when I use it, occasional business dinners or lunches off the lot — never comes to more than a couple of hundred a week, mostly less. A thousand a week I turn over to my mother to run her home. The rest — well, it goes. I'm an easy touch, and between out-of-work actors and charities and the surprising number of people who need loans — well, like I say, it goes. I'm not poor. I got about eighty thousand in my bank account, but seven million dollars — that I don't have."

"You're pulling our leg," Byron snorted.

"Mr. Britsky has a keenly developed sense of humor," Sally said.

"Max," Bert said, "I think they're referring to the fact that you do own fifty-one percent of Britsky Productions."

"I'm sure they were," Max said. "As Mrs. Upperman observed, I got a sense of humor." Snyder started to say something, but Max silenced him with an outstretched hand. "Just hold it, Sam. It's my turn. I've been quiet and listening. Now I'll talk." He turned back to Bert. "Never mind the bullshit, Bert. Wherever it is, I been there. So let's talk *tachlis*. Right? No shit anymore — the *ganse emmes*. You worked it all out before you set foot in here, you and that strange woman who was once my wife and this cookie from the telephone company. So *ahf an tisch* — you remember enough Yiddish for that. You got me by the balls, and there ain't one fucken thing I can do." The language was for Sally's benefit. "So spell it out and let's wind it up. I'm bored as hell, anyway."

"All right, Max. It's better that way."

"You're damn right it is."

"We want seven million dollars' worth of your stock — at market, to be turned over to the company to become company stock.

Then we want your resignation, since we feel these new conditions would be too abrasive for you to continue to be productive here."

"Who is we?"

"Sally, myself, Byron."

"Who gets my job?"

"I do. We'll have the votes for it."

"You won't have them. I can still swing a majority."

"No. You see, you will give us a proxy voting right that gives us the majority. No negotiating, no bargaining. The stakes are too high, and we're prepared to go down to the wire. Either you agree, or we walk out of here and drive to the office of the district attorney of Los Angeles County, turn Humboldt's statement over to him, and initiate proceedings. At that point, it is doubtful that you can survive the scandal and continue to run the company. Life is not over, Max. You still come out worth over a hundred million dollars."

"Bert, Bert, you're a patient son of a bitch. How long have you been planning this?"

"Ever since Ruby and Benny and Jake began to steal you blind. First I tried to warn you. Then I decided to use it. If Jake hadn't died, I would have sprung it next year."

"And now you and my darling Sally got it all."

"More or less."

"All right, Bert, you got it all, the whole kit and kaboodle. You also got Max Britsky on the other side, not a nice man to have as an enemy. So we'll see what the future brings. As of this moment, I don't want to talk to or look at either you or that bitch who's your partner. Freddy!"

The table had been silent, silent as a windless sea. Now Feldman said, "Yes, Max?"

"Work up the papers for this shithead. Meeting's over." And with that, he stalked out of the boardroom.

[ELEVEN]

1937
—
Requiem

MAX PASSED AWAY very quietly, sitting in the last row of the Bijou Theatre on West Broadway in New York City, about four o'clock in the afternoon in the year 1937. He was fifty-eight years old, and as the autopsy later revealed, he had two heart attacks of which he was probably unaware prior to the one that killed him. He died very quietly, slumped in his seat as if he were asleep, and everyone said it was like Max to depart without putting anyone to very much trouble.

Max had left Los Angeles two weeks after the board of directors meeting in which Bert Bellamy replaced him as president of Britsky Productions. His friends had expected Max to mount some kind of counteroffensive which would undercut Bellamy and restore Max to leadership in the company, but nothing of the sort took place. Max packed his bags and left Los Angeles, and from that moment until the day he died, he did not see or speak to any member of his family, including his mother. Britsky Productions was one of the few stocks that rode through Black Thursday and the Depression that followed with scarcely a tremor, and Max was never in want of funds. Indeed, he was quite wealthy. He took a suite of rooms at the old Murray Hill Hotel at Park Avenue and Thirty-ninth Street, and he never returned to Los Angeles. He made no attempt to return to the film business, nor did he interest himself in any other financial venture. He walked a good deal, always fascinated by the city which had produced him, astonished by the changes that had taken place while he was away. He joined the Players club, and he became a familiar figure in the lounge, a small man in a large leather chair, reading his newspaper, smoking a cigar, and sipping at a glass of beer. But he invited no intimacy, and aside from the handful of people who knew him, he was left alone.

He went to most of the openings, both plays and film, and always with an attractive woman, usually middle-aged, on his arm. The women were old friends from the days of the New York studios — bit players, supporting players, women who had been married and divorced, married and abandoned, and sometimes never married, just kicked from pillar to post — but they all enjoyed being with Max, because he spent freely and he was never judgmental and he never rubbed salt into open wounds; and some of them were a little bit in love with him but also aware that he was alone and would remain so.

About once a year, in the beginning, Sam Snyder or Freddy Feldman would come into town, and Max would take one or the other to a good restaurant and hear the news from the Coast. But a few years after Max came East, Feldman left the studio and Sam Snyder decked Bert Bellamy as a result of an argument on the studio street. For all his fat, Snyder was a powerful man, and Bellamy suffered a cut face and lost a tooth, and while he did not bring assault charges against Snyder, it was plain that Snyder's tour at the lot was over. Snyder retired, set up his own workshop, and made several significant improvements in the camera. Fred Feldman opened his own legal firm in Los Angeles, and Clifford Abel burned down the design studio at the lot and then went off on an around the-world cruise. It was never proven that he had torched the place but it was a sort of open secret.

In America, the public has a very short memory, and no one was too curious about what had happened to Max Britsky. He preferred it that way. If he had gone to a psychiatrist, he would have learned that he was living in a state of depression, but then he probably would have denied it. He would have pointed out that he did no feel particularly depressed, but neither was he very interested in anything. Since the last years of his life were Depression years, he was constantly approached for money. He never turned down a request for a charitable contribution, and he always had a coat pocket loaded with half-dollars, whereby he was known to every panhandler between Park Avenue and Ninth Avenue and south from Forty-second Street. Curiously enough, he died intestate. His fortune had shrunk to a few hundred thousand dollars — understandable, since he had Fred Feldman continue payments to his mother at the rate of five hundred dollars a week and since he had given away several million dollars.

After Max died, a reporter from the *New York Times* was sent to see Clifford Abel, who had returned to New York. Abel was sixty-two. He was quite wealthy and too old, he felt, to return to architecture. He opened a studio and looked around for Broadway plays he might design. The reporter found him at his studio.

"We're trying to put something more than the ordinary obit together about Max Britsky. I understand you knew him well?"

"You might say that. I met Max in nineteen twelve. For the next fifteen years we worked together. Max was not an easy man to know — I mean deeper than the surface. I would say that in his entire life, he had only two very close friends, myself and Sam Snyder."

"You liked him?"

"Adored him, respected him. He was a great man utterly without any sense of his own greatness."

"I wish you would explain that."

"I'll try," Abel said. "But you must think of Max as I thought of him. I saw Max, not in that damn blue serge he always wore, but in a damask robe over silk and satin. He sits upon a white horse and wears a turban pinned with diamonds and rubies, and he is followed by twelve sumpter beasts loaded with silks and spices and other things wonderful. Well, that's a bit fanciful; let me bring it down to earth. Max brought something new into the world, and because of him, for better or worse, the world will never be the same again. Oh, I know there were others, but Max was always a step ahead. Of how many men can that be said?"